Nancy

Thanks for you support! Let me know what you think.

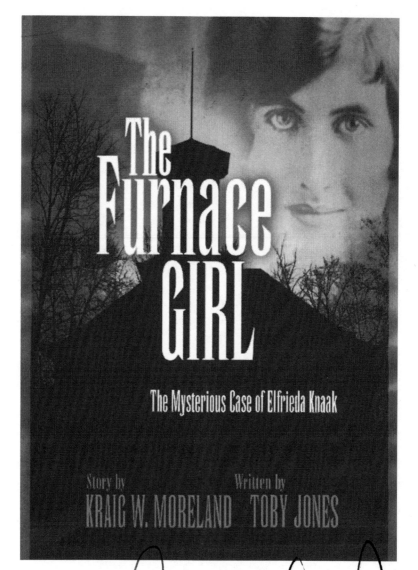

The Furnace GIRL

The Mysterious Case of Elfrieda Knaak

Story by
KRAIG W. MORELAND

Written by
TOBY JONES

ACROSS
THE LAKE

The Furnace Girl
The Mysterious Case of Elfrieda Knaak

Cover Design by Phillip Ross
Maps & Drawings by Kay Wolff
Interior Layout by Kraig W. Moreland

ISBN: 978-1-7322251-0-7

Across the Lake Publishing Co., LLC

Lake Bluff, IL

Aeroplane View
OF
LAKE BLUFF

1. Train Station
2. Orphanage
3. Village Hall
4. Merchant Block
5. Elementary School
6. Crab Tree Farm
7. Artesian Park
8. Lake Michigan
9. Cook Estate
10. Hitchcock Home

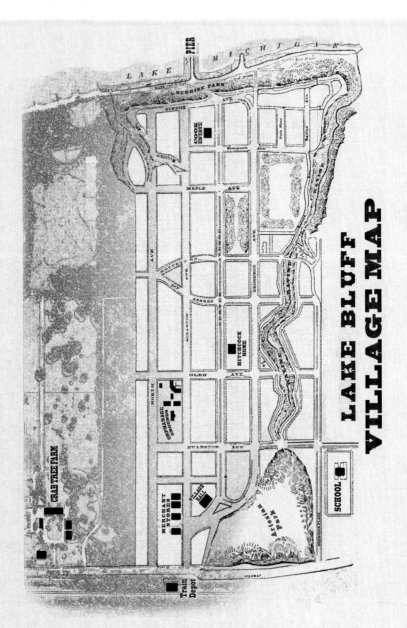

LAKE BLUFF ORPHANAGE

MAP OF CHICAGO SUBURBS

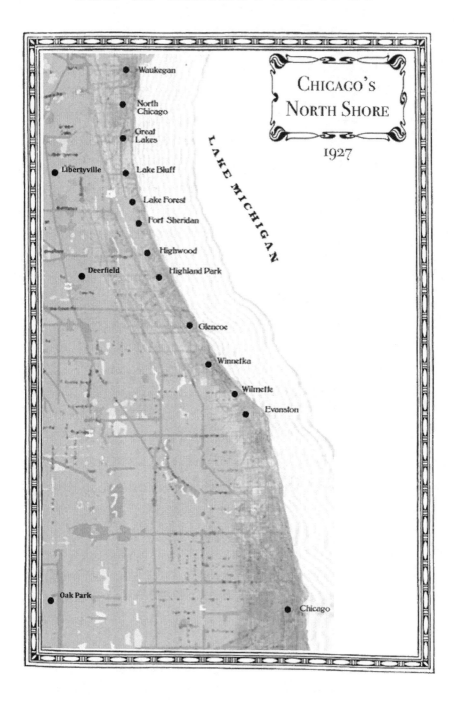

CHICAGO'S
NORTH SHORE

1927

Waukegan

North Chicago

Great Lakes

Libertyville

Lake Bluff

Lake Forest

Fort Sheridan

Highwood

Deerfield

Highland Park

LAKE MICHIGAN

Glencoe

Winnetka

Wilmette

Evanston

Oak Park

Chicago

The following is a work of fiction. It is historical in the sense that it is based upon real events and the lives of real people. In some cases the actual names of those people have been used, and, at times, actual events and newspaper reports have been used as well. But it is important to keep in mind that many of the newspapers in the late 1920s were sensationalist rags, and accounts of the Elfrieda Knaak case conflicted one another far more than they agreed.

The first purpose in telling this story is to entertain the reader. The second purpose is to put forth a plausible theory of what really happened to Elfrieda Knaak in the the Lake Bluff Village Hall in October of 1928. Today, 90 years later, her story remains one of the most intriguing unsolved crimes of the early 1900s.

We wish to dedicate this book to two groups of people. The first is our families, particularly our children, in the hope that they will always have genuine, supportive love in their lives, as they have brought such love into ours. The second group is all of those who spend their lives working with children, particularly children without loving parents. The difference you make in this world is extraordinary.

CONTENTS

Elfrieda Grace Knaak – 1928

Foreword

CHILDREN FROM THE LAKE BLUFF ORPHANAGE CARRY A GIANT
AMERICAN FLAG THROUGH THE STREETS FOR THE
FOURTH OF JULY PARADE
Photo courtesy of the Lake Bluff History Museum

In 1979, I was an eighth grader in Lake Bluff, Illinois—home of the mighty Bobcats. Miss O'Hara was our Social Studies teacher, who held court Monday through Friday in Room 103. "Miss O.," as she was called by both adults and kids in our community, made history fun, because she turned every historical event into an animated and memorable story. I was not the greatest of students and was more than a little concerned when she assigned us a three-page report on Lake Bluff's local history. Having lived in Lake Bluff since birth, I couldn't imagine that enough had gone on in my sleepy little town to fill a single page, much less meet the three-page requirement. But I would soon find out just how much Lake Bluff had to celebrate.

Lake Bluff's storied history began in 1875 during the Chautauqua movement. People from all across the country flocked to our idyllic lakefront town, seeking refreshment and rejuvenation in religion, education, recreation, and the arts. In Lake Bluff's heyday, the town boasted 30 hotels and boarding houses. Amongst its early visitors were Miss Frances Willard—founder of the Women's Christian Temperance Union—and Mrs. Rutherford B. Hayes—wife of our 19th president. Willard's influence was particularly profound, as Lake Bluff developed an active WCTU chapter.

I discovered that in 1894, The Village of Lake Bluff saw fit to turn its resources outward to orphans throughout the entire Chicagoland area. The Methodist-Deaconess Orphanage was founded in the tiny town, in an attempt to provide parentless youngsters with "the Lake Bluff experience." More than 150 children came through the orphanage annually, some leaving within the same year they arrived, while others spent much of their childhood at the facility.

Lake Bluff has always had a peace and grandeur that gives it a magnetic allure, an almost irresistible draw to this day. Families with small children flock to Lake Bluff, as it has always been an absolute paradise for children and the families who raise them. From end to end of my picturesque hometown, parents let their children run, bike, and play freely, knowing that they would be safe and looked after, for Lake Bluff is a town in which all the residents know one another. It's a place where on the Sunday before Christmas, children—still in their pajamas—run from their beds straight out to the edges of their street to receive chocolates thrown by Santa from atop one of the town's volunteer fire department trucks, with its siren blaring.

Between the Lake Michigan shore on its eastern edge and the train tracks to Chicago and Milwaukee to the west, lay a complex network of heavily wooded ravines, which traverse nearly half of the 4.05 square miles that constitute the village proper. Massive oaks and tilting birches fill the wonderful web of ravine trails. Outside the ravines and a bit closer to the lake once stood Lake Bluff's two legendary "Indian Trail trees," authentically shaped and bent oaks that served as constant reminders of Lake Bluff's Native past.

My eighth-grade research also revealed that during the most horrible years of World War I, Lake Bluff was declared "America's Most Patriotic Small Town" thanks to her tireless efforts in support of the Red Cross. Lake Bluff sent an ambulance to the front in France and could boast of having more enlisted men than any other town of its size across the entire country. This same patriotic spirit led to the town folk organizing a small parade on July 4, 1911, that would grow into one of the largest Fourth of July celebrations in the United States.

As I neared the end of my research project, I was about to conclude that Lake Bluff was the perfect community. But then I came upon a singular, horrifying event that, in some ways, has defined Lake Bluff ever since. I am referring, of course, to the mysterious case of Elfrieda Grace Knaak.

On the morning of October 30th, 1928, Miss Knaak, a 30-year-old door-to-door encyclopedia salesman from the neighboring community of Deerfield, was found naked and horribly burned in the basement of the Lake Bluff Village Hall, which also served as the police and fire station at that time. She was alive, though just barely. No one knew who this woman was or what she could have been doing in the basement on that fateful night, but suffice it to say that the discovery of this badly burned victim kicked off an investigation and media frenzy, the likes of which have never been seen since in my hometown. In fact, even today, 90 years after Elfrieda Knaak was found, her case is still considered one of the most puzzling, unsolved crimes of the early 1900s.

I still live in Lake Bluff, and, my wife Jennifer and I have raised all four of our children here. It's safe to say that nobody grows up in this town without hearing about and getting caught up in the mysterious case of Elfrieda Knaak. From the time I first heard about it all the way back in eighth grade with Miss O., I haven't been able to let it go. This peculiar and fascinating case is still a crucial part of the history curriculum at the Lake Bluff schools.

Thanks to Miss O. and the love of local history that she instilled in me, back in 2008, I began writing, producing, and directing a documentary film about another astonishing chapter in Lake Bluff's history, the Lake Bluff Orphanage. I teamed up with my friend and fellow Lake Bluff History Museum Board member Cathy McKechney. The project took me all over the country, to children and grandchildren of folks who had grown up in our town's orphanage. It even led me to orphanage staff and administrators who knew things about the orphanage and Lake Bluff that nobody else would possibly know. But that was all to be expected.

What I didn't expect during my orphanage research was a story a gentleman shared with me that I simply couldn't ignore, a story you'll come upon as your read the pages of the book you are now holding, *The Furnace Girl*.

I hope you enjoy this great tale as much as my good friend Toby Jones and I enjoyed working on it together.

Kraig W. Moreland

Abrahams, Morris law	607	Neelson, Andrew R law	901
Brookers, Cocos Fra 3945	505	Nemmers Tax Service 3945	224
Brown T W dent cen 2047	201	Palace Publishers Co Dea6111	509
Buck & Raynor druggist Sta 028	149 N Clark	Payne, D law Cen	401
Callahan & Callahan law Cen	207	Pirelli & Donato law	316
City Tax Service Bureau tax agents Can3029	810	Polk R L & Co directory pubs Was0486	815
Commercial Exchange of Illinois contra		Prout Hedley mag Har6076	210
	Can 3020 822	Quest Mfg Cotypewriter supply Wab 333	308
Giiblen, M S Fra 1860	501	Rand McNally & Co printers Wab 0363	802
Gualano A N law Ran 2349	818	Seybold, Machine Co (The)	522
Hargrave Edward J secret Service (The)	Cen1500	Stevens, Chas N pres Wab	420
		Stevens Chas N Co printers supls	112
Hargrave Edward J principal Cen	303	Trudell, A E artist Har2202	804
Hargrave, Geo E gen mngr Cen 1500	302	Western Druggist (The)	600
Hargrave Patrol & watch Service Cen 1500	300	Wetzel, A E enge Wab6811	704
Horwitz, Jack theatre tickets Dea	145 N Clark	Woodruff M P labels and tags	612
Keegan Wm Fra 1860	504	Wray Co (The) portable elevators	100
Keystone Chocolate Co Sta 8074	706	Youngma T S & Co paper	102
Marks, A law Ma 3860	407	Zeh-Rex Engraving Co wood engravers	603
McChesney & Brown (Inc) dentists Cen	203		

Chapter 1 — A Conversation With Detective Hargrave

Chicago, IL — The Hargrave Secret Service Agency — October 19, 1948

It was a gray, blustery afternoon in Chicago, when I found myself pulling into 145 Clark Street for a visit with Detective George Hargrave. I parked in front of an eight-story brick building, conveniently situated right across from the Cook County Courthouse. The nameplates and mailboxes just inside the entryway indicated that The Hargrave Secret Service Agency was on the third floor.

After hustling up three flights in the echoey, concrete stairwell, I emerged in the carpeted hallway and found the dark wooden door ᴊearing the name of Detective George Hargrave. I knocked firmly and soon heard the sound of heavy footsteps coming my way. The detective opened the door, nodded, gave me a closed-mouth smile, and gestured for me to enter. "You're a man of your word, Mr. Morgan, right on time. In my line of work I'm not used to people keeping their word," he said with a smirk. "Come right in."

"Thank you, Detective Hargrave." He offered his hand and I shook it. His was a large and powerful hand, swallowing mine almost entirely. "It's kind of you to meet with me," I added as we entered his large, cluttered office. There was an unpleasant mix of odors inside: coffee, stale cigarettes, and a hint of maple doughnuts. Behind his desk hung an unorganized cluster of framed photographs of Hargrave posing with several local Chicago legends throughout the years, none hanging even close to evenly. I recognized one of Hargrave posing with Big Bill Thompson, Chicago's mayor from back in the 30s. Hargrave's desk had two towering stacks of file folders on it, one at each of its front corners with a phone in between them. Crowded over in the corner, to his left, was a bunch of wooden chairs, as if he kept them there for those rare occasions when he hosted a meeting.

"Please, have a seat." The 50-year-old detective pointed to a hard-backed leather chair on the opposite side of his desk. He sat, and I followed his lead. He ran a hand through his thick graying hair and removed his glasses, as he glanced out the window at the softening fall colors. Detective Hargrave was a thick-set man. He had the build of a former athlete, with the emphasis on "former." His large hands grew out of long, still-toned arms and broad, swimmer's shoulders. His face, while it showed the wear and tear of years in the trenches of detective work, was still the face of a fine-looking man. There was a fatigue in his eyes, and his posture suggested it wouldn't be long before he called it quits.

Over the past 10 years, Detective Hargrave and I had a half-dozen conversations on the phone, all about this singular case. All these years, I had kept picking away at the matter I'd come to discuss like an itchy scab, and I did it because, deep down, I believed that if I got somebody in law enforcement to ask the right questions, to reexamine the critical facts, maybe they'd reopen the case and uncover what they'd clearly missed in the fall of 1928. From everything I knew about this case—and I reckoned I knew more than just about anybody—I'd always figured that if anybody was going to reopen this case, it would be George Hargrave.

"Tell me what you're after here, Mr. Morgan," the detective said in a voice that suggested decades of cigarettes and cold coffee.

I took a long, slow breath and decided to dive right in. "Look, you and I both know, Detective Hargrave, that there are a lot of things about this case that can really eat at you. But, without question, the biggest one is trying to figure out how in the world a jury could have possibly rendered the verdict they did, when they looked at all the evidence in this case. And it's not just you and I, Detective, for just about everyone who has ever taken a serious look at the facts of this case—the raw, medical, physiological facts— knows that all these findings were simply not consistent with the verdict that was returned. We're talking about a 30-year-old woman with severe burns on both feet up to her shins, on both hands halfway up to her elbows, over half her face and head. She's found barely alive, propped up next to a furnace that has a single twelve and three-quarter inches by nine and three-quarter inches opening, an opening that happens to be nearly three feet off the ground. How in the world was this woman supposed to get each arm, each leg, and her head into this small opening—each one at a time, mind you— and then have the pain tolerance to keep each of these extremities in the furnace, while they burned for a few minutes? It's ludicrous."

The detective shook his head and picked up a pencil, drumming it lightly on the edge of his desk. "I know. I know. It's the darndest thing. But, you've got to admit that, at the same time, it is the perfect case, right?" He dropped the pencil and looked up at me. "It's got everything: a beautiful, innocent victim, a washed-up silent movie actor, an idyllic North Shore suburb, it happened in the police station, and it was never solved."

"You mean not yet, Detective. Not yet," I said. "But I'm really hoping you can tell me how in the world this case became the three- ring circus that it did back then."

Hargrave resumed. "I knew those bumblers on the Lake Bluff force didn't know their asses from their elbows. Chief Rosenhagen fouled up the crime scene the moment he and that public works gardener Chris Louis discovered the woman. They threw the ashes away, for Christ's sake, the only tangible evidence that might have led us somewhere!" He cleared his throat, and I flinched, fearing some of the phlegm he was coughing up might make it across the desk onto my shirt or pinstriped tie. "When that jury's decision came down, I knew that poor Knaak family, who had already been through so much, was not going to be anything close to satisfied. Those two brothers—Otto and Alvin—called me within an hour after the verdict was announced," he said sipping his coffee. "I'd be working for them officially just over a week later." Recognizing his lapse in manners, he added, "You want some coffee?" gesturing at his thoroughly stained cup.

"No, thank you," I said. From the smell of his and the lack of anything resembling steam coming from his cup or the pot over on the sideboard, I was sure I'd be better off declining.

Looking at the enormous file the detective had pulled from the pile to his right, I thought of my own. Even twenty years after the crime, neither of our files on this case had made it into our file cabinets. Instead they stayed right out on our desks, ready and available. I've never stopped poring over my file on the Elfrieda Knaak case. It never failed; every year, right around Halloween—the anniversary of this gruesome affair—the memories would rise up inside me like a tidal wave and come crashing down upon the shores of my mind. I'd dig back through the hundreds of articles, photos, and reports I'd accumulated about the case and try, once again, to figure out how in the heck that jury ever could have missed what should have been so obvious. Of course, I readily admit that I had a significant advantage over that confounded jury of men—and over Detective Hargrave—having been in Lake Bluff on the night of October 29, 1928. There were things I witnessed and heard in the weeks surrounding this crime that the detective and the jury wouldn't have had quite the same access to. But even if I hadn't been in Lake Bluff at the time, seen what I'd seen, and heard what I'd heard, I can guarantee that I'd have looked into a number of angles that were completely glossed over or, worse yet, totally ignored in the weeks and months following the discovery of Miss Knaak's badly burned body.

All the work I did on this case in the first ten years after it happened had been done either in secret or under false pretenses. I was barely a teenager when I started poking around in this town scandal that was way out of my league. At least when I got my first job as a reporter for the *St. Paul Pioneer Press* in 1937, I finally had a more legitimate reason to be asking so many questions.

I knew that Hargrave's involvement in the case originated when he was brought in to assist the State's Attorney and the County Sheriff in the overall investigation. But ten days later, Hargrave was hired by the Knaak family to get to the bottom of what all the Knaaks were convinced was foul play. I couldn't wait to dive into the details of this case with this detective, now that we were finally face to face.

"So what do you think happened, Detective? After all these years, I have to imagine you've combed through your file on this case a hundred times. You must have a theory."

The detective leaned back in his chair, pulled a cigarette out of his breast pocket, and struck a match to light it. With the cigarette firmly between his lips, he reached both his hands behind his head, interlocking his fingers. "I still think Hitchcock did it," he said. He was referring to Mr. Charles Hitchcock, Lake Bluff's most famous citizen. He'd had a good run in silent movies in the early 1900s. He'd even played opposite Charlie Chaplin a few times and starred in a few reels made by Essanay Films in Chicago. But by 1910, all the great filmmakers and actors had gone west to L.A., and Charles Hitchcock was left behind. He spent the next 20 years piecing together a living, doing odd jobs: teaching night classes at the Waukegan YMCA, serving as the night dispatch deputy at the Lake Bluff Village Hall, and picking up the occasional booking at small theaters in Illinois and Indiana.

"They ruled Hitchcock out," Hargrave continued, "all because of that broken ankle he had and because two members of his own family—plus his loyal buddy Oscar Kloer—testified that he was home that night." The detective started rustling through some of the papers in his Knaak file as he paused. He was squinting rather than putting on the glasses that hung around his neck. "But you can't tell me that scum-sucker didn't have something untoward going on with Elfrieda Knaak! He was her teacher at the YMCA in Waukegan, but somehow saw fit to 'tutor' her on the side—in the Lake Bluff Village Hall, late at night, when nobody else was around, when he was supposed to be on duty!" The detective's face reddened, and two veins on his neck protruded. I took a slow, audible breath, in hopes of calming him down.

"Me, I still like Charles Hitchcock for the crime," Hargrave concluded. "And if Rosenhagen and Spaid hadn't looked at him as one of their own up there in that half-wit Lake Bluff Police force,

Hitchcock would have gotten a much harder look as a suspect—broken leg or not."

"Maybe nobody wanted to finger a former famous movie star like him," I said.

"The law is the law, Mr. Morgan. It doesn't play favorites," he said. "Ex-big shot movie star or not, this Hitchcock had regular, unsupervised access to the crime scene, not to mention a personal relationship with the victim, despite claiming he had no idea she was in love with him."

"But did he have a motive," I asked, "not simply to do away with Miss Knaak, but to torture her in such…such a barbaric way?"

Hargrave expelled a long, raspy breath. "I can't figure it. What could possibly possess a person—any person—to do that? Naw, I just can't figure it. But love, sex, jealousy…I've seen it do crazy things to people over the years, Mr. Morgan."

"What about Hitchcock's wife, Estelle? You ever think that she might have suspected something going on between her husband and Miss Knaak? If she did, maybe she tried to do away with her in some sort of jealous rage?" I speculated.

Hargrave looked at the floor and then out the window. "She clearly suspected something was going on between the two of them. But you've done your homework, Mr. Morgan, so I'm sure you are aware that Mrs. Hitchcock had an even better alibi than her husband; she was at work on the night in question."

I nodded, for I was, indeed, aware of this fact. Estelle Hitchcock was all the way down in Highland Park, working at a friend's music store. So I tried another tack.

"There was another woman though, Detective, someone I read about who testified at the inquest. Her name was Marie Mueller. It said in the papers she was Miss Knaak's best friend. Did you ever find out anything about her? You think she could've somehow been involved with all this?" I asked.

"That's an interesting angle, Mr. Morgan. The only questions anybody ever asked this Mueller dame, both before and during the inquest, were whether she felt her friend could do such a thing to herself, you know, light herself on fire." He shook his head, took a long, deep pull on his cigarette, and exhaled a frustrated breath. "I don't believe anybody—including yours truly—ever asked Miss Mueller where she was on that night." He took another drag on his cigarette. "But I'll tell you this: after Estelle divorces the scumbucket, your Miss Mueller runs off fifteen years later and marries Hitchcock. Seems awfully peculiar, if you ask me, like some kind of love triangle or whatnot was going on between Hitchcock, Knaak, and Mueller."

"Seems to me like Hitchcock had a lot of women who were willing to protect him. And for what?" I asked.

"You're right about that. Heck, if you want to consider Mrs. Hitchcock or Marie Mueller, then you might as well look at some of the other cockamamie people who turned up as this case unfolded. Back in November of 1928, it seemed like every day some new person of interest surfaced out of nowhere. There was an army deserter who contacted the authorities from all the way down in Texas. He claimed he was a chauffeur for a family in Lake Forest and was contacting the police to confess to the crime. But once they got him extradited back to Illinois, they found out he had been in an asylum for years and was making the whole thing up." Hargrave took a sloppy sip of coffee. "Then there was a strange letter A.V. Smith, the State's Attorney, received from someone down in Chicago, claiming he had put Miss Knaak into a hypnotic trance and assisted her as she burned herself. But unless this guy had studied with Houdini himself, there's not much chance he could have pulled that off."

"I read somewhere that Hitchcock had an association with Houdini. Might he have been able to put Miss Knaak under a spell?" I asked.

"We looked into that. Another dead end," the detective said, shaking his head.

"What about the notion that the victim was burned elsewhere and dragged into the Village Hall?" I asked. "Did you ever think that was a possibility?" He was shaking his head before I finished my sentence.

"Naw. Too many facts against that." He paused and scratched the top of his head. "There was the so-called 'Electrocution hypothesis' somebody brought to us, that Miss Knaak was electrocuted elsewhere and dragged over to the Village Hall to die. But if you've seen the pictures, the burns on her hands and feet, missing fingers and toes..." Hargrave closed his eyes and pinched the bridge of his nose. "Electrocution doesn't cause that. Plus the dragging-her-in-already-injured theory wouldn't account for the bloody footprints we found on the stairs."

"I'm not sure I follow," I said.

"The footprints we found were completely distorted. You almost couldn't tell they were footprints because of how badly damaged the victim's feet were. So the blood and prints were definitely Miss Knaak's, and there were two sets of them—the first set going up the stairs and the second set going down—but both hers. They originated by the furnace."

Piecing it together in my mind, I said, "So Miss Knaak tried to get out a couple times?"

"Exactly. And don't forget, Mr. Morgan, one of her ramblings at the hospital spoke of a 'mystery hand' that must have locked the door. That's the door on the north side of the Village Hall."

"So whoever did this locked her in?"

"Yep," the detective said as he exhaled.

Detective Hargrave shook his head and let out an exasperated sigh. "There were even some stories that never even made the papers," Hargrave continued.

"Like what?" I asked

"Well, one that circulated around town with all the locals was about this wealthy couple who operated the dairy farm up there in Lake Bluff. Some thought they were even involved."

"Are you talking about the owners of Crab Tree Farm—Scott and Grace Durand?" I asked. I couldn't wait to learn how the Durands figured into Hargrave's theory of the case.

"Now, how in the heck would you know those names, Mr. Morgan? You know more about Lake Bluff in 1928 than you're letting on." Hargrave crushed out his cigarette and picked up an old notepad from his file, flipping through the pages until he came to the information he was looking for. "Appears Mrs. Durand and Miss Knaak had some sort of unusual spiritual connection. Says here that they both believed in communicating with the dead. In fact, that old loon Mrs. Durand even wrote a book, long before all this happened, claiming that she'd communicated with the likes of Abraham Lincoln and Joan of Arc." Hargrave rolled his eyes and shook his head. "Yep, it seems our Miss Knaak spent at least a handful of evenings over at Crab Tree Farm, involved in her spiritual pursuits."

"So did this connection between Mrs. Durand and Crab Tree ever come out as relevant to the case?" I asked.

"Nope. We pursued that lead, but it never led anywhere. Plus, you've got to remember that once I started working for the Knaak family, the last thing they wanted me doing was looking into anything that would fuel this spiritual purification theory. We did establish a possible link between the victim and Crab Tree Farm from something Miss Knaak said of her attacker when she was in the hospital."

"What was that?" I asked.

"Miss Knaak said, more than once, that, 'Frank threw me down.'" Hargrave replied. "The Knaak boys were adamant that whoever this 'Frank' was had to be found. In fact, they paid me overtime to track down each and every Frank their sister might have been referring to. The first Frank I came across was a kid who worked over at Crab Tree Farm. So I stopped by there to have a talk with this young man."

"And what did you find?"

"Not much. The kid was a little slow in the head. Both Mr. and Mrs. Durand didn't even want me talking to him. I think Mr. Durand's words were, 'Stay away from that boy!' Said he'd been through enough. Their Frank was a charity case, plain and simple. He'd done a little time down at Joliet, but Mrs. Durand hired him anyway as a favor to this Frank's mother. The Durands did a lot of favors for people, Mr. Morgan. They were not your typical farm folk though." The detective paused and lit up another cigarette

"What do you mean?" I asked. Hargrave took a while to formulate his answer.

"They had a ton of money, those two. Scott Durand was a big time sugar broker, and neither he nor his wife put up with anybody telling them what they could and couldn't do on their farm, or anywhere else, for that matter. The farm was both Grace Durand's idea and her domain. She ran the place. She wanted it to be the most beautiful dairy operation in the entire midwest. But once those federal indictments came down on Mr. Durand's sugar company, people started getting suspicious about the goings on at the farm as well."

Hargrave got up from his chair and poured himself another cup of coffee. Carrying the stained, white cup over to the window, he looked over toward the courthouse. "There were a couple of shady characters who'd been seen around Lake Bluff and Lake Forest in September and October of '28. They drove around in fancy cars, smoking big cigars, and dropping enormous tips in local eateries and whatnot. We got some unconfirmed reports of them being around Crab Tree Farm." He set his coffee down to light up a cigarette.

"About all we ever got on them were their names—Pirelli and Donato, I think. Some speculated that these guys were part of Capone's operation, the big fella himself."

"But anyway," Hargrave continued, "the Durands eventually let me talk to their long-time foreman, the fella who ran their farm operation." Hargrave thumbed through the sheets of paper in his file, looking for the name. "Here it is...Alex...Alex Reddington, that's who ran the farm in '28. My notes here say he went by just 'Redd.' He sure was a nervous character, as I recall. Got all fidgety and clammed up the moment I started asking him questions. That guy seemed to be hiding something. Could never get a straight answer out of him. He did let it slip, eventually, that this Frank was in the workers' quarters sleeping the night of the 29th."

"So were there any other Franks that you found?" I asked.

"I beat the bushes on it, I tell you. I went through the Lake Bluff and Lake Forest phone books. I went through every file we had at the Waukegan office with a first initial of 'F.' The only other Franks I could find in connection to Miss Knaak were dead ends. One was a queer music teacher, a violin instructor, a real fruitcake. Frank Mandy was his name. He had a studio adjacent to Hitchcock's room at the YMCA in Waukegan. This guy was about as incapable of violence as any man I've ever known. I mean, Frank Mandy couldn't have thrown down a two-year-old, much less Elfrieda Knaak. Only reason we pursued him was his connection to Hitchcock in Waukegan, where they both taught and where Miss Knaak took classes."

As Hargrave shook his head yet again and scratched the back of his neck, I realized how much the unsolved nature of this crime still ate at him. He was picking the same scab I was, and I needed him to keep doing so.

"The only other Frank we tracked down," the detective continued, "was the owner of Compton Publishing, where Miss Knaak worked selling Encyclopedias. F.T. Compton was his name. The F was for Frank, but that guy said he didn't even know Elfrieda Knaak, nor anyone else on his sales staff, for that matter. He was what they call a 'hands-off' owner, hardly ever around the Chicago office. But then again, Miss Knaak was one of Compton's top sales agents, and the other salesmen I interviewed at the company all said Miss Knaak always seemed to be getting fed the good leads." He took a thoughtful drag on his cigarette and squinted from the smoke. "I mean, how in the heck can a woman be the top seller in an office over a bunch of experienced salesmen? Miss Knaak was a former teacher with no sales experience, and yet she outsells a group of veteran salesmen? Who knows? Maybe this Frank T. Compton was taking care of her, feeding her leads. Maybe Compton and Miss Knaak had some sort of special relationship nobody knew about, despite his claiming not to know his own top sales staff."

"Let me ask you something else, Detective, about another strange character in this case." I rifled through my notes to the page labeled "Luella Roeh, aka B. Lock." I looked at a wrinkled, yellowing photo of a middle-aged, stout woman. "I'm sure you're familiar with this other strange relationship Miss Knaak had with a Luella Roeh. Seems she also went by the pen name of B. Lock."

"Ah, yes. I remember her, all right," Hargrave chuckled. "You have done your homework, Mr. Morgan. You sure you're a reporter and not a detective?"

I laughed in response, adding, "Sometimes I don't think our two lines of work are all that different. But, Detective, I could never understand why the police didn't pursue this woman and her obvious influence on Miss Knaak. They missed it altogether at first, for B. Lock was not even mentioned in either the inquest or in the original police investigation."

"That's because the letters between Miss Knaak and B. Lock didn't even surface until almost two weeks after the jury had ruled," Hargrave replied. "In fact, B. Lock might never have surfaced at all, if it hadn't have been for one of the Knaak brothers—Alvin, I think—coming across Elfrieda's journal and all these letters from a mysterious woman who wanted to keep her real name a secret." The detective paused again, shuffling through his massive pile of papers. "Alvin brought a small box of their correspondence to my office less than ten days after the jury had made its ridiculous ruling," he said.

What did you do with them?" I asked.

"I rushed them straight over to Waukegan, to the State's Attorney's office. A.V. Smith looked them over, with their various references to 'the refining fire' and 'self-purification,' and the two of us immediately hopped in his car, drove to 413 E. Park Avenue in Libertyville, and brought B. Lock in for questioning."

"And...?" I said, feeling on the verge of something important.

"Well, State's Attorney Smith allowed me to sit in on the questioning," Hargrave said, "but the entire interrogation lasted less than ten minutes. Smith released her, because, as A.V. put it, 'all this little old lady did was talk to Miss Knaak about the concept of self-purification, and there is certainly no crime in that.' In addition," Hargrave continued, "Smith had established with his second or third question that this B. Lock had an airtight alibi on the night of Miss Knaak's misfortune, and so that was that." Then Mr. Hargrave let something slip that I jumped on like an attorney in a cross-examination. He said, "The State's Attorney then handed me that small stack of letters and called it a day."

"Wait a minute…He gave you those letters? You still have them? In your possession?" I asked.

"Sure, I've got 'em," he said. "They were never used as evidence, so they're right here in my file."

I hesitated, wondering just how direct to be. "Any chance I could look at those letters, Detective?" Hargrave didn't answer immediately. But I saw him start digging through that massive file again. "You see, sir, I've always been fascinated with the spiritual dimension of this case, Miss Knaak's penchant for mysticism, the books she read, and her obsession with self-purification."

"So, Mr. Morgan, do you think these letters and their contents are going to find their way into that twentieth anniversary spread you are doing for that paper of yours, the one you told me about when you called to set up this appointment?" He cleared his throat.

"I guess that depends on what's in them. My piece will certainly mention the spiritual dimension of this case, but I doubt it will be a focus." I paused, trying to read Hargrave's expression. "Would you prefer that I not use them?"

He had pulled out a massive file from the middle of one his stacks. It bore a single word across its front: "Knaak." Putting his glasses on with one hand, he slid a small stack of letters across the cluttered surface of his desk. "Ten or fifteen years ago, when I was still in touch with the family of the victim, I'd have asked you to keep this kind of personal correspondence out of the papers. Now, I'm not so sure. I'd just hate to stir up any unnecessary emotion for any of the Knaaks."

"I understand, and I'll respect your position on this, Detective." I meant what I said, but at the same time, I could barely contain my excitement. I'd heard and read about these letters for years. My hands were shaking a bit when I picked them up, and I saw Detective Hargrave noticing.

"Had a little too much coffee on the drive down from the Twin Cities," I said. Hargrave nodded, smiled, and I began reading the first few of their correspondences.

From Elfrieda on 8/19/28

I'm interested in the various barriers to spiritual growth. Why is it that so many spiritual pilgrims stop reaching or seem to level off at such a rudimentary level of faith? So many of the things we talk about, you and I, are never even brought up in church. For instance, spiritual purification and physical rituals of repentance; I'm fascinated by these matters and believe they have tremendous potential.

From B. Lock on 8/23/28

My dear Elfrieda, the vast majority of religious pilgrims in general—and Christians in particular—are caught in what can only be thought of as an adolescent level faith. They can conceive of nothing beyond sin and salvation, heaven and hell, when none of the great teachers—including Jesus himself—gave a hoot about that nonsense.

Think of it this way, Elfrieda. Everything in this visible world of ours is physical and tangible. The Refiner's Fire cannot be understood in such a world, by such a people, by those whose entire world is physical. You mustn't be surprised or disappointed that these teachings aren't embraced or included in 1920s American churches!

From Elfrieda on 8/28/28

You are so kind, B. It was my good fortune to knock on your red door that August afternoon! How I have longed for conversation of this kind about these matters. How will I ever thank you?

To burn one's self, to submit to fire, is to subject oneself to torturous pain. How do we endure and move through that pain to the other side?

I've hesitated to bring this up, dear B, but I work with my brother in the family pharmacy. I'm around all manner of medications most every day. I have access to several varieties of powerful numbing agents. The strength they all share is that they don't produce excessive fatigue or render the user unconscious. Please don't think less of me, dear friend, for I am only trying to find a way to pursue the path of purification. But the fear of pain is quite real for me; it is what is keeping me from moving forward to what my soul—my spirit—seems to be calling me to.

From B. Lock on 10/3/28

Think less of you? How could you even think it? I not only understand your fear, I share it, my dear. When we move beyond mere talk and conceptual discussion in these matters of purification, we arrive at the practical dimensions. I'm glad we've reached this point together. And there is no one with whom I'd rather enter the refining fire than you, my sweet friend.

For me, my marriage to Harold is, without question, my biggest barrier to spiritual growth. It has been this way for many, many years. And I am not getting any younger. I have friends who are dying. I would like to find a way to proceed with this, Elfrieda. Truly, I would. I just don't see how I can, not while Harold is around.

I rubbed my eyes and looked up at the ceiling of Detective Hargrave's office.

"Well," the detective said, extinguishing another cigarette, "What do ya think?"

I clenched my teeth and shook my head before responding. "Well, I can tell you that Miss Knaak and this B. Lock weren't alone in their fascination with the spirit world and self-purification."

"How do you mean?" Hargrave asked, flicking the ash from his cigarette into his overflowing ashtray.

"I did a fair amount of research on spiritual movements from that time period. Both Christian and cultic mysticism were flourishing in the 1920s. In fact, after the 1915 World's Fair, New England's 'New Thought' movement made it all the way out to California. That was the same time that Theosophy and Pentecostalism were spreading like wildfire. Even famous people, like the poet William Butler Yeats, were willing to talk publicly about their experiences with spiritual mediums and communication with the dead." I paused, seeing the detective looking puzzled.

He asked, "So how does all this affect Miss Knaak or fit into this case?"

"It just seems to me that the people investigating this case and preparing to rule on the cause of her injuries should have looked into this," I said. "It's my impression that pretty much everyone had heard or read about Miss Knaak's claim to have done this to herself.

But what still eats at me is that these letters weren't even available in time for the jury, right?"

"That's correct," Hargrave said, nodding. "Your point?"

"That once the letters did come to light, it seems to me that they should have been treated with greater importance."

"How so?" Hargrave asked, pushing his chair back from the desk a bit.

"I just don't see how the jury could have come to the verdict they did without any of these letters. I mean, it seems to me, Detective, that it's precisely these letters—more than anything else—that lend a certain credibility to the notion that Miss Knaak may have at least wanted to purify herself by means of fire. If B. Lock's letters had been a part of the investigation and deliberation, they might have made the shocking ruling the jury eventually rendered a great deal more plausible." I added, "But they ruled without even having them. Doesn't that strike you as fishy, Detective Hargrave?"

Hargrave rose, pulled his pack of cigarettes out of his breast pocket, banged one out, and lit up, moving across to the window. "There's a lot about this case and how it was handled that smells fishy to me. Always has." Blowing a few smoke rings up toward his ceiling, he watched their ascent. He looked at his watch and was pulled out of his musings. "Mr. Morgan, I wasn't sure how long this conversation was going to go or how much ground we would cover. But I can already tell that this could take a while. Give me a few minutes here to clear out the rest of my day."

I got up quickly and said, "Wow. Thanks. If you're sure that's OK." He nodded and picked up his phone. "I'll just head to the lavatory," I said on my way out.

I grabbed my notebook and headed out to the hallway toward the bathroom I'd seen right by the door to the stairway. I couldn't believe how this conversation with Detective Hargrave was going. He seemed as excited by it as I was. I could only imagine where it might lead.

When I heard him hang up the phone, I tapped lightly on his open door and came back in.

"I don't mind saying, Mr. Morgan, that you've got me more than a little intrigued. I mean, you seem to know more about this case than I do, for Christ's sake." Hargrave leaned across his desk and looked directly into my eyes for several seconds.

"I can't thank you enough, Detective, for clearing your schedule and spending so much time with me."

"I'll tell you just how you can thank me, Mr. Morgan," he said, still staring me straight in the eyes. "By telling me the truth about who you are and what your connection to this 'Furnace Girl' case really is."

I looked down at the floor and rolled my tongue against my lower teeth. "If I did that, Detective," I paused again, looking back across at the overstuffed file labeled "Knaak," "you might need to clear your schedule beyond just today."

He looked at his enormous file, shook his head, and said, "This case...this one case has eaten up more of my time than most of my others combined. It's still unsolved, Mr. Morgan, unsolved in the most unsatisfying way. It has eaten at me both day and night and may well haunt me in my grave. I'll clear as much time as this takes but not until you level with me on why this case is so...so personal to you."

SWIFT HEALTH CARE CENTER — LAKE BLUFF ORPHANAGE
Photo courtesy of the Lake Bluff History Museum

Chapter 2 — It's Only for a While
Evanston, IL — Church Street Station — November 25, 1927

The truth is, it's awfully hard to know where to begin. So I suppose I'll start at the beginning.

On the day after Thanksgiving in 1927, my mother packed my sister Betty and me up and dragged us down to Church Street Station in Evanston, Illinois. Helen Morgan was a slender, high-strung woman in the best of times. But on this particular Friday, my mother was in quite a state. Pacing back and forth on the station platform, her gray coat filled with air and billowed out around her with every change of direction. Poor Betty, my stubby-legged, four-year-old sister, tried to keep up with her, grabbing for the fold of her coat each time it swung out. She finally got a hold of it and hung on for dear life, as we waited for the northbound Chicago North Shore Line to arrive. When Mother finally stopped moving, Betty clung to her leg, burrowing her face into the tattered, fraying folds of Mother's coat.

As an eleven-year-old, I suppose I was tall and slender, like my mother. I wasn't particularly tall for my grade; it's just that I was always too big for the rummage sale clothes I wore. So I guess that made me look taller than I was. I remember glancing nervously around that echoey train station platform, just wishing my mother would sit down.

For the last six months, the three of us—Betty, our mother, and I—had crammed into Aunt Rose's Evanston apartment. "It's only for a while," our mother had said to us. In the last six months, Mother had said all sorts of stuff we didn't like was "only for a while," ever since Mother whisked us away from our father's South Chicago house in the middle of the night back in May.

When we finally managed to escape from Father, we took almost nothing with us: a couple of grocery sacks of clothes, the last of Mother's money, my little red ball and jacks, and Betty's faded brown, threadbare, one-eyed teddy bear. Mother wasn't even sure she had enough cash to pay the Checker cab that picked us up in front of Father's and deposited us outside her sister's apartment at two a.m. on May 7th.

"It's only for a while," Mother had said to Aunt Rose, when she opened her door with sleep in her eyes and her auburn hair tied up in curlers. She had no idea we were coming.

"Hi, Aunt Rose!" Betty said, way too enthusiastically for two o'clock in the morning. But that didn't stop Rose from pulling Betty and me into her smothering, flabby embrace.

"Come in! Come in! You are all welcome to stay here for as long as you need to," Aunt Rose said.

But after six months, even Aunt Rose couldn't continue to cover the costs of supporting the three of us any longer, particularly where doctors' appointments and inoculations were concerned. So she announced on the way home from church one November afternoon, with that big, Christian grin on her face, that, "Pastor Baddeley placed a call on our behalf to a place up in Lake Bluff that provides a wide variety of services to children just like you two." I wasn't sure what "just like you two" meant, but it probably had something to do with having a drunk for a father, a mother who wasn't much better, and clothes that were threadbare to the point of disintegration.

So that's what landed us in the Evanston train station on the morning after Thanksgiving for this sudden trip to Lake Bluff. Mother had kept trying to explain it that morning at the breakfast table, as she hurried us along. "Aunt Rose found us a free clinic, where we can get you checkups from both a doctor and a dentist.

We'll take the train there," our mother had promised, "and then get some ice cream afterwards."

The Chicago North Shore Interurban Line went all the way from Evanston up to Lake Bluff and points north. At 10:37 a.m. that Friday morning, the brown, wooden train cars squealed to a stop at the Evanston Church Street Station. Only a few passengers disembarked, and mother herded the two of us onto the crowded second car. We scrunched onto two seats facing forward.

"How long will it take to get to the hospital?" I asked.

"There won't be shots, Mama. No shots, right?" Betty begged.

Just then, the train began to lurch forward. "Here we go, now," Mother said, forcing a smile as she looked out the window. "Let's just enjoy this," she implored. "We'll be there in about an hour."

"Will it be dark when we come back?" I asked, looking upward at the wooden luggage racks above the seats.

"What about the shots, Mama?" Betty pressed. But Mother just kept looking away, closing her exhausted eyes. Betty grabbed mother's arm, as she began to notice all the strangers getting on at each new stop. They were bundled-up folks of every shape and size, packed tightly around us in the crowded car. Some of the travelers sat, but many stood, hanging onto brown leather straps that hung from the luggage racks overhead.

"I'll go first if there are shots," I whispered to Betty, "K?"

Posted above the exit doors was a list of towns, and I remember trying to read them to myself: Wilmette, Kenilworth, Winnetka, Glencoe, Highland Park, Highwood, Lake Forest, Lake Bluff, North Chicago, and Waukegan. Much later, I'd come to understand that these were all the stops the Chicago North Shore Line would make on this and all its trips. I reached into my pocket and squeezed a tiny red ball, the one I always used to play jacks. But before I got a good grip on it, it dropped out of my pocket. Bending down to retrieve it, I found that it had landed on the top fold of Mother's satchel.

"How come you brought this, Mother?" I asked. "Aren't we coming back tonight?"

She looked away and exhaled. "It might get cold," she said, putting an arm around Betty but turning her head away from both of us again. "It's some warmer things…just in case."

Betty watched the men reading neatly folded newspapers, and I noticed that several women clutched white handled shopping bags from places like Mandel Brothers and Marshall Fields. We both felt the side-to-side swaying of the train and the rhythmic "ta-dum, ta-dum, ta-dum" of the rails below.

At the Glencoe stop a tall, thin man got on board by himself. He was shouting things, but I couldn't tell who he was talking to. "Get outta my way!" he said, but no one was in his way. I put my arm around Betty. "I thought I told you to shut up! Now, shut up!" he said, but nobody was speaking. I pulled Betty closer.

He had a patchy, dark beard that seemed to have holes in it. His nose was long and crooked, and he kept picking it. "That's the dumbest thing I've ever heard!" he yelled, looking at the empty space beside him. People were moving away from him, as he continued his angry conversation. I tried to look away, but my eyes seemed to keep returning to him.

"What are you looking at?" he screamed. I bent down again, pretending to look for something under my seat.

"Lake Bluff! Lake Bluff is next!" hollered the blue uniformed conductor, passing down the crowded aisle. He had one of those curlicue mustaches and a gold chain that hung from one of his vest pockets across to the other.

Mother motioned for us to get up. "Here we are," she said. She wrung her hands, and glanced down at her far too heavy satchel under the seat.

"Will there be shots here, Mama? Will the shots be soon?" Betty whined.

I slid the satchel out from underneath Mother, struggled to pick it up, and handed it to her. Mother grabbed it from me way too quickly, and looked away immediately.

"This way." She led us toward several descending steps. I stooped to lift Betty, and she clung much too tightly to me, sinking her nails into the back of my neck. We both craned our necks in search of our mother. She'd exited the train well ahead of us, and when we entered the gray light of the outdoors, the first thing we saw was the dark brick train depot. Down the steps and to the right was our mother, whispering to the conductor, who turned to point back behind them, off to the east. He glanced at us as we descended the steps, shook his head solemnly, and walked in the opposite direction.

Mother shot us another forced smile and beckoned us toward her. I set Betty down but held onto her tiny hand. Her grip had not relaxed. Looking across the tracks to the east and then south, I saw a small, well-manicured village green. Beyond it were some shops that I couldn't quite make out. Up ahead to the left was a neat row of dark brick shops: a bakery, a pharmacy, and a hardware store, I think.

We followed Mother down Scranton Avenue, heading east, and were greeted by majestic, overhanging oaks and maples that towered above the commercial buildings. In the distance, the broad street seemed to narrow into a slate gray mass that I would later discover was the western edge of Lake Michigan.

We passed the small, brick shops on Scranton, and then the small but well kept homes with wide, manicured yards and even more of the majestic trees. Just a block beyond the center of town, we came upon several huge, red, brick buildings set way back from the road.

"Here we are," Mother said, as she led us up the sidewalk, where a sign said "Mackey Memorial Building." Two heavy, wood doors stood upon a cement stoop. Inside were clean, squeaky, marble floors beneath a high, vaulted ceiling. I remember it being eerily silent, except for the echo of footsteps that we heard in the cavernous distance. Mother led us to the main desk, where a tall woman in a pressed white shirt looked up from some files. Removing her glasses, she said, "Ah, you must be Mrs. Morgan, then?"

"Helen, yes," Mother responded. Betty let go of my hand and rushed over to our mother, again clutching Mother's leg. Mother closed her eyes and reached for the edge of the desk.

Rising from behind her large walnut desk, a tall matron with ramrod posture put her glasses back on her long nose. Stepping around her desk, I saw her plaid skirt. She said with a voice full of authority, "I'm Miss Arbuckle. Children, those chairs over there are for the two of you, while I speak with your mother for a few minutes…alone." She pointed out some small, painted wooden toys and used a small, scruffy doll made of stuffed socks and yarn, in an attempt to lure Betty away from our mother.

"Mama said we'll have ice cream after the shots and then the train."

Miss Arbuckle smiled at Betty, glanced at our mother, hesitated, and said, "Oh…I see." The matron's eyes met mine for just a fraction of an uncomfortable second.

I grabbed the doll and crossed over to Betty, took her hand, and pulled her over to the chairs. Glancing out a window beside us, I saw a large wooden playground with four swings, a seesaw, and a wooden jungle gym for climbing. I picked up Betty to show her. "Look, Betty! See the playground?"

Back at the desk, where the two women spoke in faint whispers, Miss Arbuckle took my mother's heavy satchel and set it behind her desk. She then seemed to work through some sort of checklist with my mother. Mother had her head in her right hand, as she kept wiping her nose and eyes with a hanky. Miss Arbuckle then placed a clipboard in front of my mother and handed her a pen. Mother signed it quickly and stood up.

"Come along, children," we heard Mother say, moving back toward the double doors we'd entered just minutes before. Betty ran to our mother, still holding the doll. I glanced back down the long hall in the other direction and noticed two teenagers peering at us through the crack of a barely opened door.

When we got back outside, the November air carried a chill, and I remember the sky being completely colorless. The four of us walked eastward along the main campus sidewalk, paralleling Scranton. We passed two more large, brick hospital buildings. Looking up, I saw what I was pretty sure were the heads of several children, silhouetted in the glass. I think they were watching us.

Miss Arbuckle turned left on the walkway that led up to the Swift Health Care Center.

"Swings, Mama! Let's try the swings!" Betty said, but my mother didn't even look up.

"Yes. Aren't they pretty swings? We'll give them a try after we see the doctors. They're waiting for us. Come along." Our mother kept dabbing her eyes with her hanky.

"It's only for a while with the doctor, right, Mama? Only for a while?" Betty said in her best grown-up voice. "And then we'll have ice cream." Miss Arbuckle held the door open, and Mother ducked inside without even responding.

Once again, marble floors amplified our footsteps. Across from the front desk, a couple stood smiling and whispering excitedly. "I'll bring the child right out," a nurse said, looking back at them. The husband and wife stood and took several steps in the direction of where the nurse had disappeared, then stopped, hugging each other.

Behind a desk, much like the one in Mackey Memorial, two women in white nursing uniforms stood like sentries. Miss Arbuckle approached them and gave them muffled instructions, pointing back toward Betty and me. The shorter of the two began waddling over toward us, with her partner close behind. I kept my eye on Miss Arbuckle who was watching my mother out of the corner of her eye, as if my mother were about to steal something from the desk. Over to the right of where the nurses had been, I saw another door that was slightly ajar. Three girls' heads peered out from behind it. One of them had her hand over her mouth as she stared at Betty.

"You must be Betty. I recognize that dolly you have." The waddling woman took Betty's hand firmly and added. "I'm Nurse Sanderson. I'll take you back now." Nurse Sanderson waited, while her taller, older partner made her way toward me.

"Right this way, young man. My name is Nurse Blueberg." She was tall and big-boned. Her lips were thin, and her jaw firmly set.

I nodded but didn't say anything. The four of us began walking toward a pair of heavy wooden doors, a little to the left of where the three girls had been. They were now gone. Betty asked, "Does the doctor have shots for us?"

"No. No shots today," Nurse Sanderson answered, glancing curiously at her fellow nurse. Betty turned around in search of Mother. Not seeing her, she suddenly pulled away from the nurse and cried out.

"Mama? Mama!"

I turned back toward the now empty reception area and scanned the cavernous halls in search of our mother. I didn't see her at first, but soon heard her unmistakable wail, coming from all the way back by the entrance doors, where Mother was at a dead run, running away from us.

"Mother!" I screamed. And then again, "Mother!"

Miss Arbuckle had corralled Betty and was trying to shield herself from Betty's kicking and flailing. Our mother was gone.

"Jesus," Hargrave said, looking down and shaking his head.

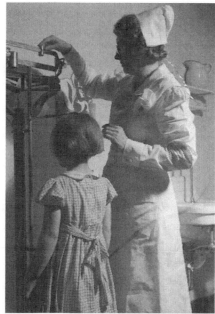

INTAKE EXAMINATION — LAKE BLUFF ORPHANAGE
Photo courtesy of the Lake Bluff History Museum

Chapter 3 — We Welcome You
Lake Bluff, IL — Lake Bluff Orphanage — November 25, 1927

"I have to see my sister! Why can't I see my own sister?" I yelled, as Nurse Blueberg moved through her endless medical intake checklist.

"Your sister is fine. You need to relax," she said, looking down at me.

"Betty is four years old! Four!" I said, half spitting. "Her mother just dumped her here. You think that's fine?" I wiped my tears with the back of my hand. "You can't keep us from seeing each other!"

Nurse Blueberg set her tongue depressor and flashlight on the noisy metal cart and let out an exasperated breath. "We've been over this, Griffin. We separate boys and girls here for very good reasons. We also separate children by age. Betty is just two buildings from here in Judson Hall, and she is fine. She passed her checkup. She has a nice room, just like you do." She paused, put a hand on my trembling shoulders, and added, "Now please, Griffin, be a big boy, and let me finish my work here."

I pictured my sister, two buildings over, sobbing uncontrollably, kneeling against the window. Did she have her one-eyed bear or at least that silly sock doll from Mackey Memorial? Was anybody holding or comforting her? Nurse Blueberg had told me that the Judson housemother was a Miss Jaeger, and I prayed that, whoever she was, she would stop at nothing to get Betty settled down.

"Where is my mama?" I could imagine Betty saying. "Where is Griffy?" I knew I had to find a way over there.

I'm sure they were telling her the same stuff they were telling me: "Betty, your brother is right next door. He's with all the other boys, just as you get to be with all of our girls."

"When do we get the i-i-ice cream with my ma- mama? Whe-when will we go to the train?" she'd be stammering between her tear-choked breaths. I wanted to scream at my mother for all her "it's only for a while" promises and lies. But first I needed to figure out a way to get over to Judson Hall and up to Betty's room.

When I finally finished the intake checkup, I was even more edgy than I'd been before. As Nurse Blueberg walked me to my partition in Wadsworth Hall, one building over and up the solid concrete steps, I thought only of Betty.

Orphan boys were staring at me from every conceivable angle. Some stood at the top of the stairs, peering down at me as they whispered and snickered. Others looked up from games of Jacks and Checkers. None of them smiled. I bit my lip, looked down, and then glanced over to the window to my right, as we turned the corner in the main first floor room of this boys' dormitory. I could see Scranton, but couldn't quite see the train station, where my mother would have already boarded the southbound North Shore Line back to the city. What was she thinking? Where was she going? Was she really leaving us here? Would she be coming back?

The partition Nurse Blueberg led me to had two beds in it, each with a chair at its foot. There was a dark wooden bedside table between the two beds with a black Gideon Bible on it. The single paned window, just behind the table, looked out the back side of Wadsworth Hall to a grassy area. On my bed, all neatly folded, were the clothes Mother must have brought in that satchel she'd hidden under the train seat. That's what made it so heavy—all my clothes and all of Betty's.

Even in this partitioned space, there was nothing remotely resembling privacy. It was really just one big room on the first floor of Wadsworth Hall, divided up by the careful placement of furniture and the occasional five-foot partition posing as a wall. Anyone who was tall or even clever enough to stand on a chair could look down into any one of the eight cubicles. I'd felt like I was being watched from the moment Nurse Blueberg left me in my partition, and, as it turned out, I was. Two sets of eyes with dirty, blond bangs above them looked down on me, as I put my stuff away. I pretended not to care. Whoever shared this partitioned space with me wasn't around, but his things were. His white sneakers looked almost twice as long as mine, but our beds were exactly the same, each with the same charcoal wool blanket folded at its foot. I glanced back up at the two blond spies, shook my head, and was saved by the 12:15 bell summoning us to lunch.

I followed a thundering herd of boys down the steps of Wadsworth Hall, behind the Mackey Memorial building, and over to the dining hall, where dozens of long tables, covered in checkered tablecloths, were lined up end-to-end, covering the entire floor. More and more eyes stared in my direction, along with pointed fingers and muffled laughter. There were pictures of Jesus and depictions of other Christian scenes I recognized from Aunt Rose's church, evenly spaced on the walls, so that no matter where we were in the room, somebody holy was looking down at us.

Just beneath a picture of a smiling apostle, I saw two boys about four feet apart with their foreheads pressed against the wall and their hands held awkwardly behind their backs. One of the housemothers stood watch over them with her long switch poised and ready.

Girls started streaming in as well, standing in their places behind each wooden chair, waiting for some sort of signal, I guess. Just then Miss Arbuckle, the lady with the ramrod posture who had taken Betty and me from Mackey Memorial over to the Swift Healthcare Center, walked in with her stiff, even stride. Her entrance seemed to quiet everyone down and improve their posture to that of soldiers standing at attention. I noticed the distinct odor of this room, a mix of floor cleaner and overcooked meat.

I was at a table near the stuffy matron, with a lot of eleven and twelve-year-olds, all from "Wads," as they called our dorm. I'd later learn that the older boys in grades six through eight lived on the first floor of Wadsworth Hall, and the younger boys in grades three to five lived on the second floor.

I scanned the large dining hall for Betty. The rows of smooth, wooden tables alternated between boys and girls, but I couldn't see Betty anywhere. With everybody standing, it was impossible to see. It didn't help that the tables closest to mine were filled with the older, taller girls, totally blocking my view of nearly a third of the room. I needed everyone to sit down, so I could see Betty, if she was even here.

A single chime of Miss Arbuckle's tiny bell silenced the room for a second or two. Heads bowed, eyes closed, and the echoing recitation began.

Bless this meat that we shall eat, this bread that we shall break.
Make all our actions kind and sweet, we ask for Jesus' sake. Amen.

No one moved, and all eyes were fixed upon Miss Arbuckle as she spoke. "Children, I am excited to welcome two new residents to LBO today, thanks be to God. Let us sing our song of welcome to Griffin and Betty Morgan." She blew into a small, round pitch pipe, and a single note came forth. At her nod, the chorus began:

We welcome you, we welcome you, we welcome you today
Oh how glad we are to have you with us while we may-hey
We welcome you, we welcome you, we'd like to have you know
That we are very glad to have you here at LBO.

I recognized the tune—Jingle Bells. I wondered if Betty would catch it. She loved that song and "Kwis-mis," as she she used to call it. But even that song wasn't going to bring her any comfort in this place.

I was startled by the noisy, echoing screech of 114 wooden chairs being pulled back from the tables, as the entire orphanage finally sat down. But I didn't sit. I scanned the expansive dining hall for my sister. I hadn't seen her since we were separated coming out of our checkups. I felt the eyes of my tablemates all over me. Every table I stared at was looking back at me. But they were all sitting down, which is probably why the next thing the entire dining hall heard was my name.

"Griffin, you will, please, be seated," Miss Arbuckle said, punching out the word "will." I heard her, but I didn't respond, at least not at first. I couldn't, for I had finally located Betty. She was nearly a hundred feet from me, at the last table over in the corner. She was clutching a teddy bear to her chest, as she sat sullenly.

"Griffin!" the voice of authority came once again, this time sharp and pointed. I nodded at Miss Arbuckle and sat down.

"Ow!" I shrieked, pulling the upturned fork from beneath the seat of my pants. Half the boys at my table covered their mouths, as their shoulders lurched in laughter. I looked down at my folded hands and felt the movement of older orphan boys bringing platters and pitchers to each table. The volume of banter resumed to its pre-prayer level.

"Great. Looks like sticky spaghetti and mystery meat, boys," a tall, pasty-faced boy said, shaking his head. "Another Friday night feast."

"You sure about the roadkill story, Danny?" a boy with beady, close-set eyes asked.

"Yep. Billy O'Neil works in the kitchen," the pasty faced kid continued. "Says Mr. Spader's brown truck makes deliveries every other week: deer, possum, squirrel, you name it. If it gets run over, shot in the ravines, or rejected by any local hunters, it winds up right here in the dining hall, and we eat it." He licked his lips and raised his eyebrows sarcastically.

"If they shoot it in the ravines, they should just leave it there to feed the witches!" the beady-eyed boy said. It produced a snicker throughout the table.

"Billy O'Neil should learn to keep his mouth shut," the boy next to me muttered, examining his meatballs for possum hairs.

"Look on the bright side, Knox. We get to wash it down with orange jello and string beans," the beady-eyed boy snickered.

I hadn't touched my food. I couldn't even think about eating. With my fingers tightly intertwined and clenched beneath the table, I kept craning my neck to see Betty. I'd seen her, but she hadn't seen me. I wanted to make sure that she saw me and knew that I was here, that I wasn't leaving her.

"You got a girlfriend over there?" asked Knox, the short, pudgy boy next to me.

I shook my head. "A sister," I said.

"Better eat up, Griffy boy," the tall, pale boy chided. "Never know what they're going to feed us tomorrow."

"Danny's right," Knox said. I nodded back quickly and picked up my bent fork. I wondered if this tall, awkward, pasty-faced kid who called me by name was my roommate, and glanced under the table at his enormous shoes.

There was a momentary silence.

"It's all in the jobs," Danny continued, without looking up from his plate. "We all get assigned chores, right? You just gotta put in for the ones that get you over to Swift and Judson. That's how you'll see her."

I took my first bite, considering his suggestion.

"Danny's right," Knox offered. "Laundry pickup, tunnel sweeping, shoveling, and trash duty," he paused to take a swig of milk. "They'll all get you over there."

"Problem is, you still won't be able to spend any time with her. It ain't like you can sit down and have a chat," said the kid on the other side of Knox. He'd laughed the hardest when I sat on the fork. He'd probably put it there. He had a ruddy, pock-marked face and a jagged scar in the shape of an upside down V, just over his right eyebrow. "Can slip her a note though," he added.

"What if she's not old enough to read, Ernie, you moron! How's she gonna read it?" Knox laughed.

"Easy, Knox," the tall one, Danny, said. "The older ones'll read it to her. They take care of the little ones over there. They remember how it was."

I looked over toward Betty again. Her eyes looked puffy. The girl next to her was cutting Betty's noodles. I had to get over to see her or get her attention somehow.

Pushing back my chair abruptly, I stood up again and coughed as loudly as I could, looking right at Betty's table. Everybody looked up in horror, first at me and at Miss Arbuckle. But I didn't care, for I had caught Betty's eye. I nodded to her and smiled before sitting back down. Miss Arbuckle said nothing.

We cleared our own plates into wooden crates, and one boy from each table shuttled them into the kitchen. It was the pudgy one they called "Knox" who had that duty at our table. Once he'd shuttled the dishes to the kitchen, he returned with vanilla ice cream for the table. Why did it have to be ice cream? I thought, remembering my mother's lie: "We'll get ice cream on our way to the train." Yeah, I thought. We'll get ice cream all right.

The Furnace Girl

LAKE BLUFF ELEMENTARY SCHOOL — EIGHTH GRADE CLASS
Photo courtesy of the Lake Bluff History Museum

Chapter 4 — Late for School
Lake Bluff Orphanage — November 29, 1927

On the last Tuesday in November, four days after our arrival, I choked down the lukewarm oatmeal and canned fruit covered with syrup, pushed my chair back, dropped my dishes in the wooden bins, and bolted back to Wads with all the other boys.

"You got your bed made, kid?" Knox said, as he slapped the back of my head and passed me at the entrance door. "Don't want Harvey to paddle ya, like she did the O'Neil twins last night. You hear 'em screamin?"

"You should talk, Knox," another kid said. "You're the biggest slob in Wads." Then one of them snorted.

I'd made my bed before breakfast, so I grabbed my toothbrush and dashed to the head. On my way, I passed our housemother, Miss Bertha Harvey, moving from partition to partition with her clipboard.

"You're all set, Mr. Morgan," she said, as I dropped my

toothbrush back in my closet drawer. I joined the hustling throng of those who passed muster and plodded down the stairs unenthusiastically for another day at Lake Bluff Elementary School, another eight hours in a place where we would never quite fit in. Betty, at least, was spared the indignity of being one of the orphans at the public school. The littlest kids—preschool through second grade—simply went next door to the Mackey Memorial building for a one-room schoolhouse with Miss Arbuckle and Miss Jaeger.

Up ahead of me on the path were a group of boys from my floor. They were the first to reach the end of the long sidewalk that stretched from the Wads front door to the east-west sidewalk along Scranton Ave. A few others I recognized but couldn't yet name were close behind them, and they all followed the gang that was heading west, the official route to school by way of downtown Lake Bluff. Lagging behind were two kids whose names I did know—Homer Haskell and Ernie Van Es. Homer and Ernie walked side-by-side, down the Wads walk, with me a little behind them and to the right. When they reached the perpendicular sidewalk, they turned left, while I turned right toward the other boys.

"Hey, kid! Why don't you come with us!" shouted the shorter of the two, Homer. I hesitated, looking back and forth between the two groups of boys. I'd heard about "the other way" to school, through the ravines and bridges, but I hadn't taken it. It was supposed to be longer, dirtier, and "full of trouble," according to Miss Harvey.

Ernie chimed in. "Aw, just come with us, kid. We won't be late...unless, of course, the witches get us!" I took one final look over my shoulder to the west and then chased after Homer and Ernie. We traveled half a block toward Lake Michigan and then took a right. The entrance to the first ravine was a single-track path that cut down toward a small creek. A series of fallen trees crisscrossed the tiny rivulet, and Ernie and Homer mounted every one, jumping from trunk to trunk, hurdling the creek this way and that, and making "whoops" and "yawps" at every turn.

I took a more cautious approach, this being my first trip through the ravine. I couldn't help noticing the houses above us, the brown and crunchy leaves below our feet, and the sounds of doors closing and mothers saying goodbye to their husbands and kids. I'd tested my balance on the occasional fallen oak and leapt over the winding creek a time or two. But my main concern—besides the witches and not getting lost—was making sure that I didn't wind up being late for my second day of school.

I heard more yelping and whooping from above, so I looked up to see a hanging bridge made of rope and wood that spanned the entire ravine. Both Homer and Ernie had climbed back up the slope of the ravine and were jumping up and down on the flimsy suspension bridge.

"It's been here since forever, Griff!" Ernie shouted.

"Yeah, Injuns built it about a thousand years ago," Homer added.

I headed up to join them, but both boys were jumping so violently on the simple rope and board structure, I feared it would give way at any moment. "Wow!" I uttered, as I joined them on the surprisingly strong but swaying structure. At its south end, Homer and Ernie leapt off and then split up in different directions. Ernie ran up a path that led up to another level of the ravine. Homer was running down toward a lower path that ran along the creek.

"Griff! Griff! Up here!" Ernie was calling to me, urgently motioning for me to follow him. "Hurry up! Climb here!" I quickened my pace, leapt off the bridge, and cringed, as my leg sank almost eight inches, completely soaking my shoe in muddy sludge. I freed my foot and bounded up the pathless way toward Ernie. I glanced back down in search of Homer, but he was long gone.

Ernie was now at a full sprint, laughing and whooping all the way, with me a good hundred paces behind. We exited the ravine and could see the school up ahead. Just then I heard the unmistakable, cocky cackle of Homer, who came into view, sitting comfortably like a dewdropper and eating an apple on the green bench, just outside the main doors of the school.

"What took ya so long, fellas?" Homer snickered, as he jumped up from the bench and chucked his apple core halfway across the adjacent playground. The bell rang out abruptly, and my jaw dropped in terror. I looked down at my mud covered pant leg and soaking shoe. Our tardy threesome raced in the main door and ran full bore through the central gymnasium toward Miss Kerrington's sixth grade classroom, which was a straight shot. In addition to squeaking at every step, I left a muddy, wet trail across the entire gym floor.

Our shoulders were heaving as we entered the classroom. The entire class was already seated and ready to begin.

"Well, well. How nice of you three boys to join us," Miss Kerrington, said. She had her glasses down toward the very end of her upturned nose. Her sleek, black hair was pulled back in a tight bun, and her thin lips were painted a deep maroon color.

Homer and Ernie kept their heads down and turned away from the teacher, but their sly smiles were more than evident to all our classmates. I, on the other hand, must have looked like I was going to faint, die of shame, and probably never speak to either of these bad influences ever again. It didn't help that my entire left leg, from my knee down, was caked with wet mud.

As I made my way to my seat, I passed the desk of David Gadd. "Couldn't pass your bed inspection, huh, orphan?" Gadd whispered to me. "Or were you last in line for the morning gruel?" he snickered.

Danny Thompson, my roommate, had warned me about kids like Gadd. "Make enough friends with the nice ones and forget the saps," he'd said. But I wasn't nearly as big as Danny was, and I wasn't too confident about my chances of making any friends outside of LBO.

"Open your math books to page 32." There were groans and exasperated exhales, as we opened our flip top desks and dug out our dark covered math texts. "We will continue to practice multiplying three digit numbers, and with our test only two days from now, we need to be sure we've mastered this vital skill."

Gadd had the right book out but wasn't opening it. He had a small scrap of lined paper out and was writing some sort of note. He crumpled it up, waited for Miss Kerrington to turn her back, and tossed it lightly, so it landed atop my book, which was already opened to page 32. I opened his crumpled note and read.

"Bet Miss Kerrington'd be your Mama if you asked her... bastard!" I brushed it aside, acting as unfazed as I could, even faking a smile. But I didn't appreciate the crack about my mother.

The girl who sat in the desk to Gadd's left and right behind me was Charlotte Stevens. I remembered her introducing herself on my first day of school. She had pretty, wavy hair and a warm smile. She'd probably seen this kind of behavior from David more times than she could count. She wrote a note of her own, tapped me on the back of my left shoulder, and handed me her note when I turned. "Nobody listens to DG. Nobody cares what he thinks. Don't you either. CS" I nodded subtly in her direction and started the row of math problems Miss Kerrington had assigned.

When the bell rang for morning recess, Ernie and Homer were among the first to exit the classroom. Instinctively, I started rushing to catch them but then remembered that they'd made me late. I paused to let the other kids by and turned toward Miss Kerrington's desk. After a deep breath I said, "Miss Kerrington, I'm sorry we were late and interrupted your class."

She looked right at me, pushed her silver framed glasses all the way up to the bridge of her nose, and replied, "Thank you, Griff. It's important to apologize, but not as important as doing better the next time." I nodded and filed out of the sixth grade classroom.

The gym was packed with kids. The fourth and fifth graders had their recess at the same time we sixth graders did. The two teachers and the principal had whistles around their necks. A third teacher was outside on the playground with those kids who were properly bundled up for the cold.

Scanning the room, I didn't see Ernie or Homer and thought about heading outside. I noticed a girl with red hair in pigtails, standing with her elbows out and her hands at her waist. She seemed to be telling a story or giving orders to a cluster of kids, fifth graders I think. They stood silently before her, oblivious to the chaos in the rest of the room.

"Griff! Over here!" I heard another girl yelling from across the gym. By the fireplace, Charlotte waved to me. She was with a couple girls and a handful of boys. "We're starting a game of tag. I'm it. Want to play?"

"OK," I said.

At lunchtime, we orphanage kids went back to LBO for our meal. It meant more walking and left little time to actually eat, but we welcomed any opportunity to break up the long school day. Plus, it meant that I could get away from the likes of David Gadd. With food at the other end of this journey, few, if any, of the LBO residents took the ravine way back. I caught up to James Ward and Knox Korly.

"Heard you were late today, Griffy," Knox chided with a light shove.

"Better hope Miss Harvey doesn't hear about it," James added ominously.

We passed the Village Hall and cut up Evanston Avenue toward Scranton. Finally, I caught a glimpse of Homer and Ernie, taking the right turn onto Scranton. They were both laughing about something, as they broke into a run toward the dining hall.

Right behind them was a big kid, close to six feet tall, with black hair. He walked almost like an adult, purposefully and controlled. I'd heard other kids talking about him. Moley was his name, Dick Moley. He was both the biggest and the oldest kid in the orphanage, not to mention the best athlete in the entire school.

I hung back and eyed the entrance to Mackey Memorial, while the other kids went hastily to the dining hall. The youngest kids in the orphanage—the kindergarteners through second graders—were still inside from their morning of school with the housemothers. I lingered as long as I could, in hopes that I might be out front when Miss Arbuckle led the little ones across the walkway to the dining hall. It could mean an extra couple of minutes with Betty.

This was one of several tricks my roommate Danny had begun to teach me in my first week at the orphanage. He had had a little sister at the orphanage too; her name was Linda. They'd been at LBO together since Danny was in second grade; he was now in eighth. After this year, he would "age out" of the orphanage. But his little sister got fostered out three years ago, and now Danny was faced with being booted out at the end of the current school year. It was a daunting prospect; I simply couldn't believe it when Danny told me.

"They're just going to kick you out of the orphanage? What will you do? Where will you go?" I'd asked.

Danny sighed and shook his head. "Beats me." After staring out the window above his partition, he added, "I got the rest of this school year to figure it out."

"What about your sister? Where is she?" I pressed.

Danny shook his head and looked down. He exhaled heavily, and I wondered if I even should have brought her up. "First she was with a family up in Mundelein. Then she was out in Glen Ellyn. But I haven't heard from her or gotten any update in almost two years." I couldn't imagine being so separated and cut off from Betty. "There's no way I'm leaving here, LBO, I mean, until I figure out where she is and how to see her," Danny said. He scratched his left cheek, just below his ear. "I wish these Christmas visits were set up right here in Lake Bluff or Lake Forest."

"What do you mean?" I asked.

"Well, this family, the Berns, I've spent the last six Christmases with them. We get along real good. They're swell people, and they sure treat me," he paused, searching for the word. "...well, like family." Again, he grew thoughtful, and his face scrunched a bit. "I just feel like if Linda ever wants to find me, she'll come here—to Lake Bluff—first, and I don't want to be far away when she does."

I was half listening and half thinking, turning every option I could think of over in my head. I felt Danny's dilemma as if it were my own, and in about a year and a half, it would be. "Have you talked to Miss Arbuckle about it? She's gotta help you! She can't just turn you out." My hands were in fists. I was pacing back and forth in our cubicle. I ached for him, but I was also terrified for myself. If Betty left this place without me, I'd lose my mind. She was all I had.

"I do talk to Miss Arbuckle about it," Danny said. "She always says, 'Something will work out.'" He got up off his bed and returned to the window. Light snow had started to fall. He drummed his fingers on the window pane. "Most days I think I believe her. I want to believe her."

I took in a breath and opened and closed my fists. "It's not right. It's not fair." I moved toward the gap in the partitions. "You're not even in high school."

The front door of the Mackey Memorial building swung open, and a row of little girls hurried out in pairs. They were the four-to seven-year-olds, each holding hands with her assigned partner. I scanned the little heads, most covered in hoods or knit caps. I spotted Betty five pairs back and fell into line beside her.

"Hey, peanut!" I said, ruffling Betty's hat and grabbing her hand.

"Griffy! Why are you here?"

"I missed you, and I knew this is where you'd be." I let go of her hand and rushed ahead of the first pair of girls to grab the heavy door into the dining hall. Opening it, I caught Betty's eye again and smiled.

"Helping?" Betty asked.

"Yes, brother Griffy is helping."

CRAB TREE DAIRY FARM
Drawing courtesy of Crab Tree Farm Foundation

Chapter 5 — Farmhands
Lake Bluff, IL — Crab Tree Farm — December 5, 1927

The brown and heavily dented Lake Bluff Orphanage truck rolled down the main driveway of Crab Tree Farm off of Sheridan Road. Driven by the LBO's main utility man Jim Spader, the truck angled toward the milk house. It listed so far back and to the right, that at times it appeared to have only three functioning wheels. I was sitting in the passenger seat of the cab with Mr. Spader, while back on the flatbed sat Danny and Knox. It was time for our after school chores.

Mr. Spader was about 50. I'd been told that he spent most of his time in the power house and the laundry at the orphanage, fixing things and keeping everything running. It was an incredible day. Usually, early December in Lake Bluff can feel like mid-February everywhere else. But this was one of those rare days when the winds had shifted, and warm air from the south gave us a day that felt like early fall.

I'd heard a bit about Crab Tree Farm from some of the Wads boys almost from the day I arrived and was anxious to get my first look at the place. They'd said it was a good place to get assigned if I could, because it would get me out of the orphanage, teach me some skills, and, on some days, get me some of the best oatmeal cookies any of the guys had ever had.

Mr. Spader jumped out from behind the steering column, and the two boys in the back hurdled awkwardly onto the dusty ground. Spader was average height and a little thick in the midsection. He ambled more than walked and always had a pipe in his mouth, even when he wasn't smoking it.

I climbed out of the passenger side tentatively, taking in the massive and brilliantly white buildings around us. The main farmhouse had more windows and porches than any place I'd ever seen. It all seemed to glisten, and I couldn't imagine how many people it took to keep the place so clean, neat, and well taken care of. There were at least nine or ten buildings, and they all looked brand new.

I heard a door open and close behind me, and I wheeled around to see a tall man, coming out of the milk house, wiping his large, calloused hands with a torn gray towel. His sharp eyes quickly passed over Danny and Knox, settling firmly upon me. I averted my eyes from his gaze and stared off toward the orchard.

"Afternoon, Redd," Mr. Spader said. Danny took that as the cue to start pulling down the three crates of empty bottles we'd brought over from LBO. The man he'd called "Redd" looked them over.

"Afternoon' yourself, gentlemen," Redd said, still staring at me, the wiry, sheepish new boy.

"Say hello to Mr. Reddington, Griff," Mr. Spader prompted.

"Hello, sir,'" I said.

"No, no. Just call me Redd," he said, waving off Mr. Spader's formality. "Griff is it? Ever been on a farm?" he asked, still wiping his hands as he squinted toward the sun. I looked down at the gravel drive and shook my head. "We're mostly a milking operation here, as I suspect Mr. Spader has explained," Redd continued.

Mr. Spader stepped toward the three of us. "Each o' you boys take a crate in and see that the bottles are rinsed one last time. Danny, mind that Griff here learns what we do and how Mr. Reddington expects it be done." He rubbed his cracked hands together and then blew in them.

"A new one, huh?" I heard Redd say, as we hustled toward the milk house door.

"Yep," Mr. Spader looked at his hands before continuing. "His mother brought him and his four-year-old sister in last Friday." He shook his head. "Would'a been nice if she'd a told 'em. Poor kids thought they was gettin' shots and checkups. The lady'd run off 'fore they got through the infirmary door. Plum run off."

"Sweet Jesus," Redd replied, just before the milk house door shut the three of us inside and out of earshot. But I stopped just inside the door and looked out the window for Mr. Reddington's reaction. If I read his lips right, he said, "What in the hell kind'a woman'd do that?" My mother, that's who, I thought.

Danny, Knox, and I were over at the washing section of the milk house, where crates were stacked up seven and eight high. Even the crates looked new, their unvarnished slats sanded smooth.

"So over here, on the left of the hoses, are the ones waiting to be washed," Knox instructed. "Those ones over on the right have already been cleaned out." We'd stacked our crates on the left, and Knox headed straight for the hose, while Danny showed me how to scrub out the bottles with warm soapy water, rinse and towel them off, and then gently place them back in the crates.

There was a shiny, white door and two windows in this section of the milk house that Danny said they'd learned to keep open, "so things didn't get all steamed up." One of the windows faced the driveway, and we heard engines approaching and the rustling of gravel. A black Ford Model T Pick-up churned its way toward the main farmhouse. No sooner did it stop, then two other cars, a green Packard and a brown Ford, pulled in beside the black one. Each car was loaded with ladies, some with hats, many with dark colored coats, and all with very loud voices. They proceeded up the porch stairs, where a woman welcomed them stiffly.

"That's Grace Durand. She owns this place," Danny said, pointing to the colorfully dressed woman opening the kitchen door from the inside. She was a short, stout woman, powerfully built. Her face was leathery and weathered, and her eyes were set in a kind of permanent squint. Her lips were tight and thin, and she wore no makeup.

"She's the boss around here," Knox added. "Her husband makes the money and pays the bills, but he don't run the place. That he leaves to Mrs. D."

I wiped a few bottles that Danny had handed me without taking my eyes off the parade of ladies heading in the kitchen door. As the last of the guests entered, Mrs. Grace Durand stepped out on the porch to speak to Mr. Spader.

"Good afternoon, Mrs. Durand," I heard Mr. Spader say, removing his cap and taking the unlit pipe from his mouth.

"Afternoon, Jim," she said. "Milk day, is it?" She squinted toward the sinking sun.

"Yes, ma' am," Spader replied. Danny and Knox had set their work aside and were heading out the door, so I followed. As the three of us hustled out of the milk house, Redd saw us and waved us over toward the porch railing.

He gestured toward us as he spoke. "Mrs. D., you know Danny and Knox." Both boys smiled and nodded. "And this here is Griff. He's new today." I stiffened and blushed, unsure of what to do. I forced a smile and nodded, as I'd seen the others do.

"Well, welcome, Griff," Mrs. Durand offered, stepping toward me, smiling. "Welcome to the best darn dairy farm in the whole midwest."

"Thank you...ma'am," I said, looking down between my shoes.

"I reckon you'll have to be getting to your guests," Redd said. "This is your meeting day, huh?"

Mrs. Durand chuckled, turning back toward the house. "Oh, yes. The Lake Forest-Lake Bluff Chapter of the WCTU, and I do believe it will be quite a lively one, quite a lively one, indeed." Her gray-green eyes glinted, as she chewed on a callous on her thumb. "I can tell you that those bootleggers had best steer clear of these parts, if they know what's good for them." She went up the porch steps spryly. Mrs. Durand opened the door but then abruptly turned back to Redd and Mr. Spader. "If you can spare the manpower, gentlemen, I'd sure like to get the last of the leaves out of my ivy and cedar hedge over on the north side." She gestured with her gnarled index finger around the corner and then turned back toward the kitchen door.

"Yes, ma'am. We'll take care of that straight away," Redd said.

"Danny, you and Knox hop to it on those bottles," Mr. Spader said. "We're going to get Griff started on leaf duty." Redd ducked into a shed, while I glanced at the other boys. Danny smiled slyly and whispered something to Knox about "letting the new kid get a look at the witches," as the two of them turned back for the milk house.

"Come with me, Griff," Redd said, now carrying a rake and a large garbage can. I followed him around to the north side of the farmhouse. There was a large bank of freshly painted windows that looked in at the grand sitting room, where nearly a dozen ladies sat in an oval, sipping tea. The ground where we stood was covered in myrtle or ivy with several low-lying cedar bushes every five feet or so. They were neatly trimmed.

"We always try to get as many of these leaves up and out of here before the snow flies, Griff." He pulled a pair of work gloves out of his back pocket and handed them to me. "Put these on, and put all the leaves you gather into this can." I nodded. "Just holler if you need anything. I'll be back and forth between the milk house and here."

I nodded again and pulled the too-big, tan leather gloves on. The bottom of the windows came up to my neck, and I noticed right away that I could hear pretty near every word that was coming from that room. Four or five of the woman were only a couple of feet from me, but since they had their backs to the windows, none of them saw me.

I looked out away from the house toward what seemed to be an orchard. Several other buildings as big, white, and as pretty as the others I'd seen shined in the afternoon light. As I started to rake, I struggled to pick out Mrs. Durand in her living room full of women. Too much of my view was blocked, but I recognized her voice. She didn't strike me as the witch type.

"That's right, Myrtle. If it's happening in Evanston and in Waukegan, Lord knows, it's happening here, or it very soon will be." Mrs. Durand declared.

One of the ladies closest to me said, "The rest of Lake County may well stick their heads in the sand as this poisonous scourge infects their men, but it's always been the WCTU's place to sound the alarm."

"And sound it we will," another lady added.

I bent down to get what the rake wouldn't dislodge and started making a pile next to the first cedar bush.

"Hey!" a girl's voice startled me. I looked up to see a sturdy, red-haired girl wearing pigtails, a red and black plaid shirt, overalls, and farm boots. It was the same girl I'd seen at recess the week before, telling a bunch of fifth graders what was what. "I'm Lily Reddington. Who are you?" She spoke firmly with her hands on her hips. She looked about my age, maybe a little younger, but there was something bossy in the way she spoke, like she was used to being in charge.

"I'm Griff...from the orphanage."

She rolled her eyes and shook her head. "I know you're from the orphanage. Every boy who works here is from the orphanage. Tell me something I don't already know."

I looked around, unsure what to say. I started raking until she broke the silence. "My daddy's the one they call Redd," she said, crossing her arms.

"Yeah. He sent me over here...to do this, I mean," I said without looking up.

The gruff, authoritative voice of Grace Durand came through the window. "I'm with Myrtle and Agnes on this one." Lily Reddington's ears perked up, and she leaned in toward the voice. "I'll be sorely disappointed if our vote on taking action be anything short of unanimous."

"Have you met Mrs. D. yet?" Lily asked. "She runs the farm," she added, crossing her arms again.

"Yeah, I know," I said, raking harder. Glancing at Lily and then pointing with my head toward the window, I asked, "What are they doing in there, all these ladies?"

"Depends. Mrs. D. goes to a lot of meetings. What day is it?" Lily said.

"Monday."

"It's the WCTU. Definitely the WCTU. That's the Women's Christian Temper Union," she said.

"What's a Temper Union?" I asked. I bent over to put my first pile into the trash can.

"They're the ones that don't want any alcohol anywhere," she replied. "And they lose their temper, I guess, when anybody drinks it."

I rubbed the back of my neck with a gloved hand. "But it's already against the law. We learned that in school. It's an amendment."

"Haven't you ever heard of bootleggers?" she asked, cocking her head to one side.

"Sure, I have," I lied. "But what good is some ladies' temper meeting gonna do?"

"Well, if Mrs. D.'s involved, something good will come of it," Lily said. I remembered Mrs. D's line on her way into the kitchen: "I do believe those bootleggers had best steer clear of these parts, if they know what's good for them."

"I got a newspaper clipping on my bulletin board about Mrs. Grace Durand taking on The Illinois Stock Breeders' Association. I can show you if you want. Those guys came right here, saying they were going to exterminate all of Mrs. Durand's cattle. Said her cows were sick or something. Mrs. D. held them off all by herself for three days with her own Remington shotgun. She's still got the gun, and I still got the article. I can even show it to you, if you want." This girl seemed to know everything, and I could tell she wasn't near finished with this story.

"Mrs. D. took those boys to court. She even sued the Governor of Illinois, along with the State's Livestock Commission. She won too—$50,000 in cash money. So," Lily continued, "if she took on the whole Illinois government, I bet she can take on these North Shore bootleggers too."

Lily leaned in toward the windows. She smiled at me, and her green eyes got really big. "Let's listen in! We can spy on 'em!" she whispered.

"I'm supposed to get all these leaves up," I said. "Doesn't look like I'm doing too good of a job though."

"I can help you. Doesn't mean we can't listen at the same time," Lily said.

I shrugged and grabbed the rake, moving over to the next bush.

"None of us wants whiskey and its accompanying debauchery in or even passing through our dear towns. As our founding sister, Frances Willard, herself, said, 'We must make the whiskey rings— and the corrupt politicians who condone them—dread our very presence.'" Whoever was speaking paused, and Lily held her finger up to her mouth. Then the voice resumed. "Our goal is clear, yes. But just how do we propose to accomplish it?"

"These are the days of the 'Do Everything Policy,' are they not?" a woman with a shrieking voice said. I stood up to see the woman who owned this voice. She had stood up to address the others. Her broad nostrils flared, and her chin jutted forward. "What 'everything' means to me is education, transportation, and law enforcement. We produce hanging signs and fliers for every church, school, business, and organization in the villages. We speak at every establishment that will have us and inform them about all the illegal activity that is already happening in Evanston and Waukegan." The shrieker paused, as if searching for her third step.

"Road blocks!" It was the now familiar voice of Grace Durand interrupting. As she did, Lily Reddington's green eyes widened, and she smiled and nodded, edging closer to the window. "We must insist that every truck and vehicle capable of transporting this poison is stopped from coming into Lake Bluff and Lake Forest and from going out, until they are searched."

"Barney isn't going to like that one bit. Where will he get the man power?" a froggy-voiced woman said.

Lily leaned toward me and whispered, "She's talking about our police chief Barney Rosenhagen."

Another voice I'd heard before retorted, "Chief Rosenhagen doesn't have to like it and neither does Lake Forest's Chief Tiffany." This woman crushed her consonants. "And as for man power, I should think we could offer our husbands and our eldest sons, if need be."

"I see you've hired a helper, Griff," Redd said, startling us.

"Hi, Daddy!" Lily said. I bent down and started grabbing leaves feverishly. I hadn't even come close to finishing the job I'd been given and regretted how much I'd allowed Lily to distract me.

"Griff, Mr. Spader is loading up the milk crates, so you guys'll be heading back soon," Mr. Reddington added.

"Ok. I'll just finish as much as I can here, sir." I grabbed the rake and went after the next bush.

"Fine," Redd said. "But nobody calls me 'sir' around here, so I'd prefer you not do it either."

"I'm sorry. I won't do it again," I said without looking up. Lily wandered over to the driveway, and I could hear her talking to Danny and Knox. I filled the metal garbage can with leaves and hauled it and the rake back around by the truck.

"Hop in, Griff," Mr. Spader said, as he took the can and the rake from me, delivering them both to the shed. I climbed in the back bed of the truck this time with Danny, Knox, and the full milk crates. Lily Reddington smiled and waved at us, as the truck sputtered up the gravel drive of Crab Tree Farm toward Sheridan Road. I looked through the back slats at the disappearing girl, until the dust was too thick to see through.

593. Y.M.C.A. BUILDING, WAUKEGAN, ILLINOIS.

WAUKEGAN YMCA
Photo postcard courtesy of the Waukegan Historical Society

Chapter 6 — Learning to Swim
Waukegan, IL — The Waukegan YMCA — December 7, 1927

Once the days shortened and the darkness of a long Chicago winter set in, the ladies who ran the orphanage scrambled to find indoor activities for all the kids who lived here. There was only so much that the housemothers could do to keep a hundred kids busy inside the cold, sterile bricks of LBO, and that's where field trips and the like came in. Betty and I happened to arrive at the children's home in late November of 1927, right during this shift from outdoor to indoor activities.

I didn't realize it at the time, but I'd learn later that the Lake Bluff community offered all kinds of support to Miss Arbuckle and her staff, so they could give us "opportunities:" tickets and transport to Chicago's museums, meals and movies downtown, and even swimming instruction at the Waukegan YMCA.

Within a couple of weeks after Mother dumped us at LBO, I was invited to participate in the "Learn to Swim" program at the Waukegan Y. Eight of the oldest boys in Wads who didn't already have their swimming certification were carted up Sheridan Road, past

Great Lakes Naval Base, to the YMCA pool. Dennis Bradley, one of our eighth graders who'd been at LBO for more than half his life, had filled me in.

"It's not all bad, six to eight weeks of getting out of this place every Wednesday for a couple of hours. They pack you a sack lunch, throw you in a couple of cars, and off you go," Dennis said.

"When do we leave and when do we get back?" I asked, thinking about not getting to see Betty at dinner, and I couldn't help but think about what Danny had said to me about not wanting to be gone if his sister came back to LBO looking for him. If Mother would be coming back for us, I didn't want to be away.

"You load up while everybody else is heading to dinner at about 6:00, and you're back by 8:00 or a quarter after," he said with his typical casual flair. Then Dennis's tone changed. "But you gotta remember, Griff, it's important that you pass, that you actually learn how to swim, or Arbuckle won't let you go to the beach with us in the summer. And if you're from Chicago, you know how hot it gets here in August, Griff. We're talking real steamers. And if you don't pass, you don't swim."

So on the first Wednesday in December, I was given the standard issue LBO stretchy, black swimsuit. I'd have to wait till we got up to the YMCA to be entrusted with the white towel. The temperature outside had dipped into the low 30s, but we weren't outside for any length of time. Loading into the two vehicles, I realized that I was one of the oldest boys in the group. Knox, Ernie, Homer, and the O'Neil twins—Billy and Bobby—all came. There was also a delicate boy named Artie with something wrong with his arm, and a loudmouth by the name of Johnny Dee who were with us.

It was about a half-hour drive straight north, and it was just cold enough for all the windows to be fogged up. We couldn't see much on the way there, except the lights from the naval base.

The Waukegan Y was an L-shaped, three-story, brick building that took up a third of the city block. We walked up the half-dozen concrete steps and quickly realized we wouldn't be alone in this building. The hallways were bustling with activity. A steady stream of adults wearing the kind of clothes I was used to seeing in church poured into Room 23. Men and women from their twenties all the way up into the forties were moving back and forth in the crowded hallways, and, as Johnny Dee was quick to point out, "the gals far outnumber the guys."

Knox was equally quick to reply, "Maybe we should take that class." He eyed a tall brunette with a long blue coat and a matching purse.

One of our adult chaperones, Mr. Lacey, sensed our excitement and called us over to him, just beyond the room we'd passed. "You guys wanna see a real-life movie star?" he asked. We all looked at each other, not sure what to make of his offer.

"Are you tryin' to pull one over on us, sir?" Johnny Dee said, glaring at our bald and bearded chaperone.

Just then a man in a charcoal suit with silver pinstripes came around the corner. He walked purposefully, theatrically, as if he were aware that all eyes were upon him. He had silver-gray hair and deep-set blue-gray eyes. Mr. Lacey dipped his head down and to the right, gesturing toward this compelling man.

"That, boys," our chaperone whispered, "is none other than Mr. Charles Hitchcock, star of stage and screen."

Watching the man strut into his packed classroom, none of us doubted what Mr. Lacey had said. He entered in a strong but measured gait, running the fingertips of his left hand over the edge of the long oak desk at the front of his classroom. This Charles Hitchcock was in constant but controlled motion, and he seemed to give off some sort of energy that hypnotized his entire class and all of us as well.

"On your feet, ladies and gentlemen. Let us begin with our vowel sounds. No lazy lips. Jaws open fully from here," he instructed, grabbing his own jaw from just under the ears. "And begin."

I was mesmerized and wanted to drop out of swimming to take Mr. Hitchcock's class, without any idea what he was teaching. But Mr. Lacey had continued on down the hall, and I raced to catch up. I got there just in time to hear the end of Homer's question, "... really a movie star?"

"Not only is that man really a movie star, Homer, but he has spent a significant amount of his life in Lake Bluff!" Lacey continued. "He and his wife live just a couple blocks from the orphanage, right down the street from the Village Hall, in fact."

"Really?" Knox asked. "Where in Lake Bluff?"

"Did he go to our school?" Billy O'Neil inquired.

Mr. Lacey smiled. "I can show you the very house Mr. Hitchcock lives in now," he said, stroking his black beard. We were heading down another set of stairs, and I could smell the pool. Steam was rising from underneath the door. "And, yes, Billy, I believe our movie star did attend at least one of the Lake Bluff schools, but back then, everybody finished up at Shields Township High over in Deerfield."

"Well, if he's such a big movie star, what's he doing teaching some class at the YMCA?" Johnny asked.

"Mr. Hitchcock's films were made mostly over a decade ago. He made a couple with the one and only Charlie Chaplin, and I know you boys have heard of him." He winked at us as he opened the door to the boys' locker room.

"Here is where we will all change," said Mr. Winfield, our other driver. "Our instructor's name is Perry Foster, a delightful young man. And while he's not a movie star, he did grow up in the Lake Bluff Orphanage."

I stepped over to Mr. Lacey. "Sir, I need to use the bathroom," I whispered.

"Oh. I do wish you'd told me earlier. We came right past one on our way down here."

"I know, I saw it. I can find it and come right back." I didn't wait for his response, though I did hear his "OK," as I rushed back through the locker room door, around the corner, and up the stairs.

Most every classroom in the building was in use, but I headed straight for Room 23. Relieved when I saw the door still open, I stood across the hall and back a ways, just out of Mr. Hitchcock's view. But I could hear his clear, extraordinary voice.

"So often in a sale or presentation, we concern ourselves solely with what we shall say…" He paused, letting the word "say" hang indefinitely. I saw the woman with the blue coat sitting in the very front row. She smiled and tilted her head, placing her pencil gently between her white teeth. Mr. Hitchcock stopped walking momentarily, looking at each face in the room methodically, building their anticipation. Finally, he continued.

"But it is rarely our words that matter most." Hitchcock turned his right hand over, so that its palm faced upward, then held it there in front of his chest imploringly, as if the hand would ask a question of its own. "Our bodies do most of the communicating in any given situation. And so tonight, we turn our attention to our gestures and what they will say to our audience. We shall also attend to our stance, our posture," he continued, moving his right hand downward, from his sternum to his thigh, calling attention to his own practiced and noble stance.

The pretty lady in the front row set her pencil down. She seemed to be studying Mr. Hitchcock, and I could see why. He was like a movie that was happening right in front of us all, and I know I didn't want to miss any of it.

"Role play!" Hitchcock clapped with each word, and his sharp claps woke me from the trance I'd been under—his trance. I had no idea how much time had passed, but I spun on my heels and ran back to the locker room. I found it empty and ripped my clothes off as fast as I could. I tugged the stretchy black suit on and ran barefoot onto the cold, concrete floor, through the steamy door, and onto the pool deck.

"Ah. This must be the long awaited Griff Morgan," said the voice belonging to our instructor. His slanted smile led me to believe I would escape any consequence.

"I'm sorry, Mr. Foster. I was in the bathroom much longer than I expected." I looked down and then glanced over at Mr. Lacey and Mr. Winfield.

"Is everything all right, Griff?" Mr. Lacey asked with an edge to his voice. I nodded silently before turning my gaze to the pool's smooth, aquamarine surface.

Perry Foster was a calm but quirky fellow. He was short and stout, carrying most of his extra weight in his middle section. His hair was blond and stringy, and there was something about him that made it very easy to believe that he'd spent some time at LBO.

"The first order of business is making friends with the water. If we're afraid of this stuff," he cupped both hands and pulled the water up to the top of his head, pulled his hands apart, and smiled as the water washed down his face, and continued, "we'll never be good swimmers. So, how does this stuff feel on your feet, your legs, your belly, your buttocks?" We snickered at the mention of "buttocks." "Artie, what do you think?"

Artie looked terrified, as if he'd been caught stealing from Miss Conkle's kitchen. He looked around the circle for help but none came. "OK, I guess." Perry laughed and slapped some water his way.

"What about you, Griff?" he asked, smiling broadly.

"It's great, just like a bath," I replied.

"Yes, but look at how huge our tub is!" He hurled himself backwards and disappeared under the water for at least ten seconds.

When he surfaced, his cheeks were full, and he took both hands and pushed his cheeks in, expelling the water in a steady stream right up at the chaperones. They backed away quickly, escaping all but a few drops.

"We need to have a meeting, boys, in my office. Come with me." He didn't move at all but simply sat down in the water, submerging to the bottom of the pool. We could see him under water, waving us toward him, but all we did was look at each other, wondering who would go first. It was Johnny. He took a big, audible breath in and then lowered himself beneath the surface. The two O'Neil brothers were next, neither wanting the other to beat him to the bottom.

As Perry came up for air, he singled out Artie and me, saying, "You two are next. Come on down!" I went down first, holding my nose and keeping my mouth and eyes shut tight. It was exhilarating when I rushed back up to the surface. I noticed that Artie was sitting on the edge of the pool with only his feet dangling in the water. He held his left arm in close against his body, bent and kind of tucked beneath his other arm. I remember Danny saying something about a horrible train accident that killed Artie's family and messed up his arm, but this was the first I'd ever seen it without a shirt covering it. His thumb seemed tucked under the other four fingers, which were all kind of clustered together. His left wrist was cocked inward at an unnatural angle. I looked away, but not before he'd caught me staring.

We dried off, got dressed quickly, and began our climb back to the main entrance. I wasn't the only one who was hoping to get another look at Mr. Hitchcock. The classroom door was open, and the students were laughing. We all paused at the doorway of Room 23, where the actor was in rare form.

"Yes, yes. Well done, Mr. Wentworth and Miss Knaak! Lovely, just lovely," Mr. Hitchcock said, patting the two students on their shoulders. "Please be seated. Oh, I see we're running out of time." Hitchcock paused, loosened his collar, surveyed the room, and smiled gently. "My dear students, I must make a change in our schedule. Two weeks from tonight we shan't be having class. I'm afraid the ghosts of my acting past have summoned me once again, this time to a little stage in Warsaw, Indiana. I'll make it up to you somehow. I promise." He pretended to pout and then broke into a broad smile. "Take note of it. Thank you. Dismissed!"

The students seemed to collectively exhale as they stood, gathering purses, coats, and satchels. They spoke animatedly to one another and began to file out. Mr. Winfield and Mr. Lacey quickly prodded us on toward the door, hoping to beat the herd of students, as they were dismissed from their classes.

"Where's Knox?" Mr. Lacey asked.

"He went to the bathroom," Ernie said.

"He's with me," Mr. Lacey said, "so why don't you go ahead with your four, Myron, and we'll catch up." Mr. Winfield nodded and collected both O'Neils, Homer, and Johnny. I was thrilled to be able to linger outside Room 23 for a bit longer.

"How come all the girls were sitting in the front two rows?" Artie whispered to me. I hadn't noticed before, but he was right.

"I don't know," I replied, without taking my eyes of Mr. Hitchcock, as he lingered in front of the desk of one of the beauties Artie was talking about, the one with the long blue coat. She had a coy, demure manner in the presence of her animated instructor.

"Finally. It's about time," Mr. Lacey said, when Knox caught up to us in the hall.

Back in Mr. Lacey's maroon Ford, we peppered him with questions about the man Knox was now referring to as "Hollywood Hitchcock."

"Have you seen any of his movies, Mr. Lacey?" Knox asked

"Of course. I think nearly everyone in Lake Bluff has. Several in fact!" He came to a stop at the intersection by the Naval Base. "One of my favorites was called 'His New Job.' It was a Chaplin film, and our Mr. Hitchcock was stupendous in it. In more recent years, since 1916, I believe, Mr. Hitchcock has been more involved in the production end of the business for The Chicago Film Company."

"So he's not an actor anymore?" I asked.

"I wouldn't say Mr. Hitchcock is not an actor anymore. It's just that he's producing pictures and photoplays, like 'To Arms,' a hilarious comedy that his company filmed over at Fort Sheridan!"

"Is he rich, Mr. Lacey?" Artie asked.

Mr. Lacey chuckled a bit. "I don't think I'd call Charles Hitchcock rich."

"Me neither," Knox chimed in. "Nobody who's rich would be teaching night classes at the YMCA."

"Good point, young man," Mr. Lacey snickered. "Now that I think about it, Charles Hitchcock also starred in a film called 'Pirate Cupid,' a romantic adventure filmed largely in our dear Village of Lake Bluff."

"Wow!" Artie and Ernie said at the same time.

"Wow, indeed," Lacey replied. "You know, you boys should ask Miss Arbuckle to take you to see one of his films as an outing some night. They show one of his films every now and then over at the elementary school gym." He turned left onto Scranton at the train station. "While 'Pirate Cupid' certainly was filmed well past his acting prime, Mr. Hitchcock still had a certain charm and charisma. Mrs. Lacey used to say that Charles's wavy, graying-blond hair, and slate silver-blue eyes were awfully hard to look away from."

"What does 'past his prime' mean, Mr. Lacey?" Artie asked.

"Well, I supposed it means that Mr. Hitchcock was getting a little old for the big screen," Mr. Lacey said.

"It means Old Hollywood Hitchcock is washed up!" Knox added.

MISS JESSIE ARBUCKLE
LAKE BLUFF ORPHANAGE SUPERINTENDENT
Photo courtesy of the Lake Bluff History Museum

Chapter 7 — Griff's Initiatives
Lake Bluff, IL — Train Station — December 13, 1927

Ever since that first trip to the Waukegan YMCA, I'd found myself thinking a lot about Mr. Charles Hitchcock. I'd learned over at the farm from Redd, Lily's father, that "Hollywood Hitchcock" actually worked over at the Village Hall as the night deputy dispatch several nights a week. Billy O'Neil and I approached Miss Arbuckle several days after our first swimming lesson to see if it would be possible for us to see one of Charles Hitchcock's movies sometime in the near future. Billy piled it on pretty thick, talking about "local history" and "the value of seeing our new town on the big screen." She seemed impressed by our "initiative" and said she'd talk to her staff about it.

After Billy left, I stayed behind to talk to Miss Arbuckle about Betty. Her office was dark and filled with oak: oak walls, oak doors, and a large oak desk. Only a couple of dim table lamps fought off the oaken darkness.

"Is there something else, Griffin?" she asked, looking down the point of her nose at me.

"Has...has my mother called...or anything? I'm just asking ...for...for Betty." I paused.

"I'm sorry, Griffin," Miss Arbuckle said, "but we've heard nothing from your mother." Her voice was cold, without expression. She turned back to her desk and retrieved a small package. "We did receive this small package from your Aunt Rose. It contains two sweaters, one for you and one for Betty." She handed the plain, brown parcel to me.

"Thank you," I said, taking it. "Speaking of Betty, I'm kinda worried about her. I mean, I don't get to see her much." I looked right at her and took in a quick breath. "Don't you think it would be better for both of us if...if we saw a little more of each other? I mean...I'm the only family she has." My throat tightened the second the words had come out.

She took her glasses off and moved over toward her window. "Your sister is doing quite well, all things considered. Her housemother reports only the normal adjustments. She seems to be eating and sleeping well." Miss Arbuckle pivoted and walked directly toward me. "I'm sure you understand, Griffin, that we can't make exceptions from our tried and true rules for you two."

"But couldn't we just eat a few meals together? We could come early and eat in the kitchen or any place you want." She tilted her head and shook it ever so slightly.

"You want private dining privileges? Will you require a butler as well?" she said. "Do you know how many brothers and sisters, and even groups of siblings we've had in this orphanage over the years?" I looked down. She placed her long-fingered hand on my shoulder. "Griffin, I know you love your sister very much. I just want all of us to give this adjustment a little time."

I backed away. "I'll try, ma'am." I opened the heavy, dark door to leave, then turned back toward her. "But she's only four. Four's pretty young for all this, don't you think?" I closed the door behind me without waiting for a response.

I walked out of the Mackey Memorial building onto the cold sidewalk that led to Scranton. I'd planned to turn left to head back to Wads, but I heard a train whistle and found myself looking down to the station. It was late, past eight in the evening. I was outside alone, and it felt good. I started walking and then running toward the Lake Bluff Train Station.

The Chicago North Shore Line train pulled into the Lake Bluff station. The first northbound passenger to exit through the steam was Charles Hitchcock. I froze for an instant and then slid behind the northeast corner of the station wall. He walked briskly along the brick walk, crossed Sheridan Road onto Scranton, and then cut over to the Village Hall. Over his shoulder was a thin, black wardrobe bag.

Tuesdays, Thursdays, and Saturdays were the nights, according to some of the guys at Wads, that the former actor worked the night shift as the police dispatcher. Lake Bluff was a sleepy village, and I'd later learn that about the only calls he or any of the dispatchers ever got were either a minor disturbance or some kid who was out past curfew. I thought back to what Knox had said about why any actor would be teaching night classes at a YMCA. I wondered what Knox would say about "Hollywood Hitchcock's" other part-time job.

Earlier this same week, our teacher at Lake Bluff Elementary School showed us some old pictures of "Lake Bluff's favorite son," as she called Mr. Hitchcock. She even showed us a summary of his rise to fame that was kept in the town archives. It said that he'd grown up near here and had grown to love this town. Apparently, Artesian Park, the endless ravines, the patriotic holiday celebrations, and the beach all held wonderful memories for Hitchcock. He reported that he knew most of the folks in town, and they all knew him too—Lake Bluff's one and only movie star. Toward the end of this summary was a quotation from Mr. Hitchcock, saying that being a night dispatcher gave him a sense that he was "taking care of the town that had taken such good care of me through many of my younger years."

I followed the actor-turned-town-deputy at a good distance and watched him enter the Village Hall. Once I saw his figure descend the stairs to the basement, I took off in a beeline for the orphanage, not sure how long I'd been gone.

Nurse Blueberg was exiting the front door of Wads just as I was entering. I hadn't seen her since my intake checkup eleven days earlier.

"Why, Griffin, where have you been? It's almost 8:15," she said, raising her eyebrows.

"Yes, ma'am. I know. I've been discussing things with Miss Arbuckle...stuff about my little sister. And I had to get this package from my aunt." I gestured with the parcel and then wiped my eyes with the back of my sleeve.

"Well, run on upstairs. I'm sure everything with little Betty will be just fine." She nodded and headed on her way, and I hustled up the stairs to the first floor of Wads.

Since 8:00 was the enforced bedtime in Wads, the common room had emptied out. But Dick Moley was reclining on a couch with some baseball magazine that had Babe Ruth on the cover.

From my first day at LBO, there was something about Dick I couldn't put my finger on. It was like he was the elder statesmen of Wadsworth Hall, and, in many ways, of the whole orphanage. He'd been here a long time and stood a full head and shoulders above most of the rest of us. Dick was an all-star athlete and somehow managed to look like one of the regular kids of Lake Bluff. Nothing about him looked or smelled like an orphan.

As I made my way over to where Dick was, I spotted an open newspaper. The headline read: *NORTHERN SUBURBS BRACING FOR BOOTLEGGERS*. I quietly picked it up and read.

> *Amid reports of increased smuggling of alcohol and other contraband through Chicago ports and thoroughfares, Chicago Police are beefing up security. With the help of federal agents, likely supply routes moving in and out of the city have been identified for possible checkpoints and barricades. Both uniformed and undercover police have been dispatched to potential delivery locations.*
>
> *Recent arrests have been made in Evanston and as far north as Waukegan, a police spokesperson for the recently formed Anti-Alcohol Task Force said over the weekend. While the perpetrators have not been identified publicly, leaks from the Chicago PD have indicated that all those being held have ties to two major organized crime rings.*
>
> *"The fact that some of our suburbs along the North Shore are seeing increased smuggling activities is both unprecedented and disturbing. I want to assure the citizens of the entire Chicago area*

*that we will increase our efforts, both in and out of the city limits,"
Mayor William Hale Thompson said Monday morning.*

*Representatives from eleven chapters of the Women's
Christian Temperance Union met in an emergency session at The
First Baptist Church on Sunday, urging local and state authorities
to take whatever measures are necessary to "save our city and
suburbs from this damaging and demonic blight."*

Dick said, "Hey, Griff. What gives? Where have you been?"

"Just talking to Miss Arbuckle is all," I said.

"You in trouble?".

"Nope. What'cha reading?" I said, nodding toward his magazine.

"Nothin' much." He pulled the magazine down to his chest.
"You better get to bed before Miss Harvey comes back around, or
she'll get you with that switch."

"Aw, I will. But what about you? Aren't you worried? It's almost
8:30."

"Naw. Miss Harvey and I have an understanding. She knows I'm
a night owl. I do gotta go iron my shoelaces though." He dropped
the magazine and ambled toward the head like it was the middle of
the afternoon.

"Night then, Griff," Dick said.

"Night," I replied and tiptoed over to my partition. I couldn't
help but wonder if Dick had his own rules or something. It wasn't
like Miss Arbuckle or any of the housemothers to make exceptions.
Heck, they wouldn't even let me eat a meal once in a while with my
own sister. Dick was a great athlete, and it would be a while before
I'd learn what brought him to LBO, what his father had done to
both him and his little sister. But it wouldn't be on this particular
night. I was bushed, and Wednesday would be a busy day with a full
day of school and then swimming at night.

Detective Hargrave shifted uncomfortably in his hard-backed
wooden chair. Tapping his fingers on the desk in front of him, he
said, "I remember those days, all the scares about smugglers in the
suburbs. It was a nightmare, so much fear about what illegal booze
would do to these pristine towns like Winnetka and Highland Park."

"And Lake Bluff too," I added, "as you will see."

CRAB TREE FARM ADVERTISEMENT
Print courtesy of Crab Tree Farm Foundation

Chapter 8 — Raising Lazarus
Crab Tree Farm — December 16, 1927

Mr. Spader maneuvered the dusty, brown LBO truck down the gravel drive toward the Crab Tree Farm milk house. He pulled as close to the barn as he could, while Danny, Billy, and I had all admired his parking expertise from the flat bed. With the ongoing run of unexpected sunshine and mid-50s temperatures, we milked these strange December days for all they were worth, holding our heads up to the glistening sun.

As Mr. Spader pumped the squeaky brakes, bringing the old truck to a stop, we popped open the back end and jumped out. Danny handed the empty milk bottle crates to Billy and me two at a time, and then managed the last few himself. I led the way into the milk house ahead of the other two, got my bottles rinsed, and was off to get my first load of full ones before Danny and Billy had even begun rinsing. Returning to the welcome warmth and brightness of the afternoon, I reached the truck and began to position my cases on the truck bed, when I heard a distant scream.

I slid the bottle crates forward and took off up into the orchard following the awful sound.

"Help! Help! Somebody!" It was a girl's voice, and I had a pretty good idea whose. I ran as fast as I ever had toward the sound.

"Help! Please! Somebody, help!" In a small clearing on the edge of the apple orchard, I saw the now familiar figure of Lily Reddington. She was standing on her tiptoes holding a stick above her.

"The bird! Help the bird!" Lily was gasping now. She'd exhausted herself. She twisted around, so her back was to me and changed the stick from her left hand to her right, all the while keeping the stick as still as she possibly could.

A small robin was caught in an intricate tangle of string. It fluttered wildly, tightening the trap it had fallen into. Then it hung limp and lifeless. Lily's stick was supporting the bird from underneath.

"If I move or he falls off this stick, he's gonna choke! He's gonna die," she said, much louder than she needed to, with me not even two inches away from her.

Lily had been exactly right. Without something supporting the bird, its own body weight would pull the bird down, and the tight string would snap the bird's neck for sure. It helped that I was taller than Lily. I could almost reach the bird without the stick. But I didn't dare try to release the only thing supporting the desperate, little robin. The bird calmed, but then, out of nowhere, fluttered madly, worsening its own predicament with every violent flap of its wings.

"Here," I said. "Hold the stick again. I'll run back to the barn and get a knife or something sharp." As I ran off, she held the stick as steadily as she could.

I reached the inside of the barn, looking madly around the tool bench for a knife. I knew right where one was kept, but it wasn't there. I heard laughter, a low, guttural chuckle. Over by the slop sink a slender man with ripped jeans held the knife I was looking for. I ran to him, still out of breath, and saw that he was covered in chicken feathers. Blood was swirling around in the sink.

"I need the knife. I need the knife," I panted.

He looked at me with a blank, vacant stare, like there was nothing behind his eyes. He extended the knife toward me, sharp end first. A strange smile emerged on his pockmarked face. I reached for its handle and grabbed it out of his right hand and took off.

By the time I finally got back to Lily, the bird looked dead, hanging lifelessly, but still supported by Lily and the stick. "Don't move and don't move the stick!" I commanded. I hoisted myself up to the first tree branch, and stood on it. I leaned out away from the trunk, out toward the bird, and started cutting every string I could see. Feverishly, I cut and cut, but none of the cuts seemed to loosen or free the bird. I finally got close enough to position my left hand beneath the bird, and motioned for Lily to take the stick away. Then I made a series of rapid but cautious cuts.

"Got it!" I said, almost in a whisper. The bird lay completely lifeless in my left palm. Dropping the knife to the ground, I jumped as softly as I could behind it. Lily was crying and came toward me tentatively.

"I can feel his heartbeat. He can't be dead," I whispered, more hoping than stating a fact. Looking straight at the bird, I saw that the creature's eyes were closed but would flutter sporadically. I ran the edge of my right hand softly along the bird's side and wing, up toward the neck. I felt something, something that wasn't supposed to be there. "Get the knife again!" I commanded. "There's still a tiny string under here. It's almost like fishing line." I used my thumb and forefinger to coax the remaining thread away from the bird's neck. The robin spasmed and fluttered, and I closed my right hand around the bird in an effort to keep him settled. I felt it go limp again and found the tiny thread with the ends of my fingers and thumb.

"When I hold this string up, get just the edge of the blade between my finger and the bird's neck." I looked right at Lily. "You can't shake or lose your focus, Lily. You don't have to actually cut this; you just have to get the sharp edge against the string, and it'll snap right off, OK?" She nodded, cracking her knuckles as she bent down to get the knife. I exposed the line and pointed with my middle finger to where Lily needed to put the edge of the blade. The robin gasped, its beak opening for a moment, and then it seemed to expire.

"There! You got it!" I exclaimed. Gently, I lay the bird down on the spring grass. It was completely motionless.

Lily got down next to me and put her face within six inches of the robin's lifeless body. "Is it…is it…dead?" she asked.

"I don't know. I don't think so. Stay right here with it. I'll be right back. I'm gonna get some water."

I raced past the barn to the milk house, where we used the hoses to rinse the bottles. Danny and Billy saw me streak by. "Griff! Griff!" they shouted. When I didn't reply, they ran after me.

In the milk house, I grabbed a tiny top from a milk bottle and was trying to fill it with water. The two boys caught up to me, out of breath. "What in the Sam Hill are you doin'?" Billy asked.

With the small cap filled, I began to walk as quickly as I could without spilling any of the precious water. "Trying to save a bird," I said. They followed me.

Lily was kneeling next to the bird, sobbing and fighting back the tears. "He hasn't moved since you left." I got alongside her and put my hand under the bird's head.

"See if you can take a little stick or an apple stem and pry open its beak." Danny and Billy were standing above, angled over with their hands at their knees. Lily began the delicate beak-opening operation, while I positioned the tiny lid of water just above it. With the subtlest motion I could muster, I trickled drops of water into the bird's beak. Its tongue was visible and flopped to one side.

The bird fluttered and convulsed, coming to. Lily's eyes widened, and Billy and Danny shouted, "Yes!" The robin appeared stunned and frightened and didn't move to get to his feet. It stilled momentarily, and its eyes closed and then opened again rapidly. Lily and I tried the water procedure again without any words exchanged. The robin was instantly responsive this time, seeming to welcome the tiny refreshment.

The four of us all backed away slightly, as the robin began to roll a bit and get to its feet. Fluttering its wings as if it had just rinsed in a puddle, the brown and orange bird hopped and shook itself some more. Just then Redd and Mr. Spader came jogging up the path.

"What's going on up here?" Redd asked. "I thought I heard screaming."

Lily glanced at the bird and then took several steps toward her father. "We saved a bird, Daddy! Griff and I just saved that bird!" She gestured at the robin as it fluttered its wings wildly and hopped three times. Then, with considerable effort, he jumped again and took to the air.

"Well, I'll be," Redd said, a satisfied smile accompanying his nod.

"Griff was amazing. That bird was a goner!" Lily exclaimed.

"You found him, Lily. He'd 'a hung himself for sure if you hadn't thought to use that stick to hold his weight off the string," I said. Lily smiled and ran across to me, hugging me like a long lost friend. I could feel myself blushing in the presence of the four others, but received Lily's hug just the same.

Mr. Spader cleared his throat. "We ought'a be getting back. Well done, Miss Lily," Spader said, as he turned back toward the path to the truck. Danny and Billy fell into step behind the two men. Lily and I took one last look for the bird, but it was long gone.

On the path to the milk house, she turned up to me and said, "Doesn't it feel good, savin' that little guy?"

I nodded before I spoke, taking in a reflective breath. I realized that this was the kind of thing I'd usually tell Mother about. "Yeah. It sure does." We walked the entire length of the path to the truck, side by side. Billy and Danny were already in the flat bed, each sitting upon a stack of milk crates.

"Hey, Lily," I said. "When I went to get us that knife in the milk house, there was a creepy guy using it. I think he'd been skinning chickens or something."

"Oh, that's Frank," she replied. "He's harmless. A little slow and, yes, creepy, but harmless."

Mr. Spader had started up the truck. Redd was over by the milk house door watching his daughter. He paced back and forth, clenching and unclenching his fists with both hands.

"Thank you for helping me, Griff," Lily said, softly.

"Thanks, yourself," I replied, still puzzling over her father's agitation.

"I think we should name him, don't you?" Lily stated.

I looked at her curiously and started to climb up onto the back of the flatbed. Turning back to look at her, I just said one word: "Lazarus." My Aunt Rose must have told us that story a dozen times in the six months we'd lived with her in the Evanston apartment. It was her favorite Bible story about the man Jesus had raised from the dead.

Mr. Spader dropped the truck into gear and we grinded up the hill back to town.

"WADS I" BOYS AT CHRISTMAS — LAKE BLUFF ORPHANAGE
Photo courtesy of the Lake Bluff History Museum

Chapter 9 — The Coming of Christmas
Lake Bluff Orphanage — December 17, 1927

It didn't take me long to realize that Saturday mornings were the best time of the week for those of us living at the orphanage. We got to sleep in a little, have breakfast, take care of a few chores, and then actually have a little unsupervised time to ourselves. For those of us in Wads, the playroom on the first floor was the place to be on a lazy Saturday morn.

Dennis Bradley had sprawled out on the lone couch and was reading another one of his gadget magazines. His IQ was "off the charts" according to the teachers at the school, and the science teacher Mr. Shelby fed Dennis a regular diet of science magazines that most high schoolers could never have handled.

In the middle of the room were a card table and four chairs. On this morning, three of them were filled by Artie, Ernie, and Dick. As usual, Dick was holding court. The biggest and oldest kid in the orphanage, he had the ear of every other kid, and not just the boys either. As an athlete, I'd heard over and over already that Dick was quickly becoming a Lake Bluff legend. A three-sport starter for the town teams in baseball, basketball, and football, Dick even had kids who weren't orphans wanting to be his friend. He was one of the best-looking kids I'd ever seen, with thick dark hair and piercing blue eyes. But beyond his movie star looks, Dick was a real charmer, complimenting the housemothers and school teachers on their clothing or their hair. One of the young female seminary students, who helped out around at the orphanage from time to time, even bought him a yellow, genuine cashmere sweater, and it wasn't even his birthday or Christmas.

"One week, boys. Just one more week," he said without looking up from the cards he held. "I can already smell it. It's nothin' like the way food smells around here."

I looked over from the puzzle table, where the O'Neil brothers and I had just completed the border on a 400-piece rendering of Wrigley Field. I had no idea what Dick was referring to. Bobby must have seen the confusion on my face.

"Christmas, dodo! He's talkin' about Christmas," Bobby said. "We all get to go to houses, real families." I'd certainly noticed that the orphanage was decked out for the coming holiday with greenery, red bows, and wreaths, and I'd heard the scuttlebutt that soon a 25-foot tree would be delivered from Hannigan's Nursery. But this was the first I'd heard of getting to leave LBO for Christmas. I wondered if anything had been said to Betty.

"Gin," said Dick, laying down his cards triumphantly.

Artie and Ernie both whined, "Aw, jeez," in defeat. Ernie rubbed his v-shaped scar, in frustration. It was like a third eye on his forehead.

An angry voice echoed from the stairwell. "All right! Who's the circus clown who put mayonnaise in my shoes!" Knox jumped down the last two steps with a thud, a sneaker in his hand. His face was bright red, and his free hand was balled up in a tight fist.

"Knox Korly, you can march yourself and that shoe of yours right back to your cubicle," said an angry Miss Harvey. Knox rolled his eyes and pointed a threatening finger at the O'Neil twins before heading back up to the group sleeping quarters.

Artie looked down somberly at the mention of the circus. In June of 1918, he and his entire family were on board the Hammond Circus Train, when it derailed and crashed, killing 86 and wounding 127 others. Artie, two years old at the time, was the only survivor in his family. Danny told me that story the second night I was at LBO, right after he'd caught me staring at Artie's damaged left arm. He also told me that Artie, at age 11, was still wetting his bed every single night. Danny told me so that I wouldn't find out some other way and add to the relentless teasing Artie already endured.

"Another Christmas in Wilmette. This year'll be my sixth," Dick said, leaning back on his chair and folding his hands behind his head. "Mrs. Hancock puts on quite a spread, boys: turkey with all the fixins, stuffing, mashed potatas, sweet potatas, corn bread, and two kinds of pies." He smiled and inhaled through his nose, as if trying to conjure the smell right then and there. "Can any of you toads top that?"

Ernie started giggling. "Can't wait to see where they're sending me this year!"

Johnny chimed in from his spot on the floor, where he'd been building and knocking down domino structures all morning. "Somewhere you don't break your leg on your way in the front door!" The entire room cackled. Injuries seemed to follow Ernie VanEs everywhere he went. He spent more time in the orphanage infirmary than any other kid on campus. In the twelve-month period alone preceding my arrival, Ernie had broken his right arm falling off a table, received eleven stitches in his head from a sledding accident, and was quarantined for a two-weeks with the mumps.

Dennis smirked and without looking up from his magazine said, "If Miss Arbuckle knows what she's doing, Ernie, she'll set you up with a surgeon's family, preferably one that lives next door to a hospital." Ernie was still giggling but had begun to redden with embarrassment as well.

Artie was awkwardly dealing the next hand of gin. His crookedly bent left arm hampered him significantly, so he never took his eyes off the cards. Dick picked up his cards as they were dealt and said, "Not sure you should talk, Johnny. Rumor has it Arbuckle can't find a family for you on account of she can't find anybody in all of Chicago who doesn't use a screw-top salt shaker." Hearty laughter came from all corners of the room, but it was actually Artie's cackle that was most audible. Red-haired, freckle-faced Johnny was notorious for unscrewing the caps of saltshakers whenever and wherever he encountered one. It was like an addiction; he couldn't help himself, not even at a formal Christmas dinner.

"Easy over there, Mr. Pee-Pee," Johnny retorted, staring right at Artie. "I'm not the one Nurse Blueberg has to deliver the extra sheets to every morning, now am I?" Johnny snickered before adding. "You probably need a special diaper under your choo-choo train pajamas!"

The laughter became muffled, uncomfortable, and awkward, as Artie looked down in shame. Dick stood up, putting a hand on Artie's shoulder.

"C'mon, Artie. Let's go up and have a look see at what Madame Conkle is cooking up for lunch." Dick looked across the room to the puzzle table. "Hey, Griff, why don't you come along too. You might get a word or two with your sister."

I nodded at Dick, shrugged my apology to the O'Neil boys for abandoning the puzzle, pushed my chair back, and hustled over to the bottom of the stairs. Dennis sat up on the couch, and once he saw that Artie was out of earshot, looked over at Johnny. I paused at the bottom of the stairs and pretended to tie my shoe.

"Johnny," Dennis said, motioning for the redhead to join him on the couch. Johnny stuck his hands in his pockets and ambled over. "Listen, Johnny, you gotta go easy on Artie. You can't be bringing up his bedwetting in front of all of us. And you know how sad he gets at the mention of trains. Jeez."

Johnny looked down, shaking his head. "But, Den," he said.

"No, Johnny. No buts here." Dennis put an arm around Johnny's neck and shoulders. "A train wreck, Johnny! Artie's whole family was lost in a train wreck." Dennis snapped his fingers sharply. "Boom! Like that! It was over. His mother, his father, 84 other people, and half his arm! All when he was two, Johnny. Two!" Dennis shook his head, "It's no wonder he hasn't stopped wetting his bed since it happened."

"I know, I know. We've all got stories, Den. But he started it." Johnny argued.

"I don't care who started it. All I'm sayin' is just lay off of Artie." Dennis took a deep breath, clenched his teeth, and continued. "We're Artie's family now—us…you, me, all of us." Dennis made eye contact with Johnny, nodded a couple times, and forced a smile. "C'mon, Johnny! It's Christmas, right? Huh?" He tousled Johnny's red mop of hair, as I hustled up the stairs to catch up with Dick and Artie.

"Well, would you look at that!" I heard Dick saying up above. I reached the ground floor windows in time to see what he was talking about: an enormous flatbed trailer behind a city truck, backing right up onto the front lawn of Mackey Memorial. Everybody had raced to the window. A 25-foot Christmas tree was about to be delivered to the Lake Bluff Orphanage, and it was snowing, heavy, wet flakes.

I caught up to Artie and Dick at the entrance to the kitchen, where we were never supposed to be, other than at mealtime. Dick had knocked on the swinging door gently and pushed it in far enough to see Miss Conkle, the legendary and grouchy cook of LBO. "What's cooking, Miss Conkle?" Dick said.

"You have no business in my kitchen at this hour, Dick Moley!" She spat her words out hastily. "Saturdays are cornbread and beans. Always has been, always will be. You've been here plenty long enough to know that." She set her flat, thick spoon on the counter, wiped her manly hands on her powder blue apron, and continued. "Now, unless you—and those two weasels hiding behind you—have some other urgent business here, I suggest you turn around and get your fannies out of my kitchen!"

"Just looking for Miss Arbuckle is all, ma'am. We'll be on our way," Dick said, giving the grumpy cook a big grin. Then he rolled his eyes at Artie and me. Somehow he'd also managed to swipe three oatmeal cookies off a tray just inside the kitchen door.

"Jeez," Artie muttered. "That lady is a regular witch. It's like she was put here just to make us miserable!" We turned back and let the kitchen door close. A din drew our attention to the front window. More than thirty girls were out in the snow-covered yard, watching the unloading of the largest Christmas tree they or any of us had ever seen. I could see that all the boys from Wads had abandoned their board games, grabbed their coats, and spilled out onto the lawn to join in the ruckus. Snowballs were flying across the yard in every direction, a blatant violation of Miss Arbuckle's winter rules. Four kids from my first floor of Wads were using the moving Christmas tree as a shield, as they lofted hard packed snowballs over the horizontal tree at a handful of younger boys from the second floor.

I heard a scream followed by some yelling and then crying. Miss Jaeger hustled out there with her unbuttoned coat billowing behind her, as she chased after the culprits from my floor.

I raced to a clearer window with half a cookie in my mouth and scanned the chaotic scene for Betty. Without taking my eyes off the front yard, I called back over to Dick. "Hey, Dick, how do these Christmas family visits work?"

Dick strode up to the window next to the one I was looking out of. "You mean for you and your sister?" he said. I nodded. "Well, Miss Arbuckle always tries to keep siblings together. Sometimes the host family can only take one kid, so when that happens…" Dick didn't finish.

"How can I find out? Ahead of time, I mean," I pushed.

Dick hesitated. "Well, talk to Miss Arbuckle, and…" Before Dick could even finish, I caught a glimpse of Betty and was out the front door after her. I bounded over to her, picked her up, and twirled her beside the now empty flatbed.

"Griffy! Griffy!" Betty yelled gleefully. "Did you see the tree?"

"You betcha, sis! Isn't she a beauty! Biggest tree I ever saw." I kissed her on each cheek and then lifted her up on my shoulders to give her a better view of things. Then I handed her the rest of my half-eaten oatmeal cookie.

The crew from Hannigan's Nursery and Jim Spader were carrying the tree like a casket. They had the top heading in first, right through the main entrance of Mackey Memorial. Snowballs still flew from one side of the tree to the other, despite Miss Jaeger's threats. Most of the children had lined up on both sides of the tree and followed the needle-shedding procession right up to the entryway but had to stop there in clusters on each side of the door. Betty, still perched on my shoulders, was the only one who could see anything, as the tree disappeared inside the large double doors of the Mackey Memorial building. But once the doors closed, even Betty was shut out.

Looking around, it occurred to me that this was the first time I'd ever seen the entire population of the orphanage in any one place, other than the dining hall. The boys and girls were all mixed together, as were the big kids and the little ones. I pulled Betty back down hard into my chest in a tight hug. "It's OK here, right Betty?"

"It's Christmas!" she squealed, lifting both arms up into the descending snow.

AN AUNT WALKS WITH HER NEPHEW AND NIECES ON LBO
VISITATION SUNDAY
Photo courtesy of the Lake Bluff History Museum

Chapter 10 — Unexpected Encounters
Lake Bluff Orphanage — December 19, 1927

Every other Sunday was family visit day at LBO. Mothers, fathers, grandparents, aunts, and uncles were all encouraged to come to the Mackey Memorial building between one and five in the afternoon, after we had all been to the required Sunday School and worship, to be with their children. The lounge in Mackey Memorial was like a gigantic living room with lots of stuffed couches and chairs. When the weather was nice, some of the more adventurous families would walk over to Artesian Park or stop down at Munch's Pharmacy for a soda.

While most of the kids at the orphanage had some adult relative come at least once in a while on a visitation Sunday, a few of us had nobody to come visit us. Johnny's situation was highly unusual. The only living relative he had was his Aunt Lucy down in Kenilworth, but she had only one leg and was legally blind, so she couldn't possibly be expected to make it to LBO for the designated every-other-Sunday family visit times. So, on whatever day Miss Arbuckle could arrange, Johnny got to ride the southbound North Shore Line after school got out and come back on the 8:03 to Lake Bluff.

Generally, some adult from the orphanage staff would accompany Johnny on the train, both there and back. His favorite chaperone was Olive Stavenhagen, an intern, who was, by his reckoning, "a real beauty!" While the lovely Miss Stavenhagen was not his escort on December 19, Johnny was happily distracted by another beauty, and this one wasn't his chaperone. As he told us the next morning at breakfast in penetrating detail, it was none other than the very same woman who had caught our eye in Mr. Charles Hitchcock's Elocution class at the Waukegan YMCA.

We had all referred to her as "the woman in the blue coat." But the morning after Johnny's train ride to see his Aunt Lucy, during which he sat directly across from her from the Highland Park stop on up, we finally had a name to go with that incredible face.

"Elfrieda Knaak," Johnny said, as if she were his girlfriend. "And you aren't going to believe what I saw," he added with his eyes widening and his nostrils flaring.

"Guess who met her at the train station, right when she got off, right here in Lake Bluff?" He baited us with silence and his smug smile. "Hollywood Hitchcock! He met her wearing his police uniform, right under the Lake Bluff sign, and escorted her—arm in arm—to the Village Hall! At eight o'clock at night!" Johnny nodded and gave us a sly grin.

"No!" Knox said, tossing his head back and putting both his hands on his forehead in disbelief. "Hollywood is old enough to be her father!"

"Maybe he is," Johnny said, with a shrug thrown in for good measure. "But I know what I saw."

"Where were you?" I pushed. "Were you close enough to follow 'em or hear what they were saying?"

"You bet I was…for at least as long as I could."

"And?" Knox asked.

"At first, it was just, 'how was your train ride?' and 'I had the train car almost to myself.'"

"Yeah," Bobby replied in a mocking female voice, "almost to myself, except for the creepy orphan kid who kept staring at me!" The rest of us howled in laughter.

Johnny shook his head. "C'mon, guys! It's December! She had the long blue coat on, buttoned all the way up to her neck, a paisley scarf, and some black boots on."

"Forget the clothes, Johnny," I said. "What happened? What did you hear?"

Johnny squinted a bit, trying to remember. "Hitchcock had his deputy's uniform on, see, and Elfrieda said he looked good in it. But he joked that it made no sense to even have a uniform for this job."

Johnny continued. "Then Miss Knaak thanked him for taking time out of his busy schedule to work with her."

"What kind'a work do ya think she was talking about?" Bobby asked.

"She told me on the train that she sells encyclopedias door to door," Johnny said. He paused momentarily, and then his eyes widened, as he remembered something else. "When they got close to the Village Hall, Miss Knaak asked if anyone else would be in the building so late at night, and Hollywood said 'not usually.' Then she told him she was cold and asked if it was cold in his office."

"Hah!" Knox interjected. "I bet old Hollywood promised to keep her nice and warm." He smiled and raised his eyebrows snidely.

Johnny shook his head. "Uh-uh. He told her that his office was 'the warmest spot in town.'" Johnny cleared his throat and wiped some dangling snot off the end of his nose. "Then I saw Hitchcock pull out his key and open the door for Miss Elfrieda."

The five of us who had surrounded Johnny during his story fell silent for a few moments. We heard the door to the dining hall open, and Miss Arbuckle came in with a boy we'd never seen before. He was a short little kid with stringy black hair, and he looked like he hadn't had much sleep. He kept wiping his eyes and seemed to want to hide behind his bangs.

"Looks like we got a new one, boys." It was Dick from the table next to ours. Arbuckle was going over the mealtime protocol and introducing him to the other housemothers.

Knox brought us back to Johnny's story. "So what do you think the two of them could be doing down in the basement of the Village Hall that late at night, when nobody else is around?" There was a strong suggestion of impropriety in Knox's tone, which he further emphasized with his folded arms.

"He's her teacher," Billy said. "Maybe he's giving her some extra help?"

His brother Bobby chimed in. "Or maybe she wants to become an actress, and Mr. Hitchcock is helping her." He paused and then added, "We all know she's got the looks to be on the big screen."

"It could have something to do with the encyclopedias," I offered. "Maybe he used to sell them or is good at selling things."

Knox shook his head knowingly. "Fellas, whatever is going on down there in that basement room, it can't be good."

Knox never seemed to trust anybody, especially older women. He had a way of rolling his eyes, shaking his head, or even crossing his arms that seemed to suggest that nobody else was seeing the sordid truth that he already knew. The kid wasn't but a couple of months older than I was, but somehow Knox knew things that even the thirteen-year-olds among us hadn't considered. He'd grown up on the south side, not far from my father. I found out much later that his mother had been a prostitute. That is what had brought him to the orphanage in the first place, along with two other boys from his household. Technically, they were all half-brothers, having come from different partners of his mother. But the entire time I was at LBO, Knox never acknowledged that he even knew these other boys, much less that they were related.

I'd hoped to walk to school by myself after breakfast on the morning of Johnny's train ride revelation. I wanted to think through what he'd said about Miss Knaak and Charles Hitchcock without all the morning chatter. But Miss Arbuckle asked me to accompany the new kid to school on his first day. I'd only been at LBO about a month and couldn't figure why she'd pick me to shepherd this scared little kid. It was all he could do to lift his eyes up from his tattered shoes. No matter what I said, all he'd do is shrug. So when I asked him if he'd mind stopping by the Village Hall for a second, I expected the same. But this time I didn't even get that, so I proceeded with my plan. I wanted to get a look at the side of the building where that door down to the basement was.

"Hey, Griff! You guys are gonna be late!" Artie called to me from across Center Avenue. I nodded, nudged the kid I was chaperoning, and we hustled to catch up with the others. I felt sorry for the kid but had no idea how to reach him. As it turned out, he only lasted at LBO for about nine days. Some aunt of his from Nebraska came for him, and he vanished just as quickly as he'd appeared.

CHARLES W. HITCHCOCK ENTERTAINMENT POSTER
Print courtesy of the Lake Bluff History Museum

Chapter 11 — A Night at the Theater
Crab Tree Farm – December 22, 1927

After finishing my after-school bottle-washing duties, Mrs. D. invited me into the kitchen for a snack. She was an odd lady, wrinkled and gruff on the outside, but kind and soft to all of us from the orphanage who worked for her. All the rumors about her oatmeal cookies were true. A tall glass of fresh milk and a couple of those cookies gave us a taste we didn't get too much of at LBO.

The other luxury I'd get from time to time when I was at Crab Tree was a chance to read a newspaper. Mr. and Mrs. Durand subscribed to several newspapers, and they encouraged us to read during our lunch and snack breaks. As I brushed some cookie crumbs off the *Chicago Daily Star* I was reading, a headline caught my eye.

CHARLIE HITCHCOCK GAVE A DELIGHTFUL PERFORMANCE AT WINONA LAST NIGHT
Proclaimed by All as One of the Most Pleasing Programs Ever Rendered Here

If Charlie Hitchcock ever returns to Winona Lake, he will be assured of a capacity audience. His entertainment last night was unquestionably one of the most delightful ever given at Winona and was enjoyed by an audience that nearly filled the auditorium. From the instant he stepped upon the stage until he concluded his program, amid shouts of delight, there was not a moment of lagging interest. The audience was convulsed with laughter, as this capable impersonator, actor, and humorist gave his readings, told his funny stories, and actually impersonated the characters he sought to portray. There were no tiresome waits for changes of costume. Hitchcock needed only his sparkling wit and humor to delight this Indiana audience. He concluded his program in a most unique and original manner. The scene was set in a Democratic ward in Chicago, and all present were asked to pretend they were Democrats. Out stepped the ward boss, black cigar in mouth and mighty gavel in hand. He introduced the candidate for ward alderman, who was the speaker for the evening. Mr. Hitchcock first portrayed the ward boss and then became the Irishman with flaming hair and green necktie. As the Irish candidate uncorked his oration, he beat the table with his gavel and called for words of approval. The audience responded, and through Mr. Hitchcock's clever handling, nearly all joined in the frolic, and, in fact, became a part and party to the entertainment itself.

"What are you reading, Griffin?" Mrs. D. asked in her raspy voice.

"Oh, just a review of a performance Mr. Charles Hitchcock gave down in Warsaw, Indiana, last night." I showed her the page.

"Lake Bluff's very own Charles Hitchcock," she said. I caught a shake of her head and just a trace of a smirk as she said it.

"Have you seen many of his films, ma'am?" I asked.

"Oh, yes. I'm afraid we all have." Again, her tone made it sound like more of a burden than a blessing. She glanced down at the article. "I can't imagine that playing the Winona Lake Theater can hold a candle to his days down at the Chicago Theater or making films with Mr. Charlie Chaplin."

I paused for another bite of the last cookie. "How old would Mr. Hitchcock be, Mrs. Durand?" I asked, remembering Knox's remark at breakfast about his being old enough to be Miss Knaak's father.

"He must be in his mid-40s by now." She reached for a cookie for herself and then tucked another in my jacket pocket. "But however old he is, we can safely say that he is washed up as an actor. I would venture to say that his one night stand down in Winona would scarcely pay for his petrol to get there and back, the poor fellow!" She chuckled.

"Thank you for the cookies, ma'am. They are the best I've ever had."

She smiled, and her thin, cracked lips pulled tightly against her large teeth. "You, my sweet boy, are so welcome. I can't have my best workers going hungry!"

I took another look at the newspaper article and wished I could take it with me. "Ma'am, do you think after you and Mr. Durand finish reading this paper I might be able to have this article?"

She laughed and flipped her hand back toward me. "Take it now, Griffin. Take it now." I ripped it off of its page and folded it carefully in the same pocket of my jacket where Mrs. D. had slipped my cookie.

I never lost or let go of that article. I came upon it in my burgeoning "Elfrieda Knaak" file just before Halloween in 1938, when I was 22-years old, working my first newspaper job. I was surprised by my own reaction as I held this brittle, yellowed, and poorly written review of Charles Hitchcock's one-man-show in Warsaw, Indiana, over a decade after I'd come across it in the Durand's kitchen. It was like I was a kid again, and all I had to go on was my imagination. So for the next ten minutes or so, I imagined Hitchcock, the beleaguered, washed up actor in the tiny, second-rate Winona Lake theater, all the way back in December of 1927.

I pictured him in a dimly lit dressing room, behind a dark wooden stage, sitting alone on a stiff wooden stool. I imagined the mirror before him, bordered with twelve evenly spaced light bulbs, only four of which worked.

The Furnace Girl

In his right hand was a worn brownish-beige makeup sponge, while in his left was a round container of stage makeup. He pursed his lips as he examined himself in the dim, cracked mirror. His face showed every one of his 44 years. It was his eyes that bothered him most, all the cracks in the outside corners. Not even the the thickest stage makeup could lessen those.

I imagined a sharp knock upon his door. "Mr. Hitchcock! Mr. Hitchcock. Five minutes. Just five minutes to curtain."

"Thank you, five," he replied in the theater-speak he had used daily for nearly seven years back in his prime. The lingo came back to him without effort or even thought. He smiled at himself, shaking his head wistfully. "Well, this is it, Charles," he said to his reflection. "It's not New York nor Chicago, but it's a house of paying customers nonetheless."

The seasoned actor rose and grabbed his black top hat, flipping it easily in his two soft hands.

"Two minutes, Mr. Hitchcock! Two minutes," the voice repeated. "We're almost at places, and I'm here to escort you."

Charles opened the door and tipped his hat to the short, plump stagehand.

"Right this way, sir," the stagehand gestured stiffly with his extended left arm.

"And how is the house tonight, kind sir?" Hitchcock inquired, trying not to sound concerned.

The stagehand glanced at his pocket watch and winced. The actor caught it and sighed to himself. "Well, for this close to the holidays, it's a pretty good crowd, sir. We're about half full."

Hitchcock shook his head with resignation.

"Here we are, sir. Our host will introduce you, and we'll part the curtain. Break a leg." The stout man nodded respectfully at Hitchcock, started to leave, but then turned back briefly. "And, sir...it really is an honor to have you here...no matter how many seats are full."

"Thank you, young man," Hitchcock replied with a wink. "I'll see if I can deliver a performance worthy of your praise." As the stagehand disappeared into the backstage darkness, Charles Hitchcock closed his eyes, as was his custom before a show back in the Essanay Studios days down in the Chicago's theater district. He pictured Charlie Chaplin and their 1915 film together, 'His New Job.' In that hilarious piece, Hitchcock had played a receptionist for a boss who was interviewing candidates for a position. Chaplin, in his inimitable way, played one of several candidates interviewing for the job. Chaplin was unruly and ill-behaved in the waiting room, and Hitchcock, as the receptionist, had to reprimand him repeatedly. What fun they had had. Chaplin was a genius with

an unparalleled sense of timing and gesture, and yet he had offered high praise to Charles! "Terrific to work with," Chaplin had said to one reviewer.

Hitchcock's reminiscence was interrupted, as he suddenly heard his own name.

"Please join me in welcoming world famous actor, star of stage and screen, from Lake Bluff, Illinois, Charles Hitchcock!"

As the faded, moth-eaten, blue velvet curtain was parted by the very same stagehand who had summoned Hitchcock from his dressing room, the actor might have heard polite but tepid applause from the Winona Lake patrons. As always, the bright lights, aimed directly at him, made any visual contact with the audience difficult, but even so, Hitchcock could see large, dark pockets of empty seats throughout the tiny, 200-seat venue.

He began with one of his favorite, time-tested bits—an impersonation of US President Calvin Coolidge. Hitchcock contorted his face and managed to seemingly broaden his lithe body, as he recited one of Coolidge's most famous addresses. The crowd erupted in laughter and applause, and Hitchcock drank in their adoration. It fueled him, as he launched seamlessly from sketch to sketch.

His one-man show would have provided him with no rests, no gaps of any kind. There were no costume changes, no makeup alterations, and no time behind the curtain. So Hollywood Hitchcock would have to conjure such changes by the sheer force and creativity of his gestures, facial expressions, bodily contortions, and tone of voice. Hitchcock may have been out of practice, but he was not rusty. By his third bit, Charles Hitchcock would have been drenched in his own sweat.

For more than an hour, the Lake Bluff, Illinois, resident kept them wanting more. In his final sketch, the political one the reviewer had highlighted, Hitchcock somehow managed to bounce back and forth between a Chicago ward boss and an Irish alderman, the two of whom were embroiled in a political argument. As Hitchcock banged the gavel to end the skit and cue the closing of the curtain, the hundred and four Hoosiers from Warsaw, Indiana stood and clapped as loudly as they could.

The exhausted actor stood behind the closed curtain for at least thirty seconds, before slipping through the part to take his well-earned bows. He nodded appreciatively and smiled, his silver-gray eyes glinting in the bright lights. He blew a few kisses to each third of the house and then angled back into the dark of the empty stage.

The plump stage manager patted him on the back and led him back to the dressing room. "Wonderful, Mr. Hitchcock! Truly wonderful," he said. "They loved it! They absolutely loved you, sir!" He unlocked the dressing room door and opened it for the star.

"I thank you, sir," Charles replied. Closing the door behind him, he collapsed onto the stool facing the cruel mirror. He put his silver-haired head into his hands and exhaled a loud sigh. Looking up, Charles Hitchcock saw only his tired, heavy face in the poorly lit mirror, grateful for the burned out bulbs.

Several minutes later, two thud-like knocks startled the actor.

"Yes...come in," Charles replied. The door opened quickly and the chief administrator of the Winona Lake Theater entered, carrying the till for the evening.

"Mr. Hitchcock, you were fantastic! We haven't had an actor of your caliber here in a long, long time." He wiped his brow with the back of his suit coat.

Charles smiled politely and nodded. He couldn't help glancing in the till box anxiously, wondering if his share of the take would cover the petrol for his trip home.

The venue administrator continued. "We had just over a hundred patrons in the house tonight, but twelve of them were our guests." He pulled out the bills and set them on the table and then poured the coins into his own hand. "After our expenses, we have $23.75 for you, Mr. Hitchcock." He handed Hitchcock the cash and then stood to shake his hand.

"It has truly been a pleasure for all of us here at Winona Lake, sir. We hope you will come back, this summer, perhaps. I know we can promise you a sellout after the way you knocked 'em dead tonight." The large man cleared his throat, wiped his brow again, and continued. "There was a reviewer here from The Warsaw Union who loved it. Couldn't say enough about your performance."

"Thank you. Thank you. Yes, I'll have my assistant look at our summer schedule, and see if we can work something out." Hitchcock showed him to the door, feeling just a twinge of guilt for lying about having an assistant.

Alone in the room once again, Hitchcock grabbed his bag, tucking the night's paltry take into his pants pocket, and looking back one last time into the dimly lit mirror. "This is what it has come to, Charles, a half-full theater in Warsaw, Indiana, and $23.75." He shook his head and ran his right hand through his silver-gray hair. "If only Mr. Chaplin and the Essanay crew could see me now."

The disappointed and exhausted actor buttoned up his coat, pulled his fedora on, and paused one final time to tip his hat to the worn-out, graying man in the mirror. Charles Hitchcock headed out the backstage door to the parking lot and into the cold, December night.

"If I didn't know better, Mr. Morgan, I'd swear you were trying to soften me up on Hitchcock," Hargrave said.

"No, nothing like that," I replied, shaking my head.

"Well, it isn't working," he said, getting up and refilling his coffee cup. "I still like Hitchcock for the crime, no matter how washed up he was." He paused and turned toward the window. "In fact, I say he was more likely to commit the crime precisely because he wasn't able to fill theaters anymore." He crossed his arms and nodded for me to continue.

EVANSTON METHODIST CHURCH CHRISTMAS PARTY
FOR THE LAKE BLUFF ORPHANAGE
Photo courtesy of the Lake Bluff History Museum

Chapter 12 — Christmas Gifts
Lake Bluff Orphanage — December 24, 1927

Betty and I sat nervously at the desk of Miss Jessie Arbuckle. Betty wore an adorable, handmade, red jumper that a woman from the Lake Bluff Methodist Church had made especially for her. Betty's curly hair had matching ribbons that her housemother, Miss Jaeger, had tied for her right after breakfast. Tucked in her left arm was her ever-present, one-eyed teddy bear.

I sat to Betty's right, wearing my best brown pants—only two small holes in them—a creamy white shirt, and suspenders. My light brown hair was neatly trimmed, thanks to Jim Spader. He'd given all the LBO boys haircuts in the last few days, in preparation for today's Christmas visits.

At first, I'd been a little worried about being summoned to this meeting with Miss Arbuckle. I'd heard the horror story about when Charlie DeWitt, another recently departed Wads boy, had tried to run away just before Betty and I arrived. His "meeting" ended with an abundance of swats upon his hindquarters that left Charlie unable to walk or even sit down for almost a week. And, a couple of days after that, he was on his way down to the Glenwood Military School in Chicago. There were other scenarios running through my head, everything from Betty and me being fostered out to separate families, to some crazy news about our mother. In the end, an hour and a half before the meeting, Danny put my fears to rest.

"She's just going to talk to you two about the Christmas home visits down in Wilmette," Danny said. "It's what she does with all the first year kids, and most of it will be about manners. She wants to make sure you and Betty say all the right 'pleases' and 'thank yous,' and that you don't grab at whatever gifts your family has for you."

When Miss Arbuckle entered her dark wooden paneled office and closed the heavy, oak door behind her, I sat up as straight as I could and reached for my sister's little hand.

"Good morning, you two," she said, smiling. Reaching for a file on the back corner of her mahogany desk, she noticed Betty's hair. "My, Betty, you look so grown up and pretty today!"

Betty blushed and looked at me. I gestured with my eyes and hand for her to say thank you. Instead she just giggled awkwardly and tugged on her hair. "Thank you, Miss Arbuckle," I offered on Betty's behalf.

"Oh, before I forget, I have a nice Christmas card for each of you from your Aunt Rose." She handed us each a white envelope.

"Aunt Rose!" Betty said clapping her tiny hands together.

"Yes, isn't that nice? Now, today is a big day for you and all our children," she began. "We are sending you to have a Christmas celebration with a wonderful host family. This very nice family has been working very hard to provide you two and one other girl from LBO a merry Christmas."

"Will there be presents? And Santa?" Betty blurted out. I winced.

"Oh yes, Betty," Arbuckle replied calmly. "That is why I wanted to talk to you and Griff. Many nice people have been working very hard to get all this ready for you and all our children." She lowered her head and body and leaned across her broad desk to be right at Betty's eye level. "I need to be sure that you and your brother can be very polite and well behaved today. Can you do that, Betty?"

Betty glanced at me and nodded energetically. "Santa gives presents when we are nice. Not naughty though." She switched from the nodding to a vigorous shake of her head at the naughty part. I looked down at my folded hands, now resting on my lap, a bit embarrassed by my sister's antics.

"Saying 'thank you' and waiting your turn are very important today. I know I can count on you and your brother to be especially good today, right, Betty?" Miss Arbuckle paused, sat back up in her chair, and opened up the file on her desk.

"Now, when you get to Wilmette, the two of you will be going to the home of a nice family named the Freidles."

Betty interrupted. "Will Mama be there? With our family?" she asked, hopefully.

"No, Betty," Arbuckle replied matter-of-factly. "Your mother will not be there. But Mrs. Freidle is a very nice mother." The matron of LBO put her glasses on, tilted her head back, and consulted her file again. "The Freidles have a girl named Rita who is eight and a boy who is just about your age, Griffin" she said, removing her glasses and looking at Betty. "And Carol Ridley, who lives in Judson with you, Betty, will be going there with you. Won't that be nice?"

Miss Arbuckle looked at me, tentatively, and I sensed she was preparing to broach a tougher topic. "You will be riding the train down to Wilmette with sixty-one other children from our orphanage." She saw me look down and take Betty's hand again. Betty looked confused and pulled her teddy bear close to her chest.

"Will we see Mama on the tra…" Betty began, but I interrupted before she could finish.

"We know about the train," I said, willing the conversation forward.

Nodding to me, Miss Arbuckle added, "The Freidles will pick you up at the Wilmette train depot and take you three back to their lovely home. You'll have a nice dinner with them, open some gifts, and then they'll deliver you back to the train station in time to return with the rest of us on the 5:17 train." She paused again, replacing the file and looking at both of us briefly. "You will have so many reasons and opportunities to say 'thank you' today, all right?"

I straightened up and adopted the most formal and adult tone I could muster. "It sounds really swell, Miss Arbuckle. Thank you for putting all this together for us." I glanced at Betty and then back at Miss Arbuckle. "We won't let you down, ma'am."

She rose from behind her desk and set her glasses down upon it. "I am sure you won't. Well, we need to get going."

Of the 109 current residents at the orphanage, 48 had their own families or relatives to spend Christmas with. While Sunday was the regular visitation day for parents on an every-other-week basis, with Christmas falling on a Sunday in 1927, parents and legal guardians were asked to come a day early to pick their children up by 9 a.m. This would allow the orphanage staff to manage the chaotic enterprise of getting the other 61 of us to the train station, "tagged" with the orange badges given to us by Mrs. Roy L. Haskin of the Wilmette Methodist Church, and then onto the southbound North Shore Line by 10:22.

For several years, Georgia Haskin had organized and executed all the logistics of this trip, in cooperation with Miss Arbuckle. Mrs. Haskin recruited the host families—all from the Wilmette Methodist Church—paired them up with appropriately aged LBO kids, communicated the gift lists, and even accompanied the children on the train, both leaving and returning to Lake Bluff. Jessie Arbuckle had often referred to Mrs. Haskin as "a saint." In many ways, this Christmas visit day was not one the orphanage staff looked forward to, given the logistical nightmare of getting so many of us to Wilmette and back. But Georgia Haskin made it much more manageable for everyone.

Dick Moley did not look forward to this day either. His mother had died giving birth to his sister Linda, who had also been at the orphanage with him for the first couple of years. His father, Miles Moley, remarried quite quickly and lived less than three blocks from the Lake Bluff Orphanage with his new wife Liz and her three children. But their "arrangement" was that Miles was to have "no contact whatsoever" with Dick or Linda, in order to assure Liz that Miles had really made "a clean break" from his past. It seems that this pledge to his new wife was the one promise Miles Moley had actually managed to live up to.

But then, a few years ago, Dick's little sister got fostered out, and Dick hasn't seen her since. To make matters worse, every Christmas Visit Day, Dick got to watch almost half of his orphanage cohorts get picked up by their birth parents and relatives, while he could only relive his father's unfathomable and selfish decision all over again. Rather than being able to walk to his own father's house, Dick would board the train and ride 40 minutes to visit a well-meaning and generous family named the Hancocks, a family Dick had no emotional connection to. But, as he'd said to his Wads buddies just two Saturdays ago in my hearing, "Nobody can put on a spread like Mrs. Hancock: turkey with all the fixins, stuffing, mashed potatas, sweet potatas, cornbread, and two kinds of pies." I suppose Dick was grateful to the Hancocks, but it certainly couldn't have lessened the anger he felt toward his father every single Christmas, every Sunday family visit day, and every other day as well.

On that Saturday in 1927 and on a good many days since, I wished that I could redefine the word "orphan." It shouldn't mean a kid who doesn't have any parents; it should mean a kid who was unlucky enough to be born to a couple of idiots, who never should have been allowed to be parents in the first place.

It was a bitterly cold morning, as we walked, two-by-two, up Scranton to the train station. Sixteen degrees minus the wind chill made it feel like four degrees. At the front of our line was the proud figure of Miss Arbuckle. Behind her were five pairs of children followed by Miss Jaeger, then five more pairs, another housemother, all the way back to Mr. Spader, who brought up the rear. We were on a "strict schedule," as Miss Arbuckle had put it, so no dawdling was permitted. In a strange and annual breach of LBO protocol, this was the only outing where siblings were allowed to walk together, regardless of age and gender. So at least I got to hold Betty's little hand, knowing that this would be her first time at the train station since the day—exactly a month ago—when our mother had brought us to Lake Bluff for our "checkups." In the months and years since this Christmas outing, I've often thought about this small but significant concession on Miss Arbuckle's part—to let Betty walk with me and to bring her teddy bear, which she had buttoned up inside the front of her wool coat.

The two-and-a-half block walk to the train station was brisk and uneventful. Mrs. Haskin was there, awaiting our arrival. She wore a long black coat and a fashionable hat with a scarf attached that tied under her chin to keep the hat from blowing off in the blustery Chicago wind. She was of medium height and powerfully built. She held a clipboard with dozens of bright orange tags attached to it.

We stayed in our perfect rows, as Miss Arbuckle went over all the final details with Mrs. Haskin. We all leaned and craned our necks to the left and right, trying to see what lay before us. After several minutes, the two women exchanged nods and Miss Arbuckle blew her whistle sharply.

"Children, this is Mrs. Haskin, a real live angel from the Wilmette Methodist Church." She spoke in a virtual shout to be heard over the wind and the trains. "You will stay in your pairs as she makes her way through our lines, attaching an orange tag to each of you. The tag will have the last name of the family you will be meeting and going home with once you arrive in Wilmette. After receiving your tag, you will wait until one of the orphanage staff takes you to board the train." She cleared her throat. "Once aboard the train, you will sit down immediately and remain seated until you arrive in Wilmette, where Mrs. Haskin will give you further instructions for disembarking."

The tagging process began with remarkable efficiency. The older kids were extremely helpful and reassuring to the first timers. I caught on as quickly as I could and gently but firmly directed Betty. Our tags, which were clipped on by Miss Arbuckle, said, "Freidle."

"Griffy! Ice cream on the train, but no shots?" Betty whispered.

Smiling down at her, I replied, "No, peanut. No ice cream and no shots. Just a fun trip, a lot of food, and presents at the end."

"Oooo, presents!" she squealed.

"And we will be together the whole time, and Carol too." I glanced behind us, where Carol Ridley was standing. I took both girls' hands and boarded the train.

We sat in the third seat on the left, on the station side of the southbound train. I turned around to see our train car now completely filled with orange-tagged kids of every shape and size from the Lake Bluff Orphanage. Out the window, beneath the white and green Lake Bluff sign, stood Miss Arbuckle and her three housemothers. Only Mr. Spader had actually boarded the train to assist Mrs. Haskin, who had assured Jessie that she had "everything under control."

The four women at the depot platform waved and smiled as the southbound 10:22 pulled out of Lake Bluff right on -time.

"Willl-mette! Willl-mette is next!" the conductor called, as he passed through our car. Mrs. Haskin rose immediately.

"Here we are, children. Thank you for your excellent behavior and cooperation on our journey! Miss Arbuckle will be so very pleased." She worked her way to the exit doorway. "We will get off in the very same manner as we boarded. We'll start at the front of the car and work our way back, moving two by two. My husband, Mr. Haskin, will be waiting for us right under the Wilmette sign. Each of you will report to him, and he will connect you with your host family."

Despite Mrs. Haskin's calm and assuring voice, there was nervous energy and anxiety throughout the train car, as we disembarked and began speculating about which people out there might be "our families" for the day. Clutching Betty's and Carol's hands as they descended the stairs, I quickly spotted the smiling Roy Haskin, holding his own clipboard and smoking a pipe. He wore a fuzzy gray overcoat, black rubber overshoes, and a black fedora. His white mustache and reddened cheeks rose together in a smile, as we approached. His wife had begun shuttling children to their families, who were waiting at the south end of the Wilmette depot.

"Hello! Hello! Welcome!" Mr. Haskin said, as he shook my hand and pulled me close to read the name on my orange tag. "Ah, the Freidles! You three are in for a real treat!" He bent down to touch both Betty and Carol on the tops of their hats. He turned to his left and called, "Georgia! Fetch me the Freidles, dear!"

My two charges and I turned to the south end, where a tall, handsome man approached with a gangly boy just behind him. "Here we are! We are the Freidles. Welcome!" The man reached the girls first and knelt down to give each of them a hug, while his son leaned awkwardly toward me.

"Hello. I'm Mitch. Are you Griff?" the boy asked. I nodded.

Mr. Freidle, an enormous man, rose and extended his massive right hand to me. "We are so pleased to meet you, Griff. Come! Come this way! Let's get you home and warm!" He gestured through the boisterous crowd, and I grabbed a hand each from Carol and Betty and pulled them through. Mr. Harold Freidle led us to a shiny brown Model T with four doors. Mr. Freidle and Mitch each manned a door and opened them for the girls and me. The three of us slid comfortably into the back seat, while the Freidles got situated in front. Betty and Carol were wide-eyed and looking in every direction but said nothing. I felt the smooth seats and took in the fine details of the car.

"We're just a few blocks over on Lake Avenue, so we'll have you there in a jiffy. Mrs. Freidle and Mitch's sister Rita are so excited to welcome you." He kept his eyes on the road. "They're cooking up a storm, or they'd have come with us."

Betty and Carol's mouths were wide open in amazement, but they remained silent. I noticed that Betty had unzipped her jacket, so that her little bear could breath and see the sights as well. Her left hand was still clinging to mine, but her right was holding Carol's.

Wilmette shared many similarities with Lake Bluff: beautifully manicured homes, massive oaks and maples, and a downtown that fanned out from the train station. But everything seemed to be on a bit grander scale.

Pulling into the driveway at 1232 Lake Ave., the Freidle home was beautifully decorated for Christmas. It was a three-story, dark red home, with a garage to the left of it. This garage, into which Mr. Freidle pulled his car, still had room for four bikes, a massive tool bench, and more fishing equipment than I had ever seen.

Before Mitch and his father could even get the three of us out of the back seat, Mrs. Freidle and her daughter came rushing out the front door. They both had beautiful, blond hair. The daughter's hung clear down to the middle of her back, while her mother's was pulled up in a tight bun. Mrs. Freidle wore a long, plaid, flannel skirt and a deep green sweater. She welcomed Carol with a toothy smile, a gentle hug, and then moved onto Betty, offering the same and adding, "You brought a special friend with you, I see. Does your bear have a name?" Betty just giggled.

Mrs. Freidle presented her daughter. "This is Rita, who just turned nine. She has been so anxious for you to get here!" She turned and eyed me. She shook my right hand with both of hers. "Merry Christmas, Griff! We are so happy to have you with us today." Realizing how cold it had become, she added, "Oh, my! Do come right in!"

The entryway was warm and inviting. Giant black and white squares of marble formed the floor, and straight ahead and to the left was a carpeted staircase. To the right of the stairs was a small kitchen with a table completely covered in food. I smelled the turkey and gravy and realized how hungry I was. I thought back to Dick Moley's description of the spread at his Christmas family.

"Rita," her father said, "Why don't you show the girls around. Mitch and I will give Griff the men's tour." He put his arm around me and steered me toward the staircase. "We want you to feel right at home here, Griff. Anything you want to do or anything you need, please, speak right up."

"Yes, sir. Thank you," I replied. Mitch scooted past me on the broad staircase, just as we reached the second floor.

"My room is over here, if you wanna see it," Mitch said, opening the heavy oak door. There was a huge bed that seemed unnaturally high off the floor. It came almost all the way up to my waist. Next to it was a large, wooden desk, almost the size of the one in Miss Arbuckle's office. Some matching wood bookshelves rose up behind it. "I have a lot 'a baseball cards if you wanna see 'em." Mitch pointed to three picture book albums on the shelf closest to the desk's surface.

"Sure," I said. I thumbed through the first, well-organized album he handed me, feeling the shiny finish on each card. I saw many of the most famous players in the game: Lou Gehrig, Babe Ruth, Ted Lyons, Roger Hornsby, and Hack Wilson.

"Let's take Griff upstairs, shall we, Mitch?" Mitch nodded, smiling, and rushed to the doorway. But I was confused, for we already were upstairs.

In the hallway, Mr. Freidle opened a door I hadn't noticed before. He flicked on a light, and I could see another, much smaller stairway leading upward. I followed the father and son up these curious stairs, until they opened to an unfinished attic space. Against the far wall, a long table housed several radios.

There was a big piece of plywood anchored to the wall, probably three feet high and seven feet long, with many knobs, needles, and meters attached to it. Mr. Freidle began flipping a series of switches, and little red lights began to flicker. He motioned for me to come closer.

"These are ham radios, Griff." He reached for a set of headphones and placed them around his neck loosely. "Mitch and I can talk to people all over the United States on these."

"Don't forget Britain and France, Father," Mitch added proudly.

His father chuckled. "You believe that, Griff? We can talk through these little machines to people who are oceans away." He smiled and put a second set of headphones on my head. "Shall we show him, Mitch?" The two Freidles took seats, and I stood between them, fascinated. The two operators adjusted knobs, and static began to emerge. There was a little, brown, box-looking thing with a black tapper on the top. Mr. Freidle held his headphone to his left ear, while he tapped out some sort of code or message with his right hand. Mitch had his hand on a big knob that said "Frequency" under it. After about a minute, Mr. Freidle seemed to hear something in his left ear.

"Try 180, Mitch." His son dialed the frequency knob to 180. Soon strange tones, beeps, and fuzz emanated from the machine but then slowly faded. I began to make out voices. Adjusting one more knob to the right and then back to the left, Mr. Freidle began to speak.

"This is V-dash-seven-four-zero-niner. V-dash-seven-four-zero-niner. Over." He paused to listen, still tweaking a couple of knobs.

A static-filled voice from the radio replied, "This is V-dash-one-five-one-seven. I read you, seven-four-zero-niner. Come in. Over."

Mitch and his father nodded their heads and smiled, turning toward me. Mitch adjusted my headset so I could hear everything they were picking up.

"This is Liberty Station, seven-four-zero-niner. We copy you, Anton! Do you read me, over?" Static filled the silence in the attic, as the three of us waited.

A voice punched through the static. "Yes, Liberty Station, you have Clock Tower one-five-one-seven, live in London, over." The British accent was unmistakable. My eyes widened and my jaw dropped. I looked excitedly at my hosts. Mr. Freidle patted me on the back, and Mitch smiled and nodded as well.

The voice came again. "Liberty Station, what is your business tonight, over."

"Clock Tower, we send our Christmas greetings from Chicago, Illinois, over." Freidle said. "And we have a very special guest with us, Mr. Griff Morgan. He's never seen a ham radio before, over.

"Indeed, Liberty Station! Indeed! Merry Christmas to you, Griff, and to your hosts, over."

"This is Liberty Station signing off." They powered down the radio and removed their headphones. I was utterly speechless and grinning ear to ear. "We better get downstairs, or the girls will think we flew to the moon!" Mr. Freidle said. I headed for the door with them. At the top of the stairs, Mitch turned to me and tapped the side of his head.

"Huh?" I asked

"You'll probably want to take those headphones off before we head back downstairs," Mr. Freidle said, winking at me. I slid them off, feeling foolish, and ran them back over to the table. I lingered, taking another look at the nobs and needles. I ran my hand gently over the frequency wheel, before turning to catch up to my hosts.

"Do you talk to people up there every night?" I asked, as we reached the second floor.

"I'm up there three or four nights a week, when the weather is clear," Mr. Freidle said. "Mitch joins me when his homework is done and on the weekends as well."

"Do you talk to the same people ever?" I pressed.

"You bet. We run into the same people from time to time. That's how we know Anton. It's part of the fun."

Mr. Freidle had turned left as we reached the second floor. He then turned right, down another, even longer hallway. "Let's check on the girls." He knocked on another oak door. "Rita?" He opened it to reveal three girls lying side by side on their stomachs on Rita's white, ruffled bed. It was canopied with lace and was every bit as high off the ground as Mitch's bed had been.

"Griffy!" Betty said. She stood on the bed, holding her arms out to me. I crossed to her quickly, enfolding her in my best big brother bear hug.

I whispered, "No shoes on beds, right?"

She smiled. "Miss Jaeger says that, Griffy."

"You girls having fun?" Mr. Freidle asked.

"Very fun! Very!" Betty said. Rita and Carol smiled in agreement and got off the bed.

"We'd better head downstairs and see if we can help Mother with the feast," Mr. Freidle suggested. I was still carrying Betty, and Rita put Carol on piggyback. Mitch led the way, and Mr. Freidle followed Rita with a hand on Carol.

The walls on the way down to the first floor had beautiful sketches of Rita, Mitch, and both parents. Near the bottom was a beautiful rendering of all four of them.

"There you are!" Mrs. Freidle said, coming out from the kitchen in her holiday apron. Santa was eating a Christmas cookie on it. "I was beginning to think I'd have to eat all this food myself." She bent forward, putting her hands on her knees. Betty and Carol approached her, staring at her apron. Betty reached a hand tentatively toward her.

"Santa," Betty said, wide eyed and pointing.

"Yes, Betty! We love Santa here." She took her hand and walked Betty around the corner to the living room. Without saying anything, Mrs. Freidle pointed.

"A tree! A beautiful tree!" Betty exclaimed. "And presents too?"

"Yes, presents too," Mrs. Freidle said, putting an arm around Carol.

The Christmas tree was a full, broad, perfectly shaped Douglas Fir. It practically reached the ceiling and was covered in silver and gold balls spaced an inch and a half apart, reflecting the multi-colored lights that shone all around them.

"Santa knew you, Carol, and Griff were coming here, and he brought some presents for you!" Betty's eyes widened. "So why don't we have our supper, and then we'll come back here by the tree to see what Santa brought, OK?"

Mitch and Rita led the way into the formal dining room. The dining room was lighted by two candelabras, each holding five candles. The china settings at each place were sparkling in the candlelight, and, to the left of each plate was a green cloth napkin, perfectly rolled and held by a brass ring with a tiny pine cone on it.

"I love Christmas!" Betty said.

"Me too!" Carol added.

"So do we," Mr. Freidle agreed, gesturing for everyone to sit down. "Let's offer thanks." He bowed his large head and began. "Heavenly Father, we are truly thankful this day for the birth of your son, Jesus. As we prepare to celebrate and remember his birth, we are particularly grateful that you have brought Griff, Carol, and Betty to our home. May they feel a part of our family, just as all of us are a part of yours. Bless this food to our use and us to thy service, through Christ, our Lord. Amen."

Mr. Freidle began to carve the sixteen-pound, perfectly bronzed turkey. He used shiny silver carving utensils. Pinching each carved piece between his fork and knife, he placed a piece on one of the plates that had been passed to him and then handed it to Mrs. Freidle, who stood at his right. She measured out small, evenly spaced helpings of the side dishes on each plate—mashed potatoes, string beans, cranberry sauce, and dinner rolls. Then she would whisper a name to Rita, who delivered the plate, being sure to serve it from the right.

I received my plate and remembered again what Dick had said about the food at the Hancock home, where Dick would be at this very moment. I wondered if the Hancock home was in this same part of Wilmette. Mitch appeared at my right with two silver pitchers, filling one of my glasses with water and the other with milk. "Thank you," I said, nodding at Mitch.

"Let's dig in, folks," Mr. Freidle instructed, seeing everyone had been served. Neither Betty nor I began. Both of us seemed lost in the wonder of this room, this home, and this family. I scanned the entire table, the flickering candles and the warm glow that seemed to bathe the entire scene in soft light. Betty's eyes were fixed on Mrs. Freidle.

"Thank you, Mrs. Freidle," Betty said.

Smiling and putting a hand to her mouth, Mrs. Freidle blushed. "You are so welcome, Betty, so very welcome."

After dinner, the dishes were shuttled to the kitchen by Mitch, Rita, and me, while Mr. and Mrs. Freidle entertained the two little girls around the Christmas tree. When the three others of us joined them, Mrs. Freidle selected a present for each of us guests. "Let's see what Santa brought this year!" She set a beautifully wrapped gift on each child's lap, beginning with Carol. The gifts, while different sizes, were identically wrapped in red paper with golden ribbons tied in perfect bows. I put a gentle hand on Betty's knee as a reminder to wait and to be polite.

"Thank you, Mr. and Mrs. Freidle," I said. Betty and Carol nodded.

"We need to see what they are first, boy," Mr. Freidle said with a wink.

Carol and Betty each received jumpers with flowers along the seams. Betty's was royal blue and Carol's was maroon.

"I believe there is something else in those boxes," Mrs. Freidle said. The girls reached in beneath the tissue paper to find a pair of knee socks that matched the jumpers. The girls looked at each other and giggled. "Thank you!" they said together.

I felt a nudge on my left shoulder. It was Mitch, looking down at me from behind the couch and nodding as he pointed at my unopened present. I found the taped lines and unwrapped the gift carefully, without tearing the paper. I moved slowly and deliberately, in no hurry for any of this to end.

The box was both deeper and taller than the boxes the girls had opened. I reached in to find a leather baseball glove with a real baseball tucked in its fold. I'd never seen a glove up close, and had certainly never held one in my own hand.

"Try it on, Griff," Mr. Freidle said.

I hesitated for a moment, caught up in the leathery smell. I glanced up at the family and took in a much-needed breath. When I looked back at the ball glove, I bit my lip, afraid I was about to cry. So I bit down even harder and slid my left hand into the amazing glove. There were three sections inside—one for my thumb, one for the first two fingers, and a third for the other two fingers. Mitch grabbed the ball from the webbing and flung it back down toward the glove. Startled a bit, I bobbled it, but held on, using my right hand.

"Atta boy!" chuckled Mr. Freidle. "A regular Lou Gehrig!"

Again, needing air, I said, "Thank you…thank you all so much."

"Aww, you bet, Griff. We are so glad you like it and that you came to be with us," Mrs. Freidle said.

Rita took the girls up to her room to try on their dresses, while Mitch took me out to the garage where Mitch's own glove was. "We're going to have a catch out on the drive, Father," Mitchell shouted over his shoulder back toward the living room.

"Right-o, son. Right-o," Mr. Freidle replied. I heard the footsteps of Emmaline and Harold Freidle heading back into the kitchen to tackle the dishes.

When Mitch and I returned from the driveway, it was nearing four o'clock. It wouldn't be long until we'd be taken back to the Wilmette train station. Mitch went in to help his parents finish up the dishes, and I said, "I'm going to check on Betty." I climbed up the stairs as quickly and as quietly as I could. Reaching the second floor, I looked and listened down the hall. Hearing the giggles, I walked softly to the attic door and turned the knob as silently as I could. I closed it behind me and crept up in utter silence. There, spread out before me, was the ham radio. I'd forgotten to ask why it was called a "ham radio." Picking up the headset that Mr. Freidle had used, I placed it carefully on my head. They were still plugged into the plywood apparatus.

"Clock Tower, this is Liberty Station four-zero-niner, over," I said, just above a whisper. I reached for the knob I'd seen Mr. Freidle fiddle with and pretended to turn it."

"Yes, Liberty Station. This is Clock Tower. I read you, over," I said, in my best British accent. Looking just to the left of the ham set-up, there was a window I hadn't noticed before. It was high on the attic wall and looked out at the darkening sky. Though the sun hadn't yet set, the moon was up and two stars flanked it. I stared at the sky for several minutes. When I looked down, I realized I still had the new ball glove on, and the baseball was still in the webbing. Using my free hand to remove Mr. Freidle's headset, I placed it carefully on the table. I ran my right hand over the surface of the plywood, touching two of the needle gauges, and then tiptoed back to the stairs.

I heard the girls' excited voices coming from down on the first floor. Taking a peek in Rita's open bedroom door, I saw Betty's teddy bear on the bed. I fetched it, turned off Rita's light, and pulled the door shut behind me. Descending the final flight of stairs, I stopped at each drawing, the one of Rita, the one of Mitch, and, finally, the one of the entire Freidle family. I tucked Betty's bear in my baseball glove on top of the ball and ran my right index finger along the drawing, tracing the outline of the four smiling figures, a family.

Mr. Freidle's voice echoed from the hallway to the kitchen. "The Freidle taxi to the Wilmette station will be leaving in four minutes! That's four minutes, people!"

Coming around the corner of the stairway, I saw Betty and Carol in the kitchen, modeling their new dresses. Mrs. Freidle, Rita, and Mitch were all admiring the show. But after Mr. Freidle's four-minute warning, they all began to hug and say goodbye. I heard the car starting up in the garage, took in a big breath, took one last look into the now empty dining room, and joined the others.

At the Wilmette train depot, all the LBO kids had formed a line that stretched back from where Mr. and Mrs. Haskin stood. The Haskins busily checked off each child's name, using the orange tags to verify their count. Mitch and Mr. Freidle stood with Carol, Betty, and me, saying their goodbyes.

Mr. Freidle put his long, powerful hand on my shoulder, turning me to face him. Smiling down and nodding, he said, "You remember, Griff, that we will always be here for you and your sister." Mr. Freidle paused, moving his hand down from my shoulder in order to shake hands. "We will be here next Christmas and for as many years as you and Betty are at the Lake Bluff Orphanage."

"Thank you, sir." I swallowed. "It's been a....a....perfect day."

"Enjoy that glove, now," Mr. Freidle winked and Mitch gave me a little wave, as we turned to join the line of orphans boarding the train.

As we found our seats and I got Betty and Carol situated, I looked out at the platform and noticed that none of the host families had left. They were lined two and three deep, scanning the train windows for "their" kids. As I looked through our train car, all the LBO kids were doing the same thing. Nobody was sitting and all of us seemed to be bunched on the same side of the train, squirming and leaning in search of our host families.

Mr. Freidle was easy to spot. He was a good six inches taller than anyone else there, and his hand, twice the size of any of the others, waved wildly in our direction.

"Children! Children!" Mrs. Haskin yelled. "Sit down! Sit down at once! The train will be moving any moment."

I watched as boys and girls my age and younger hung their heads and returned reluctantly to their seats. The conductor blew his whistle, and the electric train pulled away from Wilmette station and the cheering waves of well over a hundred people.

317 E. CENTER AVENUE — THE HOME OF CHARLES HITCHCOCK
Photo courtesy of the Lake Bluff History Museum

Chapter 13 — Trouble With the Law

Lake Bluff, IL — January 28, 1928

I really can't explain, not even after all these years, why I chose one of the coldest nights of that winter in '28 to begin what would become my regular habit of sneaking out of the orphanage late at night to walk the streets of Lake Bluff. It must have been fourteen below with the wind chill when I cleared the corner of Wads and started moving from tree to tree in the shadowy night.

There was always a sudden rush of adrenalin for me, once I got clear of the enclosed walls of the orphanage, and it had nothing to do with the sub-zero temperatures. It's not an overstatement to say that we often felt like we were in prison at LBO. Early in my years as a reporter, I came across an article that had been written about the orphanage in the 1930s, and in describing a boy who had died at LBO, the paper referred to him as "an inmate at the Lake Bluff Orphanage."

So any chance that those of us with wanderlust got to clear the walls of this place and get out, especially in an unsupervised way, we would seize upon. Lots of boys snuck out of Wadsworth, usually in pairs or threes. But I preferred to go it alone. I needed time to think and to figure things out, things like how to get more time with Betty and how to get the two of us out of the orphanage together, without the foster care system separating us.

The other thing I found myself doing on the quiet, sleepy streets of Lake Bluff was looking inside the beautiful houses and imagining what it must be like to live in one of them. On this particularly frigid January night in 1928, I headed east, toward the lake, and the closer I got to the water, the bigger the houses got, and the colder I felt. The east-west streets in Lake Bluff were like wind tunnels. The roads weren't paved back then, so the dirt, sand, and crushed gravel would get picked up and carried by the wind. You could feel it pelting your face. I tugged on the black knit cap I had received from the Methodist church a couple of weeks before and made sure my navy pea coat was buttoned up all the way.

Up ahead, near the intersection of Scranton and Maple, I saw a man walking a dog. I avoided him by cutting through some yards to get back toward town. It was between 10:00 and 10:30, and most of the houses were dark, but I saw one with some smoke coming out of its chimney and headed toward it, hoping for a little heat. A light was on upstairs, and I walked up the driveway toward the chimney. I knocked my knee against something—a rake or a shovel—and it slammed against the side of house. A light came on by the front porch, and I took off through some yards and started heading back toward LBO, when I heard an unmistakable voice from right behind me.

"It's quite late to be out running through yards, young man." I froze at his words and knew in an instant who was speaking them. It was the clear, perfectly enunciated voice of Charles Hitchcock. I turned around slowly, as he continued. "You do realize that you are right across the street from the home of Lake Bluff's Chief of Police?" He pointed across the street and diagonally to Chief Barney Rosenhagen's house.

Deputy Hitchcock, even back then, when I was a shrimp, was shorter than I expected, standing less than two feet from me. Everything he'd done in his YMCA classroom was so big—animated and dramatic. But here, he wasn't much bigger than my roommate Danny Thompson. His expression was stern but not at all menacing.

"Who are you, and what are you doing out so very late on this dreadfully cold night?" He crossed his arms and cocked back his head. His words vaporized and were blown west by the wind.

"I...My...I'm... Griff Morgan," I stumbled. Hitchcock's eyes widened.

"I'm not familiar with the Morgan family, and I know most everyone in this town." The actor straightened his arms and tightened his gloves. "What street do you live on, Mr. Morgan?"

"Scranton," I said as I exhaled. "I don't have a family...I live at the orphanage."

"Oh...I see," the night deputy said, lowering his eyes. "I don't suppose Miss Jessie Arbuckle will be any too pleased by the news of your current whereabouts, will she?"

"No, sir," I said.

"Well, I am not on foot tonight, at least, so I can offer you a warm ride back to your quarters, Mr. Morgan," Mr. Hitchcock said, pointing down Prospect, across the street and a couple houses down from the Rosenhagen home, where his silver-gray Packard sat. As we walked toward it, I felt him slow down as we passed in front of the police chief's home. Maybe he was hoping Chief Rosenhagen would see us and make a note of Deputy Hitchcock's able detective work.

Once we were both inside the car, we sputtered westward down the street, the Packard struggling against the cold and wind. "I knew a boy who grew up in your orphanage. Tommy Hillman...he was a friend of mine when we were both a bit older than you. We were at the Shields Township High School." Hitchcock grew somber as he pictured his childhood pal. "We ran around together most every day after school. We spent one entire summer running the ravines and getting in all kinds of trouble."

"Trouble?" I repeated, unsure what an officer of the law would have done to get in trouble.

He laughed dramatically. "Oh, nothing like that, though, come to think of it, he did speak of sneaking out at night from time to time when he lived at LBO." I wondered if he ever got caught and what punishment he faced. "If I may ask, Mr. Morgan, what...brought you to the orphanage? Did you...lose your parents? Did something happen to them?"

Without looking at the deputy, I thought about what to say. "My mother took us away from my father...and then about six months later, she dumped us here."

Mr. Hitchcock shook his head. "I'm sorry. Perhaps she'll be back when her fortunes improve."

I hoped so, but all I said was, "Is this your car? It's a beauty."

Mr. Hitchcock chuckled. "Oh no. I'm nowhere near owning my own automobile." He patted the steering wheel with his left hand. "This beauty belongs to my good friend Oscar Kloer. He is kind enough to loan it to to me on particularly cold patrol nights."

We turned left off of Prospect and both heard the low rattle of a single vehicle approaching from the east. It was a black Packard that seemed to catch Hitchcock's attention, a much newer model than his. It was barely moving, almost at a crawl. Two men with dark fedoras were inside, the passenger looking straight ahead, while the driver seemed to look directly at Charles Hitchcock. There was a hint of a smile on the broad man's lips, and I saw him nod at Deputy Hitchcock in an almost ominous greeting. There was something uneasy about the encounter, and I could see the discomfort in the actor's face, as I turned around in my seat to watch the slow moving Packard disappear into the darkness.

"Do you know them?" I asked.

He hesitated, then shook his head. "No, Griffin, I don't. But something tells me I should."

We came to a stop directly in front of Wadsworth Hall. I heard myself exhale, far more audibly than I intended. I waited for him to move, but he remained perfectly still. He looked up at Wads, toward the first floor, I think. Then he spoke, softly. "Do they still use the paddle on you boys?" I'd heard about the housemother's paddle but hadn't experienced it. I did know, however, that getting caught sneaking out was the shortest route to a sore buttocks.

"Yes, sir," I said, looking down at my folded hands. I glanced at my captor out of the corner of my eye and could see that he was still staring at the first floor. He pulled out his pocket watch, an Ingersoll Yankee.

"10:45," he stated, looking at me for the first time in quite a while. "What do you suppose the chances are of you getting in there and up to your bed without being noticed?"

"Sir?" I asked. "I don't understand."

"Well, I could take you up to the door and ring for Miss Harvey." He paused and took a breath. "Or, we could handle this another way."

"What other way?" I asked.

"I could use some help from time to time, over at the Village Hall, and sometimes at my home over on Center." He reached his right arm toward me and rested it on my shoulder, looking me right in the eye. "We could make an arrangement. I could pretend that your little excursion tonight never happened, and you could pretend that you have a part-time job working for me." He looked back over my shoulder at Wads.

"So where is the escape hatch, a first floor window on the back side of Wadsworth?" He smiled and raised his eyebrows at me.

"Yes, sir," I replied. "The northwest corner."

He nodded. "Well, you'd best be going. And I'll see you over at the Village Hall Tuesday on your way home from school." He lifted and lowered his eyebrows again several times, punctuating his nodding.

"What will I tell Miss Arbuckle and Miss Harvey? About the work, I mean," I asked. "I already have chores I do both at the orphanage and over at Crab Tree Farm."

The actor patted me on my shoulder. "Leave that up to me. Now, you go on, Mr. Morgan. And good luck!"

I got out of the Packard and closed the door as softly as I could. I glanced up and down Scranton and then made a dash for the northwest corner of Wads. I came to the window I had propped open with a stick, but the stick was on the ground. The window was shut.

I tried to pry it open, first with my hands and then with a thin, sharp stone, but it wouldn't budge. Looking up at the second floor windows, there was not a single light or sign of life anywhere. There were three doors to the building—one on the front, one on the back, and one on the north side. I knew they would all be locked but tried them all anyway, tugging as firmly and as quietly as I could. After the third refused to give, I took off at a dead run for the Village Hall. If I could get there before Mr. Hitchcock went downstairs, maybe he'd help me. I cut from Scranton up Center. I came around the corner and heard voices. Ducking behind a tree, I saw the back of Charles Hitchcock. He was approaching the curb, where a black Packard was idling, the same black Packard we had passed only a few minutes ago.

As the window lowered, I saw the large driver with his black fedora and the glow of his lighted cigar. Mr. Hitchcock looked away nervously, unsure of himself. He took a couple of breaths, and leaned down toward the window.

"Good evening, Deputy. A little cold for a stroll, huh?" the voice from the driver's seat said. Though he smiled, there was something ominous in the man's broad face. Then I noticed his passenger, almost completely enshrouded in the shadows. I saw only his silhouette, slender, still, and staring straight ahead, not acknowledging the deputy's presence at all.

"Is there something I can help you with, gentlemen?" I heard Hitchcock ask.

The large driver looked on up the road before answering. "Maybe you can." He paused and then repeated himself. "Yes, maybe you can." I saw him glance at his silent passenger before continuing. He took a long, slow pull on his cigar and then flicked the ash onto the curbside. "You are the night patrolman for this fine town, am I right?"

Hitchcock tensed. There was something creepy in the way this stranger spoke to him, like he knew something Hitchcock didn't. The deputy seemed to be looking past the driver and spokesman to the shadowy, silent man beside him, who still refused to turn his head. There was just enough light to see his profile. I leaned to the other side of the tree and could finally make out the passenger's almost translucent skin, stretched tightly across his face like an onion.

I heard the deputy purposely raise his voice as he leaned toward the vehicle. He seemed to be addressing his response more to the passenger than the driver. "Yes, I am." Hitchcock said. "Do you gentlemen have something to report or a matter of concern tonight?"

A slow, subtle grin began to emerge on the driver's face. He glanced over to his passenger friend before turning back to Hitchcock. "No. We're not the reporting kind, if you know what I'm saying." He let his words hang there and returned his gaze to the road in front of him.

"Are you men passing through? Visiting someone, perhaps?" the deputy continued.

"You're here, what, three nights a week, Mr. Hitchcock?" The words came as if from a cave. It was the hollow, breathy voice of one who had recently had a tonsillectomy. Hitchcock seemed to flinch, and I think I flinched with him. In the cold, I could see the air disappear from the deputy's lungs and wondered if the trail of my breath could be seen coming out from behind my tree.

For a couple of guys Hitchcock had said he didn't know, they sure seemed to know an awful lot about him and his schedule.

At last I could see the gaunt, taut face, which was every bit as ghastly as his voice, like he had just emerged from the grave. His translucent skin seemed to be stretching to the very breaking point. Everything about the man was gray and oniony. Hitchcock broke away from the close set eyes and glanced up and down the street again nervously. He put one hand in his pocket and the other on the roof of the Packard, saying nothing. "We've taken enough of your time."

Hitchcock saw the window roll up smoothly. The Packard drove away almost as slowly as it had arrived. I ducked as close to the ground as I could, digging my shoulder into the tree trunk, and slid around it to stay shielded from the car, as it made its slow way up Center in the cold darkness.

I'd worked my way around toward the Village Hall side of the tree and saw the deputy, paused at the door and drawing something out of his coat pocket. It shined in the porch light, a glimmering silver. He untwisted its top and took a long hard slug of its contents. It was a flask. He shoved it back in his pocket and began fumbling to get his key in the locked door.

"Mr. Hitchcock! Mr. Hitchcock," I called out. He wheeled awkwardly, dropping his keys.

"Good God, Griffin! What on earth are you doing here?" He bent to pick up his keys. "You nearly gave me a coronary."

"I'm sorry, sir. I'm sorry, but...the window...at Wadsworth Hall...it's stuck. And so are all the doors. I can't get in."

"Oh my! We're certainly in a pickle now, aren't we?" He checked the ring of keys he had in his other hand and then shook his head. "Come in with me, and we'll warm up a minute. Then I'll see if we still have a set of keys for the orphanage downstairs."

He unlocked the door and took the descending steps two at a time. I followed him, glad for the warmth. As he opened his office door, I saw where the heat was coming from. Nearly a third of the tiny, barren room was taken up by the furnace and water heater. I got as close to it as I could, while Mr. Hitchcock looked through his makeshift desk drawers for the keys. The black, cast-iron furnace bore the name of Weil-Mclain, and I was grateful for its heat.

"It has to be in here somewhere. I've seen the blasted thing before," the deputy said. Removing his coat, he knocked an old newspaper off of his desk and onto the floor.

"Ah-hah! We're in luck, Mr. Morgan!" He turned to me holding the large skeleton key. He leaned down to grab the newspaper.

"Let's see if we can get you home, young man," he said. "You must be awfully tired."

"Yes, sir," I said. And I followed him toward the door.

ELFRIEDA KNAAK OF DEERFIELD, ILLINOIS
Photo courtesy of the Lake Bluff History Museum

Chapter 14 — A Complex Character
Lake Bluff Orphanage — February 15, 1928

The first time I met Miss Elfrieda Knaak was in early February of 1928. It was a Friday afternoon, just after school, when I saw her trudging up the steps of the Mackey Memorial building, lugging a big case of books behind her. I recognized the long, blue coat and black boots, and I ran from the steps of Wads over to assist her.

"May I help you, ma'am?" I asked, reaching for the box before she could even reply.

"Well, what a gentleman you are," she said, smiling and releasing her grip on the heavy case. "Now, you let me get the door for you," she said. I nodded and followed her in.

"You'll be wanting to see Miss Arbuckle, ma'am," I offered, heading down the same hallway my mother had brought Betty and me to back in November. As we neared the reception desk that formed a sort of barrier between the hallway and Miss Arbuckle's office, we heard two loud thwacks, followed by a muffled cry of pain.

A few seconds later, the heavy oak door from her office opened, and out came Bobby and Johnny scowling and walking gingerly with their hands on their behinds. Miss Arbuckle came out just behind them with her paddle still in her right hand. I was setting Miss Knaak's heavy box on the reception area desk.

"Thank you, Griffin," Miss Arbuckle said, nodding and quickly leaning around to place her paddle on the inside wall of her office.

"Thank you, indeed! Griffin is it?" Miss Knaak said, extending her hand for a shake. "I'm not sure if you give out gold stars around here, Miss Arbuckle, but this young man is certainly deserving of one." She smiled at me, and I looked down between my shoes. "I'm Elfrieda Knaak."

"Nice to meet you, ma'am." I replied, glancing at Miss Arbuckle before adding, "I'll be leaving now."

"I hope to see you again soon, Griffin," Miss Knaak said, as I headed for the door.

I would learn later, as we all would, that Elfrieda Knaak had come to make the first of several deliveries of a complete set of encyclopedias, which had been purchased by Mr. and Mrs. Durand from over at Crab Tree Farm. It was just two nights after my encounter with the salesman and her heavy case of books that Miss Arbuckle stood up at dinner for a "special announcement."

"Children, we live in such a generous town with so many wonderful neighbors. Mr. and Mrs. Scott Durand from over at Crab Tree Farm, from whom we get our milk and our apples, have given us a complete set of Compton's Pictured Encyclopedias." She paused to look around the old dining hall. After a deep breath and a smile, our matron continued. "Encyclopedias are wonderful educational tools for students of all ages. Whether you are writing a report for school or simply wanting to improve yourself, these books are your bridge to knowledge." She removed her pointy glasses and smiled. Then she went on to explain where the collection would be kept and how we were to go about using them.

Still at the dinner table in the dining hall, the banter began. "So you've seen 'em, right Griff?" It was Johnny who asked me.

"Yeah. I helped Miss Knaak bring them in," I replied.

"Did you talk to her?" Homer asked.

"Did you ask her about Hitchcock?" Knox pressed.

I shook my head. "C'mon, guys. You think I'm just going to bring that up out of the blue?"

"What's she like?" Homer asked, and I shrugged my shoulders.

"I'm dying to know what she does with Old Hollywood Hitchcock down in his office!" Knox exclaimed, rubbing his hands together.

Less than a week later, we would all have a chance to get a much fuller picture of Elfrieda Knaak. Miss Arbuckle had arranged for her to come back to LBO on a Thursday night for what she called "cultural enhancement." Right after dinner, when the last of the dishes had been done and every single table had been wiped down with soap and warm water, Mr. Spader and a few of the older, stronger boys came in the rear entrance door of the dining hall, lugging several volumes each of the new black and gold encyclopedias. Once they had lined the ten volumes up in alphabetical order at the front of the room, we heard the main door open in the rear of the room. In walked Miss Elfrieda Knaak, followed by Miss Arbuckle, who had held the door for her. Every eye in the room was on the radiant Miss Knaak. Her brown hair was shoulder length and curled under, with her bangs pulled around to the back by a ribbon. While she was several inches shorter than our matron, she was still a striking figure. She wore a black, pleated skirt that came just below her knees and high-heeled shoes that click-clacked on the shiny maple floors of Hobbs Hall. She smiled and seemed to make eye contact with every table of kids as she passed by.

When they reached the front of the room, standing just behind the lined up encyclopedias, Miss Arbuckle reached into her pocket for her whistle and put it to her mouth. But it slowly dawned on her that we were already completely silent. She smiled at the surprise, returned the whistle to her pocket, and began.

"Boys and girls," she said, "I am so pleased to introduce you to a new friend of LBO. Miss Knaak works for Compton Publishing in downtown Chicago, the company from which we got this incredible set of encyclopedias." The matron gestured to the books, lined up like soldiers at attention. "As a part of our regular Thursday night cultural enhancement program, I've asked Miss Knaak to familiarize us with this impressive collection. So I'd like you all to be on your very best behavior and to tune your listening ears in as carefully as you can. But before we turn the program over to Miss Knaak, don't you think we should all stand and welcome her to LBO, as is our custom?" She nodded to us forcefully, gesturing with her hands for us to rise. She blew on her pitch pipe and counted us in. "One...two...three!"

> *We welcome you, we welcome you, we welcome you today*
> *Oh how glad we are to have you with us while we may-hey*
> *We welcome you, we welcome you, we'd like to have you know*
> *That we are very glad to have you here at LBO.*

Miss Knaak's eyes widened, and her jaw dropped in wonder, as she clapped as vigorously as she could. "My, my, children! What a lovely song! I am so thrilled to be here and feel about as welcome as I've ever felt anywhere!" She turned to Miss Arbuckle. "Thank you so very much, Miss Arbuckle, for that nice introduction and wonderful song." Miss Arbuckle nodded and went to sit down about halfway back and off to the right side of the room, where she could keep a watchful eye on us all. I wondered if she needed to do that, given the fact that pictures of Jesus and practically all twelve of the apostles had us surrounded and were staring down upon us from every conceivable angle.

"Children," Miss Knaak began, "I must tell you, before I go any further, that while I may have delivered these wonderful books to your home, I am not the one who gave them to you. Mr. and Mrs. Scott Durand of Crab Tree Farm paid for this wonderful collection of books and asked that they be kept here at Lake Bluff Orphanage to help all of you learn and grow. Isn't that terrific?" She looked at all of us and began to clap, and we joined in.

As the applause died out, she bent down and reached into her large handbag and pulled out a large card. It looked to be about 18 inches by 12 inches. "I thought, if it is all right with you, Miss Arbuckle, that we might have every one of these amazing children sign this card as a thank you to the Durands." Miss Arbuckle nodded heartily.

The thank you card was passed around, and for the next fifteen or twenty minutes, Miss Knaak showed us the kinds of things we could do with these shiny, heavy books. She showed us pictures of sharks and dolphins, tigers and tiger lilies, and she even showed us where we could look up all sorts of information about some of the

US Naval ships that were docked just a few miles north of us at the Great Lakes Naval Base.

She had a soothing voice, and it made us feel safe and protected. I could tell she spent a lot of time around kids. She moved throughout the room and looked at most every one of us as she spoke. She showed girls pictures that girls would like, and showed boys the stuff we wanted to see as well.

The presentation flew by, and the next thing I knew, we were clapping again. Miss Knaak sat up by the books, and a big group of kids flocked to her in no time. I spotted Betty tugging on the pleats of her skirt. I rushed up to make sure my sister wasn't being obnoxious, but our guest seemed almost smitten with her. By the time I pushed through the adoring crowd, Betty had crawled up into her lap and was reaching for the ribbon in Miss Knaak's hair.

"Betty!" I said in a loud whisper. "Betty, come here! Let's let Miss Knaak talk to the other kids too!" I reached for her, and Miss Knaak seemed to recognize me.

"Why, you are Griffin, that nice boy who held the door for me and helped me cart these books in last Saturday!" she said. I must have blushed and looked away. "Is this your sister? What an absolute charmer!" She pinched Betty's cheek and picked her up again. "Do you know that you have the best big brother in the world?"

"Griffy! Yes! He's my big brother!" Miss Knaak grinned and shook her head with delight.

Miss Arbuckle had the four housemothers in tow, and they began lining us up so we could return to our respective dorms. Betty and I lingered long enough to hear Miss Arbuckle say, "That was so terrific, Miss Knaak. I can tell you were a classroom teacher before you started selling for Compton's. Please know that you are always welcome here. Do come back."

"If you really mean it, Jessie, I'd love to come back with a couple of my fellow Sunday School teachers from my church in Deerfield. We love working with children and could come back any time for a craft project or a..." Miss Knaak was interrupted by a persistent tugging on her skirt.

"Thank you, Miss Knaak for the nice books!" Betty said.

"You are so welcome, little angel!" Betty hugged her new friend's leg with all her strength. I pried her loose, apologizing to both Miss Knaak and to Miss Arbuckle, as we rejoined the lines to Wads and Judson.

≈

I would see Elfrieda Knaak three more times during my year at the orphanage, four if you count the night of October 29. Most of what I know about Miss Knaak came years later, in the 1940s when I became a reporter. Elfrieda taught Sunday school at the Presbyterian Church in Deerfield from the time she was 17 until she was 30. Her students adored her, and thinking back on her first visit to LBO, I could see why. She graduated from the University of Chicago and became a schoolteacher at Glen Flora Elementary up in Waukegan, where she taught for four years.

She was incredibly hard-working. She spent her mornings at the pharmacy but then would head out just after lunch to sell encyclopedias door to door for the Compton Publishing Company. Lugging those sample boxes on buses and off trains, up and down neighborhood streets, and all over Chicago's suburbs was all in a day's work for Miss Knaak. I can still remember the weight of the one box I lugged a mere 25 feet that February day in '28 when she first came to LBO. But even after her mornings at the pharmacy and afternoons on her sales routes, Miss Knaak's day was still not done. Several evenings a week, she would then take yet another train ride all the way up to Waukegan, where she would seek to improve herself by studying elocution and salesmanship with the once famous Mr. Charles Hitchcock.

My reporter's sense is that no one would subject herself to this kind of schedule without some deep, inner drive and determination. Knaak's strong Christian faith must certainly have played a role in fueling that inner strength and resolve. And yet, the more I dug into this unusual and ultimately tragic life, the more I came to see in Elfrieda Knaak a certain hunger, a restlessness, a longing for something she couldn't quite name.

Even as a seasoned reporter, I had a hard time over the years reconciling some seemingly contradictory parts of Miss Knaak's life and personality. Her Deerfield High School Annual noted that she was "timid, even shy in the company of others." But that same annual noted that she was "involved in Drama Club" and often had "major roles in school productions." Later in life—and still shy by nature—she left teaching to undertake door-to-door sales as a career.

It was learning about her books and her reading list that would lead me to see her as a restless heart. According to both friends and family, Elfrieda always had some volume or another of spiritual mysticism in her purse. In what would turn out to be the last several months of her life, that book had been *Christ in You*, a work of anonymous authorship that sought to point its reader toward a more intimate and mystical union with the Divine.

Clearly, Miss Knaak didn't simply read these books; she devoured them, taking extensive notes and marking all over them as well. Not long after she was discovered in the basement of the Village Hall, investigators found this passage from *Christ in You* bookmarked and underlined:

> *I tell you, it is impossible to know true joy—the heights of joy— until you have known the corresponding depths of pain. This is the process known as "the Refiner's Fire."*

It was a haunting passage that would weigh heavily in the debate about what may have happened to this complex character.

The Furnace Girl

SIR OLIVER LODGE IS RIGHT — SPIRIT COMMUNICATIONS: A FACT
BOOK WRITTEN BY GRACE DURAND OF CRAB TREE FARM — 1917
Courtesy of the Lake Bluff History Museum

Chapter 15 — Ghost Stories
Lake Bluff Village Hall — February 21, 1927

I got pretty good at sweeping floors, thanks to Mr. Charles Hitchcock. He had me sweep everything: the furnace room floor, the stairs leading down to the furnace room, the Village Hall lobby, the chief's office. He even had me come to his house to sweep.

"Our little arrangement," as he called it, had its advantages. It got me out of the orphanage and gave me time to think. Over time, I came to believe that Mr. Hitchcock was not so much punishing me with these duties as trying to relieve me of the monotony over at LBO. What he didn't realize, however, is that he was also providing me with some information that, eventually, helped me with this story—with the facts of the case.

I think it was my second or third time working for Mr. Hitchcock when I came across a book, opened on his desk, with some passages marked.

Spirits do not belong perpetually to the same order. They are destined to attain perfection and, as they do so, they progress up through the different orders. This advancement is achieved through incarnations, which are undertaken either as special missions or as trials leading to purification. Physical life is an experience spirits must undergo many times before reaching this goal. These lives can be understood as cleansing exercises from each of which spirits generally emerge in a more purified state.

It was a book called *The Spirits Book*, written by an Allen Kardac. I could tell it wasn't a library book, and it wasn't Deputy Hitchcock's book either. It had some handwriting both in it and on some separate pages that were tucked inside it. It was a woman's handwriting, some of the most beautiful cursive I'd ever seen. And it didn't take me long to find out who the woman with the beautiful penmanship and the unusual book was. Her name was on the inside cover of the book: Elfrieda Knaak, the woman from the classroom, the woman with the blue coat, the woman on Johnny's train, the woman who brought us and taught us about the encyclopedias, and the woman who, in many ways, is at the center of this tale. There was another passage that was all marked up.

On leaving the body, the soul returns to the spirit world, where it exists as a free spirit (i.e., free from the limitations of the physical world) and where it will stay for an indeterminate time until it enters a new incarnation.

I read these marked sections over and over, trying like heck to make sense out of them. But I always kept an ear cocked toward the stairway in case Mr. Hitchcock returned. These passages were way beyond my understanding. I remember thinking at the time that Miss Knaak and Mr. Hitchcock must have been interested in spirits and ghosts and the like. And I'd already seen how interested the deputy was in cleansing and purifying things, given all the floor sweeping and scrubbing he had me doing all over the place.

"So then, Master Griff," the voice of my boss echoed from the bottom of the stairwell. I snapped the book shut and stepped toward the furnace with my broom. "How goes the sweeping, my young friend?"

"Fine, sir," I uttered.

"I believe I will have you feed both the furnace and the boiler next," he said, eyeing the big, black beast in the center of his tiny room and the smaller boiler furnace over in the corner.

"I'm just about out of time, though," I said, looking at his desk clock.

"Yes, yes, I suspect you are. Next time then." He glanced at the desk and moved the book I'd been snooping through aside. "Do you like to read, Griffin?" he asked without looking at me.

"Yes, sir," I replied, as I grabbed my coat from the hooks, just to the right of the giant furnace. "Shall I come back here on Thursday after school?"

"No. Let's make it at my house on Thursday, just down Center Avenue, 317 to be precise."

Hargrave cleared his throat to interrupt me. "I can see now why you've been so interested in the B. Lock letters and the whole spiritual angle of this case. I had no idea that there had been this level of conversation about spiritual matters and purification between Miss Knaak and Hitchcock."

"I don't think anybody was aware of it, Detective."

He scratched his head a gazed out the window. "Do you suppose this means she really may have tried to burn herself in that furnace?" he asked.

"It's possible that she tried," I said.

The detective closed his eyes and pinched the bridge of his nose with his thumb and index finger. "Continue, Mr. Morgan. Continue," he said.

When I got back to LBO, there was a hullabaloo on the first floor. Dennis, Johnny, the O'Neil twins, and Knox were in a huddle arguing about something.

"I did not wet my bed!" Johnny said, stomping his foot on the hardwood floor.

"Listen, Johnny," Dennis said, "you can't expect us to believe your cockamamie idea that somebody else peed in your bed."

"Yeah," Billy said, "like somebody's just going to sneak up on you, while you're sleeping in your bed and then just pee all over it."

Billy shook his head and scrunched up his face. "And not wake you up?"

"Look, fellas," Johnny responded, "You can think whatever you want. But I didn't wet my bed. I stopped doin' that when I was about four." Johnny stormed away, pushing me out of his way as he headed out the front door.

Dennis shook his head and crossed his arms. "I think God is punishing Johnny for all the grief he's been giving Artie for wetting his bed."

"What happened?" I asked.

"Apparently, Johnny's bed sheets were yellow and wet when he woke up this morning," Knox said. "Then his roommate started laughing and telling the whole dorm about it, starting with his buddy Artie Spellman."

"And given all the public teasing Johnny's given Artie about still being a bedwetter, Artie's had the time of his life," Dennis added. "He even told some of the older girls in Judson."

I sat with Artie at dinner that night. He had a smug grin on his face as he lapped up the chicken noodle soup. I bet he looked at Johnny at the table across from ours a dozen times during the meal.

"So you really think Johnny wet his bed, Artie?" I asked.

"How else do you think his bed got pee all over it?"

"Beats me," I said. Artie just kept smiling.

"Maybe it was a ghost," Artie said, as he got up to put his bowl in the dish bin.

WINTER SLEDDING AND SKATING ON THE
ORPHANAGE PLAYGROUND
Photo courtesy of the Lake Bluff History Museum

Chapter 16 — Warming Up

Lake Bluff, IL — The Home of Charles Hitchcock — February 23, 1928

I came to find out, thanks to some snooping by my orphanage cohorts, some conversations I overheard while working for Mr. Hitchcock, and some police records I've been able to track down in more recent years, that Charles Hitchcock used to meet Elfrieda Knaak for private tutoring sessions in the Village Hall.

The way I had it figured, Miss Knaak would have had to come by train during Deputy Hitchcock's night shifts. She worked most every day, running between the family pharmacy and her door-to-door sales. And I can't believe either she or Mr. Hitchcock would be willing to execute such an arrangement during the daylight hours. Johnny, Billy, and I had all seen Miss Knaak walking from the train station over to the Village Hall just after the 8:00 or 9:00 p.m. train. Most times, it seems Mr. Hitchcock escorted her over himself.

One Thursday after school, I was shoveling snow over at the Hitchcock place, and his daughter Charlene brought me in for some hot chocolate. I heard some yelling down the hall, just as I came in. It was coming from one of the bedrooms, I think. Charlene shook her head, like it was nothing out of the ordinary.

"Here they go again," she said. I saw Helen, Mr. Hitchcock's other daughter, come out of her room, across the hall from the yelling, plugging both ears.

"If you have any better ideas for me to make the extra money we need to live in this house, I'm all ears!" the former actor shouted.

"Better ideas than meeting with single women half your age in your office, while you're supposed to be watching over our village? I'm sure I can come up with something!" I heard a door open and then slam shut, followed by the hard clicking of heels on the hardwood floor.

Mrs. Hitchcock came around the corner scowling. She saw me and pushed her face into a tight smile. "Why, Griffin, I didn't know you were here." I looked down into my hot mug.

"Charlene got him some hot chocolate," Helen tattled.

"Well, isn't that nice," the red-faced matron said, heading into the dining room.

I thanked Charlene for the warming drink and headed back out to the finish the sidewalks.

I pictured Miss Knaak entering the furnace room, just out of the frigid winter air, her blue coat pulled up tightly around her neck.

"It's freezing out there!" she would have noted, brushing the remaining snow from her coat. Ever the gentleman, Charles Hitchcock would have helped her out of it and hung it gently on one of the two metal hooks that hung just beside the door frame.

"Step over here, my dear." I could see the debonaire actor gesturing toward the monstrous iron furnace. He would have slid the one and only chair in his little hovel over to Miss Knaak.

Would they have been scared, nervous of being discovered down there? If the deputy's wife knew about their arrangement, who else might have? Did Hitchcock have any unexpected visitors come by during a typical night of work?

Miss Knaak was a student of Mr. Hitchcock's, in his Elocution and Salesmanship class. It's possible that he just helped her with her schoolwork, the way I sometimes stayed after class to work with my teacher. But there was that book, that Alan Kardac book about spirits and purification.

"I've been anxious to speak with you about Mr. Kardac's book," Charles Hitchcock might have said.

One time I found a letter Elfrieda had written to Mr. Hitchcock. I'd been shoveling coal from the pile outside the Village Hall down into the coal chute. When I finished, I came back inside to make sure none of the coal had missed or fallen from the box next to the furnace. It was a real mess when that happened, and Mr. Hitchcock did not like messes. I saw a sooty piece of paper that had fallen back behind the coal chute box and between the furnace and its boiler. I brushed the black dust from it and began trying to make sense of it.

I understand your confusion, Charles, with Mr. Kardac's emphasis on purification and with my "fascination" about it, as you called it. You seem to think of spiritual purification as being only for the ardent sinner, but I believe that purification is for us all. Remember when Jesus was at table with sinners and tax collectors, he said, "Those who are well have no need of a physician. I came to seek and to save the lost"? That's just it, I suppose, Charles. I see all of us as lost, as searching for something. Don't you? Aren't we all looking for something, longing for some fulfillment that is forever just beyond our grasp?

I've met the most incredible woman! It was on my sales route. She invited me in—you see, the sales techniques you're giving your students really do pay off! Anyway, we seemed to talk about everything—other than encyclopedias, that is. I believe she may be a prophetess or a luminary of sorts. We've begun a regular correspondence, and I'm quite taken with her depth of understanding, spiritually, I mean.

Her name is Luella Roeh, though she goes by "B." She writes quite prolifically, but I'm not sure any of her work has been published yet. It wouldn't surprise me, though, if all of what she writes winds up in print someday. It's quite remarkable, really. She has opened my eyes and my heart to something wonderful...

I put the shovel back in the Hitchcock's garage and started to walk back toward town. If I hustled back to the orphanage, I'd still have a little time with the guys from Wads before the dinner bell. I wanted to see Ernie. Word came down last night that Ernie had been fostered out. Miss Arbuckle had told him to have his things packed, for he was to be picked up sometime this evening. It wasn't the first time Ernie had shipped out to a foster home. The last one, just over a year ago, had only lasted about five weeks. Apparently, a farm family up near Gurnee was looking for some cheap labor and thought a foster son might fit the bill. They worked Ernie day and night but still couldn't get enough out of him for their liking. They returned Ernie in a state of physical exhaustion, with bandaged hands and blistered feet.

Kids moved into and out of LBO so fast; it hardly seemed worth getting to know somebody. Right about the time you thought you'd made a new friend, you'd go over to his cubicle and some kid you'd never seen before was already in his bed. Kids like Dick Moley and Danny Thompson were the exceptions. I found out years later that the average length of stay at LBO was eight months, which meant that some of the kids were only there two or three months.

The little kids went the fastest. Adopting parents always said, "the younger the better," I'd heard. So it was kind of a shock that a twelve-year-old like Ernie was leaving. I was going to miss him. His cubicle was just two down from mine.

What really worried me, though, was that someone would come along and take Betty away. I couldn't let that happen. I just couldn't. Danny told me once about a guy who arrived here with three little sisters. The youngest one got fostered out within two weeks, so this boy told the other two sisters that they needed to pretend to be sick at least two days a week, to get in that infirmary anyway they could, so that the adopters wouldn't take them away, like they'd done with their baby sister.

I would not be separated from Betty. I couldn't let that happen.

On my way back to LBO, I heard a yell.

"Griff! Griff! Over here!" It was Danny. With him were Artie and Knox.

"Where you guys going?" I asked, crossing the street toward them.

"The ravine," Knox said. "There's tons of snow down there, and it's perfect packing for snowballs."

The three quickened their pace, and I hurried to keep up. Soon we were running, and Danny angled down to the path. That's when the whooping and shenanigans began. Knox tripped Danny from behind, and Artie flung a handful of unpacked snow awkwardly toward my face. As Knox stepped first onto the frozen creek bed at the ravine's base, cracks rang out, and jagged lines emanated from wherever his foot met the ice. We followed Knox down the icy path, producing cracks of our own, but the ice held.

Artie said, "Remember that time when..." and then screamed, "Ow!" A hard packed snowball caught him square in the face. None of the three of us had thrown it. I was in the back of our line, and nobody had even bent down to make a snowball, much less throw one.

"Take that, you stupid orphan!" The voice echoed through the ravine. It came from above us on the left bank. David Gadd stood proudly, a good forty feet above us. Two other town kids flanked him, pointing down at us and laughing.

"Take cover, guys. Find a tree, and make as many snowballs as you can. Now!" Danny ordered. But Artie wasn't moving. He was covering his face with his good hand and fighting back tears. I bent down and pulled him off the ice and over to the closest tree. I slid to his left to the next one and started packing snowballs. The snow was perfect for it. I glanced around my tree and up to the spot where Gadd and his henchmen were, still gloating.

"At the count of three, grab as many of your snowballs as you can and run about halfway up the hill. We'll never be able to pelt 'em from this far below," Danny instructed. "But don't stay out in the open. Move tree to tree." Artie was still working on his first snowball, his bad arm not cooperating.

"You can use some of mine, Artie." I said. "C'mon."

"One...two...three...Go!" Danny said, barely audibly. We each took a different line up the steep ravine bank, ducking in behind trees. "Same thing," Danny said, "only now we fire at them from four different angles and all at once." He paused and took a peek around at the enemy. "One...two...three...Now!"

I chucked my first snowball as hard as I could, but it had nothing on it by the time it got up the hill. It fell lamely at their feet. Knox's and Danny's had the same trajectory. Artie's throw barely made it halfway up.

"Oh, boy! We're in real trouble now, fellas," Gadd mocked.

"Yeah. We better run before one of their snowballs actually gets within five feet of us," one of his buddies said." I grabbed two of my snowballs and ran back down to the creek. Using a giant oak for cover, I stomped on the ice as hard as I could, and on the third time broke through. I soaked two of my snowballs in the freezing water, and then sprinted back up the ravine. Danny had led the others in a futile charge upward, the only result being that the three of them got pelted by a barrage of snowballs. But looking up the embankment, I couldn't see anyone. It was totally silent. Then Gadd appeared again, completely alone. He had his arms crossed and his feet apart, posing.

"Now's our chance boys," Danny said. "It's just him. Let's charge."

"But what if…" I started to say, but Danny drowned me out.

"Now!"

Knox led the charge, with Danny close behind. I waited to make sure Artie was with us and then took a circuitous route around the left flank. Just as Danny and Knox cleared the top edge, Gadd took off and five other town kids emerged from behind trees and charged—two at Knox, one at Danny, and two at Artie. They were trapped. I saw Gadd slip out from behind his tree with a cocky grin on his face. He laughed when he saw three orphans getting white washed. What he didn't see was me, nor did he see my perfectly packed ice ball, as it punished his smug face. I held onto my second one and ran for Artie. I chucked it at the back of one of the guys who had pinned him down. No sooner had I let it fly, when I got crushed by a cross body block from Gadd. He and the other kid I'd tagged with the second ice ball were on me, and I couldn't breath. Gadd's hit had knocked the wind out of me. His pal was yanking my coat up over my head while Gadd shoved snow up my shirt and down my pants. I couldn't see or move to defend myself.

I heard Artie crying and gasping from what I imagined to be the same treatment. Then it was Gadd's voice again. "How's it taste, orphan?"

The white washing intensified, and I was both freezing and soaked. I couldn't find my breath. Gadd said. "Probably better than that gruel they serve you bastards!"

Then he lowered his voice, offering it just to me. "You orphans may be allowed to come to our school, but you are never allowed in our ravine again. Never! You hear me, you stupid bastard?"

"Get off of them now!" It was the familiar voice of Dick Moley. I felt the weight of the two boys get off of me, and I pulled my coat down off of my face. Moley stood alone. His imposing physique cut these bullies down to size. He walked over to Artie and shoved both of his tormentors over the edge of the ravine, and they tumbled another 20 feet down.

"You all right, Artie?" Dick asked. Artie sniffled and nodded unconvincingly. There was a trickle of blood beneath his nose and a blotchy spot by his chin. "Any of these kids ever touches you or even looks at you the wrong way, and I want to hear about it, OK, Art?" Dick continued. Again, Artie nodded. Knox and Danny were back on their feet, trying to get the snow out of their clothes. Not one of the town bullies said a word in Moley's presence. Dick stared each one of them down and then turned, and we followed him.

My stomach and neck were burning from the snow they'd stuffed under my clothes. It felt raw, like rope burn. I tried to walk without a limp but wasn't succeeding.

Nobody said a word until we could see the orphanage up ahead. Then Dick broke the silence. "Fellas, you let me explain what happened to Miss Arbuckle. I'll tell her how you guys were fooling around in the ravine, when, surprisingly, the ice broke and you fell through. She doesn't need to hear about these jerks from town."

Artie looked at me with concern all over his face. I nodded to reassure him, though I was just as scared as he was. Dick was a great guy and all, but Gadd and his townie friends could get to us anytime they wanted to, when Dick was at basketball practice or with one of his many girlfriends. This town wasn't safe for regular orphan kids like Artie and me. But we followed Dick and the others inside, pretending that his story was the truth.

LBO MAINTENANCE MAN WITH KIDS OUTSIDE
THE LAUNDRY BUILDING
Photo courtesy of the Lake Bluff History Museum

Chapter 17 — Milk Trucks
Crab Tree Farm — March 12, 1928

It was an unusually warm day for late March, and I sat under the same apple tree where Lily and I had rescued Lazarus back in December. My farm coat was spread on the ground beneath me, and I had my lunch laid out upon one of its sleeves. The sun felt great on my face, and I'd closed my eyes. With school out for spring break, I was spending a lot of hours working on the farm and spending every moment I could with my sister.

I loved Crab Tree Farm. Working for Redd and Mrs. Durand had become the best thing about living in Lake Bluff. "Mrs. D.," as she liked us to call her, had begun saving certain farm chores for me. She knew I'd learned to love the milk house work. Thanks to Lily, I'd learned more than a third of the milk cows by name. I'd learned which ones had to be squeezed hard—like Negress, Brunette, Donna, and Chance—and which responded to an easier, more gentle touch—like Truth, Lucky, Medley, and Sprite. There was even one called Morgan, my last name. She was missing a chunk from her left ear from when she tangled with a fence post. I'd learned the entire bottling process and all that it took to sterilize a bottle adequately. Redd was a patient and firm teacher, and I owe him an awful lot for all that I'd learned in just a few months on the farm.

In March, there wasn't much to be done with the apple production, so I was already looking forward to the fall, when the four varieties of Durand apples would come ripe, and I would have a go at my first harvest.

I bit into the ham sandwich Mrs. D. had made me and heard footsteps coming up the orchard path. It was Lily. She wore dungarees, an old flannel shirt, and a tan, unzipped work jacket.

"Sleepin' on the job again?" she said. Her smile was one third smirk and two-thirds pure farm girl. She had a small sling over her shoulder with her lunch inside. "Mind if I join you?" Lily started to lean down but then paused, waiting for my consent.

"It's a free country," I said, sitting up.

"Not to mention my grandma's orchard." She bit into a sandwich with bits of lettuce hanging out the edges.

"I still don't get why you call her your 'grandma,'" I said.

"I told you! My daddy has worked for her and Mr. Durand for almost seventeen years. We're like family to them. Plus, I was born right here on the farm, on Mrs. D.'s birthday." She pulled a banana out of her sling and started peeling it. "I'm the granddaughter she never had," she boasted, smiling again.

"But what about her son, Mr. Durand, the one who lives over on Woodland?" I started in on the other half of my sandwich. "If he's got kids, they'd be her grandchildren, not you," I concluded.

Lily took off her coat, folded it up, and propped it behind her. "I don't think she likes her son so much. I've heard 'em fighting when he's around." She looked down at me, and I looked away, still working on my lunch. "My daddy says that when Mr. Jack Durand is around, we need to make ourselves scarce, so we don't add to Mrs. D's 'consternation,' whatever that is."

There was a stick lying to Lily's right. She picked it up and began to poke at some of the leaves on the low branches above her. "Tell me some more LBO stories. You haven't told me any in awhile," she prodded.

I heard the snapping of some tree branches and a rustling back behind us. I turned far enough around to see the backside of man in torn dungarees bent over in the low lying brush.

He stood slowly, holding some sort of hunting spear in his right hand, emitting a guttural grunt. It was the same guy I'd taken the knife from in the barn on the day we saved Lazarus.

"Frank, what are you doin'?" Lily yelled.

He jolted back, like he had seen a ghost instead of a couple of kids. He looked in both directions and took off toward the barn without a single word.

"What is with that goof? And why do the Durands keep him around here? " I asked.

"Frank is just slow," she said. "He's harmless. Mrs. D. lets him work here because no other place would hire him for a job. And Mrs. D. is friends with his mother. He handles most of the slaughtering of the livestock around here when it's time."

I looked in the direction he'd headed. "Harmless or not, I wouldn't want to be on the other end of that spear he has."

Lily elbowed me in side. She shook her head and then continued. "I want more stories about the orphanage! C'mon, Griff, tell me a good one."

"Well, both Ernie and Homer got a whoopin' the other day." I found a stick of my own and started making patterns in the dirt path. "Mr. Spader caught 'em sneaking back in the first floor Wads window past midnight."

"Mr. Jim whooped 'em?"

"No. Mr. Spader would never hit any of us. He just told our housemother," I said. "Miss Harvey took care of the whoopin' herself."

"You ever snuck out?" she asked.

"Sure," I said, squinting in the sunlight.

"Have not!" Lily challenged, as if on the attack.

"Don't believe me. I don't care." I reclined again.

"Where to?" Lily pressed.

"No place. Just walking." I yawned and scratched the back of my head. "I like walking up and down the streets by the orphanage when it's dark. I like to look at the houses."

"Why? What are you looking for?"

"I'm not looking for anything special. I just...I like picturing the families." I scrunched my nose up and covered my mouth with my left hand. "Sometimes, if the lights are still on, I can see people or their shadows." I took a bite of my pickle and chewed on it for a while. "And I make up stories about 'em...in my mind. Like I'll see a mother and a father, maybe with a baby fussing." I closed my eyes and gathered the image. "And I'll come up with why the baby's crying and what the mother is saying to him as she holds him."

Lily sat up straight, looked over at me, and cracked her knuckles a time or two. "Take me next time, why don't ya?"

"Huh?" I asked, squinting at her in the sun.

"Take me with you, when you sneak out. I wanna come."

I shook my head and grinned as I did. "I could get in enough trouble already. Can you imagine what I'd get from old Bertha Harvey if I was out with a girl?" I chuckled and continued to shake my head.

"That's only if we get caught," she offered boldly. "And I never get caught."

I eyed her skeptically. "Are you saying you sneak out past bedtime?"

"Yep. Did it just this past weekend." She looked at me and then turned away. "Saw somethin' too, and not just in my imagination." She crossed her arms and widened her eyes in some sort of mock challenge to me.

"What did you see?" I asked.

"A bunch of men down at the lake." I held both hands out in a pleading position, and Lily complied by continuing. "Some nights I can't sleep...and so I walk. Mostly just around the farm and stuff. But that night, I walked all the way down the back side of the orchard, to where the property runs down to the lakeshore."

I'd leaned so far toward her, I was practically in her lap, and my face flushed with amazement. "And what did you see?"

"A boat and two trucks...milk trucks. There were nine guys in all, five in the boat and two at each truck. They were workin' real fast and with only the lights from the two trucks and a couple of flashlights to go by."

"So were the trucks bringing something to the boat?"

Lily shook her head. "Nope, the boat was bringing something in from the water. I saw big crates and some barrels. And I heard bottles clinking around too."

"A boat was bringing stuff to shore and then the trucks were picking it up? Right here on Mrs. D.'s land?" I scratched my head, trying to put it all together. "Did you tell your father?"

"No! Then he'd have known I was out and all the way down there in the middle of the night."

"Maybe I should be asking you to take me with you the next time you sneak out!" I smiled and shook my head.

"We could take turns."

We both rose and grabbed our coats, as one of the farm trucks climbed up the orchard path from the milk house. It was Lily's father.

Redd leaned out the open window, smiled, and said, "Lunchtime is over, folks." He raised his fist with the thumb stuck out and motioned for us to hop in the back. "We got 27 more cows to milk, eight crates of empty bottles to sterilize, and a whole bunch of buckets to clean."

We brushed the dirt and leaves off our hind ends and hopped up onto the flatbed. I remained standing in the bed, as had become my custom, bracing myself on the side panels, trying to see where Crab Tree Farm dipped down to the lake. Then I hunched down beside Lily, saying directly into her ear, "But where did those trucks go? Did you see? Once they were loaded up, how did they get off the farm?" "They didn't come up this way, is all I know."

PHOTO OF ELFRIEDA KNAAK (right)
WITH HER BEST FRIEND MARIE MUELLER (left)
Photo courtesy of The Chicago Tribune

Chapter 18 — Craft Day
Lake Bluff Orphanage — April 14, 1928

Most Saturday mornings, our Wads gang finished our after-breakfast chores as quickly as we could, so we could take over the rumpus room for games, puzzles, and some long-awaited down time. But on the second Saturday of April, Johnny, Knox, and I were given a "special" assignment. Miss Arbuckle had asked the three of us to help the younger kids with some sort of craft project. Apparently some "special guests from Deerfield" were showing up at 10 a.m., and we were instructed to report back to the dining hall then.

Craft Day was not a particularly enticing prospect for the three of us 12- and 13-year-olds, so we walked down the central stairs of Wads, across the soggy grass, and up the Dining Hall stairs as if we were on a funeral procession. Our death march was accompanied by the teasing voices of the O'Neil twins, Ernie, and Danny.

"Hope you girls have a swell day cutting pipe cleaners and construction paper!" Danny said.

"Yeah, maybe you can sew up my stockings when you get back!" Billy added.

Knox snarled and Johnny shot them the middle-fingered salute. But our attitudes improved significantly the moment we opened the swinging doors of the dining hall to discover that the guests from Deerfield were Miss Elfrieda Knaak and two of her friends.

"Is that who I think it is?" Johnny said, widening his eyes.

"If you think it's Hollywood Hitchcock's favorite pupil, then I guess so," Knox whispered with his usual dose of sarcasm.

"Let's grab that table up near the front," I said, "so I can be near Betty." I'd spotted my sister right up front, sitting on her folded up knees. She was staring at Miss Knaak, watching her every move.

Elfrieda Knaak had continued to be a regular topic of conversation among us, particularly given my ongoing arrangement with Deputy Hitchcock. Johnny, Knox, and the others were constantly grilling me about what I'd discovered during my various sweeping and raking jobs at Hitchcock's home and office. Knox just wouldn't let up on his theory that something was going on in that furnace room that "could cost Hitchcock his job and Miss Knaak her reputation." His constant eye-rolling and suggestions of impropriety were lost on many of the Wads' guys, but it had become plain annoying to me. Once I'd heard what his mother had caught his father doing in the neighboring apartment, I tried to write Knox's theory off as his singular obsession. But I think there was also something about Miss Knaak's appearance that Knox found irresistible.

On this particular Saturday morning, as Miss Knaak and her two friends were pulling supplies out of two large boxes, I noticed Miss Knaak's navy skirt and long, sand-colored sweater. She was fashionable, with her matching navy hat, and a real looker as well. Knox's eyes were locked in on her, so much so that I'm sure he never even saw the several colors of construction paper, the cardboard tubes, the countless pieces of string already cut to a specified length, and the growing pile of Crayola crayons she and her cohorts were setting on the demonstration table.

One of her helpers wore a drab skirt, knee socks, and a high-necked blouse. She was an old grandma, wearing pointy glasses with a chain around them. The other helper wore fashions similar to Miss Knaak's. She was slender, probably in her late-twenties, and her brown hair was curly—almost kinky—a real looker too.

The room was about one-third filled, since this particular craft day was just for the seven and under kids. Several housemothers stood guard, evenly spaced around the outside edge of the tables.

"Good morning, children!" Miss Knaak said, smiling broadly. "I am so pleased to be back here with you at your beautiful home." She brought her hands together and interlaced her fingers. "I was here, just over a month ago, helping you get familiar with your new encyclopedias, and I was thrilled to hear from Miss Arbuckle that they're getting lots of use. But today I'm here with my two good friends, Mrs. Solomon," she gestured to the grandma on her left, "and Miss Mueller." She nodded to the younger woman on her right. "We're here today to help you make something beautiful!"

"Beauty-full!" an unmistakable voice cried out. It was Betty. The room erupted in muffled laughter, but Miss Knaak transformed it with her welcoming smile.

"Yes, Betty, that's right!" Betty glowed and put her tiny hands over her mouth.

There was something genuinely endearing about Miss Knaak. It actually felt like she'd rather be here in this room than anywhere else in the world. Her training and experience as a classroom teacher set everyone in the room at ease.

"Children, how many of you have heard the story of Moses and the burning bush?" Miss Knaak asked. She looked around the room, making eye contact with someone from every table, nodding her head when she saw a raised hand. "Well, my friends and I are here to help you make your very own burning bush, and do you know why?" She paused, again looking around the room. "Because we want you always to remember that God is alive and still speaking to regular people like us! That's what Moses learned that day, tending his uncle's sheep, and we need to be reminded it of it too." Her two partners smiled and nodded. Miss Knaak then nodded to them and gestured to the neatly stacked piles of supplies that lay in front of them on the table.

"My partners, Mrs. Solomon and Miss Mueller, will be coming around now to deliver supplies to each of your tables. Your housemothers will bring you the scissors and glue, and, of course, we all know how careful we must be when using scissors and glue. We'll need to take turns and share, which I know you all know how to do, right?" She looked over at the three of us and then added, "Oh, and we are especially lucky to have three big-boy helpers too!"

"Griffy!" Betty shouted, turning me beet red. "My big brother Griffy is here!"

"Boys," Miss Jaeger whispered, "why don't you spread yourselves around to different tables, and be as helpful as you can." We nodded and split up. I bee-lined to Betty's table, partly because I missed seeing her and partly because she'd be less likely to yell my name across the dining hall if I was right next to her.

Mrs. Solomon brought over a cylindrical container with two pairs of scissors and a couple of bottles of glue inside. She set it on the middle of our desk, just as Miss Mueller placed a stack of brightly colored construction paper, eight cardboard tubes, and a handful of string in neat piles. About the only thing missing from Danny's prophecy was the pipe cleaners.

"Fire," Miss Knaak continued, "is brightly colored. So you'll see that your paper choices are red, orange, and yellow. You can cut your paper up in all kinds of shapes. Sometimes fire looks jagged and angular, but at other times it's more smooth and wavy." She walked between our table and the one where Knox was, as she offered more creative options. "Try to imagine your fire as alive, as talking to you, just as the fire in Exodus 3 spoke to Moses thousands of years ago."

"What's the cardboard tube for, Miss Knaak?" Betty's friend Heather Madsen asked.

Miss Knaak approached her, leaned over gently, and said, "Great question, young lady! Think of it as a log and glue your colored flames to it." She patted Heather gently on the back. Betty leaned her way, and Miss Knaak touched the side of Betty's cheek gently and smiled down upon her.

The sounds of scissors, and rolling tubes began to fill the dining hall. As I watched these little kids diving into their project enthusiastically, I tried to remember being that young but couldn't. Then I looked back to the table where Johnny was "helping," with a cardboard tube in each hand held up to his eyes, as if they were binoculars. He had another one sticking out of his empty shirtsleeve like a third arm.

"That's enough, Johnny," I heard Miss Jaeger say. "You boys are here to help, not cause disruption." I heard Johnny exhale louder than he should have, before grabbing a pair of scissors to start cutting out flames.

Knox had jumped up from his table and walked across the room to where Miss Knaak stood, even though Mrs. Solomon and Miss Mueller were much closer to his table. I watched as he slid up to her, puffed out his chest, and asked his question. As he raced back to his table, Miss Knaak spoke up.

"Boys and girls, this young man just asked an excellent question." She looked but Knox was gone, already sitting at our table whispering to several of the little ones. "I need to tell you what the string is for," Miss Knaak said. Leaning over a table of girls, she lifted up a tube that already had several flames glued to it. "There are two ways you can use the string. If you'd like to be able to hang your fire, you can glue two loops of string at each end of the tube like this." She demonstrated. "Or you can cut the string and glue pieces of it on the upper edges of your flames to suggest smoke or even white hot coals." She smiled and looked all around the room. "Be creative and have fun with this. And remember—God is in the fire, speaking to you!"

I found myself staring at Miss Knaak, trying to find some key to her connection to Deputy Hitchcock. I thought back to some of those underlined book passages of hers that I'd seen down in the furnace room office. I even remembered that first night of swimming lessons at the Waukegan YMCA, when we all noticed her in the front row of Mr. Hitchcock's elocution class.

"Boys and girls," I heard a woman's voice say. It was the tired voice of Mrs. Solomon. She pointed at our Crayolas and said, "You can write on your flames if you'd like. Exodus 3 or something from the story that helps you remember its message."

"Ok!" Johnny said, trying to sound like a five-year-old. He grabbed a marker and wrote something quickly. A few seconds later, he was flashing his message to me: "I want some of Miss Conkle's cookies!" Not to be out done, Knox had written on his flames as well: "Saturday mornings are for sleeping in!"

The craft morning was winding down. The housemothers were seeing to it that all the tables were clean and ready for our upcoming lunch. Miss Knaak and her assistants had loaded all of the leftover supplies in their bags and were saying their goodbyes. Betty was never more than a few inches away from Miss Knaak, and at times she was practically wrapped around one of her legs, the same way she used to grab our mother's leg. Miss Knaak was unfazed by Betty's clinging. I worked my way up to the front table to pry Betty loose, apologizing to Miss Knaak.

"Don't be silly, Griffin! Your sister is an absolute angel." Then she moved close enough to whisper to me, "In fact, I'd take her home if I could." She winked and smiled.

"Can I help you and the other ladies get these boxes out to your car?" I asked.

Her eyes widened and her jaw dropped. "My, aren't you a gentleman! That would be just fine, Griffin." I nodded and picked up the first box.

"Griffy helping!" Betty said, clapping her hands together. I saw out of the corner of my eye that Knox had followed my lead. He picked up two smaller boxes, and we followed Miss Mueller out the dining hall doors. We passed Miss Arbuckle, who nodded approvingly at Knox and me. She always seemed surprised when any of us Wads boys did something nice.

When we reached the door to the outside, I set my box down and held the door open for Knox, Miss Mueller, and Mrs. Solomon. Then I waited for Miss Knaak to catch up to us. She came around the corner, and I heard her talking with Miss Arbuckle.

"It's a wonder Glen Flora Elementary ever let you get away!" Miss Arbuckle said.

"It was our pleasure, Jessie, truly. We'd love to come back any time. I mean that." She saw me holding the door and said, "I'm coming, Griffin. So sorry to make you wait."

"That's OK, Miss Knaak. No hurry." I held the door as she passed through. Knox and the other ladies were already out at the green Ford, loading in the boxes.

"Miss Knaak," I said. "I'm working several days a week for your teacher, Mr. Hitchcock." She stopped and tilted her head at me in surprise.

"How did you kn...." She seemed to catch herself. "Well, that seems enterprising of you, Griffin. Good for you." We walked toward the others at the street.

"I do some odd jobs for them, both at the Village Hall and at his home, with Mrs. Hitchcock." I watched her face instantly tighten and her steps cease.

"Well, isn't that nice? I'm sure he appreciates that." Immediately, Miss Knack turned away from me and hurried to the car to help the older Mrs. Solomon into the back seat. My buddy Knox came over to me, his face making it clear that he'd seen me talking to Miss Knaak. He wanted to know straight away what had been said. Miss Mueller and Miss Knaak called out their thanks and goodbyes to us. We nodded and waved, as we headed back up the lawn toward Wads.

"What were you saying, Griff?" he asked.

"I just told her I was working for Deputy Hitchcock doing odd jobs."

"What did she say?" he asked.

"Not much," I said. "But she didn't look too happy when I mentioned Mrs. Hitchcock."

"I knew it! She's jealous that Hollywood goes home to his wife!" He turned back toward the street to get a final look at Miss Knaak. "What did you say? What did she do?" Knox pressed. We entered Wadsworth and started up the stairs.

"Nothing. I just told her I was working for him. She seemed kinda surprised that I knew him and that I knew she was his student."

Knox's eyes widened. "I bet she's wondering if you know about those Village Hall meetings!" He elbowed me in the side and laughed.

"I don't know," I said. "I don't even know why I said anything to her. I just sort of blurted it out."

And with that, the woman who in less than a year would be known throughout America, drove away.

Detective Hargrave stood up suddenly, slapping the desk between us with his left hand. "You actually knew and talked to Miss Knaak, on several occasions even! Christ, you probably knew her better than anyone on the police force or on the Coroner's Jury, for that matter!"

For a moment, I felt like I'd been caught stealing or something. I looked down between my knees and held my two hands out and upturned in a "so-what-do-you-want-me-to-do-about-it" gesture.

"So she really acted that uncomfortable when you mentioned Hitchcock and his wife?"

I tried to picture the moment all those years before. "I think so. That's how I remember it, as one of those really awkward exchanges."

"Christ!" he said again, shaking his head in a kind of exasperation.

WADS BOY WITH A LAKE BLUFF STRAY DOG
THAT OFTEN SPENT TIME ON THE ORPHANAGE GROUNDS
Photo courtesy of The Lake Bluff History Museum

Chapter 19 — A Midnight Walk
Lake Bluff, IL — April 26, 1928

It was the two O'Neil brothers who first showed me the northwest window in the first floor of Wads. And despite being nabbed by Deputy Hitchcock back in January, I hadn't given up my late night outings. In fact, I did them more and more regularly.

"It can't even be locked," Billy snickered, the first time he showed me the escape hatch.

"And when you're outside, you're at the back where nobody can see you." Bobby had shrugged. "It's down around your feet."

I'd done just what they said pretty much every time. Getting out was the easy part. Staying invisible on the streets of Lake Bluff and then climbing back in without anybody seeing or hearing you was the much tougher challenge.

It was 9:50 p.m. on an April night, a Thursday. I only had about ten minutes to get to the corner of Blodgett and Sheridan Road, where Lily was to be at the stroke of 10:00 p.m. Fortunately, it wasn't very cold, just over 50 degrees with clear skies. The moon was high and almost full. I could see it as I bent down to pry and then prop the window open for my escape and eventual return.

The lawn felt damp with dew, as I slithered out the window onto the back lawn of Wads. I always stayed close to the building as I stood up to make my way around to the Scranton side. An engine's rumble and headlights from the east froze me. It was the now familiar black Packard rolling slowly down Scranton. I could just make out the two men inside and saw the orange glow of a cigar from my frozen perch behind a lilac bush. They were creatures of the night, as reliably present as the darkness they inhabited.

When the coast was clear, I broke into a run toward the post office, but stayed up as close to the houses and their shadows as I could. I used every tree and shrub to keep me invisible from the street. Though it had been several months, I still feared I'd hear the actor's voice behind me or feel his hand grabbing my shoulder.

I angled north toward Sheridan Road. This way, I'd avoid most of the downtown area, easily the most lighted place at night, not to mention the most likely place for the Lake Bluff Deputy Dispatch to be. Since getting nabbed in January, I'd been a lot more careful with these excursions, and there was no way I would take any unnecessary chances with Lily joining me.

I saw her shadow near the little house closest to the intersection. I waved as I ran across Sheridan Road to meet her.

"Hey," I said, out of breath.

"Hey, yourself," Lily replied. "Where to?"

I stuck my hands in my pockets and pointed with my head back toward town. For several minutes, neither of us said anything. Lily spoke first.

"Do you have a favorite route or streets you like best?" She slid a few stray strands of her auburn hair back behind her ear.

"Nah. I just look for houses with lights still on is all." I picked up the pace and decided to cut through the yards. Lily followed, trying to figure out where in the heck I was heading.

"Did you tell anybody you were going out...or that you were meeting me?" she asked.

"Danny, my roommate. But he sleeps so heavily and mumbles nonsense from his pillow. I'm never sure if he really gets what I'm telling him." Looking to the east, I spotted some light coming from a brick house. "There," I said, pointing. "Let's see what's going on over there."

We came to a long, narrow lawn, flanked by two driveways. It was a small, brick bungalow. Its porch light was still on, and I motioned to the driveway on the left. We headed up stealthily. Nearing the house, I stepped off the drive onto some soft, silent grass. There was a hedgerow, and we tucked ourselves into it. A side door led into the kitchen, where a black-haired man sat, while his wife flitted around him busily.

It was weird having Lily with me, looking into the same kitchen window I was. She must have seen the middle-aged blond woman, hustling back and forth, appearing to be busily preparing something. But whenever I'd glance at her beside me, I got the sense that Lily's attention was fixed on me, and that made me nervous. With zero wind on this Thursday night, Lily must have heard the couple's voices, just as I could, but neither of us could make out any words.

"Do you know what they're saying?" she whispered, leaning in toward me.

I didn't move or react in anyway. She must have wondered if I'd even heard her. "Griff...what are they talking about?" she said.

Without turning aside, I replied, "Not the point." I wasn't used to being interrupted. I started thinking I'd made a mistake bringing Lily along. But the next thing I knew, I'd started in.

"I don't spy. I imagine," I said, biting my upper lip.

"Imagine what?" she inquired.

"They've got a young boy and a younger girl, thirteen and six. They're leaving tomorrow for a weekend trip. The mother is packing lunches. Each person gets his favorite sandwich." I paused, but just for a moment. The husband had gotten up to leave the room and was hugging his wife. "He was telling her about his boss. He was offered a promotion today and a big raise. But they'd have to move to get it." I craned my neck a bit as the mother moved from one window to the other. "They were talking about what would be best for the kids. Donny, their son, plays baseball. His mother is worried that the team and the school downstate won't be nearly as good."

Just then the kitchen went dark. The woman had finished and was heading up to bed with her husband. Without saying anything or even realizing what I was doing, I had slipped out of the bushes and down the driveway. Lily followed along.

We were silent for an entire block, as we moved westward. But then something startled Lily.

"What's that?" she whispered pointing to a tree by the intersection. "Something moved over there."

I leaned around her cautiously, catching the movement she had seen. "Oh, it's just Bandit."

"What?" Lily asked, as the dark, scrawny mutt ambled across the street toward us.

"Bandit. Come here, boy. C'mon, Bandit." I leaned down to scratch both ears of the mangy stray. "You're my buddy, aren't you, boy?"

"You two know each other, then?" Lily asked, rolling her eyes.

"Oh yeah, don't we, Bandit?" I stood back up and resumed walking, with Bandit heeling by my side. At each intersection, I looked around for light. "It would be great to have a home, your own room, and your own parents," I said, not sure if it was to Bandit or to Lily.

Lily looked at the street sign, realizing we were heading back toward Crab Tree Farm. Then I said, without even thinking, "How old were you when your mother…when she passed away?"

"Two," she said, startled by my sudden question.

"That's sad," I offered, turning back toward Blodgett Avenue.

"I know," she hesitated, looking through me. "But I'd rather have her dead than just gone like your mother."

I didn't say anything. I just nodded ever so slightly, feeling the truth of Lily's remark. "What about your father?" I asked. "Do you like living with him?"

She clenched her teeth and cracked her knuckles hard, looking up at the night sky. "It's OK…but not when he drinks."

"What's he drink?"

"Booze. Whiskey," she said, walking ahead of me.

"Well, where does he get it? And doesn't he know Mrs. D. runs the WCTU?"

"Of course, he knows that." Lily stopped to tie her shoe. "I don't know where he gets it, but it never seems to run out."

I turned back to the dog to pet him and asked, "Why does he do it, do you think?"

She exhaled a long, loud breath. "At first, I thought he missed my mother, that he was sad or something. But he's always talking about how much pressure he's under. Even though Mrs. D. runs the farm, there's something he does for Mr. D. that he never really talks about. I reckon that is the part he doesn't like."

Then, all at once, Lily grabbed my arm and looked straight in my face. "Your mother...Do you think she'll ever..."

"No," I interrupted resolutely. "She's not comin' back." I looked back at Lily. "That's why I'm here...why I take these walks. I need to make a plan." I bent down again to scratch Bandit behind the ears.

"What kind of a plan?" she asked nervously.

I looked at her with what must have been disappointment, or maybe impatience. Whatever it was, it was a look Lily didn't recognize, and she sure didn't like it. She crinkled up her face in a way I'd only seen a couple of times out at the farm.

"To run away," I said, irritated. I picked up my pace and looked straight ahead. Lily had to jog every couple of steps to keep up. Her face was as tight as her two fists. She must have had a thousand questions. But as we arrived at the entrance to the farm off of Sheridan Road, she only asked me one.

"When?"

I hesitated. Looking up at the moon, I shook my head. "I don't know, but it better be soon. Betty's best friend Heather Madsen just got fostered out yesterday. Betty could be next. Cute little girls don't last long at LBO."

When I got back to the window at Wads to let myself in, I saw a light in the far corner of the room. Sitting there in one of the high backed reading chairs was Dick. It had to have been 11 p.m. on a school night, and Dick was just sitting there in his striped pajamas reading a sports magazine.

I climbed in as quietly as I could, pulling the window shut behind me, and tiptoed over toward him.

"Are you...is everything all right?" I asked.

"You bet," he said. "Have a nice walk?"

"Yeah. I guess." I looked up the stairs. "Are the housemothers all asleep?"

"They better be. They got a big day tomorrow." He turned a few pages without looking at me.

"Well, good night then," I whispered, heading toward the stairs.

"Good night," Dick replied.

GRACE DURAND OF CRAB TREE FARM WITH HER GUERNSEY CATTLE
DN-0002644, Chicago Daily News negative collection, Chicago History Museum

Chapter 20 — Voices in the Night
Crab Tree Farm — May 19, 1928

"You have no idea how crazy Mrs. D. can be!" Lily said. "She's nice and everything and acts pretty normal at the farm and all." Lily finished washing her hands in the milk house sink. "But if you lived here and saw her all hours of the day and night, you'd know just what I mean."

I took my turn at the washtub, trying to scrub off the sticky milk and udder residue. "She's always real nice to me." I toweled off my hands. "What's your father say?"

"He says that her son Jack has 'frayed her poor nerves to the breaking point.'" Lily headed out the rear door and I followed her.

It was a bright Saturday afternoon, and the May sun was still high in the sky. "I guess that Jack has been arrested several times, and Mrs. D. has to keep getting him out of jail. Daddy says that with the Durands being such a prominent family and all, the son's shenanigans are hurting their family's reputation." Lily picked up a rotten apple off the path and threw it back toward the milk house.

I'd later learn that Jack Durand was, indeed, a notorious trouble maker. From an early age, he'd run with a wild group of boys who got in all kinds of trouble down in Lake Forest. These other kids, like Jack himself, were all of privilege, rich and wild. Their parents were not going to abide having their kids getting hauled in by the cops for reckless behavior every other week.

From the Durands' standpoint, Jack's final straw had come in 1921 when he was 18 and managed to steal over $1,500 worth of whiskey and wine from a family with whom he was living. Mrs. Durand ordered him to leave that home and their Crab Tree Farm permanently. Jack moved to another friend's house in Lake Forest, and apparently his wayward path only continued. His beleaguered, high-profile parents sought to keep his criminal exploits out of the papers but never quite succeeded. Jack was eventually charged for a jewelry theft from an estate in Lake Forest and fled the area. Police tracked him down out in California, where he was working in blackface as an entertainer at a Venice Beach, California street show.

"Mr. Durand is the president of a really big sugar company," Lily continued, as she carefully pried two cookies out of the front chest pocket of her overalls and handed one to me. "Mrs. D. made us these. Oatmeal and raisin."

"Thanks." I gobbled it down in two huge bites. "You been out at night lately?"

"Sure, I have. When you gonna sneak out again?" she goaded.

"Miss Harvey's been on the warpath. She caught the O'Neil brothers sneakin' out last week and beat 'em both so bad, no one's dared go out since." I looked back at the Durand house and saw Mr. Durand under a tree whispering something to Redd. Redd was clenching and unclenching his hands again, and Mr. D. was leaning hard toward him, pointing his finger. Lily hadn't seen them, and I didn't point the two men out to her.

"Danny's been warnin' me that there might be a snitch among us over at LBO," I said, moving to Lily's right so she wouldn't see her father.

Lily sighed. "I wish you'd figure out a way to come back out." She elbowed me in the side. "I'm gonna go out tonight."

"Why?" I stopped and looked at her squarely.

"Mrs. D. usually has the same four or five ladies over on Saturday nights. They come real late." She nibbled at the edges of her cookie. "I don't know what they do in there, but they light candles and pull most of the drapes shut. And two Saturdays ago," she paused to swallow, "I even saw your deputy dispatch guy—Hitchcock—drive back and forth by here, first on the Sheridan Road side and later by the Blodgett entrance."

I scratched my head and peered off in the distance for an idea. "What time you gonna be out?"

Lily's face brightened, and she spoke quickly. "The ladies usually come around 9, and Daddy gets to bed by 9:30 or 9:45."

"I'll come about 10:00, if the coast is clear back at LBO."

Lily took a step toward me, nodding excitedly. "Meet me at the big elm tree right behind the milk house." She pointed to it. I waved in acknowledgment and headed back up the driveway. I heard a stern, deep voice across the driveway and over to my right. I stopped abruptly and ducked behind a tree to my left to listen.

"I want out!" one of them said.

"How many times do I have to tell you?" It was the voice of Mr. Scott Durand. "There is no getting out with these guys!"

"I just want to go back to running your farm, Mr. Durand. That's all." It was Lily's father, Redd. He was pleading. "My daughter needs me. I can't take these kinds of chances, sir."

"Yes, Redd, your daughter does need you. And it's this little side job that is going to allow you to take the best possible care of her."

"I understand that these men are paying me to help with these deliveries," Redd said, sounding fatigued. "But if something happens to me or if the police get wind of this, I won't be able to do much of anything for Lily."

"Our agreement with them calls for you to be taken care of in perpetuity, Redd. You know what that means?" I heard one of them expel a big breath. "That means even if something were to happen to you, the payments don't stop. They go to Lily."

I heard movement and the two men came into view, heading back toward the main farm house. I stayed off of the noisy gravel and slipped between the trees lining the left side of the driveway and out toward Sheridan Road.

$$\approx$$

Later that night, I lay in my bed, under the covers, fully clothed, including my shoes. The light was out, and I was just waiting for Miss Harvey's 10 p.m. bed check.

"You sure about this, Griff," Danny whispered.

"Yeah." I swallowed.

"What's so important about tonight? Danny asked. "Harvey's been on the prowl. You ever think about the fact that Saturday night is the most obvious night to try something like this?" He slipped into a volume just above a whisper. "You know how many people are out there, all around town on a Saturday night?"

"Sshhh!" I whispered. "I'm not stupid. I'll be fine. Just remember, if Harvey comes in, all you have to…"

"Pretend I'm asleep!" Danny interrupted. "I know. I'm not stupid either."

A loud, announcing knock on our cubicle wall silenced us. In walked Miss Bertha Harvey, flicking her light on us. She looked at both our beds, sure to see both heads, both faces, and both sets of eyes. "Nighty-night, boys. See you at breakfast at 8:15 in your church clothes." She turned her light off and shuffled on with her rounds.

I took in a deep breath, exhaled it in relief, and waited for eight more minutes. I got up as quietly as I could and angled my ear into the opening to the hall, listening for the last of the housemother's footsteps. I took one last breath and exited quietly, without another word to Danny.

I stayed as far to the right side as I could, where the floorboards were the quietest. I leaned around the corner to see the window at the northwest quadrant of the room. I crossed to it, cloaked in shadows, jimmied it open, and eased out. I pulled an eraser from my back pocket, one that I'd swiped from school, and used it to prop the window open.

Working my way to the southwest edge of the building, still in the shadows, I scanned the adjoining yards and took off at a swift jog. I headed toward Evanston Ave. and then over to Blodgett. I was at the entrance to Crab Tree Farm in less than seven minutes. I only saw two cars on the way, but they didn't see me. And I'd seen no one on foot.

I snuck from tree to tree, never setting foot on the Durand's actual driveway. Glancing at the main farmhouse, I saw closed curtains and almost no light, just an eerie glow. To the right of the kitchen entrance, I saw three cars that weren't usually there. Cutting toward the milk house, I saw the elm tree, and Lily revealed herself.

"You're early! Not even 10:30 yet."

"Did I miss anything?" I asked.

"Nope. Nothin' except Frank and one of his campfires."

"What do you mean? Frank the animal killer?" I asked.

She nodded with a roll of her eyes as well. "He makes a fire out behind where the farmhands sleep and then sits real close to it, just staring at it for hours on end."

"Is something wrong with him?"

"Who knows? My daddy says he's slow in the head is all. But one of the other farmhands called him a 'jailbird' once, when they didn't know I was around." Lily turned back toward the main farmhouse and pointed. "I can't wait to see what's going on in there."

"With this hot of a night, there have to be some windows open, even if the drapes aren't." I said. I glanced back toward the guest cottage. "Where's your father?"

Lily nodded toward the cottage. "In there. He's had a lot to drink, so he's snoring."

"Even though liquor is illegal, your father seems to have no problem getting it." I said.

"Yeah." She shook her head and glanced back at their cottage. "And he seems to get it by the case, and it never runs out."

I started walking over toward the main farmhouse. Lily fell into silent step behind me. We worked our way to the east side of the house, opposite the kitchen entrance. The trees were most highly concentrated on the sunrise side. Plus, it was where the large family room was, the most logical spot for Mrs. Grace Durand's covert gathering.

We crept around and crouched down beneath an open window. I put my index finger to my mouth. It was very quiet. I was right; the windows were open. The light breeze moved the dark curtains into the room and gently out again, in a wave-like motion. I inched my head up to the level of the sash, trying to peek inside. Everything was blurry, in some sort of haze. I saw candles, dozens of them, flickering. But I couldn't see any people at first. Finally, after standing there a couple of nervous minutes, I heard one.

It was the familiar voice of Mrs. D. Yet something about it was different. She sounded like she was almost pleading in a slow, rhythmic cadence.

"Come…now….Speak…from the beyond."

Both Lily and I rose up and peeked in from opposite edges of the same window, willing the curtain to sway just enough so we could see something, anything. The haunting voice of Mrs. D. continued.

"Oh…Spirit we await…your direction." She paused. "Cynthia, your mother…is here now…Give her what she needs…Speak Cynthia…Speak." The altered voice of Grace Durand trailed off. I motioned with my right hand for Lily to crouch back down to the ground. When she did, I took two silent steps toward her and stood behind her but leaned over her. I slid my right hand in between the window frame and the curtain. Using the back of my hand, I pushed gently on the curtain and finally saw what I was looking for. There, in a circle on the floor, were five women. A single candle was in the middle of their circle, and each participant had a candle in front of her. My gaze stopped on one woman whose head was bowed but she was facing us. She looked familiar and far younger than the other four. Her brown hair was shoulder length and tied back in a ribbon. I knew I had seen her before. It was Miss Knaak!

I stepped silently to the left, around Lily, but maintained contact with the curtain. I nodded for Lily to come up and have a look. She looked at me fearfully and hesitated. Then she slowly rose. She steeled herself for what she was about to see. At first, I'm pretty sure she saw only the candles, like I had, candles on every table, on every surface. But in a second, I could tell from her face that she'd seen the circle, five heads now bowed in prayerful silence. Mrs. D.'s torso was weaving back and forth, with her legs crossed beneath her. The other women sat still.

"Ahhh! She's here!" It was a scream, coming from the woman directly across from Mrs. D. "My Cynthia!" The woman began to cry. Her shoulders heaved, and her body jerked, as if she were being stabbed. "I'm sorry, baby! I'm so sorry!"

Lily shot up, right in front of me, knocking my chin with the top of her head. She was trembling, not realizing that she had pushed the curtain almost fully open as she'd risen. I grabbed her hand and tugged her back away from the window, releasing the curtain slowly back to its closed position. Almost involuntarily, Lily backed away even further from the house with both hands covering her mouth. I motioned for her to get down, and I did the same. I looked around quickly and then motioned with my head for us to move back around to the milk house. Once there, in the shadowy darkness, at the trunk of the elm tree, I spoke first, breathlessly. "What the hell was that?"

"Creepy…It was…so creepy." Lily was still shaking. "They were talking," she shook her head back and forth with her eyes closed, as if trying to rid herself of the image inside it. "To dead people, Griff. That one woman was talking to her dead daughter." She sniffled and wiped her eyes with her sleeve. "I met that lady once. She was crying on Mrs. D.'s porch. It was right after her daughter—Cynthia—died." She looked down at the ground and then up at me, thinking. "She was twelve…her daughter…Cynthia…was only twelve when she died!"

"How'd she die?" I asked quietly.

"Her mother, that lady in there, had too much to drink and ran her car into a wall." Again, Lily shook her head and closed her eyes. "Cynthia got crushed. When I was looking in there, Griff, that lady had her arms around her…her imaginary daughter, like this." Lily hugged an invisible child.

"I read about this once," I said. "And some of the Wads boys were talking about it." I tried to remember the word Ernie had used. "Say-yonce or see-ance, I think."

"Whatever it's called, it's just creepy." She turned to me and poked her index finger into my ribs. "I told you! I told you Mrs. D. was a crackpot. She wasn't just in there; she was leading that, that…whatever it was."

I leaned toward Lily. "Did you see the one woman in there who was a lot younger than the others, next to Mrs. Durand, I think? I think it might have been Elfrieda Knaak, the encyclopedia lady."

"Who?" Lily asked.

"Elfrieda Knaak," I said. "She had long, brown hair pulled back. She was right across from us, facing our window."

"Oh, her. Yeah. She comes here almost every Saturday. She always has a pretty ribbon in her hair."

"I want to go back and get another look at her," I said.

"What? I'm not going back there. Those ladies are crazy, talking to the dead. No thanks!" she said, crossing her arms and shaking her pigtails back and forth.

"Suit yourself," I said, sneaking back to the open windows in a low crouch. As I came up slowly beneath the window with the billowing curtain, I heard a different voice.

"Father, Father, I miss you so," the younger, crisper voice said.

"Come, Spirit. Come!" the other ladies chanted in unison. I rose up slowly and parted the curtain. It was Elfrieda Knaak, seated and facing the central candle.

"Dearest Father, I must hear from you. Please…let me hear that you are all right, that my two brothers who died so young are with you and safe in the beyond."

The candles seemed to brighten and flicker.

"He is here," another voice said, but I couldn't tell from where it had come.

Miss Knaak began to weep. Her head fell into her hands and her shoulders trembled up and down. "Ple….please Father…Just let me know that all is well…that your spirit is at rest." She paused and wiped her eyes as she straightened up. "I'm doing my best…we all are. Theodore is trying to do what you would have done with the pharmacy…I…I was teaching but now I'm…well…I'm…selling. They're books, Father, good books, spiritual and educational books."

Again, Miss Knaak broke off and wept. Her head shook back and forth until she collapsed onto the floor. The others slid toward her, and Mrs. D. placed her hand on the middle of her back.

"Now, now, child," she said, moving in a rhythmic, rocking motion with Miss Knaak.

I was startled by something back and to the right of where I was. I dipped beneath the window and backed quietly toward Lily.

"What was that?" I said, as she came out from behind a tree. We both turned and took a step toward the east. It was a car motor. I looked at Lily and our widening eyes locked. In a second, without a word, we both took off at a dead run, up the path and into the orchard.

There was just enough moonlight to light our way. Lily was fast and cut in front of me. "This way," she said in an urgent whisper, as we crested the hill that brought Lake Michigan into view. It was a dark, blue-black, silent mass. We saw the lights at the exact same time and stopped, sliding to the ground silently.

Two trucks were idling with their back wheels six feet from the water. A single, low-slung, fishing boat had drifted to where the water gave way to sand. Lily whispered, "Stay down and follow me."

She cut across the path we were on, angling down and to the right, toward the water. Lily moved agilely from tree to tree, and I stayed two trees behind her, moving exactly as she did. I couldn't tell how close she planned on getting to the vehicles and to the dark figures that were now coming into view.

Then Lily, laying down, was peering around an apple tree trunk. I slithered up to the tree next to hers and could begin to make out the voices.

"Keep it moving, fellas. Forty down, forty to go." A tall man, standing on the shore between the two trucks, was calling out the orders. Eight others were in constant motion. Two were on the boat, lifting heavy cases off a pile and swinging them to four others, who would shuttle them through knee-deep water back to the two trucks. I could barely make out two more sets of hands, one poking out of each truck, to receive the delivered cases. The hands grabbed one crate at a time from one of the four men on the ground, disappeared momentarily, and then reappeared in time for the next one.

I remembered that article that Dick Moley had given to me, the one about bootlegging. But all I whispered to Lily was, "What is it, do ya think?"

"Don't know," Lily replied even softer. "But it's the same ones I saw before, the trucks and the boat."

"They're almost done," I interrupted. "We gotta see how they get out of here."

Lily nodded, then added, "Then we gotta figure out what's in those cases." She got up quietly and slowly. "Stay here until they're long gone." Before I could respond, Lily had disappeared into the darkness.

I nervously resumed my watch and crept forward on my belly, two more trees toward the trucks. I could make out other voices now.

"We'll have about an hour and a half to get down to the warehouse on Cicero," a man with a raspy, hollow voice said. The boat started its engine and started moving out from the shore. It was pointed north and fought against the waves. Two of the men on the shore picked up some sort of panel or door off the sand, and began to connect it to the back of one truck and then repeated the process with the other one. The tall man in charge picked up what looked like a final, stray crate and walked up into the first row of trees. The trucks started up their engines, their passenger doors opened and closed, and the tall man was the last one to board. He no longer had the crate in his hands.

The truck headlights arched around and seemed to be pointing right toward me. I held my breath and kept my head down, burrowed into the dirt. The two trucks, in single file, drew nearer to my tree but then veered to the left and headed toward Blodgett.

I didn't move for several minutes. I prayed that Lily would show up soon.

"Hey," she said, no longer in a whisper. She was almost completely out of breath. "They went out one of the orchard paths...the one that bends left out onto Blodgett." She bent over, resting her hands on her thighs, trying to catch her breath.

"Where were you?" I asked urgently.

"I was right off of that path...the one they went out." She looked toward it and pointed. "I figured if you were here and I was there, one of us would see something."

"And what did you see?" I blurted out, unable to contain myself.

"Milk trucks, just like ours. Three guys in the first one and four in the second one."

"Did you see the back of either truck?" I asked.

"What do you mean?"

"The last thing I saw before they started leaving was two guys putting some sort of door or panel on the back. I just wondered what it was or what it looked like."

"Just like ours. Everything about the trucks was just like our Crab Tree trucks."

I was silent for a while, trying to recall the particulars in that newspaper article I'd read months ago. I looked up at the nearly full moon and said, "I gotta go. I have no idea what time it is, but I better get back." I started up the orchard path but froze. "Wait a second," I said. "I gotta check something." I ran down where the men had been and looked around the base of the trees, and then I saw it. It was the one crate I'd seen the man intentionally leave behind. I dragged it out from the tree a bit in hopes that the moonlight would illuminate it.

"What is it?" Lily asked.

"I don't know, but it's one of those 80 boxes that just came off that boat." I looked at its rough wood and examined the thin cracks between each board.

"Did they forget one?" she asked.

I shook my head. "No. This one was left on purpose."

"What for?" she asked looking up at me.

"I'm not sure," I hesitated. "Someone they need to thank maybe."

Lily leaned down and got close to the crate. She tilted the crate enough to hear the glass containers clinking together inside. She stepped away from it, shaking her head, and turned toward the dark lake. She crossed her arms and her entire body tightened.

"What?" I said, placing a hand on her shoulder.

"I know who it is they want to thank." She turned back toward the crate and pushed it with her foot back against the tree trunk. She dashed up the orchard path without a goodbye, and I raced after her. As we neared the guest cottage, I moved over to the right onto the quieter, softer ground, and Lily peeled off toward the cottage door.

I crawled back into Wads by way of the northwest window. It was pitch black, so I felt my way from chair to chair and used the long back of the couch to guide me toward the stairs. I crept back up the quiet side of the stairway, holding my breath in order to hear any movement. My greatest fear was running into Miss Harvey at the top of the stairs or finding her sitting on my empty bed with her switch in her hand.

As I came up over the top stair, there was still very little light, although the moon seemed to be shining in some of the south side windows facing Scranton. I heard a footstep and froze. I took two steps backward and ducked beneath the edge of the stairwell wall, looking around the edge toward the source of the sound. I saw a boy tiptoeing out of Johnny and Bobby's room, but he was smaller than either of them. When I saw the limp, bent left arm, I knew it was Artie. He angled across the room and down two more cubicles and slipped into his own room.

I waited until I knew he was in bed and until the steady silence confirmed that no one else was up and about. I slid past my room and ducked into Johnny and Bobby's. They were both sound asleep and nothing seemed out of sorts in their room. I let out the breath I'd been holding as silently as I could and crept back into my cubicle.

I pulled out the clothes and blanket I had stuffed under my sheets, tucked them back under my bed, and climbed into bed. My mind raced from the seance to the smugglers and then to Artie sneaking out of Johnny and Bobby's room. I knew that no sleep would come on that May Saturday night.

WADSWORTH HALL BOYS — FIRST FLOOR LEVEL (OLDER BOYS)
Photo courtesy of the Lake Bluff History Museum

Chapter 21 — Life After LBO
Lake Bluff Orphanage — June 8, 1928

Danny and I were in our room in Wads. Friday night ice cream and game night had ended. It had gone longer and later than usual, since school had just gotten out for the summer.

Danny was on his bed, lying on his stomach, skimming through the latest *Science and Invention* magazine. He had only a t-shirt and skivvies on. I was on my back, wearing the red shirt the Freidles had sent me for my birthday back in February and a pair of pajama shorts. I also had my left hand in the ball glove they'd given me for Christmas and was playing catch with myself. Throwing the ball straight up, I was trying to get it as close to the ceiling as I could without hitting it.

There was a tap at the cubicle opening, and in walked Dick. "Boys," he said, nodding at us.

"What brings you to these parts, Dick?" Danny asked without looking up from his magazine.

"Boredom. Pure, Friday night boredom!" He plopped down hard on my bed, intercepting my fly ball on its way down. "Griffy, when you've been here as long as I have, going on eight years, ice cream and game night is just not as entertaining as it once was."

I groaned and cocked my head back as I shook it. "As long as you have? What about as long as I have?" He shook his head. "Less than a year here, and I'm already sick of it," I said, sitting up. "Say, why don't you guys sneak out with me tonight?" I looked at Dick and then at Danny.

"No-sir-ee, Mr. Morgan," Dick said, tossing my ball over to Danny. "We're trying to punch our tickets out of here for keeps."

"Yeah," Danny added, "we need Arbuckle and all the big cheeses in our corner, not paddling our behinds." He stood up straight and performed a mock salute. "I'm not giving them any reason to send me to Glenwood Military School for Boys, sir, no sir!"

Remembering their predicament, now that they'd graduated from eighth grade, I frowned and furrowed my forehead. "So what are you going to do, when you leave here?"

Danny smirked and surprised Dick with a baseball to his shoulder. "Well, Mr. Three-Sport Jocko, here, may soon be adopted by the Lake Forest High School basketball coach." My eyes widened and my jaw dropped. Danny continued, "But yours truly, Mr. Can't-Walk-and-Chew-Gum-at-the-Same-Time, has not received any such offers."

"Aw, cut the pity party, Danny," Dick said, chucking the ball at Danny's thigh. "I keep telling you, with your brain and your grades, there is no way Arbuckle is going to send you out of this school district. I can guarantee you that she's working the phone, talking to Mr. Shelby and all the other science or math teachers, trying to find you a local family."

"We'll be all right, Griffy boy," Danny said, half-heartedly. "Have no fear."

I bounced up abruptly and started pacing.

"Uh-oh," Dick mocked. "Looks like young Griff is agitated!"

"Guys, it's not right, you having to leave, just 'cause you finished junior high." I stopped and eyed both of them. "It's not your fault you got crap for parents and no relatives around to take you in." I regretted my words the second they escaped my mouth, realizing that Dick's father lived a couple of blocks away and was choosing not to see him.

Dick had taken over the entirety of my bed. He interlocked his fingers behind his head and released a deep breath as his head hit my pillow. It was easy to see why every girl in the orphanage and most of the local girls at school dreamed of being his girl. He was tall, dark, and handsome. At age 13 he had the bearing of a returning war hero.

"It's just the rules, Griffy boy," Dick said. "It's how they've always done things here. Besides, we need to make room for the little kids...like you and your sister." Danny drilled me with a fastball to the buttocks.

"Ow!" I said, scowling. "I'm no little kid, and you can leave my sister out of this."

Danny picked up the ball off the floor and said, "Sit down, Griff. You're wearing a hole in the floor and making me nervous."

"Yeah," Dick added. "Why don't you sit down and tell us about this farm girl honey-pie of yours." Danny laughed and nodded in agreement.

"Why does everybody keep saying she's my girlfriend?" I protested.

"Oh, I don't know," Dick said, raising and lowering his shoulders. "It couldn't be because you sneak outta here to see her every week."

"Yeah, or that you're always the first one on the list for milk duty every time the chore list gets posted," Danny said. "You're in the presence of LBO's number one lady-killer, Griff. Just look at him stretched out on your bed. Ask him anything you want about the dames. Anything."

I closed my eyes and let out an exasperated breath. "You guys ever think that it might just be less boring over at Crab Tree than in this hell-hole?" I sat on the floor and leaned against the cubicle wall. I motioned to Danny to toss me my ball. "I don't think I'll be here much longer than either of you anyway." I looked down at the pale floor.

Dick sat up and cast a sideways glance at Danny. "What are you talking about, kid?" Dick asked.

"What do you think I'm talking about?" I shot back, without looking up from the floor.

"We don't know. Why don't you tell us?" Dick said slowly, with the pronunciation of an elocutionist.

I started tossing the ball up with my right hand and catching it in my left. The mitt was over by my bed. "I'm thinkin' about leavin'."

"Thinking about or planning to?" Danny asked, looking at me and then over to Dick.

Dick straightened up and leaned off the bed, reaching one of his leading rebounder arms all the way toward me to intercept my ball in mid-air again. "Answer the question, big man," he said.

I took a loud, deep breath, closed my right eye, and said, "Both."

"And does your little sister know about this?" Dick asked.

"No. Betty doesn't know. Betty doesn't need to know," I said.

"So, you're just leaving her here...like your mother did?" Danny said.

I shot up toward Danny, cocking my right fist. "I said leave Betty out of this!" Both Danny and Dick shook their heads in disbelief. "Wherever I end up, my sister will be with me. Neither of us is ever getting left behind by anybody, ever!"

"You gonna talk to us about this, Griff? Let us help you? Or are you gonna just do it your own way and get caught?" Dick said.

"C'mon, now, Griff. Take a deep breath and tell us your plan," Danny said. "Three heads are better than one." He patted the spot on his bed next to him for me to sit. I looked at Danny, then at Dick, and finally at the floor between them. I sat down on Danny's bed, folded my hands in the space between my knees, but said nothing for more than a minute. Dick and Danny glanced at each other and waited patiently.

Angry footsteps approached, the unmistakable stomps of Miss Bertha Harvey. Dick looked at Danny's alarm clock. "Holy crap!" he muttered, seeing it was after 10 p.m. He froze, knowing it was too late to get back to his cubicle without being seen.

Bertha Harvey appeared at the opening of our cubicle, filling it up with her broad shoulders and stout build. She had her switch in her right hand. She wasn't smiling. "Boys, boys," she said, wagging her head in disappointment. "I trust we all know what time it is?" She looked at each of us, tapping her switch upon her upturned left hand.

I spoke up. "Yes, Miss Harvey. We sure do." I rose slowly and looked down to the floor regretfully. "This is all my fault."

She looked at me skeptically. "Oh, I see. So you forced Mr. Moley, who is nearly twice your size and strength, to stay in your cubicle past curfew?" She looked briefly at Dick. "Congratulations, Griff."

"It wasn't exactly like that," I looked up and faced her. "You see, I've been crying, sad about something...and these two were trying to help me." I walked over to the chair at the foot of my bed, grabbed its back, and bent over it. "So, if you're gonna need to swat somebody, it ought'a be me."

Dick stood up and stepped toward me. "Naw. It's my own fault. I'll return to my cubicle at once, Miss Harvey. You can do as you see fit."

"Yes, I will do as I see fit," she said, emphasizing the second "I." She blocked Dick's path to the doorway. "Sit back down, you two, and tell me about this sadness."

I didn't hesitate. "I just don't see why they have to leave here when they finish eighth grade. They…they don't have any parents. There's no place for them to go. Kids like me, the younger ones, we need them around." I looked at Dick and Danny.

Miss Harvey rubbed her cheek with her left hand, and the trace of a smirk began to appear on her dour face. She ran her tongue across her upper teeth, as if she'd just started a joke and was about to deliver the punchline. "We have rules here, Mr. Morgan, time-tested rules at that. As a Methodist-Deaconess institution, the people who pay for these beds, for your food, and for everything here have policies that we all must abide by."

"Of course, Miss Harvey," I replied, nodding. "It's just that…they help me. They help me with school work, with the other kids…like they were just doin' now, when you came in."

"I'm glad for that, Griff. And you will be the helper soon." She looked over at Dick. "I just hope that when you are helping the younger, more impressionable boys, you'll be better at telling time than Mr. Moley, here, is." She began tapping her switch again. "Back to your cubicle, Mr. Moley, quietly and quickly." Dick exited and was followed closely by Miss Harvey.

I shook my head and plopped back onto my bed. "This place is a prison. You two are lucky to be getting out."

Danny pulled off his t-shirt and climbed into his bed. "You're only lucky to get out if you got some place better to go." He rolled back over to look at me. "And you and your sister don't. So until you do, don't even think about running away, you hear?"

I nodded slowly but said nothing. He turned off the light and climbed into bed. I lay there on my back staring at the dark ceiling. When I heard Danny roll over again, I whispered, "Dan…you remember me telling you about the family I went to for Christmas?"

"Sure," Danny responded. "The ones who had the ham radio and gave you that ball glove."

"I was thinkin'..."

Danny interrupted. "Let me guess. You were thinking that maybe you could run away to their house? That maybe they'll take you in, and you and your sister can have a real family and live happily ever after?" His words dripped with sarcasm.

I was too surprised and flustered to speak.

"Here's something you probably ought'a know, Griffy boy. Whenever a kid runs away from here and actually makes it out of Lake Bluff, you wanna know where the first place Arbuckle goes to find 'em is?" He paused. I froze. "You guessed it, the kid's Christmas family down in Wilmette. And you should probably also know that it's almost always the Christmas family down in Wilmette that turns the kid in. Oh, they love having us orphans for an afternoon once a year, sure...but not for good." Danny turned back over, facing away from me.

Moisture welled up in my eyes, and I bit down hard on my lip, as I pulled the covers up, completely over my head.

LAKE BLUFF ORPHANAGE BENEFIT
Photo courtesy of the Lake Bluff History Museum

Chapter 22 — The Magical Palace Fundraiser

Lake Bluff, IL — The Horace & Ethel Cook Residence — June 16, 1928

I didn't realize it until many years later, when I became a full-fledged newspaper reporter, but the 1920s Lake Forest-Lake Bluff telephone directory was a veritable "Who's Who" of Chicago's business and political communities. There were judges from the 19th District Court, the President of The State Bank of Lake Forest, the head of the Chicago Mercantile Exchange, the aforementioned sugar magnate Scott Durand, and the soon-to-be-famous Lake County Coroner, Dr. Manfred Traynor, just to name a few.

What didn't take me nearly as long to come to grips with was the fact that even during the height of Prohibition, alcohol was abundantly present in the estates and large residences of Lake Bluff and Lake Forest. Such widespread drinking on the local scene took place, at least, in part, because it wasn't technically illegal. While the 18th Amendment made it illegal to sell and distribute alcohol, it never prohibited the consumption of it. If the liquor came from either one's private stock or from some other unpurchased source, it could flow freely. And flow freely is exactly what it did in places like Lake Bluff and Lake Forest in 1927 and 1928. The elite in these North Shore towns could amble up to the bar in any lavish neighborhood estate and, knowingly or unknowingly, wind up with a glass in their hand containing spirits that had come from the infamous Alfonse Capone.

Several of the wealthiest residents of these two towns had fairly direct business dealings with "The Big Fellow," as Capone was often called. Even Crab Tree Farm proprietor Scott Durand was eventually indicted on the charge of "conspiracy to violate the laws of prohibition." The indictment specifically linked Durand to the Capone liquor syndicate, claiming that Scott Durand's sugar company, S.S. Durand & Company, had provided Capone with over 30 million pounds of sugar for his illicit alcohol racket. So it isn't hard to imagine some conversations around the bar at any of the majestic estates in Lake Forest, Lake Bluff, or even at the fledgling Onwentsia Club between a circuit court justice, a head of a major corporation, the Lake County Coroner, and someone who might have had direct and personal ties to some real live bootleggers.

It was in late June of 1928 that my path would cross with many of these business and political powerbrokers. On a Saturday afternoon, the entire population of LBO was all dressed up and standing in the massive foyer of Mackey Memorial. Miss Arbuckle was dolled up like we'd never seen before; she even had eye shadow and rouge on! Her high-heeled shoes made this extraordinarily tall matron look that much taller. She smiled as she began her most impassioned and lengthy pep talk ever.

"Boys and girls, today is a special and important day for all of us at the Lake Bluff Orphanage." She paused and seemed to make eye contact with every single one of us. "Some very kind and generous folks from Lake Bluff and Lake Forest have planned and put together an amazing party for all of you." Excitement and anticipation spread through that echoey, marble-floored hallway like electricity. I saw Betty and her friend Carol's eyes widen, as they put their hands up over their mouths.

"We will be walking over to 700 Center, to the beautiful home of Mr. and Mrs. Horace Cook. The Cooks have decorated their spacious home like a castle for your party today. There will be games, snacks, fizzy drinks galore, and even a performance by a world famous opera star. There will be servants, circus performers, and all manner of fun things for you to do. There will also be a lot of grown ups there, men and women who have paid, not only for this party, but for food, supplies, and clothing that we will be using here at LBO for years to come." Miss Arbuckle paused again and paced back and forth across the line that separated her from our crowd of spellbound and excited orphans.

When she resumed, her tone became more serious. "Now, I know that all of you will be on your best behavior today, minding your manners, remembering that you are inside someone else's home, where you will use your inside voices and where you will never run." Here she turned and looked directly at the cluster of Wads boys to her left. "It is just so important that all of us make this afternoon and evening a demonstration of our very best behavior." She paused and nodded at us. "Can I count on you, boys and girls?"

"Yes, Miss Arbuckle!" we said, all in unison.

"Very well," she smiled and exhaled. "Now, then, we will walk in two lines, all the way down Center to the Cook Residence. I will lead and Miss Harvey will bring up the rear." And with that, all 107 of us were paraded down Center to the home of Horace and Ethel Cook.

The Cooks lived in a mansion. Even in a town of oversized and amazing houses, this one stood out. I'd noticed it several times on my day and night time excursions through Lake Bluff. It was right on Sunrise Park, where Center intersects with Sunrise Avenue, with nothing but the park and some majestic trees separating it from Lake Michigan. The Cook property—including the garden on the east side—took up darn near an entire city block. It even had an enormous turret, complete with a cone shaped roof, making it as close to a real castle as any of us at the orphanage had ever seen.

On this particular Saturday afternoon in late June, that patio— and the sidewalk leading up to it—served as an alluring entryway to a magical palace. There were flaming torches lining the walkway off Center, and two sentries were stationed at the main door, dressed like Buckingham Palace guards. Our entire brigade from LBO walked up that walkway with our housemother-chaperones and passed between the two statuesque guards.

"Griffy, look!" Betty said, as the two of us entered the Cooks' foyer.

"It's swell, isn't it, peanut?" I said.

Just inside the door, a tall, beautiful, blond woman stood in a glittering, white ball gown. Betty's jaw dropped, as this real life, fairytale princess began to speak to us.

"Welcome, children. Welcome. I'm Mrs. Cook, and I am so glad to welcome you to our magical palace today."

"I've never been in a real palace before! It's beauty-ful!" Betty said.

Ethel Cook bent down toward Betty, grinning broadly. "Well, aren't you the cutest and sweetest child! Thank you." She stroked the side of Betty's head gently. "Now, you promise to have the best day ever in my palace! There's so much to do!"

"I promise! I promise!" Betty replied.

Standing beside Mrs. Ethel Cook was an even more beautiful woman in an even more elaborate gown. She was tall, thanks, in part, to her very high silver heels, and had long, blond hair, wrapped around her head in an upward direction. Glittery silver earrings dangled from her ears, and as she angled her head down to greet us, her ruby red lips parted, revealing perfect, sparkly teeth.

"Are you a real princess?" Betty said, gawking up at her.

"I am Marion Claire, and I grew up right here in this house," she replied. "This woman next to me is my mother, and if she is the queen of this castle, then, yes, I suppose that makes me a princess."

Betty reached out to touch Miss Claire's red beaded gown. I grabbed her hand and pulled it back just before she made contact with Miss Claire's leg. "Come on, Betty. There's a big line of people behind us waiting to meet the princess and her mother." Miss Claire smiled and nodded at me, gesturing with her gloved right arm for us to enter.

Immediately before us was a massive spiral staircase with an ornate chandelier suspended above it. Colorful streamers hung from it and from the railing of the bannister just beneath it. Men in black tuxedos and white gloves were serving the guests—orphans and patrons alike—from large oval trays. Some had tall, slender glasses half filled with gold, bubbly liquid, while other trays had triangle shaped pastries with toothpicks in the middle.

Just then, a few eighth grade girls I recognized from school swooped down the stairs and whisked Betty and several of the other younger girls away. From the way they were dressed, they must have been the children of some of the benefactors who were hosting and supporting this party. They had sparkly dresses, earrings, and grown-up shoes. I'd seen one of them with Dick Moley after a basketball game once. Her name was Madeline, and she'd looked like royalty in her after-school clothes. On this afternoon she was a heart-stopper. I watched her as she moved gracefully up the spiral staircase with Betty at one hand and another Judson youngster in the other.

Dick and Danny had told me this party was an annual affair. A different family hosted it each year with a different theme. But no matter where it was, it always raised over a thousand dollars to support the orphanage. That's undoubtedly why Miss Arbuckle gave us her longest ever "be on your best behavior" speech, before leading us over to the Cook's palace. She was having a hard time getting beyond the majestic foyer, as she was swarmed by men and women wanting to shake her hand, kiss her cheek, or say something to her. Something seemed different about Miss Arbuckle in this setting. She was less in charge and not nearly as intimidating as she was at LBO. The way she moved was stiff and awkward. Her head jerked when one of the adults called to her. It was almost as if she were more nervous about being at the Cooks than we were.

There were all kinds of games, drawings, and prizes throughout the three-story magical palace. I saw jugglers, magicians, clowns, and even a few fairies. But, as I often did in crowded places, I wandered off by myself pretty quickly. The hallways were broad and dimly lit. The doors seemed massive and heavy, like something you'd see in a medieval castle. I came to an open door that led into the Cooks' library, where a half-dozen men were smoking cigarettes and cigars, and drinking lemonade and iced tea. I was pretty sure, however, that their drinks were spiked with something else. Homer Haskell had warned me to be on the lookout for giggle water, because last year's party "smelled like Kentucky bourbon."

The ornate library opened out onto a side porch, which was pretty packed on this warm, early summer evening. Miss Arbuckle had said that many of Lake Forest and Lake Bluff's "most esteemed citizens" would be here, and I could tell that that was exactly who these people were. One man, dressed in a stiff, black suit, kept gesturing wildly with his drink. He'd pivot around every now and then, taking note of his growing audience. Everybody called him "Judge." His belly pushed outward against his shirt and suit coat, and his large angular face was reddened with sweat. He kept wiping his sweaty forehead with the sleeve of his suit coat.

One of the other similarly dressed men in the judge's expanding circle was a taller and much quieter man. I'd heard the judge introduce him as "the President of The State Bank of Lake Forest," but didn't catch his name. He wore spectacles and a neatly trimmed mustache. His shoulders slouched, and his little head seemed to sink between them.

Just then I saw the one and only man I would recognize on this memorable evening. It was Mr. Scott Durand, the owner of Crab Tree Farm.

"Evening, Judge," he said. Mr. Durand stood on the judge's left. I'm sure he wouldn't have recognized me even if he'd looked my way. He wasn't around the farm much. Mr. Durand wore a pinstriped suit with an ascot instead of a tie.

"Quite a place, huh?" Mr. Durand said.

"Scott! Great to see you," the judge replied, putting his chubby left arm around Durand's shoulders. "I am awfully impressed with the things I'm hearing about S.S. Durand and Company. The sugar business seems to be booming." Just then, one of the tuxedo-wearing servants brought a full drink to the judge, who gladly swapped his empty glass for the new one. The judge winked at the servant, as he stirred the brown liquid with his fat index finger. He raised his glass toward Scott's and the bank president's, saying "To the Lake Bluff Orphanage."

"To the orphanage, indeed," both men responded. After a generous sip, Durand continued. "I don't mind telling you, Judge, that this whole prohibition debacle has been the best thing to happen to the sugar trade in years." Durand took another swallow.

The judge backed up toward the floor-to-ceiling, mahogany bookshelf, the one that I was at the other end of, and leaned against it. He took a slow sip of his icy drink, eyeing the room for a moment. "I think it's clear to everyone at this point, Scott, that there is no future in the 18th Amendment." He gestured with his drink around the room. "The great experiment has run its course, with all due respect to your wife and the WCTU." The judge wiped his perspiring forehead with the back of his navy blazer sleeve. "The problem is, Scott, a hell of a lot of money is being made by the bootleggers who are beating the system." The large man belched.

The mention of bootleggers reminded me of that article I found that night I came home late after talking to Miss Arbuckle and found Dick still up. The article noted how suburbs like Lake Bluff were being used to smuggle whiskey down into Chicago.

"And the longer this failed experiment goes on," the judge continued, "the more my docket is going to be overstuffed with accused bootleggers and the associated criminality that accompanies their illicit trafficking." The judge shook his head. "Not to mention the number of phone calls and visitors to my office from some of the very people who are benefitting from the illegal alcohol business."

"I'm sure you have no shortage of suitors, Judge," Durand smirked and raised his glass. "But probably not the kind with whom you'd care to have your photo taken." After a generous sip, Mr. Durand continued. "Being in the sugar business, I am in the unique position of benefiting from increased alcohol production and consumption, whether it is legal or not."

The judge smiled knowingly and nodded. "I suppose that is true. You've always had a knack for playing both sides where profit is concerned."

Just then, I noticed a tall, slow-moving, bald man approaching the judge and his constantly growing audience.

"Hello, Judge. Evening, Scott," the bald man nodded to each of them.

"Well, if it isn't our County Coroner! How are you, Manny?" the judge cackled.

"Quite an occasion. I'm privileged to be a part of it," Dr. Traynor offered, sizing up the room and its many wealthy patrons.

"Just as every Catholic family needs a priest, any gathering with this many old codgers probably needs a coroner," the Judge said, slapping Dr. Traynor on the back. The three laughed.

"Pity your bride couldn't make it tonight, Scott," Coroner Traynor said. "How is the old loon?"

Scott Durand shook his head, smiling. I half expected him to punch the bald coroner for calling his wife a "loon," but the sugar baron seemed unfazed by the jab. "She's fine. Just fine, Manny. But you and I both know, that if my wife were here tonight, there'd probably be milk in these glasses of ours."

"I'll drink to that," the judge offered, raising his glass. Then, the judge pulled the coroner closer and lowering his voice said, "Are you as glad as I am, Mr. Coroner, that the Valstad Act only prohibits the sale and distribution of alcohol, while allowing for the drinking of alcohol purchased before the 18th Amendment went into effect?"

"Yes, indeed, your honor," Traynor replied.

At the time, most of these stuff-shirted men just seemed rich and important to me. But in five short months, I would think back on this night and the conversations I overheard as having a role in what would become Lake Bluff's biggest scandal.

"People thought I was plum crazy at that meeting of The Onwentsia Club's board, when I suggested that no board member be allowed into that clubhouse without contributing at least two cases of liquor from his private stock," the judge said, again wiping his forehead. "I'm pretty sure that anybody who has set foot in the club since has begun to see the method to my madness."

Manfred Traynor smiled and nodded. "And when one of those penguins with the drinks returns with a refill, I'd be happy to drink to both your method and your madness, Your Honor."

Mr. Durand spoke up again after a prolonged silence. "I can assure you, Judge, that you and the club will never have to worry about running out of high quality beverages, no matter how long this 18th Amendment hangs around."

I looked around the library and realized that I was the only kid in the room. I made my way out toward the patio, still catching snippets of the judge's conversation.

"Now, Doc, do tell me, how is that jury of yours shaping up?" the judge asked.

Considering the question for a moment, the coroner glanced up at the ornate, high ceiling. "Pretty well, Judge. We've pulled in an electrical contractor from Lake Forest. One of our other recent recruits has his own filling station, also in Lake Forest. And our newest addition is a a plumbing contractor, who recently did all the updates over at the Lake Bluff Village Hall."

"Yes, that's good. Very good. As I've said before, Manfred, it's always beneficial to have local businessmen on a board or a jury like yours." He cleared his throat and lowered his voice again. "Their favors are easily repaid," the judge winked.

Dr. Traynor nodded and sipped his drink.

"Griffin!" a familiar voice startled me from behind. It was the authoritative and scolding voice of LBO.

"Oh, hello, Miss Arbuckle. Have you seen Ernie Van Es or Homer Haskell? I was with them, but they disappeared." I looked around as if searching for them.

"I'm sure they did disappear, just as you should have when you accidentally entered this particular room," she said. "This section of the house is clearly not for children, I can assure you," she said, waving angrily at the smoke all around us.

"Jessie! Look everyone! LBO's chief matron is among us!" I heard the judge say.

"Jessie!" one of the women on the patio yelled.

"Miss Arbuckle, we are so fortunate to have you and your youngsters here!" the County Coroner added.

Miss Arbuckle was clearly uncomfortable with the attention but tried to smile and nod to her admirers. I took the opportunity to slip through the tall crowd, out to the patio, and back around to the main entryway, in search of some of the Wads boys.

"Griff! Griff! Get a load of this!" It was Homer, and he was pointing inside a doorway that I couldn't quite see into yet. Once I could, I saw a woman whose face, hair, arms, and legs were all painted silver with sparkles. She was wearing an extra-large gingham jacket with dozens of pockets all over it. The younger kids were taking turns walking up to her and reaching in whichever pocket they selected and pulling out prizes.

"You want a turn, Griff?" Bobby asked.

"No thanks. I'm going to see if I can find Betty." I said. "Hey, where's Artie? I haven't seen him since we got here."

"That's 'cause he's not here. He's locked up back in solitary at the penitentiary."

"What?"

"Didn't you hear?" Bobby said, narrowing his eyes and holding both palms up. "Turns out he was peeing in Johnny's and several other kids' beds in the middle of the night. Wanted to make it look like he wasn't the only kid who still wet his bed." I immediately recalled the Saturday night in May when I'd seen Artie sneaking from Johnny's cubicle back to his own.

Bobby continued. "Miss Harvey caught him in the act, with his fire hose in his hands, if you know what I mean."

"Jeez," I uttered, unsure what else to say.

Leaving the small room, I proceeded up the spiral staircase and followed the squeaky laughter of girls' voices into a sparsely-furnished den of sorts. The walls of the room were covered in candy, and three girls were blindfolded, feeling their way toward the candy-covered walls. When I got far enough into the room, I could see that one of them was Betty. I held my breath and smiled as I watched.

Some of the girls watching were trying to assist Betty and the other two girls. "Over there, to the right!" someone called.

"No! Not that way!" another yelled.

I realized that Betty still didn't know her left from her right, and neither did the girls trying to direct her. Somehow, Betty made it to the wall and felt around gently for candy. The taller, dark haired girl, who was also blindfolded, was sweeping her arms against the wall, getting as much candy as possible with every motion, while Betty gently took only a piece or two and started back to the center of the room, saying something. I moved toward her in hopes of making out her gentle words.

"Would someone else like a turn?" She had half removed her blindfold, so only one eye remained covered, and smiled broadly. One of the mothers in a ball gown and tiara came to her aid and took the blindfold to give it to another girl. Betty adjusted to the light and, after rubbing her eyes, saw me.

"Griffy! You're here! Did you see the candy?" She held out her two hands with three small pieces of candy in them.

"Yes! Yes! I watched you, Betty! You were great! I'm so proud of you!" She immediately offered me one of the pieces of candy.

"Here, Griffy! For you!"

"Oh, no. No thank you, sis. That candy is for you!" I said, gently tousling her hair. "Would you like to come see the rest of this palace with me?"

She grabbed my arm. "Yes! Right now!"

There was a juggler at the top of the stairs, and a string quartet had begun playing on a small stage just off of the grand foyer. It seemed as though all of the other rooms had emptied into this theater of sorts in the time that I'd been upstairs. And as we walked down the turning staircase, the music stopped abruptly, and Mr. Cook was on the stage calling for everyone's attention.

"Mrs. Cook and I want to thank all of you for coming to this very special event. We are so thrilled to be a part of this effort to support one of Lake Bluff's most precious treasures. You know, my family has lived in this house going all the way back to when LBO was known as the Methodist-Deaconess Orphanage in 1894. We've seen the campus grow from one building to five and so many wonderful children pass through the incredible facility." Mr. Cook paused and looked around the room. "Before we bring up Miss Jessie Arbuckle—the reason we are all here tonight—it is my distinct pleasure to introduce, all the way from Milan, Italy, a now world-famous Opera star, Lake Bluff's own—not to mention Ethel's and my daughter—Marion Claire!"

There was an eruption of applause, as the woman in the red beaded dress, who had greeted us at the front door, flowed onto the stage. Men whistled and women hooted. Miss Claire blushed and nodded gracefully to her adoring, hometown crowd.

"Thank you. Thank you all so much." She waited for the raucous cheering to die down. "It is so grand to be home. As Daddy alluded to, I have been touring in Europe these last several months, singing in some famous, historic halls. But singing here tonight is truly special for me, for it means that I have a chance to contribute to a cause I believe in with all my heart. Our orphanage has served children right here in Lake Bluff for over 30 years. I had schoolmates and friends from LBO, and I know many of you did too." She paused and looked around the room. Her eyes seemed to linger on Betty and me. "The children we have here tonight came to Lake Bluff from..." she paused in search of the right word. "...disadvantaged backgrounds. But thanks to people like Miss Jessie Arbuckle and generous folks like you, these children have every reason to be hopeful. And speaking of hope, I would like to dedicate one of the most hopeful songs I have ever sung to the children of the Lake Bluff Orphanage and to all of you good people who support it. It comes from Puccini's opera Madama Butterfly and is called 'Un Bel Di,' 'One Fine Day.'"

She nodded to the violinist and the quartet began. I'd never heard an opera singer before, except maybe one time on the rumpus room radio. Her voice was like a soaring bird. My body was in the Cook ballroom, but she took my mind somewhere else—up into the sky or on a beautiful mountain peak. She was singing in another language, Italian someone said. Yet I felt like I understood what she was saying without recognizing a single word.

I don't know how long the song lasted. I just know that Betty never moved a muscle. She stood holding my hand, completely transfixed by the beauty of Miss Claire and her voice. When she finished, there was a brief period of absolute silence, like the whole crowd was waiting to exhale. Then the room exploded. Hands clapped, feet stomped, voices shouted, and the entire castle shook. Marion Claire blushed and must have curtsied a dozen times, but the crowd just wouldn't stop. She covered her mouth with her white-gloved hands, and I think she started to cry.

Her father Mr. Horace Cook joined her on the stage, beaming with pride. He wiped both eyes with his white handkerchief. "Honey, that was wonderful, just wonderful," he said.

Mr. Cook turned to the crowd, while holding his daughter's hand, and said, "I'm going to have Marion stay here, as we bring forward the Director of our Lake Bluff Orphanage, Miss Jessie Arbuckle. Jessie, where are you? We have a special gift for you and all your terrific kids."

Immediately, the patrons applauded, and the tall, austere woman ascended the steps to the stage. She was blushing. She was a good eight inches taller than Mr. Cook, and she hunched a bit, so as not to dwarf him.

"Look, Griffy! It's Miss Arbuckle!" Betty blurted, loud enough to be heard in our corner of the room.

"Yes," I whispered, picking her up.

Mr. Cook hugged Miss Arbuckle awkwardly and turned her to his side. Mrs. Cook also approached, smiling and holding an envelope. "Jessie," she said, we are so thrilled to have you running our beloved orphanage. If these children who are here tonight are any indication of what you and your staff are doing, all we can say is 'Well done!'"

There was resounding applause, punctuated with "Here, here!" and "Outstanding!"

Eventually, Ethel Cook gestured for quiet and continued. "We are so thrilled to present you with this token of community support, a check from The State Bank of Lake Forest for eleven-hundred dollars!" The cheering and applause was thunderous. Miss Arbuckle wrung her hands and shook her head. She seemed to be fighting back tears.

Just then, Marion Claire stepped forward, toward Miss Arbuckle, holding another envelope in her gloved hand. "And this, Miss Arbuckle, is an additional three-hundred-and-fifty dollars from my recent Italian tour." She gracefully handed Miss Arbuckle the envelope and slid back to her father's side. Applause erupted again.

"I don't know where to begin," Miss Arbuckle said, her voice fluttering. "On behalf of everyone at the Lake Bluff Orphanage, thank you. Thank you all so very, very much." As she continued, I felt a familiar hand on my shoulder. Miss Harvey was herding us—all the orphans—to the edge of the theater room. The four housemothers were quietly lining us up, so that we'd be ready when our cue came.

"...And as is our tradition," Miss Arbuckle continued, "we'd like to thank all of you by singing our Welcome Song, so you will always know that you are welcome at LBO." She nodded in our direction and smiled.

A chord was struck on the Cook family harpsichord, and we began.

We welcome you, we welcome you, we welcome you today
Oh how glad we are to have you with us while we may-hey
We welcome you, we welcome you, we'd like to have you know
That we are very glad to have you here at LBO.

The applause echoed around the large room and clear out into the foyer. Judges, doctors, bankers, businessmen, and even a coroner cheered for us that night. I'd never seen Miss Arbuckle so full of gratitude, joy, and even a touch of pride.

The Furnace Girl

MACKEY MEMORIAL BUILDING — LAKE BLUFF ORPHANAGE
Photo courtesy of the Lake Bluff History Museum

Chapter 23 — An Unexpected Visitor
Lake Bluff Orphanage — August 5, 1928

Nearly half of the kids at the orphanage had either immediate family or relatives in the greater Chicago area. Such relatives were welcome at LBO on alternate Sundays from after church until 5 p.m. Many of the visitors were not parents but designated relatives doing the best they could to approximate parents. Knox, for example, lost his father in the war, and his mother was in prison. So it was his grandmother on his mother's side who made it up to see Knox about once a month. She was a crotchety, old, battle axe whom Knox more tolerated than enjoyed. Johnny didn't have anyone to visit him, but he got to go down to see his blind and crippled aunt a couple of times a month. My roommate Danny had sporadic visits from his mother. She was a drunk who managed to show up each time she "found Jesus," only to disappear for three or four months whenever she lost him again. When Danny's mother did turn up, she was always nice to me and even took me along to eat lunch with them once or twice down in Lake Forest.

Sunday visit days were the worst for those of us who never had any visitors. Betty and I were in that category for our first eight months at LBO. Aunt Rose had written us a half-dozen times, telling us that she was trying to come, but her extensive Sunday commitments at the First Methodist Church down in Chicago seemed always to be in the way. Betty went from asking about Mother several times a day during her first few weeks at the orphanage to only bringing her up when she saw all the other girls from her dormitory going off with their relatives during Sunday visits.

Acting on the advice of both Dick and Danny, I'd told Betty way back in January that I didn't think we'd ever be seeing our mother again. I agreed with Danny that it would probably be easier for both of us just to move on. I had no doubts that our mother had already moved on from us.

Speaking of Dick, I eventually figured out that the housemothers and Miss Arbuckle always cooked up something for Dick to do away from the orphanage on family visit days, so he wouldn't have to watch all these parents and relatives spend the afternoon with their kids, while his own father sat on a couch in his own house less than three blocks away. Dick would go swimming, go to the movies, or even get to ride the train down to Chicago.

It was Sunday, August 5, at 1:15 p.m., a non-visit Sunday a full nine months after I'd arrived at LBO, when Artie came running up the Wads stairs at full tilt, completely out of breath, to tell me I had a visitor.

Wheezing and doubled over, he tried to speak. "Griff…Griff…your mother's here."

"What?" I asked in total shock. I rushed to the window and looked out. The campus was empty. It wasn't even a visit Sunday. Artie worked over at Mackey, sweeping, mopping, and cleaning up. That is where he'd run from.

Artie, still out of breath, resumed his report. "This lady…in a dress…comes in…" He was still gasping for air. "She smelled like smoke…and she tells Arbuckle that she's your mother and she wants to see you." I just shook my head and sat down on my bed.

"Miss Arbuckle tells her it's not a visitation day and that she should'a looked at the schedule." Artie paused to take in some much needed air before continuing. "Your mother didn't like that one bit, but Miss Arbuckle kept going right at her. You know how she always tilts her head down when she gets aggravated and then glares over the top of her spectacles? Well that's what she did to your mother. Then she goes, 'If you had read or responded to any of our correspondences of the last eight months, you'd have seen our regular visitation schedule several times.' She was being real sarcastic and stuff." I could only imagine.

"Your mother was practically breathing fire," Artie reported. "She started being all demanding, which I've never seen anybody do to Miss Arbuckle before. Your mother says, 'I've come a great distance, and I demand to be taken to my son immediately.' Your mother's nose was sweating and her hands were clenching her white purse real tight.

"So Miss Arbuckle sits down and starts explaining the whole visitation policy all over again, like she's talking to some little kid. She says parents have to sign up and call ahead and all, and how she and the other housemothers have to make all kinds of arrangements and stuff. But your mother, she just stood there with her arms crossed and just kept demanding to see you." Artie shook his head before continuing. "Then your mother demands to see the supervisor! But Miss Arbuckle is the supervisor, and that's what she said, kind'a smiling when she said it."

Artie's tale was interrupted when Miss Harvey came into my partition looking both somber and nervous. "Griff," she said, working her hands together like she had a bar of soap inside them, "you are wanted over at Mackey. Miss Arbuckle says...you have a visitor."

"Oh. Thanks, Miss Harvey. I'm just going to change and clean up real quick, and then I'll head right over."

"I think that would be fine, Griff." She glanced at Artie. "Just don't dawdle, OK?" I nodded and she left. Then I looked at Artie and nodded for him to continue.

"Then things got silent and tense for a long time. Your mother got all flustered and started looking around the Mackey foyer. She pulled out a cigarette, and Miss Arbuckle tells her there's no smoking here. Your mother chucked the cigarette down, right on the floor, and turned her back on Miss Arbuckle.

"So then Arbuckle asks what your mother's business is, and your mother didn't like that one bit. 'I can't imagine, how that could be any of your concern, Miss Arbuckle,' your mother says, real snippy like. Then she starts going off about how parents who come to visit their children shouldn't have to tell anyone 'the nature of their business with their own children.'" Here Artie paused a long, long time. He looked at me, like he was worried how I might take the next part of the story. I widened my eyes and held up both hands, urging him to continue.

"Miss Arbuckle got real close to your mother's face and started talking real slow, emphasizing every word, every syllable. She said, 'When a mother drops her children off in such a hurry...lying to them...and then goes off for eight months without replying to our posts or paying her portion of either child's bill, we have every right to inquire as to the nature of her business.'" Artie paused again and started rubbing his hands together nervously. Without looking at me, he said, "I don't think you're gonna like this next part at all, Griff." He was shaking his head, still looking down. "But your mother said...she was...she was gettin' married...and she wanted to tell you that herself." Artie looked up at me tentatively, gauging my reaction. Truthfully, I don't think I had much of one. Nothing really surprised me anymore where my mother was concerned. I just shook my head and looked down at the floor.

"Then Arbuckle was just asking her how this 'new arrangement' was going to affect making payments and stuff. But your mother wouldn't get into that. She just kept demanding that Arbuckle go and get you because she didn't have all day. That's when I ran over here, Griff." Artie looked down at the floor, and neither of us said anything for a while.

I got up, pulled on a nicer shirt, patted Artie on the shoulder, and said, "Thanks, pal."

When I got over to the main door of Mackey, Miss Arbuckle was there, waiting outside for me. She gave me a gentle smile, and I looked down at the ground, stopping next to her. She put a hand on my shoulder and said, "I'll be here in my office and will come right out the moment you need anything, you hear?"

I nodded. "Thanks, ma'am," I said. "I'll be all right," I added, with no idea whether I would be. We entered the front door of Mackey Memorial together, and the foyer was filled with light. The August sun was streaming in, and I couldn't really see my mother, just her silhouette. I took several tentative steps toward her dark shape and stopped, but Miss Arbuckle walked right past my mother and me, saying, "I'll be in my office if there is anything that either of you need." She glanced back at me, nodding reassuringly, crossed behind her desk, and disappeared into her office. I noticed that she kept her door open.

Neither my mother nor I moved. She seemed shorter than I remembered and wore a floral skirt that came just below her calves. Her white shoes were shiny and pointed. Her hair was fancier than I remembered it, still brown but longer and pulled up in a bun, held together by a fancy, pearly pin. She clutched that white purse, but I had nothing to do with my hands, so I quickly stuffed them both into my pockets and looked out the window.

"What do you want?" I asked, without even looking at her.

"I want to see you. I miss you, son," she replied. She sounded so fake. She took two hesitant steps toward me, and I turned full on to face her. An uncomfortable silence descended. She glanced back at the chairs. "Come and sit with me, Griff." She turned to head to the chairs, and I watched her without following. As she sat, I think she noticed that I hadn't moved. "Griff...please. Don't make this harder than it already is."

With my hands still in my pockets, I looked straight down at my feet and shuffled reluctantly toward the empty chair. I sat without freeing my hands, slouched, and stared out at the playground. Four girls from Judson and two more from Swift were playing. Betty was often out there on sunny Sunday afternoons, but, thankfully, not today.

"How are you, son? Are they treating you well here?"

"Just tell me what you want!" I demanded.

"You are not to take that tone with me, young man! Maybe they let you talk that way around here, but I am your mother, and you are not to speak that way to me." I bit down on my lip and shook my head disdainfully. I heard her let out a frustrated breath.

"I don't want to speak to you at all," I said. "So if you could do the speaking and we could get this over with..." I stopped and gave her an impatient look.

My mother was silent, wringing her hands over and over. "Ok," she tried to proceed. "I'm here because I have some very good news." She looked at me hopefully, but got no reaction. She smiled as best she could and started to reach toward my knee but drew her hand back, wisely. "I've met a wonderful man, and we've decided...We're going to get married."

I stared blankly at my pathetic excuse for a mother. Turning back toward the window, I saw that four of the girls had gone. Two swings were still moving and twirling, as if their occupants had just left. I had no idea what my mother's news meant. "Don't you have to get divorced from Father before you can get married again?" I looked directly at her. She blushed.

Sighing and shaking her head, she replied, "Yes, you do, and yes, I did. You know what a troubled man your father is. That's why I had to get you and your sister out of there, Griff." She met my gaze with a pleading expression. "I have never once doubted that that was the exact right thing to do for us."

"For us?" I said. "For us? And what about dumping us here? What about telling us we were going to have a checkup and then running out the door without saying goodbye...without explaining...without telling us if we'd ever even see you again? Was that 'the exact right thing for us' too?" My face was burning up, and my fists clenched, making the muscles in my forearms contract and bulge.

My mother crossed her arms and looked away. "It was the hardest decision I've ever had to make." She wiped her eyes, but I certainly saw no tears. "I...I had no way to support you and Betty. No job, no money, no home. I had gotten to the point, the lowest of low points, where I had to admit that this place would be better and safer for you and Betty than any place I could have provided for you on my own." She paused and looked down at the floor. She closed her eyes. "It's the hardest and worst kind of decision that a mother could ever have to make." She paused, wiping her eyes and nose again. "When you have children of your own someday, I believe you will understand."

"When I have children of my own—especially if one of them is a five-year-old daughter—I'm pretty sure I'll remember her birthday and at least send a card if I'm not going to go visit her."

Helen Morgan blanched but didn't respond.

"April 13th, Mother. Does that date ring any bells? That's when your daughter was born. But you didn't even send a card." I shook my head and stood up to leave. "I'll tell her you said hi. It's pretty clear you won't be telling her yourself."

"You aren't being fair!" my mother said. "You have no idea what this has been like for me."

I wheeled toward her and raised my voice to a scream. "I'm not being fair? I'm not being fair? I'm twelve! Your daughter is five! You ran off and dumped us both here! And I'm not being fair?"

Miss Arbuckle burst out of her office and rushed toward us. My mother saw her approaching and stepped back from me.

"Miss Arbuckle, my mother is telling me that I haven't been fair. So I guess I'd better go back to my room now." I stomped over to the front door of Mackey Memorial, pushed it open, and took off down the steps and across the lawn toward Wads. I could feel my mother's eyes watching me, but I didn't look back.

Artie told me later what transpired after I left. He'd come back over from Wads and was in one of the back rooms of Mackey when he heard the yelling, but by the time he got up to the foyer, I was gone. The first thing he saw was my red-faced mother, adjusting her purse in her trembling hands, over and over again. Then, Artie said, my mother turned to Miss Arbuckle and said, "I'd like to see my daughter."

At that, Artie reported, "Miss Arbuckle removed her glasses and gave your mother a head shake like I had never seen before. Then she said, 'I'm afraid that will not be possible.'"

Artie remembers my mother's face "contorting as she screamed, 'She is my daughter! How dare you keep her from me!' Your mother's shoulders shook up and down. Then she said, 'This may be my last chance to see Betty for quite some time.' Your mother was begging, Griff. 'Please…Miss Arbuckle … please,' your mother kept saying. 'Just a few minutes with my Betty.'

"But Arbuckle said, 'No!' that she couldn't allow it 'under these circumstances.' She tried to tell your mother that Betty was doing fine, adjusting to this place…that she has friends and a routine and all. Then Miss Arbuckle put her hand on your mother's shoulder real gently. She said something about how 'an unexpected, emotional visit like you just had with your son, would not be in your daughter's best interests.'"

I don't remember exactly how I felt about Miss Arbuckle before Artie told me all that he did about the day of my mother's visit. But I know for a fact that I became Miss Arbuckle's number one fan after that August Sunday when Helen Morgan came to LBO.

"After this, your mother was sobbing uncontrollably and began to wail," Artie reported. I don't think I needed Artie to tell me that part, because I'm pretty sure I actually heard Mother from all the way over at Wads. Artie continued. "Miss Arbuckle guided your mother back toward her office. Then she said, 'Please, Helen, come back and sit down. I'll get you some water and we'll sort this out, all right?'

"Your mother didn't resist. She kept blowing her nose and wiping her eyes, as Miss Arbuckle led her into that old, oak office," Artie said. "She poured your mother a glass of water and offered her a fresh hanky too."

Several minutes passed in relative silence, as Artie remembered it, with only the muffled sounds of my mother's grief. "Eventually, Miss Arbuckle said something about some difficult questions that had to be talked about. She asked about your mother's wedding plans and stuff. Your mother said she'd already gotten married to this other guy and that they were moving to Nashville, Tennessee. Miss Arbuckle wanted to know if they'd be able to start paying for you and Betty, 'cause they owed a lot of money. She also said something about how your Aunt Rose was making small, partial payments as best she could, but nowhere near what was owed."

God bless Aunt Rose. The woman had next to nothing and was still making payments to ensure our well-being.

"Your mother said 'no' about making any payments. 'Not at first. My husband has two children who will be moving with us.'" Artie stopped. He knew that part was going to sting and it sure did. "Your mother said she hoped that they might be able to support you and Betty after a while." I remembered how Mother always used to say that everything she put us through was "just for a while."

Artie explained, "Miss Arbuckle started going over some forms she wanted your mother to sign, forms about 'relinquishing her parental rights.' She slid these papers toward your mother.

"Then your mother stood up real quick-like, Griff," Artie said. "She was shaking her head real hard, but couldn't even speak. Her face got all red again, and she covered it up with her handkerchief. But Miss Arbuckle just remained seated and reached across the table and filled your mother's water glass.

"Miss Arbuckle kept trying to explain these forms to your mother and how if she'd just sign them, it would help the chances of finding a home where you and Betty could stay together.

"Your mother stood and was crying and stuff, and she said, 'How could I ever agree to sign away my motherhood?'

"That's when Arbuckle explained that you only had another year or so here, Griff, and how you might get sent down to Glenwood

Military Academy, where Betty could never go. She kept saying that you wouldn't be allowed to stay here 'under any circumstances.' She handed your mother the glass of water and the papers again, saying, 'With your signature, we can begin now, seeking a foster placement where the two children might even be able to stay together.' She started telling your mother how great a big brother you are, Griff, and how good you treat Betty and stuff. Miss Arbuckle kept repeating that 'this really is the best course of action, Mrs. Morgan, it truly is.'

"Your mother was real flustered and pushed the papers back across the desk without signing them. Then she started to leave, and Miss Arbuckle followed her out. Then your mother told her to, 'Please relay to Griff that my husband and I will be moving south to Tennessee. Tell him that it's a wonderful new job for us, simply too good to pass up.' Then your mother nodded kind'a awkwardly and began to leave.

"Miss Arbuckle followed her out and asked, 'What about Betty?' But your mother kept walking across the marble floor. Finally, she stopped and, without turning around, said, 'I suppose I'll leave that for you to sort out.' And that was it," Artie said. "She was gone."

"Jesus, Griff...I don't know what to say," the detective said. "You want to take a break or something?"

"No, no. I'm all right," I said. Sometimes it felt like I was talking about somebody else's life. "I think I'd rather press on, if that's OK with you." The detective nodded solemnly without saying anything.

I would never see my mother again and neither would Betty. But I've sure thought about her from time to time. When my one and only child, Artie, was born in 1947, I wondered where she was, if she was even alive, and if she'd care to know that she had a grandson. Part of me has always held her responsible for what Lily and I had to see that October night in 1928. If she hadn't dropped us off at LBO, I never would have had to see what I saw.

I suppose, though, that the passage of time, becoming a father, and doing the kind of reporting I've done over the years has softened my heart a bit where Helen Morgan is concerned. My mother, like many single mothers, was faced with some horrible choices in this life, and I'd like to think that she did the best she could. I want to believe that, anyway. But my mother's choices and actions have always haunted me more for Betty's sake than for my own. None of what our mother did to us ever made a lick of sense to Betty, and unlike me, Betty wouldn't live long enough for her heart to soften toward our mother.

LAKE BLUFF BEACH PIER
Photo courtesy of the Lake Bluff History Museum

Chapter 24 — A Day at the Beach
Lake Bluff Orphanage — August 11, 1928

The mid-August humidity sat upon Chicago's North Shore like an overweight bully. Those of us who lived at LBO had only one defense against it: heading out to the east end of Center to Sunrise Park and down the 150-foot, steep ravine path to the beach. Even on the hottest of summer days, the Lake Michigan water temperature rarely climbed above 67, making it the perfect place to cool off.

The problem for us was we couldn't just run down for a swim any time we wanted. We had to wait for Miss Arbuckle and the other adults in our orphanage community to schedule a swim. Only then, and under the strict supervision of at least two adults, would we be allowed to wade and frolic down in the Village Park in Lake Michigan.

Saturday, August 11 was just such a day. Miss Arbuckle called Roderick Stavenhagen, a seminary student from Garrett Biblical Institute, who was more than happy to take a group of us swimming.

He and his sister Olive, a part-time caseworker at the orphanage, were loved by all the children at LBO, and Miss Arbuckle had been looking for a way to reward us all for our hard work around the sweltering orphanage grounds in the past couple of weeks. So she announced the outing at Saturday breakfast, with this particular invitation being limited to those of us eleven and up, who had proven our competence in swimming. Given the 89-degree temperature on this particular August day, I had never been happier to have my YMCA swimming certification, earned back in January and February with Perry Foster. After an eruption of whistles and whoops, an unusually tolerant Miss Arbuckle asked for a show of hands to determine how many would be going.

"This is going to be berries!" Knox said, rubbing his stubby hands together.

"I was drowning in my own sweat last night," added Billy. "I'm stayin' in the lake 'til dinner!"

"You comin', Dick?" Dennis asked Dick Moley. "It's a swell day for a swim."

"Not this time, I'm afraid," Dick replied, stretching his long arms above his athletic frame as he yawned. "Football practice. Season starts in less than a month. Plus I'll be moving out in a couple days. Got a lot to do."

"Didn't I tell you guys that All-Star Mr. Everything Dick Moley would move in with one of the varsity coaches once he aged out of this place?" Dennis said, shaking his head. We'd all heard of Dick's good fortune, but it still stung to hear it again.

There was no doubt that I wanted to go swimming, but I knew from the announcement that Betty wouldn't be going. I'd enjoyed spending more and more chunks of time with her on Saturday afternoons. But I just couldn't miss this chance to cool off and get out of this baking, hot prison. I played with the last spoonful of gruel and turned toward Artie. "You coming, sport?"

"Aww, I don't know," he said. "How long you think they'll let us swim for?"

"Don't know. An hour or so, I guess." I knew how I could get Artie to come, so I added, "You don't wanna miss seeing Olive Stavenhagen in that red suit of hers, do ya?"

The often-dour Artie grinned and nodded. "Naw, I suppose I don't, not that hotsy-totsy."

Miss Arbuckle stood again and a hush descended throughout the Hobbs Dining Hall. "Swimmers will report to the front steps of Mackey Memorial at 12:30 in proper attire and check in with the Stavenhagens. Towels will be provided down at the park by Mr. Spader." She looked around the entire dining hall before continuing. "It is absolutely necessary for all swimmers to be cautious, communicative, and to follow all the usual water safety procedures. No one will swim alone or in a manner separate from the chaperones. After your tables are cleared, you are dismissed."

I was on clean-up duty with Dick. We quickly filled the wooden crates with plates, glasses, and silverware. Then Dick led the way into Miss Conkle's kitchen, where Johnny and Bobby were washing dishes unenthusiastically.

"Nobody'll be more ready for that dip than me!" Johnny declared. "Berries! I'll be first in line at 12:30."

"First to see Olive Stavenhagen in her swimsuit, ya mean," Bobby snickered.

"Enough of the shenanigans, boys. We've got dishes to wash!" came the ornery voice of Miss Conkle from the far end of the kitchen. "The only swimming you two will do will be with my mop and bucket if you don't get to work!"

Dick smirked, as he pushed back out through the swinging door. I was a single step behind him.

Just after noon, I took Artie down to the front yard of Mackey with one ball glove I'd borrowed from my roommate Danny, plus my own glove and ball I'd gotten from the Freidles. Ever since the snowball fight with David Gadd and his gang, I'd been trying to teach Artie to throw with his good hand. We had a lot of ball games at the school yard and down by Artesian Park, and I noticed Artie would never play. I thought if I could help him throw and catch— even with his bad arm—maybe he'd join in.

When I first started playing catch with Artie, his throwing motion was awkward but adequate, provided I didn't get any farther than about twenty feet from him. The problem was that he couldn't catch. Artie couldn't work or maneuver the glove with his bad arm at all. He couldn't even get it on his badly bent left hand. I'd grown tired of just rolling the ball back to him all the time after he'd thrown to me, so I concocted a way he could hold the closed glove under his left armpit while he threw and then stuff his right hand in the glove before I threw back to him. It was a clunky maneuver for him, and people passing by, who weren't aware of Artie's disability, might have thought it pretty odd. But for those of us who knew Artie and all he'd been through, we just wanted him to have a chance to participate in something athletic with us. As for Artie himself, he wasn't exactly approaching this day's catch with enthusiasm. He was spared by the arrival of the Stavenhagens and the swimming crew at about 12:20.

Artie gladly volunteered to run the gloves and ball back up to my bed, and by the time he returned, there were twenty-three orphans, including the two of us, sitting in the grass in front of the Mackey Memorial steps: thirteen boys and ten girls. We'd all reported into the tall, athletically built Roderick Stavenhagen, who held a clipboard and a pencil, duly recording the name of each of us in his two columns, one for girls and one for boys. Roderick had a nickname for all us boys. Johnny was "Tweedle-Dee," the O'Neil twins were "Bilbo" and "Bobsey," and for some reason I never figured out, he called me "Ferg." But he recorded all our real names on his clipboard. The girls were spared his inane puns. Miss Arbuckle would never tolerate such levity, especially on a swimming trip.

Roderick and his sister Olive were both thick-haired brunettes. Their hair was so shiny, that it glistened in the noonday sun. Roderick had wide-set swimmer's shoulders, though there was something bookish about him that almost canceled out his apparent athleticism.

At 12:30 sharp the group lined up in pairs to walk the half mile east down Scranton, where we would then cut a block over to Center, until we came to Sunrise Park and the dirt path that descended through the ravine to the beach. The August sun was directly overhead as our journey began, and the dirt road and path baked beneath it.

As our group neared the halfway point, Jim Spader sputtered by in the brown orphanage truck, loaded with towels. I chuckled at the listing vehicle. It didn't matter what was in that old thing; it rattled like a string of tin cans and leaned so far to the right, I never could quite understand what kept it from tipping all the way over. I wondered how many times I'd ridden in the back of that thing over to Crab Tree Farm in the nine months I'd been at LBO.

"It's gonna feel swell," Artie said, without looking at me. "The water, I mean."

The closer we got to the lake, the larger and more majestic the homes became. The lawns opened up like city parks, and the houses seemed two and three times as far from the sidewalk. Many of these homes were ones I'd looked at and shown Lily during my late night walks.

"Looky over there!" Artie yelled, pointing across the street. A black and white mongrel of a dog approached our traveling group with a stick in his bared teeth.

"I think he's a stray," one of the girls surmised from up ahead of us. But I knew better.

"Nah, it's Bandit!" I said.

"Bandit?" Artie snickered. "What kind'a name is that?"

"I've seen him rifling through people's garbage," I replied. "He always seems to come out of the barrel having stolen something. Plus he's got those markings on his face that look like a robber's mask."

"I've seen him around here a bunch of times too," Johnny added in his know-it-all tone. "Watch this!" He approached the dog, lowering his body, and grabbed the stick in a single motion. He then chucked it two driveways down Center, and the dog took off after it in a dead run. Most of the orphans kept walking east, but Johnny, Artie, and I hung back, as the dog brought the stick to Johnny in mere seconds.

"Atta boy!" Johnny said. "Now drop it, boy. Drop it!" The dog dropped the stick, and Artie reached for it.

"Let me have a try," Artie said, waving the stick in front of Bandit's nose, while simultaneously petting the back of his neck with his crippled arm. Then he hurled the stick to the east, alongside the walkers. As the stick struck the street, Olive Stavenhagen saw us lagging behind and hustled back toward us.

"Let's let the dog be, boys. We've got some swimming to do," Olive said.

Johnny replied without missing a beat, "But this dog loves to swim!"

"Yeah! Can Bandit come, Miss Olive?" I asked. "He's a swell dog."

Olive looked at the dog who had returned with the stick. Seeing no collar, she said, "That fella looks like a stray to me. We'd best leave him be."

"But maybe he needs a home," Artie pleaded. "Can't Bandit just come to the beach with us?"

The dog's ears perked up, as if he knew he was being talked about. "No more stick-tossing. We'll leave the dog to his own devices. Let's catch up to the others," Olive declared, settling the matter.

The last couple houses before the ravine trail were massive, stone structures. They stood atop a hundred and fifty foot cliff. Each home was the size of the Wads dormitory or the Mackey Memorial building. The last one we passed was the Cook home, where we'd been for the fundraising party back in June. No matter how many times we saw places like this, I don't think any of us could even conceive of a family living in one of these palaces.

"Who in the heck would live in a mansion like this?" Billy asked.

"I can't figure it," Dennis replied. "Somebody with a lot of money and a lot of kids."

"What I can't figure is why anybody would choose not to come swimming on a day like this," I replied. "It's hotter than Miss Conkle's oven out here."

Our group began the gradual descent at the end of Center, angling down to the lakeshore. The sounds of splashing and voices drifted up through the tree-lined path, as twenty-three excited orphans and our two chaperones quickened the pace.

As the terrain leveled off and the water was a mere twenty feet away, Olive tooted on her whistle—one of Miss Arbuckle's, no doubt—and gathered the group around her.

"We're here to have fun and enjoy this amazing beach. But we aren't the only people here, so we must be courteous, well behaved, and, most of all, safe. The girls need to stick with me and never separate from your partner. The boys should stay with Roderick and with your partners as well. If you hear my whistle, no matter where you are, you must come into shore and to this very spot at once, right in front of this gnarled tree." She pointed behind us to a single, wind-bent willow. "We are to be back at the orphanage by 2:30, so we'll need to be out of the water by 2:10."

Jim Spader had unloaded the towels and stacked them just to the right of the tree.

"Who's ready for a swim?" Roderick asked with a clap, and every boy headed for the water, two-by-two, with me and my partner Billy in the lead. Only Danny was spared having a partner, given our odd number and his well-known status as a strong swimmer. We angled toward the pier to our left. Olive waited for the boys to clear the area and removed her dark-colored shirt. She smiled at the girls, and they followed her into the lapping water.

The Lake Bluff Village Beach was crowded, and more and more families came down the hill as the afternoon temperature climbed. Roderick and the thirteen of us pasty-skinned boys in our black, stretchy swim trunks waded out alongside the pier. Many of us had our arms held high above our heads, while others splashed joyfully. Olive led the string of girls in a game of follow-the-leader, snaking in and out the other swimmers, staying in the shallows.

But we boys moved ever deeper, and Roderick was in his element. He loved kids, and it radiated off him. Several rambunctious town kids were hurling themselves off the pier, landing quite close to us. Roderick steered us safely away, farther from the pier. Billy was leading the rest of us in a Navy call-and-response marching chant that a visitor from the Great Lakes Naval base had taught us earlier that spring. Johnny could barely contain himself, as he played the role of drill sergeant to perfection.

I don't know but I've been told—
    I don't know but I've been told
Better to die than wind up old—
    Better to die than wind up old
I can ramble I can roam—
    I can ramble I can roam
But nowhere I've been compares to home—
    Nowhere I've been compares to home.

We were yanked out of our chant, as a thundering herd of a dozen or so teenage boys ran from the shore out onto the pier, stripping off their shirts as they ran. They screamed like Indians on the warpath, turning the heads of every bather and swimmer across the entire beach. Chasing behind them was Bandit, the stray dog we'd played fetch with on our way down Center Ave. In rapid succession, they threw themselves off the pier and made monstrous splashes and waves for a good twenty feet. They landed far closer to us than Roderick was comfortable with, and their splashes created a sort of deluge around us, separating many of our pairings.

$$\approx$$

At 2:05, the shrill sound of Olive's whistle caught everyone's ears. "Boys," Roderick called, "it's time to head in."

"Last one to the tree is a rotten egg!" Billy said, and the race was on.

I got the early lead, but Johnny tackled me from behind, dunking me in the water.

"Enough, now, you rascals! Let's get to shore," Roderick prodded, smiling at the pack of us.

Olive Stavenhagen had already lined her ten girls up. They were wrapped in the identical white towels from LBO. Billy muttered under his breath to me, "Shucks. I told you we should'a come back before the whistle, before Olive had the chance to towel up." I elbowed him in the ribs and laughed.

Roderick pulled his clipboard from the base of the tree and checked off all ten of the girls. "Ok, boys, let's make sure everybody's here before we make our ascent back up to Sunrise Park." He wiped the wetness from his forehead and bangs with the back of his left hand and began to work down the list alphabetically. "Dee I see, yes. Morgan, yes. O'Neil, O'Neil, yes and yes. Spellman …" There was a pause. "Artie?" Roderick looked across the group and leaned around but couldn't see Artie. We looked at each other and then behind us. We had our backs to the lake.

"Boys," Olive said with a forced calm, "When did you last see Artie?"

"He was right between Griff and me when those guys were dive bombing off the pier," Billy said.

"And who was Artie's buddy?" Olive asked. There was an edge to her voice.

No one said a thing. All of us boys knew, and Johnny looked straight down at the ground. Olive nodded to the rest of us once she understood, took a deep breath, and began to speak.

"Johnny…can you remember when you last saw Artie and where exactly you were?"

"Yeah. I saw him when we were doing that marching song," Johnny said.

I jumped in. "Yeah. We were right over there, halfway out the pier," I said, pointing.

I'd turned completely around, away from the group, to scan the water. Roderick ran to the lifeguard station, and Olive blew her whistle one time sharply.

"I need all of you over here at the tree sitting down! Now!" Olive commanded, shedding her towel.

A different, much louder whistle came from the direction of the pier. Then a deep voice yelled through the megaphone. "Everyone out of the water now! We need the entire swimming area cleared on the double!"

"Artie? Artie?" Roderick's voice rang out, as he ran out onto the pier.

Again and again came the name, shouted, screamed, and repeated.

"Artie! Artie!" It was a sickening sound, and the entire beach knew exactly what it meant.

Olive was in the water now. A group of men had joined her, and one of them was trying to organize the others into a human chain.

"Griff, no!" shouted one of the girls, as I tore into the water. Johnny joined me almost immediately. "We'll help you find him," I said. "We're not leaving. Artie's here. He's gotta be here!"

Olive looked back over her shoulder from her position in the human chain. Back on the shore, parents had huddled close to their children. Out on the pier, some of the boys, who had caused all the commotion earlier, were sitting with their legs hanging over the edge. Other clumps of people were standing out toward the end of the pier, struggling to see down through the murky water.

Johnny and I had made our way out to Roderick and were wading beside him, looking frantically. Several fathers had joined us.

"Here! He's over here!" The shout came from one of the boys up on the pier. He was pointing about fifteen feet out from the end. Two of his friends ran out to where he was on the pier and covered their mouths. Roderick swam hard to the spot.

About four feet beneath the surface was a small, pale, and lifeless body, face down. His arms and legs were extended. Roderick plunged beneath the body and brought it to the surface. The lifeguard helped him tow Artie to shore. They lifted him and turned him onto his back, setting him gently on the sandy beach. The lifeguard told Roderick to run for help and then began his methodical efforts to resuscitate the lifeless form of Artie Spellman.

I watched Roderick take the hill path at a dead run and took about four hard steps to catch him, but then I stopped. I just stopped and turned back to the lifeguard. Everything got still, and I just seemed to freeze in that spot. I wasn't cold, but I hugged myself and started to cry.

"C'mon, Artie! C'mon! Breathe, boy! Breathe!" Johnny said, almost to himself.

Olive's whistle sounded, and she motioned to Johnny and me to come join the other 20 children from LBO. Johnny walked toward them with his head hanging down, making his way to the bent willow tree. But I shook my head and walked toward the lifeguard, who was pressing down hard on Artie's chest and blowing air into his mouth.

As I turned to scan the beach and shore, I saw frozen huddles of four, six, and eight, families and clusters of kids, wrapped in towels and watching the lifeguard, as he tried to bring my friend back. I looked up the hill toward Center, knowing it was a solid half-mile run to the police and fire station. Roderick Stavenhagen, the bookish seminarian, though he had an athletic build, was not much of an athlete. I prayed that God would give him winged feet just this once.

At the edge of the shore end of the pier stood Bandit, moving back and forth, agitated. He didn't seem to know what to do or where to go, only that something was wrong, terribly wrong.

Finally, the clanging of the fire engine bell was heard atop the hill, and soon the squad came running down the dirt path that no fire engine could descend. As the two men reached the lifeguard and checked Artie's vital signs, I saw what everyone on that beach saw: the shaking head of the officer. The lifeguard, exhausted and ruined, collapsed on his knees and began to pound the sand with both fists. I glanced back toward the willow tree for a moment and locked eyes with Olive Stavenhagen for a second or two. But the next thing I knew, I was running. I hauled up that hill as fast as I'd ever run before.

"Griff!" I heard Olive call. "Griff, come back here! Now!" But it was in vain. I was gone, and only Bandit had darted up the path behind me.

A half an hour later, the Stavenhagens had returned twenty-one orphans to Miss Arbuckle. I'd arrived just minutes before with my stray dog, having run aimlessly through the entire village of Lake Bluff twice. When I finally collapsed in the foyer of Mackey Memorial, Miss Arbuckle had held me in her arms, trying desperately to get me to tell her what had happened, but all I could seem to say, between my tears and breathless sobs, was "Artie...It's Artie."

Miss Arbuckle had sent word to the housemothers, so they'd be ready to meet the returning swimmers on the lawn. Every child was hugged by all four of the housemothers, and every one of those women, except Jessie Arbuckle, wept.

On the wide, front lawn of the Mackey Memorial building, a huddle of sobbing children were asking questions without answers, when, slowly, from the east, the brown Henney from the Wenban's Funeral Home passed the Lake Bluff Orphanage. It was heading toward town on Scranton, moving more slowly than I'd ever seen a car go. There was no hurry to get the breathless, lifeless body of Artie Spellman to the funeral home. There were no parents to inform, no siblings, no extended family to tell; the Hammond Circus Train wreck of 1918 had seen to that. Artie was gone. He was just...gone.

The following day, after church and when lunch was not quite finished, I snuck out of the dining hall early, headed over to Wads, and up the stairs. I walked past my partition and over to Artie's. I paused before I went in and tried to remember the last moment I'd seen Artie's face. I think it was when we were marching behind Billy and Johnny, singing that blasted Navy chant. I remember looking behind me and seeing him with his damaged left arm tucked behind his side.

When I went around the partition opening, where I knew Artie's bed was, there was a boy lying on it. There were clothes in Artie's hanger and a suitcase under Artie's bed, though none of it was Artie's.

"Who are you?" I asked. He was a long, scrawny boy with a pock marked face and thick black hair.

"Who's asking?" he said, sitting up and crossing his arms.

"I'm Griff, Griff Morgan. This is…my friend's room. You're on his bed."

"It's my bed now," he said. "And you're in my partition, Griff Morgan. And right now you're interrupting my nap." He rolled away from me, and I turned to leave without saying another word.

But it wasn't the first time this sort of thing had happened. My own roommate Danny told me that I moved into his room less than a day after his previous roommate got fostered out. As Danny put it, "This place is, after all, an orphanage." But I would have appreciated a little more time to get used to Artie being gone. I think we all would have.

RESIDENCE OF SCOTT AND GRACE DURAND — CRAB TREE FARM
DN-0065430, Chicago Daily News negative collection, Chicago History Museum

Chapter 25 — Clearing the Way
Crab Tree Farm — September 22, 1928

I sat on the rough, wooden milking stool—the one Lily and I had carved our initials into—and reached my sweaty arms underneath the bloated udders of Chance, one of the more uncooperative cows. I had a vice grip hold on her udders and had to squeeze with all my might. Then I would watch and listen, as the chalky liquid pulsed into the shiny, silver bucket. Chance and I both would need a break once this particular bucket was filled. My hands were cramping up and her teats were inflamed. She let me rub some Bag Balm on her gently, and I kept some on my chafing hands as well.

When that bucket topped off, I backed away from Chance, who kicked so wildly with her back left leg, that it knocked my stool over. Spooked, I kept an eye on the riled up cow, backing away more by feel than sight. I grabbed the upended stool and set it down next to Lily, who sat milking a much gentler, slightly larger cow named Truth. I positioned myself so she could continue milking, and we could speak quietly, without being seen or heard by others.

"So are you going to help me or not?" I asked, looking at the broad black and white flank of Truth.

Lily kept her eyes on Truth's tender udders, let out an audible, resigned breath, and said, "You know I will." She released both hands from the udders, rubbed her palms on her pants, just above the knees, and turned to me. "I just want you to think through everything…and not just how not to get caught. Not getting caught is the easy part, Griff." She repositioned herself on the stool. I handed her the Bag Balm, and she gently massaged some onto Truth's udders. She leaned back into the side of Truth, and found her rhythm again, but Truth was not cooperating.

"Yeah. I know. But it's got to happen soon," I said, massaging my own sore hands, hyper extending each finger and cracking my knuckles. "Ever since Dick Moley and Danny Thompson left…and Artie…I can't think of LBO as any sort of home." It had been over a month since Dick moved into his new home with the Lake Forest High basketball coach and a full two months since Danny had left. He'd been fostered out to a disastrous situation that lasted two weeks, and from there, he'd been shipped out to the Glenwood Military School.

"I wish you lived here with us, Griff. Mrs. D. loves you, and my daddy goes on and on about what a great worker you are." Lily smiled as she grabbed the bucket handle and pulled it out from under Truth. "You're a natural-born farmer, if there ever was one."

I chuckled and turned away from her gaze. "This farm is the best part about living at LBO, that's for sure. You and your father have made it that way." I glanced at her empty bucket. "What's the matter with Truth?"

"Don't know. Think she's drying up. I'm gonna let Mrs. D. know later." Lily stood up and looked around the milk house to make sure we were alone. "Griff, there's something you gotta see." She picked up her stool and headed toward the rear door. Lily set her stool on the small, leaning stack of stools, and I followed suit with mine. She exited the milk house and angled left toward the guest cottage. The truck was not in the drive, so she must have known that her father was gone, but I had no idea where or for how long.

We kicked off our muddy boots and entered the Reddington cottage in our stocking feet. She led me straight to a closet, right off of her father's bedroom. Opening the door, she leaned down and removed a pile of towels and rags that seemed to be covering a wooden box.

"Look what I found," she said, stepping back. It was a small crate of whiskey. I recognized the crate immediately. I winced and shook my head.

Placing a hand on Lily's shoulder, I said, "So that's what those guys were doing, smuggling booze from that boat onto those milk trucks!" I said it more for her sake than for mine. I suspected this ever since finding that extra case down where the orchard meets the shore. But we hadn't spoken of it, and I wasn't sure she was ready to.

"Yep." She turned and looked at me, and I saw her teeth clench as she tilted her head down. I knew she was about to cry.

I hesitated, placed my hand on her wrist, and just said what I was thinking. "So...your father is...helping them?" I asked.

"Well, they needed somebody to help get their alcohol on and off this farm without Mrs. D. or anyone else finding out about it." She reached into the closet and started repositioning the rags, so her father wouldn't know the crate had been disturbed.

"Are you scared, I mean for your father?" I asked, trying to read Lily's face as to how far I should push. "Why is he helping these crooks, do you think?"

"I don't know what he's doing or why he's doing it," Lily said, closing the closet door and shaking her head. She crossed right in front of me, brushing against my hip and heading back out onto the back porch. "I just know that if he gets caught, we'll lose everything."

I pulled on my boots as fast as I could and hustled to catch up to Lily, who was already heading back over to the milk house.

In the noisy restlessness of the milk house, Lily changed the subject. "So when are you going to do this, go to Wilmette, I mean?"

"I know I want it to be on a Monday. I'll need at least two days when I don't usually see much of Betty anyway. I can't have her worrying about me. I'll get word to her that I'm sick and in the infirmary with something contagious. That'll be why she can't come see me." I set my milking stool down next to Lucky, and Lily leaned on a cedar post. "The trains run more regularly on weekdays than on the weekend, so I should be able to get down to Wilmette and back before she figures out that I'm gone."

The front door of the milk house swung open and the voice of Redd rang out. "Anybody home?"

"Over here, Daddy," Lily replied immediately, moving with her stool over between Medley and Sprite, the next two cows in the milking line. "Griff is here too."

"Hey, Mr. Reddington," I chimed in.

"How goes the milking today, farmhands?" Redd grabbed several ropes and harnesses off the wall as he moved toward the rear of the building.

"I think you better check on Truth, Daddy. She's not producing, and I can't tell why."

"Will do, hon. Hey, Griff, After you finish up with Lucky, I could use your help out by the truck."

"Sure thing," I replied, as the back door opened and shut with Redd's departure.

"I want to get down to Wilmette in the next two or three weeks." I stood up and turned to Lily. "It would be great if you could help me."

Without getting up from Medley, Lily replied, "Of course, I'll help." I nodded at her and hustled out the door after Redd.

Redd was beside his truck, reaching in through the slatted side panel, tying some ropes to the hooks on the inside of the truck bed as fast as he could. Seeing me jogging toward him, he said, "Pull these ropes back through the back gate and straighten them up all the way. I need to see how long they go."

I grabbed the two heavy, gritty ropes, each over two inches in diameter, and pulled them back away from the truck's rear. I was a good twenty feet back when the slack was all taken up. "How's this?" I asked.

"Perfect, Griff. Just perfect," he said, tying off the last of the knots up by the truck. "I've got to haul some fallen trees off the path back in the orchard, and I've got to get it all cleared out yet this afternoon."

"Mr. Reddington, I've got this assignment at school called 'Local Hero.' I'm supposed to write a report about a person from Lake Bluff who's doing a lot of good." I tightened up my belt and looked back at the milk house. "I was thinking about writing mine on Mrs. Durand, not just because she runs one of the grandest dairy farms in Illinois, but also because she's trying to take on the smugglers who want to ruin us with alcohol." I looked directly at Redd's face when I said it. "What's that group she's in? They protest alcohol and drinking and stuff." I craned my neck again, trying to catch a glimpse of Redd's reaction. There was none, not even a hesitation. He didn't even flinch.

"That would be the WCTU—The Women's Christian Temperance Union."

"Right, that's it," I said, though I'd known the answer before I asked the question.

"I'm sure Mrs. D. would be happy to talk to you about that, Griff." He nodded toward the Durand's house. "She's not only directly involved in the WCTU, but I believe she is the head of the local chapter." Redd removed his hat, tossing it in the bed of the truck, and started reeling in and coiling the first of the two ropes I'd stretched out for him as quickly as I'd ever seen anyone do it. "She's a big fan of yours, Griff. She'll help you with your project," he said, out of breath. Redd wiped his face with the dusty cloth that always hung from his back pocket and added, "I'd like to read that report myself when you finish it."

I coiled the second rope, working back toward the truck. "Great! Thanks, Mr. Redd."

"Hop in with me, and let's see if we can haul this fallen tree out of the way—pronto." Redd hopped into the driver's seat, and I ran around the back of the truck to the other side and yanked open the passenger door.

Redd drove right up the main orchard two-track, the very one that Lily and I used most every day. We drove right past the tree where we'd resurrected Lazarus and on up to the peak of the orchard, where the lake came into view. Redd went over the apex and began the bumpy descent down toward the spot where Lily and I had seen the two trucks and the boat back in May. I felt myself tense up and begin to hold my breath, just as Redd slowed the vehicle. We approached a fallen tree that blocked the path toward the water.

"Here's our project for the afternoon," Redd said, as he angled the truck off to the left of the path.

I jumped out of the passenger side and immediately felt the breeze off of Lake Michigan picking up. There were two to three-foot waves and just a touch of haze off the water. I looked down to the spot where the unloading of the booze had occurred, trying to see if there were tire tracks or any other indications of fairly regular use. From this elevation in the apple orchard, I could see that this huge oak had fallen from the extreme west edge of the orchard. It had fallen diagonally across the orchard and was blocking the path that led from the water up to the Blodgett entrance to the farm. I suddenly understood what the urgency was to get this particular part of the path cleared up. It was a Saturday, same as the night the delivery came through that Lily and I had witnessed. There was no way that crew could get their "milk" up the hill and to Blodgett with this tree in the way.

Neither Lily nor I had determined yet how frequently these late night deliveries were taking place. I'd had a hunch a while back that the conversation I'd heard between Redd and Mr. Durand was about their relationship with these smugglers, but now I knew for certain who was making sure the bootleggers way through Crab Tree Farm would always be clear.

I turned back toward the tree and noticed that it had already been sawed into three pieces of about twelve feet each. Redd pulled two saws out of the flat bed.

"I think we can drag these pieces behind the truck, but it will be a lot smoother if we cut the branches off first." He handed me a crosscut saw, handle first, before grabbing the other for himself. "The bottom section here has no branches, so we're all good on that one." He walked up the hill and to the west, away from the water. "But these two higher sections need to be trimmed up before we drag them out."

I followed Redd up to the top section of the fall. He had begun sawing limbs and branches off, and I did the same, but from the other side of the path. I was grateful for the breeze, as this late September day had an Indian summer feel to it. The temperature had been in the high 70s most of the day, and I'd been sweating way more than I expected, even in the shade of the milk house. I enjoyed the physical and rhythmic nature of sawing, and most of the limbs we were removing were only two to four inches in diameter. We worked swiftly and efficiently, mostly in silence.

Finishing the top section, we moved down to the middle of the fallen tree. The limbs were larger in this section, closer to six inches in diameter. I positioned myself with my back to Redd, so I could glance down to the sandy shoreline. I regretted not going down there to examine the ground and see how worn it was when we'd had the chance earlier in the week.

"Let's drag these limbs we've cut over there," Redd said, gesturing to the right of where the truck was parked. "Let's make sure they are parallel to the path and a good foot or two off of it."

I set my saw against one of the apple tree trunks and began to drag limbs to the area Redd had pointed out. In less than ten minutes, the limb pile was finished and sufficiently out of the way, and the two of us began the process of tying the first twelve-foot trunk section with the ropes we had secured to the flat bed. Redd was a wizard with knots and had the first and biggest section ready to haul in no time.

"Stay back here, Griff, and just be sure it's moving freely once I start going." Redd started toward the car door, when he stopped and turned. "Just give me a big wave if something goes wrong." He waved both hands over his head wildly. "Like this, 'cause you know how loud this old truck is. And if the log here is running smoothly, staying behind the truck and on the trail, just wait here. I'll take it down the hill, untie it, and come back for the next one."

"Ok," I nodded, backing away until I was about ten feet beyond the log. Redd dropped the truck into gear and started forward slowly. The last two feet of slack went out of the ropes and the log started dragging behind, steady and straight. As the Crab Tree Farm truck cleared the peak of the hill and began its descent toward the milk house, I turned and ran as fast as I could down to the beach, where nearly four months ago, we'd seen the boat and the two trucks. I slowed as I neared the water and bent down to where I remembered the trucks being. Sure enough, there were two faded sets of tire tracks for about twenty feet. Then up the hill, running away from the shore, they converged into one set, heading straight toward Blodgett Ave. The tracks up there were a bit deeper. Just off the edge of the tracks, I saw something shiny. I ran to it and saw that it was a license plate. It must have fallen off one of the fake milk trucks. I hid it in some brush beside a small oak, where I could show Lily later.

I took off again at a dead run, this time heading back up to where the two remaining logs were. I sat on one of them to catch my breath, just before the Crab Tree truck came back up the orchard trail, swung around in a tight arc to the left, and back up toward the twelve foot logs. Without hesitation or showing any fatigue, I jumped up into the flat bed, grabbed the two ropes and jumped them back down, walking them out to where Redd waited. But this time he wasn't alone. Mr. Durand was with him. He had fancy clothes on, a suit but no tie, and wore a cross expression on his face.

"Griff, I believe you know Mr. Durand?" Redd said.

"Yes, sir," I replied, nodding at Mr. Durand and removing my hat.

"There's no time for formalities here, Griffin," the proprietor said. "Redd here has a very urgent deadline to meet with these trees, and I came to remind him the importance of this particular job." He patted Redd's back a few times, and I noticed how hard his open hand struck Redd's back. Mr. Durand nodded at me and walked back around the truck and down the path to the farm house.

"Who uses this road or this part of the path?" I asked. "Besides you, I mean."

Redd took his hat off and looked out over the water, wiping his forehead with the back of the arm in which he held his hat. "Well, in the fall the pickers do. This time of year it's pretty much just us, Mrs. Durand and I, I reckon." He turned back toward me and cocked his head. "Why do you ask?"

"No reason. Just seen some tire tracks down near the water, but I've never seen you or Mrs. D. drive that far down."

"We'd best get the rest of this mess cleaned up," he said. Redd pulled the two ropes off the flatbed and tossed them back for me to straighten.

"I think I'll talk to Mrs. D. about my school assignment when we're all done here," I said.

"You do that, Griff. She'll be happy to help," Redd replied.

2226 The Station, Lake Bluff, Ill.

LAKE BLUFF TRAIN STATION
Photo courtesy of the Lake Bluff History Museum

Chapter 26 — Forgotten Things
The Lake Bluff Train Station — October 23, 1928

It was late afternoon on a Tuesday toward the end of October. I remember it being one of those brilliantly colorful days, when the leaves were all on fire. I'd walked straight from school over to the Village Hall to do some sweeping and other chores Charles Hitchcock had assigned to me. The reason I remember this particular day so clearly is that Miss Knaak was in the furnace room—during the day. I had never seen her anywhere near the Village Hall during regular working hours before, not with so many other people in the building too.

I remember Mr. Hitchcock being really uncomfortable about it.

He kept sending me out of the dingy little room to do all sorts of meaningless things elsewhere in the building. Hitchcock's office was a tiny space, with barely room for a make-shift desk and a single chair. The floor was mostly dirt, no matter how often I swept it. It was no place for a well-dressed lady like Miss Knaak.

It was clear he didn't want me around when his student was there, and there wasn't room enough for me anyway. So I'd been upstairs emptying the trash and sweeping out Chief Rosenhagen's office, when the clock above the chief's desk showed 5:00 p.m. I had to go because I had table-setting duty at the dining hall, and that job had to be done by 5:15, or Miss Conkle would paddle our behinds. I took the stairs down to the furnace room two at a time and found the door ajar, but not open more than a few inches. I knocked to find Deputy Hitchcock alone at his desk, writing something down. Miss Knaak was gone.

"Mr. Hitchcock, I need to go. It's after five."

He looked up and replied, "So it is, Griffin. So it is." He paused and glanced around the room, when something caught his eye, right behind the door, next to where I stood. It was a handbag. "Oh my! I see Miss Knaak has forgotten her handbag. Griff, can you grab that and run your fastest over to the station? See if you can catch her before she boards her train," he said. "She'll need that."

I considered telling him about table-setting duty, but all I said was, "Sure." Grabbing the handbag, I turned to take the stairs and heard him say behind me, "Good show, Griffin. Now scram!"

I made it across Sheridan Road to the train station in a minute and a half. As I came around the southwest corner of the building, I saw something that froze me in my tracks. Sitting on a green bench, right next to Elfrieda Knaak, was the huge, thick man, who always drove the black Packard, the man who'd done most of the talking with Mr. Hitchcock that night I was caught out past curfew. He was right there, not fifteen feet in front of me, with a newspaper on one side of him and Miss Knaak on the other.

People were trickling into the station, some to get on the train to Chicago, and others to pick up loved ones coming up from the city. I did my best to blend in with the sparse crowd and eased my way over toward the green bench. I knelt down behind it, pretending to tie my shoe, and strained to hear what this horribly mismatched couple was saying to each other. I could see the roll of flesh on the back of his neck, and he had one of his arms around the back of the bench. I looked at his fat hand and sausagey fingers, as they tapped on the top edge of the bench behind Miss Knaak.

I leaned around the legs of the person standing in front of me and saw one of those encyclopedia crates, like the one Miss Knaak had brought to LBO that day I had helped her into Mackey Memorial.

"What are you carrying a box of bricks around for, ma'am, if I may ask?" I heard him say.

Elfrieda chuckled. "They're just encyclopedias, but at the end of a long day, they certainly do feel like bricks." I stood up silently and slowly for a better view.

"Ah," the bull said, nodding, "so you're in sales?"

"Yes, I suppose I am. But given that my box isn't getting any emptier, I must not be very good at it." She flinched a bit, as if catching herself in the very pattern of thought she'd hoped to avoid. I noticed a more positive tone when she continued, "Are you a reader, sir?"

He lifted his newspaper and smiled. "This is about all I have time for these days." He leaned forward and to his right, around Miss Knaak, as if seeking a better view of her books. "But I, too, am a salesman."

"Are you, indeed?" she asked, turning her torso to face the large figure beside her. "What is it that you sell, Mr. ...?

"Pirelli, Sal Pirelli." He extended his fat hand and Miss Knaak offered hers, along with a smile and a nod. I wanted to warn her, to tell her not to trust this guy. "I'm in the transportation and services business," he continued.

"I'm Elfrieda Knaak, and I can tell you that no matter what you sell, Mr. Pirelli, this 1927 edition of Compton's Pictured Encyclopedias will deepen your understanding of the world, of the product you sell, and it will enhance your ability to converse intelligently with all of your customers." She leaned over and pried open her sample box. As she did so, several business cards spilled onto the brick walkway right at Mr. Pirelli's feet. He began to pick them up, while Miss Knaak quickly and deftly, removed her trusty "E-F" volume from her sample box and happened to open it up to the "Fi" page.

When she looked over at Pirelli, he was thumbing through the business cards he'd picked up. "Crab Tree Farm, Grace Durand, Alex Reddington, are these people you have business with, Miss Knaak?" I noted a hint of concern in his deep voice.

"Well, I'm in conversations with them, and they've been very supportive of my efforts so far. Now, Mr. Pirelli, let's suppose..."

He interrupted her. "What about this one? A Bureau of Investigation agent? You in some sort of trouble, Miss Knaak?" I noticed Pirelli slide the agent's card up his sleeve rather than back into the box of books.

Miss Knaak laughed. "No, no. That man stopped by the pharmacy my family owns in Deerfield looking into some sort of crime involving drug stores down the road in Wheeling." I wondered if Pirelli still had that card up his sleeve or if he'd moved it into a pocket. But the sales pitch continued. "Suppose that you are selling your transportation services to a purveyor of…" she looked down at the page she had opened to in her volume… "Firearms." She held the volume open and set it on Mr. Pirelli's broad lap, so he could see it. "If you were to read this one entry, an entry of barely more than a page, you would know a lot more about shotguns than you did before reading it. Now, just think how much more effectively you would be able to talk to your customer, Mr. Pirelli."

Pirelli nodded and raised his eyebrows. "Impressive, Miss Knaak. Very impressive." He returned the volume to her and straightened his tie, just beneath his square jaw. "I believe you may have undersold your salesmanship skills." He looked at his watch and then continued. "Do you have a business card of your own, in case I decide I need a set of these?" He returned to her the business cards he had picked up, all except one.

Miss Knaak smiled and reached into her coat pocket. "Here you are. If you don't live too far away, I'd be happy to set up a time to come to your home or office and give you a full presentation."

Pirelli answered, "I am most certainly interested, and if you don't mind me asking, I'm curious where you developed your skills in sales."

"That's easy," she said, without hesitation and with a sheepish smile. "Mr. Charles Hitchcock has helped me in ways that go beyond words." She looked down at her sample box and clasped her hands together nervously. "I have taken his elocution and salesmanship classes, which are absolutely riveting. He's a former actor, you know, with countless films to his credit." I pictured Hitchcock in that cop film he made in Lake Bluff. "He's also been kind enough to tutor me. In fact, it was Mr. Hitchcock who steered me to the good people over at Crab Tree Farm."

"Is that right?" He slid his left hand into his coat pocket and glanced around furtively. "I can tell that this Mr. Hitchcock has had more than the average influence on you. Perhaps I will have to look in on him myself."

"Oh yes, you should," Miss Knaak continued. "I can't recommend him highly enough." She paused briefly, and seemed to consider her next words. Elfrieda looked away for a moment. "We share other interests as well."

The bell clanged on the North Shore Line southbound train, and both Pirelli and Miss Knaak turned to see its approach. "Well, this is me, Mr. Pirelli." She rose and then bent over to pick up her samples box.

"May I help you with that, Miss Knaak? I could get it onto the train for you," Pirelli offered.

"No. No thank you. This is something I am more than used to." She smiled and nodded once more to him. "Mr. Pirelli, I do hope to hear from you soon. You have my card."

"Yes, I do. Have a pleasant evening." Pirelli stood and watched Miss Knaak move toward the train behind a thick, disorganized cluster of travelers. Without waiting to see her board, Pirelli quickly turned and walked back to the station parking lot, where, no doubt, his pasty and gaunt partner sat waiting for him in the passenger seat of their long, black Packard.

I rose and bolted forward with the handbag tucked under my right arm like a football. "Miss Knaak! Miss Knaak," I called, bobbing and sliding between the rushing throng. "Miss Knaak," I yelled, seeing the back of her head. She turned and paused against the tide of people, and I reached for her arm.

She turned sideways to let some people pass and then saw me. "Your handbag, Miss Knaak," I said.

"Griffin?" she said with a puzzled look on her face.

"Deputy Hitchcock sent me over with this. You left it at the Village Hall." I extended the purse toward her.

"Oh my! How can I ever thank you?" She hugged me with her one free arm, and I set the handbag on top of her encyclopedia crate. "Please convey my gratitude to Charles...I mean to Deputy Hitchcock, won't you Griffin?"

"Yes, ma'am," I said, nodding. I turned and started running full bore to the dining hall, already imagining the paddling I was sure to receive.

≈

When I got to the front stairs of Wads, Miss Harvey was waiting with her arms crossed. I slowed from my sprint as I approached the bottom of the stairs.

"Are you aware of what time it is, Mr. Morgan?" she said, glaring at me but not moving a muscle.

"I am, ma'am," I replied. "I'm really sorry. I was working for Deputy Hitchcock. He sent me on an important errand, and it made me late." She still hadn't moved at all. She seemed to be staring over toward Hobbs Hall.

"No matter the errand nor the person sending you on it, you know that being late for dinner is cause for consequences." She finally tilted her head toward me and narrowed her eyes. "You have two minutes to walk around the edges of this yard looking for the switch that I shall use on your behind. You can bring it to me in my office. The clock has started," she said, turning and entering the dormitory.

I sighed and began my search. I'd heard about these lashings and even heard the screams of some of the recipients. Knox had told me that once Miss Harvey had sent him back outside three times to find a "more suitable switch." "Don't bother bringing her a softie," Knox had said. "She'll send you back out for a stiff one and then give you three times as many swats."

I headed over behind the laundry where the tallest switches were swaying rhythmically with the late October breeze. I heard footsteps behind me and turned to see Mr. Spader.

"Evening, Griffin," he said.

"Hello, sir," I replied, continuing my search along the edge of the yard.

"Looks like you are heading for a sore buttocks," he said, preparing his pipe with tobacco. I nodded without speaking. "Well," he continued, "my advice is not to hold your breath. Steady, deep breaths relax the muscles, and the more relaxed you are when the switch comes 'a calling, the less pain you'll feel." He puffed hard on his glowing pipe. "I'll head back over to Hobbs and set aside a full plate of food for you, Griffin."

I plucked out my switch and turned to see this kind soul, as he ambled back toward the dining hall. "Thank you, Mr. Spader," I said, loudly enough to be sure he heard me. He waved a hand without turning around, and I ran back to Wads and tore up the stairs to the housemother's office.

Miss Harvey was recording my offense in her black, leatherbound journal. There was a column for the date, a column for the time, and a big space for a description of the offense.

"Well, let's see what you've brought me, Mr. Morgan." I handed her the switch. "Oh, yes! An excellent choice—good length, tightly wound. Yes, I believe this will do just fine." She walked slowly over to the far corner of her office, next to her desk. I followed, feeling my chest tighten.

"Bend over, Griffin." I remembered Mr. Spader's words and started breathing as deeply and as evenly as I could. I bent forward and placed a hand on her desk. "Ten minutes late, a swat for each of those minutes, and two more for trying to blame your tardiness on your employer."

I swallowed hard and closed my eyes. Just breathe, I told myself, but don't scream. Don't give her the satisfaction.

She widened her stance and wound up fully. The first strike was like a sharp whip, and the next several bit even harder. I opened my eyes at the sixth, trying to see Miss Harvey's face. I wondered if she enjoyed these moments of exercising her authority. Either way I strengthened my resolve to remain totally silent through the remaining six whacks. They came quickly.

She set the switch on the desk and said nothing. She gestured that I should leave with the back of her right hand, as if she were shooing a fly, and so I did.

WADSWORTH HALL "WADS BOYS" AND HOUSEMOTHER
Photo courtesy of the Lake Bluff History Museum

Chapter 27 — Walter Spitzer's Milk Run
Lake Bluff Orphanage — October 25, 1928

We had a lot of new kids coming into the orphanage on what seemed almost a weekly basis. Every time a bed emptied due to a kid getting fostered out, somebody's birth parents getting their act together enough to reclaim their kids, or the appearance of some well-meaning aunt or uncle, the bed was filled in less than 24 hours. There was a waiting list a mile long to get into LBO, which none of us could believe. To us who had been there a while, LBO felt like a prison.

But when a new kid came, we all tried to welcome him, at least when the housemothers were around. A real effort was made to make the new kids feel like the orphanage was going to be a good place. Miss Arbuckle and Miss Harvey were always reminding us to "extend ourselves" in any way we could. The younger new kids got a ton of kindness and welcoming attention. I still remember and appreciate all the things the other girls did for Betty when we arrived. From little Heather Madsen giving Betty her favorite teddy bear, to

Miss Arbuckle letting me walk with Betty down to the train station on Christmas visit day, there were glimpses of compassion even amidst the strict rules. Everyone understood how hard coming here was on the little kids. But that sense of welcome didn't last long. In a matter of weeks, even the new kids knew that LBO was simply a place to endure.

Older kids, especially boys, were another story, especially when the veteran boys got the new kid alone. The ones who arrived around fourth grade or later were subjected to a variety of initiation rites. Walter Spitzer, for example, was a sixth grader, who moved into Wads on a Saturday, and by the following Thursday, he'd been issued a challenge from the likes of the O'Neil brothers and Homer.

"You see, Walter, all of us have to make living here a little more fun, and sneaking out after bedtime is just one of the things we do." Homer rubbed his hands together.

Bobby picked up the thread. "We call 'em milk runs, Walter. Rosenthal and Helming's is a little grocery store, right on Scranton, the same street we're on right here. You can't miss it. There's a big open field behind the shop, where you'll see a whole bunch of wooden crates filled with milk bottles." He looked around the rumpus room to be sure Miss Harvey wasn't in earshot.

Reluctantly, Walter spoke in a shaky, cracking voice. "I don't understand the milk bottles. They're empty, and we have milk here in the kitchen, don't we?"

All the guys tried not to laugh, and about half of them succeeded. Homer shushed us and continued. "The empty milk bottle you bring back is the proof, Walter. It shows us that you fulfilled the quest." Homer gestured around our little circle in the cluster of couches and chairs. "Everyone you see here had to pass the same test, when we first came here. Right fellas?" There was a chorus of "Yeps" and "You bets," though I only knew of a few kids who'd actually been put through this particular test.

"But we didn't do it because it was a test," Bobby said. "We did it 'cause it's fun. You'll see!"

"Yeah," Knox added. "But there are a few things you'll want to keep in mind." His eyes widened, and he smirked a bit at the rest of us. "Like the fact that Miss Harvey does two to three bed checks a night, and we're never quite sure when they're going to be."

"And," Johnny piped in, "You never know when old Jim Spader will be out snooping around or coming back from that fishing hole he frequents."

"And I have to do it tonight?" Walter asked.

"Yep," Homer chimed back in. "Thursdays are better nights for sneaking out than weekends. And this particular challenge has to be completed in your first week in Wads."

With all the older, bigger kids surrounding and then closing in on him, Walter had gotten the picture that there was no getting out of this quest. So he nodded reluctantly and went up the stairs with the O'Neil twins, so they could show him the window and school him on the instrument he'd need to prop it open.

At 10:30 p.m., I heard Walter quietly making his way down the central staircase on his way to Rosenthal and Helming's. I felt nervous for him, remembering the first time I had snuck out and how that had ended up, returning in the company of Deputy Dispatch Charles Hitchcock. While I'd experienced plenty of kids going through this particular initiation rite, I felt anxious about this one. I didn't like Walter's chances of coming home with the bottle without being caught. And we all knew that if he got caught, we'd be caught. The housemothers and Miss Arbuckle would come down hard. It wouldn't just be the switch.

Usually, these milk runs took a new kid anywhere from five to seven minutes to complete. The only exceptions were when a particularly cocky kid would get cute and decide to wander around the downtown area or head over near the skating pond. I had a pretty strong hunch Walter would be back in a big hurry. He seemed like the nervous type.

It was almost eleven when a breathless and crying Walter Spitzer tumbled into his cubicle, just two over from mine. I began to hear agitated voices and snuck over to the cubicle he shared with Knox.

"Settle down!" Knox was saying in pushed whisper. "You're OK. Nobody saw you, right?"

"I...I...I don't think so," Spitzer stammered, struggling to get enough oxygen.

"What happened?" I asked. "Can you just tell us what happened?" I put my right hand on the back of his shoulder, trying to calm him down.

"I got down there...real fast...to the grocery." I felt his shoulders heaving up and down, while his head shook back and forth. "I saw the crates and was just grabbing one of the bottles when...when I heard footsteps coming up the alley. I ducked behind the crates and saw some guy—maybe a watchman or...or a delivery guy or something. He had a uniform on." Walter expelled a big breath of air, and his shoulders slumped over. He was quiet but trembling for more than a few seconds.

"Then this black car pulled up alongside him, right on the grass of the field, real quiet-like. The driver's side window went down slowly, and I heard this big voice said, 'Payday.'"

"Payday?" Knox asked.

"Yeah, 'payday.' The guy who was walking stopped and turned toward the car. I saw him look up and down the street, and he even looked over by the crates, where I was, like to make sure nobody else was around. Then this guy in the car, the guy with the big sounding voice, stuck his arm out the window and waved this brown envelope toward him. I heard him start tapping the envelope against the door of the car." Walter crumpled over onto his bed and started sobbing uncontrollably.

"Sshh!" Knox said, terrified that we were going to wake Miss Harvey, if we hadn't already. I rested my hand on Walter's knee. It was really wet.

"Can you just tell us what else happened, Walter?" I asked in a gentle whisper. "Then we can all just go to sleep."

Walter took a deep breath and nodded his head. After a few seconds, he sat up to continue. "When the guy on foot got close enough to the car, he reached for the envelope. But before he even touched it, the two back doors of the car burst open, and two men sprang out at the man who was walking. They punched him and...and...then they held him, like they were spreading him apart, like they were going to rip him in half. Then the driver got out, this huge guy, as big as a bull. And he had this pipe wrench or something."

"Jesus," Knox said, under his breath.

"The two guys from the car had the walking guy spread across the back end of the car, and one of them was pressing the man's face into the car real hard and then started slamming his head into the car. The big guy, the one with the pipe, told the other guy to knock it off, to take it easy. Then he said something to their prisoner about an agreement. And then I heard him say, 'We trusted in your discretion.'"

Walter's breathing got really rapid, like he was hyperventilating. "The guy who was pinned down started screaming something, but with his face crushed into the car, I couldn't make out what he was saying. So the one guy holding his head turned it to the side, the side facing me, and then spit it the man's eye. Again, the big one with the wrench told his henchman to knock it off or he'd get clobbered too. Then the main leader leaned closer to hear him. 'I haven't told anyone! Nobody knows anything about this!' the guy they'd caught kept saying over and over. Then he said, 'I swear it. I swear it!'

"Then the huge guy started tapping the pipe into his open hand. He said, 'We had an agreement, an agreement we kept faithfully. We have counted on your absolute secrecy and discretion.' Then he said something like 'You've been blabbing to somebody' and 'You must see that this threatens our entire operation.'

"Then the huge guy, standing right behind the man who was spread apart, nodded to the two guys holding the man.

"'Please! No! Please!' the guy who was held down started to scream. Then they mashed his face into the car again, so his voice got real muffled. I think he said, 'I've said nothing...ever! Nothing!'

"The big guy with the pipe wrench snickered and said, 'I wish we could believe you. But I had a visit with your little friend earlier this week.' The two men had to spread their prisoner out even further, while the big guy moved to the left of the guy who was pinned against the car. He gritted his teeth, wound up, and hammered the long wrench into the man's left leg, just below his knee."

Walter doubled over, like he'd been the one who'd been hit, but then stood up, looking down toward the floor. He'd peed all over himself, and it was running all the way down the side of his shoe. Knox jumped up, grabbed something out of one of his cubbies and ran to the bathroom. I thought of Artie and how, if he were still alive, this might get blamed on him.

"Don't worry about the pee, Walter," I said. "We won't tell anyone. Honest." He winced in embarrassment. "So is the man still over there – the one who got beat up?" I asked. Walter immediately started shaking his head back and forth.

"They threw him in the car and drove off real slow and quiet like."

Knox returned with two towels, one wet and one dry. He tossed the dry one to Walter, who immediately started wiping his pants. He threw the wet one down on the floor where the pee was most visible. Knox said, "You'll want to wipe those shoes off and that wet floor too."

Just then, Billy stuck his head in. He raised his eyebrows when he saw the towels and the puddle. "Hey, looks like we got another bedwetter, huh, fellas?" he whispered.

"Get out!" I hissed. "You want us all to get caught, moron?"

"Let's just try to get some sleep now," I whispered. "And, Walter, we don't want to tell anybody about this, OK? We don't want Miss Harvey to learn that you were out."

Knox added, "I've got a milk bottle hidden in the bottom of my closet. I'll show the guys in the morning, and we'll leave it at that." Knox looked at me, and I nodded. I patted Walter on the back one more time and crept silently back to my cubby.

In my bed, on my back, I knew that sleep wouldn't come. I tossed and turned all night, with my mind racing with images from Walter's story—the black car, the bull with the rippling neck, and most of all, the walking man, the uniformed watchman, the beaten one who they threw into the car. I had a feeling Deputy Hitchcock wouldn't be at work on Saturday.

"Hitchcock's broken leg!" Hargrave erupted. "For Christ's sake, the bum swore under oath that he fell off a ladder!"

"I know," I said, not wanting to add fuel to the detective's fire.

"But at least somebody got to give him what he deserved." Hargrave had his right hand clenched into a fist and was pounding it into his left hand repeatedly. "If only we'd known about this connection during the investigation! We could have really nailed him."

I felt like I'd taken one of Hargrave's punches in the gut. It was guilt, plain and simple. I'd kept my mouth shut, and there'd been consequences. "I know, detective...and I'm sorry," I said, swallowing hard after getting the words out. "But, as I've said before, when we get to the end of my tale, you'll know why I didn't ...couldn't come forward."

MISS MARIE MUELLER — ELFRIEDA KNAAK'S BEST FRIEND
Photo courtesy of The Chicago Tribune

Chapter 28 — Elfrieda's Decision
Chicago, IL and Points North — October 29, 1928

Hargrave stretched his arms upward, and cracked his neck a couple of times. "I didn't think there was any way this cold case could get any more fascinating, but I must admit, Griff, you have made it so." He looked in his empty coffee cup and got up to refill it once again. "Continue, please. I need to hear how this ends."

The last normal, healthy day of Elfrieda Knaak's life was October 29, 1928. While it was unfolding, there probably wasn't anything particularly unusual or noteworthy about it. But once she was found so badly burned, once she became "The Furnace Girl," every moment, every hour, every detail of October 29 would be dissected and interpreted for a long, long time to come.

The Lake Bluff Police, working in conjunction with State's Attorney A.V. Smith and Lake County Sheriff Lawrence Doolittle, produced a timeline, thinking it would lead to some suspect, some witness, some something. That timeline wound up in the LBPD file and a couple other places, as I recall. I've still got a copy in my file.

7:40 a.m.   Victim at work at Knaak Pharmacy in Deerfield, Illinois.

10:30 a.m.   Co-worker notices nothing unusual or out of the ordinary.

10:33 a.m.   Victim walks home to prepare for an afternoon of office presentations.

12:00 p.m.   Victim leaves her home, walks to bus station and rides to the Highland Park Train station to take a southbound train to Compton Publishing.

1:30 p.m.   Victim arrives at 58 E. Washington St. /Compton Publishing to participate in "Presentation Day" with other sales staff. Victim is one of five top sales people chosen to deliver a presentation to sales staff. Several co-workers' report victim as happy and in great spirits. Company President, Mr. James Carter, praises victim's presentation.

4:18 p.m.   Victim places call to station 528 in Deerfield to her sister Ida Knaak. Ida reports that call was about plans for their sing-along that night, indicates that Elfrieda had purchased new sheet music and was normal and happy.

4:50 p.m.   James Carter returns victim's blue coat to her in the main office room of Compton Publishing.

5:40 p.m.   Victim places call to Station 532 in Waukegan to a Marie Mueller. Miss Mueller reports the two caught up and talked about regular things and boyfriends. Mueller notes that victim was "fine at first but did get quieter, like something was wrong, once I started telling her about my private tutoring sessions with Mr. Hitchcock."

7:43 p.m.   Victim arrives at Highland Park Train Depot and places call from phone to Station 772—Lake Bluff Police Station—no answer.

8:10 p.m.   Victim is told that the bus she takes 2.5 miles west to her home has been re-routed and that the next bus to Deerfield won't arrive for several hours.

8:15 p.m.   Victim places a second call from Highland Park Train Depot to station 772— Lake Bluff Police Station— again no answer. Victim then returns to station attendant and purchases a round trip ticket from Highland Park to Lake Bluff and asks attendant to store her briefcase with the station attendant.

8:30 p.m.   Victim is seen boarding northbound North Shore Line out of Highland Park. Train station attendant reports victim as agitated and confused.

9:03 p.m.   Victim is seen disembarking from the train in Lake Bluff by station attendant but is not seen nor heard from again until she is discovered at 7:01 a.m. the next morning in the Village Hall.

"Like you, Detective, I have been over and over this timeline so many times, and the piece I've kept coming back to is the 5:40 p.m. phone call. Marie Mueller was Elfrieda Knaak's closest friend. While Miss Mueller may not have shared Elfrieda's spiritual bent, the two shared most everything else, including a fascination with Mr. Charles Hitchcock.

"When the police timeline notes that Miss Knaak got quiet after Mueller began discussing her 'private lessons,' the lessons referred to are undoubtedly Marie's private tutoring sessions with Mr. Hitchcock. Both women had been in a couple of his classes at The Waukegan YMCA, but only Miss Knaak had availed herself of the private instruction Mr. Hitchcock offered, until the second week of October in 1928.

"I seem to remember calling you about this, Detective, because I think I was trying to put together some of these puzzle pieces and just couldn't break through it."

Hargrave nodded and said, "Yes, I interviewed Miss Mueller on behalf of the Knaak family about a week after the Coroner's Jury inquest. She wasn't particularly helpful, as I recall, mostly because the darn woman just couldn't stop crying. She was an absolute emotional wreck."

"What were you able to get out of her, Detective?" I asked.

"I pressed her as hard as I could on the nature of her relationship with Mr. Hitchcock."

"Whose relationship with Hitchcock," I interrupted, "hers or Miss Knaak's?"

Hargrave chuckled. "Yes, that clarification is well worth making, Mr. Morgan, particularly in light of what I mentioned earlier—Miss Mueller's eventual marriage to Mr. Hitchcock." He stroked his chin and leaned back in his chair. "Miss Mueller was a bit more forthcoming about Miss Knaak's connection with the Deputy, calling it 'spiritual,' and 'professional,' referencing the encyclopedia sales and whatnot. But Miss Mueller did finally get around to the fact that both women had a certain attraction to the former actor."

I asked the detective another question. "Did she say anything, anything specific, about what she had said in the phone conversation just before Miss Knaak got quiet?" I could hear Hargrave's breathing for a few moments before he replied. He was consulting his notes.

"Yes…yes, she did. She told me that she recalled telling Elfrieda how much she was enjoying being with Mr. Hitchcock one-on-one, without the rest of the class present. Miss Mueller also said something about feeling like she and Mr. Hitchcock were getting closer than she ever imagined."

"So what did you make of all this, Detective?" I asked, having no idea what he would say.

"Not a lot. It's a bit like B. Lock, I suppose. It's interesting, but unless you can put Marie Mueller or Charles Hitchcock at the crime scene, none of it means a thing." He leaned back in his chair again and ran the fingers of both hands through his gray hair in frustration. "I suppose it's possible that Miss Mueller was trying to protect

Hitchcock during these proceedings, you know, provide some cover for him and whatnot."

"But what about providing a motive for Miss Knaak?" I said. "Perhaps Miss Mueller also provides the motive for Knaak to burn herself—the Refiner's Fire, and all?" I pressed.

"I'm not sure what you mean, Griff," Hargrave said.

I struggled to find the words. "It's just that…What I mean is…If the two women, even if they were friends, were rivals for Hitchcock's affection and attention, perhaps this phone call put Miss Knaak over the edge somehow."

Hargrave was silent. He started running his left hand over the inside cover of his Knaak file. "Put Miss Knaak over what edge?" the detective asked. "What are you saying, Mr. Morgan?"

Then it was my turn for silence, as I considered my words very carefully. "What if hearing that her friend, Detective, her best friend, was getting closer to Charles Hitchcock made Elfrieda feel that she needed to declare or prove her love for him somehow? What if that fear, perhaps even the image of Miss Mueller and Hitchcock alone in the Village Hall basement, drove Miss Knaak to do something desperate?" I paused to let the entire weight of my line of questioning sink in.

"Desperate how? What do you mean?" the detective asked.

"She changed her plans, Detective. Miss Knaak was on her way home, to sing with her sister Ida, remember? She'd purchased sheet music. She'd called her sister at 4:18 p.m.—according to the timeline—to confirm those plans. But at 8:15 she buys a round trip ticket to Lake Bluff, having made two unsuccessful phone calls to the Village Hall's evening dispatch office, the very office where Charles Hitchcock works, the very room where she would be found burned beyond belief the next morning." My hands were trembling, my voice was quivering. I felt like I needed some air.

After a deep breath, I continued. "I think it's important first to establish what Miss Knaak was doing at the crime scene, what her reason for being there was. I believe that Elfrieda Knaak went up to Lake Bluff that night voluntarily, intending to prove her love to Charles Hitchcock. That she showed up at the Village Hall and somehow got into the night dispatch office, and there was the furnace."

"C'mon, Griff!" the detective said. He cleared his throat and then coughed. "Finish your story. How does your crime scene unfold?"

"What did Miss Knaak say again and again, both on her way to the hospital and in the hospital?" I hesitated to see if Hargrave would answer. He didn't. "She said, 'I did this to myself.'"

"But we've been over and over this Mr. Morgan, and we both agreed that Miss Knaak never could have done this to herself," he said. "Are you telling me that now you think she put herself into that furnace, limb by limb?" He expelled a loud breath.

"All I'm saying is that she...she started to," I said. "Marie Mueller's growing intimacy with Charles Hitchcock along with B. Lock's notion of the refining power of fire set the events of October 29, 1928, in motion. That's what I'm saying."

LBO POSTCARD
Photo courtesy of the Lake Bluff History Museum

Chapter 29 — Running Away
Lake Bluff Orphanage — October 29, 1928

At about 7:45 p.m. on the night of Monday, October 29, I handed a carefully written note to Ernie. "You've got to make sure my sister gets this tomorrow afternoon—after dinner, not before!" I put my hand on Ernie's left shoulder, looking him straight in the eyes. This was too important to trust to his often goofy, off-the-cuff demeanor. "Ernie, pay attention! No one can see this note except Betty and Ceilia Graham. Nobody else. Betty can't read, so Ceilia will need to read it to her."

"I got it. Relax," Ernie said, trying to be convincing.

"The note's a lie, Ernie" I said. "A lie! It says I'm sick and have been in the infirmary all day. If any of the housemothers, Nurse Sanderson or Blueberg, or any of the blabbermouth kids around here get a hold of it, my whole plan's dead. So only Ceilia and Betty can see this. You got it? Don't leave it somewhere or drop it, and, whatever you do, don't tell Homer. Your roommate couldn't keep a secret if he was gagged and locked in his own jail cell!"

"Griff, pipe down, OK?" Ernie replied. "Just get to bed, so your plan has a chance to work."

"All right." I nodded nervously. "And thanks, Ernie."

"Good luck, Griff." Ernie hesitated. "I hope your plan works out the way you want it to." But I could tell he didn't think my plan stood a chance.

Again, I nodded at him, took in a long, deep breath, and headed back into my cubicle. I checked through my small, leather travel satchel one last time: three sandwiches, two apples, a pack of gum, and a canteen of water. I'd been swiping food items, one at a time, from "Commandant Conkle's" kitchen for the last four days. She'd almost caught me in the act of stealing the second sandwich, when I returned to her kitchen, thinking she was in her office to stay. But she came back to check on some bread, just as I was pocketing the ham and cheese. The only other items of note were a carefully folded piece of paper with the Freidles' street address on it and the baseball glove they'd given me. I know Danny thought it was a dumb idea going there, but I had to try. I was running out of time, and I wasn't running away. I was just sneaking down there to have a talk with them to see if they'd consider taking Betty and me in once I aged out in another year.

I looked out my first floor Wads window at a cold, clear October night. The moon was full, and I was glad there was no rain. But the temperature in the low 40s wasn't what I'd hoped for. I had a long-sleeved, wool, knit shirt, a stocking cap, Aunt Rose's sweater, plus the farm jacket Mrs. D. had gotten me. That would have to do. I tucked it all under my bed.

Just before lights out, I climbed under the covers fully clothed with my shoes on. Glancing again at the bed next to me, I saw the shape of the second kid sleeping in Danny's bed since he'd been sent down to Glenwood Military Academy in August. "Jeez," I muttered, shaking my head. I turned off the light on the bedside table and waited in the dark.

At 9:22, I heard the heavy, authoritative footsteps of Miss Harvey, doing bed checks, no doubt. I turned onto my side, so my face was away from the cubicle opening where she would enter. She came around the corner and shined her light right at my bed.

"Goodnight, Mr. Morgan," she said, well above a whisper. I didn't reply, staying perfectly still. Then there was a thud under my bed, followed by a rolling sound. I stiffened. One of my apples had fallen from out of the satchel. I heard Housemother Harvey take two steps further into my room, directly toward me. I reached under my pillow for the baseball I always slept with, rolled myself over toward Miss Harvey and groaned. Squinting toward the light she held, I showed her the baseball and said, "Sorry. I always sleep with this thing, but I guess it fell off my pillow. Hope it didn't wake anybody other than me."

"Go back to sleep, Mr. Morgan…without the baseball this time," she said and shuffled out of my cubicle. I let out an audible sigh and spun onto my back, with my arms folded behind my head.

When the hallway sounds of footsteps and "Good nights" died down, I waited a few more minutes, got out of bed silently, and felt underneath it to get my satchel, the wool shirt, and my hat. The apple that had fallen was against the leg of the bedside table. I picked it up, placed it more deeply inside the satchel, alongside my ballglove, and strapped it shut tightly. I jammed the hat inside the sleeve of my wool shirt and tied it around my waist. I put the jacket on without buttoning it and slung the satchel over my right shoulder. Taking a quick look out the window, I noted the unusual brightness of things due to the full moon. It would make it a lot harder to go unnoticed out there, but once I got down to the train tracks, it wouldn't matter. I took a deep breath, swallowed hard, and headed for the top of the stairs.

Suddenly, there was a muffled scream and then the word "No!" I backed into my cubicle and stood perfectly still. It was Francis Ward and another of his nightmares. He slept in the next cubicle over, and his night terrors were legendary. Again, I heard the unmistakable steps of Miss Harvey, this time accompanied by the sounds of Franny's crying. I gasped in exasperation, first because he was delaying my escape and then because I suddenly realized I hadn't remembered to stuff my bed with the dummy. Setting the satchel down on my bed, I bent down under the bed that I still thought of as Danny's, even though some kid named Michael was in it now. I slid out "Dufus," as we'd named him. I picked him up carefully and put him into my bed, pulling the covers up over him, being sure to cover the tape ball head as well. Satisfied at the body-sized bulge Dufus created, I slung my satchel back over my shoulder and tiptoed to the doorway. I heard the low, calming voice of Miss Harvey, singing "The Lord's Prayer" to Frances. As she sang, "Forgive us our debts," I took in a deep breath and made a break for the stairs.

Without making a sound, I headed for the northwest window. Propping it open first with the stick used to keep it open in the summer months, I reached under an end table for the same eraser we all had used dozens of times to keep the window open for our late night returns. I lowered my satchel down to the lawn and then slid through behind it. I carefully dislodged the wooden prop, placing it on the floor inside the window, and then lowered the window silently. Out of habit, I set the eraser where it would keep the window open just enough for a set of fingertips, even though I wouldn't be coming back, at least not tonight.

"Who's there?" came the voice from around the corner on the west side of the building. It was Jim Spader. I smelled the tobacco smoke from his pipe and crouched behind the bush to his right. A window opened above me on the second floor.

"Jim? Is that you?" said Miss Harvey.

"Yeah. Just thought I'd heard something out here."

"As did I," the housemother replied. "I'll do a quick room-to-room sweep and be down in a few minutes." She closed the window. I could make out Mr. Spader's steps heading away from me, around to the front of the building. The crisp leaves crunched in rhythm under his weight. I panicked and ran my fastest to a tree and then zigzagged from tree to tree, cutting toward the houses that backed up to Wads and the other LBO buildings. I tucked in as close to the houses as I could and then headed west through the yards toward Evanston Ave. But with the light from the full moon and the bright lights of Evanston, I decided to take Center instead.

Still up in the shadows of the houses, I heard someone coming. It sounded like someone on crutches, but if it was, he was going awfully fast. Hidden behind bushes and an oak tree, I listened to the clacking rhythm on the concrete and the shushing of oak leaves, as whoever it was hurried past. I remained in the shadows of the hedge, terrified of being seen. The rhythmic sounds moved toward the Village Hall, and I leaned around, hoping to see something, but there was only sound. I came out from the shadows and stood, curious and still.

Part of me wanted to follow the dying sounds, but I knew I was already late to meet Lily. I threw caution to the wind and cut straight for the train tracks. I crossed Sheridan Road and soon hopped over the tracks, just south of the station, working my way toward the line of trees just west of the tracks.

"Griff! Over here!" Lily whispered from behind the tree line, about fifty yards north of the train station. I couldn't see her until I was less than five feet from her. Though the moon was full and bright, throwing its light most everywhere, she managed to stay hidden behind a cluster of thick-trunked trees.

"Hey," I said, out of breath.

"Are you OK?" Lily asked. "Did you run the whole way?"

I shook my head. "I didn't run much at all. But I'm sweaty and can barely breathe for some reason." I bent over and leaned on my knees. I sucked in a couple of big breaths, trying to get air, and suddenly retched and then retched again, but nothing came out.

Lily put a hand on my back softly, feeling both the heat and moisture I was giving off. "Are you OK?" she repeated.

I responded by retching again, and this time I threw up as well. It wasn't much. I straightened up and wiped my mouth with the back of my coat sleeve. I shook my head and spit twice. Turning away from Lily, I wiped my eyes with the back of my left hand.

"Are you...are you crying, Griff?"

"No!" I snapped. "Let's get going."

Lily had a satchel over her shoulder and she removed it. "I have some things for you, for your trip." She pulled out a thick, checkered cloth that contained four of Mrs. Durand's oatmeal raisin cookies, my favorites. But I had no appetite for them or for anything else at that moment. She also had several carrots and a handful of snapping peas from the Crab Tree Farm garden. I hadn't removed my satchel, so Lily moved behind me and undid its strap, down near my left hip, and slid the additional items in. As she did, her left hand rubbed against the bottom of my shirt. It was soaked with sweat.

"Griff? What is it?"

"Nothing! I just want to get going! I gotta get down to Wilmette before sunrise." I spit again, trying to rid my mouth of the taste of vomit.

"No, Griff. No" She turned me to face her. "You can't go like this!"

"I have to go!" I practically shouted. "I don't have any choice! This is my last chance." My hands were clenched and shaking. "I am not going to Glenwood Military School. I'm just not!"

Lily took a hold of my left arm, just above my wrist, gently but firmly. "It's not your only choice." She took in a breath and steadied herself. "I...I don't even think going to Wilmette is a choice. Those people...you've had one dinner with them, Griff! How can you expect them to take you and Betty into their family, just like that?"

I yanked my arm away and started walking south. Lily's words joined Danny's in a mocking chorus. I felt Lily behind me, and she grabbed for my arm again. "Griff! Wait a minute! Just wait!"

Out of the darkness a spotlight shone directly on us. We froze in its hazy light, covering our eyes. It came from the Lake Bluff Train Station. "Hey! You kids are not supposed to be here. It's after 11:00 p.m."

"Run, Lily! Run!" I took off into the woods behind us, west of the tracks. A train whistle sounded, coming from the north, so I grabbed Lily's arm and pulled her down behind a tree with me. "We'll wait for the train and then run south behind it. He won't be able to see us."

She nodded, knowing that the rumbling and approaching noise would swallow her words before they even came out. Lily brushed against my arm again; and we both noticed that it was even more soaked than before. Lily bent forward to see my face. I was leaning over, away from the tree, and the retching began again. The train was roaring up behind us. Lily steeled herself, stood up, and yanked me right up with her. She motioned for me to follow her, and we headed south in a quick jog, in the direction the train was heading. By the time the last car of the electric train passed us, we were several hundred yards south of the train station, safely away from the station lights and our pursuer.

I'm not sure how I looked, but I felt terrible. There was enough light from the Sheridan Road street lamp for Lily to see my face and for me to see her reaction to it. I knew my eyes were puffy and red. I felt heavy, nauseous, downcast, and lost. She reached for my hand and held it gently. I didn't fight it or pull away this time. We walked across Sheridan, holding hands, and entered Artesian Park. Cutting across the field that would be the ice rink when winter came, we made it to the warming hut. Lily led us to a bench, and we both sat.

She looked around and then up at the full moon. "I have an idea. Will you promise me you'll at least listen to it, Griff?" I didn't respond. My eyes were closed tightly, and I felt the throbbing of a headache. "Mrs. Durand loves you, Griff. She told my daddy you are a great worker." Lily turned straight toward me. "My daddy says the same thing all the time. The main farmhouse is like a hotel." She paused, afraid to say what she'd come tonight to say. "I think you and Betty could maybe live there. I really do."

I opened my eyes, and my teeth were clenched tightly together. I reached for my satchel and opened it. I pulled out the cookies wrapped in cloth and offered one to Lily. She smiled and took one. I took one too but still couldn't bring myself to bite into it.

"I don't know...I just don't know!" I stood suddenly and threw the remaining cookies down hard against the warming hut floor. "Damn it! I don't know anything anymore!" I said, practically screaming.

Lily placed a hand gently on my back and took a loud deep breath, prompting me to do the same.

"I'm tired. I'm just so tired," I said. "I don't know what I'm going to do." I looked up at the bright moon and a smattering of stars. "What am I going to do, Lily?"

She exhaled audibly, put her hand in mine, and said, "I don't know...But I think, for now, we should just get you back to LBO and figure out the rest later." I looked down at my tattered shoes and felt tears forming in my eyes. Lily stood and I felt her arm wrapping itself around mine, pulling me closer to her. I exhaled and then nodded in silent resignation. We headed northeast toward the Lake Bluff Village Hall.

Cutting across the field, toward the downtown area, we had the lights of the village to brighten our path. But seeing we were exposed, I tugged Lily's shirtsleeve, pulling her over into the shadows. With a well-lit street to cross, right in the middle of the downtown area, there was only so much we could do to stay hidden. There was one bright light on outside the Village Hall.

As we crossed Center and cut to the left, heading toward Crab Tree Farm, Lily whispered, "What's that?" She pointed to a glow coming from the back side of the Village Hall basement. Before I could even respond, we heard a muffled scream and then another.

We hurried up the front lawn of the Village Hall and around toward the back, where there was a below-ground window. We both froze momentarily, noticing a strange, orange glow emanating from it. We resumed our approach and got down on all fours. Then there was another scream, a slap, and then a scraping sound. Lily and I both held our breath and bent down to the window but couldn't' see anything. I gestured silently to the other side of the building, where the coal chute was. When we got there, I reached for it quietly and pushed it open as gently and as quietly as I could. Immediately, we heard men's voices, one of which sounded familiar somehow.

"The lady likes fire, boys," the deep voice from the cellar said.

"We can help you finish what you started, if you like it hot, pretty lady," another added. "Hey, boss, you ever see a lady wanna set herself on fire before?"

"Shut up!" the boss's rebuke rang out. I'd heard his voice before. But where?

There was a muffled woman's voice. She was trying to scream, but a hand or something we couldn't quite see prohibited it. Lily looked at me with terror in her eyes. I bit hard on my bottom lip and slid over to another below-ground window. From that angle I could make out a pair of legs with dark pants and two-toned, brown and white leather shoes. Another pair of pinstriped slacks came into my limited view, and I gestured for Lily to look from where I was looking. Lily gasped, and I covered my mouth to keep from doing the same thing.

From a slightly different angle, it looked like it might have been three men holding a woman—a naked woman—who struggled mightily against them. She was nearly three feet off the ground, parallel to it. Her right arm was completely black, charred, and smoldering, hanging lifelessly. For a fraction of a second, we saw a thick, powerful hand over her mouth, and then other hands seemed to be forcing her toward the furnace opening. Lily and I watched in horror, as the woman's hand, wrist, and elbow, clear up to the shoulder, disappeared into the orange glow. She was screaming, but nothing came out, as the fat, bulbous hand smothered all sound.

"Let her go! This is madness!" It was the unmistakable voice of Charles Hitchcock. "She knows nothing, I tell you. Let her go! I swear to you, she knows nothing! This is a horrible mistake you are making! I demand that…" A resounding slap silenced the actor.

Only his faint whimpering could be heard from the far corner of the room.

Lily grabbed my wrist and sunk her nails into my skin without even realizing it. She jumped up and backed away from the window. I held my breath and bent down just a little further, forcing my neck so low in an attempt to see something, anything to make sense of this horror beneath us. I saw the back of the woman's head pressed down against the opening of the furnace, with a fat man's hand underneath it. The hand suddenly pulled away, and the back of the woman's neck dropped against the furnace with a thud, right on the crease of the furnace opening. I winced and grabbed the back of my own neck.

One of the other voices spoke, the one who'd laughed about the lady liking fire. "Well, if your little friend doesn't know anything, what was she doing here—in your office—naked?" the man said, snickering. "She was mumbling something about proving her love and sticking parts of her body in the fire. Your little stool pigeon girlfriend here is running out of time to tell us what else she knows and what she was doing carryin' a Bureau of Investigation agent's business card with her." He slapped the woman hard in the shoulder. "Your love is blindin' you, Mr. Movie Star! You think she's a door-to-door salesman? She's a snitch, and we got proof!" The thug slapped the captive again on the edge of her thigh.

"Hey! Take it easy, huh?" the voice belonging to the man with fat hands and the brown and white shoes said. "She's barely conscious already. She'll be gone soon, and we'll let that ace police chief Rosenhagen sort out how this happened." The man paused and walked to his left. Then he spoke again.

"This is a nice coat, ma'am. I think it might just fit my wife," he said.

"Yeah," the snickering one agreed. "And I don't think the deputy's stool pigeon girlfriend will be needing it anymore. She's plenty warm now." Again, he snickered. Just then I saw the coat clenched in the fat hand. I heard the unmistakable sound of a key falling onto the ground and saw the fat fingers pick it up.

All at once, I felt warm breath by my neck and heard panting. Bandit, the stray dog I'd seen so many times around town, licked me and then barked. I pushed back from the furnace chute in horror, stood up quickly, and knocked the coal chute, as I took a hard step toward Lily. I froze.

"What was that?" one of the henchmen from down below said, jerking his head toward the coal chute. I started to run, and my left foot slipped on a root, driving my knee down hard on the concrete walk. I winced but clenched my teeth, swallowing all sound. Holding my breath, I glanced down to see my pants ripped at the knee and felt blood running down my leg. Just then the man with the voice I recognized spoke again.

"That's enough boys. Leave her be," the driver ordered. "The Big Sleep will come for her soon enough. We may have company outside."

Lily and I silently made our way around the east side of the Village Hall and onto the front lawn. All I could think to do was run. I grabbed Lily's hand and turned toward Center. We'd only taken two hard steps when we hit a thin, bony wall.

"It's a bit late for a couple of youngsters to be out on a school night," said the breathy, damaged voice. It was a gaunt, pasty-faced man, dressed in a dark suit. He had a hand on each of our shoulders. While he wasn't squeezing tightly and was sickeningly thin, I knew he could break both of us in half if he wanted to. The man looked all around us, and as he confirmed that we were alone, a sickening smile formed on his face.

"I'm thinking both of you could be in some real trouble," he rasped, "out past curfew, carrying on in the downtown area." He looked at Lily and then straight at me. His skin looked like an onion, thin, papery, and like it was stretched too tightly around the bony skull beneath it.

"Y...Ye...Yes, sir," I said. "W-w-we both are in for it ... wh ... when we get home." I glanced at Lily who was a mess.

"Nothing's gone the way it was supposed to tonight," she said. "Nothing! So...if...we could just get back to the farm, like nothing ever happened..."

"The farm?" the man rasped, tilting his head down toward me.

"Yes," Lily interrupted. "My grandma's farm, Crab Tree Farm...We..."

"Are you one of the Durands, young lady?" He raised an eyebrow, and a trace of concern formed on his thin, oniony lips.

"Yes, well no. Sort of...sir." Lily looked at me.

"We both work for Mrs. Durand," I spit out. "But Lily's middle name is Grace—after Grace Durand. She and her father have lived with the Durands her whole life."

"I see," said the throaty, hollow voice. Looking down at Lily, he asked, "So your father would be Alex Reddington?"

"Please, sir," Lily begged. "Don't tell him. He'll whip me good if he hears I snuck out again."

The ghoulish man turned back toward us, and I prayed he would not speak again. I couldn't stop shaking, and hearing the muffled screams in the Village Hall behind us wasn't helping.

"I'm in so much trouble!" Lily wailed turning to me. "I never should've offered to help you run away," she whimpered, glaring at me through strands of red hair and tear-drenched eyes. She shook her head, as if trying to rid it of the horror we'd just witnessed.

The screams had stopped, and we heard a door open behind us. It was the side door of the Village Hall, and a big man came out, holding a coat over his arm. He held the door for three others, one of whom was on crutches. I watched as one of the men ordered the man on crutches to lock the door to the building they had just exited from.

"Now, now," our ghastly captor began. "Let's leave all talk of trouble. Young lady, you've got a bit of a walk ahead of you. If you and your friend here can get home in the next five minutes without being seen, we all might be able to put this...troublesome night behind us." He glanced up Center, desolate and silent, and then looked up at the full moon. For a moment, I thought he might howl at it, but instead he just continued. "I will hold off on alerting your guardians for now, provided you both forget that you ever came here tonight. Do I make myself clear?"

I nodded my consent as vigorously as I could and took Lily's hand. "We'll go straight home."

Lily pulled away from me and took off, cutting across the village green, angling toward the Sheridan Road entrance to the farm. I watched her only for a second before taking off at a dead run the other way.

[handwritten margin note: Why he couldn't tell anyone what he saw.]

OFFICER EUGENE SPAID INSPECTS THE SCENE
Photo courtesy of The Chicago Tribune

Chapter 30 — The Crime Scene
Lake Bluff Village Hall — October 30, 1928

As a kid in the orphanage back in 1928, I remember information about the crime and crime scene sort of trickling in, both at LBO and at our school. No matter how hard the adults tried to shield us from this horror, in the end they could only do so much. Even when Miss Arbuckle and the other housemothers wouldn't tell us anything, we worked out a system with a kid from school. Ricky McSwain was a newsy who hawked papers down at the train station and at the corner of Scranton and Sheridan Road. With all the news about Miss Knaak, we asked Ricky to hold back one copy of his paper at the end of his day, and we snagged it from him on his way home in the late afternoons.

The entire Chicagoland area was flooded with countless newspaper reports and radio broadcasts—on a daily basis—for weeks after Miss Knaak was found. And in the 29 years since it all went down, I've accumulated an enormous file. I swear I've gone over my notes regarding the crime scene like a drunk to his bottle.

Official police reports indicate that Miss Knaak was discovered by Chris Louis, the village gardener. According to Chief Rosenhagen's own testimony, on his way up the sidewalk, he crossed paths with Louis. The two exchanged their usual morning pleasantries and proceeded to enter the building by the east entrance. Rosenhagen reported that, "a blast of cold air hit us, as the door to the building closed behind us." The chief immediately concluded, "That old furnace must be out again." He then asked Louis "if he would mind running down and getting the furnace going."

This is where I came to grips with just how ill-suited to this moment—not to mention the weeks to come—Lake Bluff's Police Chief Barney Rosenhagen was. He was good-hearted man, a hard-working German immigrant with expertise in water and sewer systems. But Barney Rosehagen had absolutely no police nor investigative experience—none.

Chris Louis, both by the chief's and his own report, began to descend the stairs, while Chief Rosehagen headed up the four steps to the right that led to the main police office. Noticing "an unusual darkness" in the stairwell as he descended, Louis returned to the top of the stairs to turn on the light switch, so he'd have some light down below to work with once he got to the furnace room. But the switch apparently did not respond to his "several flips." So Louis descended in almost total darkness.

Louis testified that the door to the night dispatch office was "closed but not locked." As the gardener pushed it open, he took several steps into the room. Louis reported that a few shafts of morning light came in through the coal chute above and from the small window on the backside of the building. Approximately eight feet in front of him on the floor, propped against the wall, was what Louis called "a ghastly figure." It waved at him, at which point Louis turned, lunged for the door, and dashed up the stairs, screaming.

Hearing the gardener's screams, Chief Rosenhagen testified that he came around the corner and almost crashed into Louis on the landing by the outside door they had entered together only moments before. Rosenhagen described Louis's face as "contorted" and said that the gardener's hands were "shaking uncontrollably."

Louis's report was initially a single word: "Ghost!" But he was later able to add, "There's a ghost down there," as he pointed down the stairs.

The chief reportedly walked down the same darkened staircase to open the night dispatch office door. He flicked on the light switch once inside the furnace room itself, which threw light into the entire room.

Rosenhagen remembered gasping, as he saw an "ashen, phantom figure" sitting against the wall beside the furnace. The figure was alive, according to Rosenhagen, because it was "moving its left hand oddly, maybe waving." The chief stepped tentatively toward what he was beginning to realize was "a naked woman who was badly burned." The chief reportedly turned back toward the open door and yelled up to Louis for a blanket and ordered him to call Wenban's Funeral Home for the ambulance.

It was soon after yelling to Louis that the chief was able to hear the hollow, gasping voice of the burn victim, begging for water. Rosenhagen leapt to his feet and looked around the room for anything to quench her thirst. He raced toward the door, reaching it just as the gardener returned with a blanket.

Grabbing the wool, army-issue blanket, the chief apparently barked at Louis again to "get some water and that ambulance."

Louis, who had already reached Wenban's by phone, reported that the ambulance would arrive in the next ten minutes.

Rosenhagen testified that he placed the blanket around the figure "to cover her nakedness." The chief had seen horrific burns on her arms, legs, and the side of her head. Rosenhagen also noted that all of the victim's fingers on one hand were missing everything from the last knuckle on up. Similarly, he testified that her feet were "completely blackened, sooty, and missing the end of her toes."

When Louis arrived with the glass of water, the chief remembered holding it gently to the woman's lips. Aspirated sounds reportedly came from her mouth, as the chief struggled to get water into her throat. He also noted that the victim's eyes "fluttered and closed," and her head "slumped, pulling her whole torso off the wall," joining her legs and feet on the floor.

Rosenhagen said that he looked around the room for something to place beneath her head. Seeing a man's sweater on the hook beside the door, he ordered Louis to bring it to him. As he slid it under the victim's head, he must have realized that they were in over their heads, for he ordered Chris to "get upstairs and call Eugene Spaid." Spaid was the only other officer on the Lake Bluff Police force. Louis sped up the stairs and made the call.

Chief Rosenhagen later reported that he found the crime scene "inexplicable." He saw nothing disturbed nor out of place. There were no signs of struggle, nor was there even the slightest damage to the room. But he did note, once the lights in the stairway hall were fixed, that there were bloody footprints going in both directions, up and down the stairs that led from the back entrance down to the furnace room. "They seemed to originate from the furnace heading up the stairs. At the top, by the door, there was even more blood. Then the tracks seemed to turn around and go back to where we discovered the body." He further testified that he eventually noticed a pair of women's shoes, neatly placed beside the wall, and, next to them, a purse and a wristwatch. There was no blood in or around the shoes, and the footprints were clearly those of a barefooted person, albeit someone with badly disfigured feet.

It was the purse, of course, that would provide the identity of the victim in the form of an empty envelope addressed to "Miss Elfrieda Knaak, 66 Deerfield Ave, Deerfield Illinois." The return address indicated that the letter had come from the Chautauqua Equipment Co. in Valparaiso, Indiana. The only other thing Rosenhagen reported finding in the purse was a round trip North Shore Line train ticket from the Highland Park station to Station 22 (Lake Bluff), with an accompanying claim check for a checking room the victim had used to store her encyclopedia sample case down at the Highland Park train station.

By this time, some ten to fifteen minutes after discovering the victim, the chief admitted to "not being sure" whether Miss Knaak "had expired, fallen unconscious, or was merely sleeping." He recalled stepping over to the furnace to examine its open door, a door which, significantly, was almost at the height of the chief's waist. He testified that he bent to look inside the twelve and three-quarters by nine and three-quarters inch opening, but saw nothing out of the ordinary—no glow, no smoke, and no heat—only the typical morning mountain of gray ash.

Two different reports corroborate that the two men from Wenban's Funeral Home arrived at the Village Hall at 7:19 a.m. and descended the stairs, carrying a rolled up stretcher.

The drivers remembered Chief Rosenhagen asking them if the victim was dead.

One of the ambulance workers, George Wenban, testified to touching the side of the victim's throat gently with two fingers, procuring a pulse, and then determining that the victim was, in fact, taking in and expelling air.

Immediately after he made these important determinations, George remembered his brother Frederic asking "What, in God's name, happened here, Chief?"

"I have no idea," the chief reportedly responded, just as Eugene Spaid, his assistant, entered the room.

Spaid testified to having "no idea what I was walking into. I just know I came as fast as I could and asked my usual question, 'What have we got?' Before anyone had even answered, I saw the charred remains of a woman, who was barely alive, being raised up on the canvas stretcher, carried up the stairs, out the door, and toward the Wenban's vehicle."

Spaid testified that he was asked by the chief, while the two were still in the Village Hall, to ride in the ambulance with the victim. "The chief's concern was that the victim might not make it to the hospital, and he wanted me to note anything she might say, if she were to regain consciousness."

The Wenban brothers loaded the victim into the back of their brown, 1927 Henney. Both brothers testified that the victim did, in fact, regain consciousness and began to speak before Rosenhagen and Spaid got down to the ambulance from the Village Hall.

"We called the chief," Frederic said, "and told him to come out to us at the curb on the double." Neither of the Wenbans could make out what the victim was saying.

Once Rosenhagen was leaning into the rear of the Henney, he reported making out only a single word. "She kept saying 'Hitch.' It was aspirated and broken, but it was definitely 'Hitch.'"

George, who reportedly overheard this utterance, added that it seemed to him that the victim was actually trying to talk to this person, as if "Hitch" were in the ambulance and she was calling to him.

But there was no time to parse this single syllable, for the Henney driver had to transport the victim at once. As the vehicle began to pull away, Rosenhagen yelled, "Write down every word she says, Eugene!" Spaid heard this from inside the back of the ambulance.

Spaid reportedly slid as far forward as he could and positioned himself as close to the charred victim's head as possible. "She seemed to be moving in and out of consciousness, from a state of relative stillness, to an all-out thrashing back and forth," Spaid had told the Coroner. "But at one point, she became very animated. Her eyes opened, and she seemed to be looking right at me. She said, 'Hitch? Oh, Hitch.'"

Spaid leaned in closer, trying to look "as calm and unfazed by her hideous and blistered face as I could." He said he simply responded, "What? What's that, Miss?" But he never got a response. "Her eyes just closed again and she seemed to slip away."

Hospital records indicate that the Wenban ambulance pulled up to the emergency entrance of Lake Forest Alice Home Hospital at 7:36 a.m. The two attending physicians, Dr. Rissinger and Dr. Proxmire, met the Wenbans at the entrance and helped carry the victim inside, as Officer Spaid and Frederic Wenban filled them in.

Frederic Wenban later testified that, "I told the doctors that the victim was Elfrieda Knaak, a white female from Deerfield, who had been found at 7:01 a.m. that morning in the basement furnace room of the Lake Bluff Village Hall. I told them that she was horribly burned over nearly half of her body, including half her head." Frederic also remembered Dr. Proxmire saying, "Good God! Who could have done this?"

Just before Frederic left the hospital, the victim once again thrashed and opened her eyes. Wenban testified that, "the patient gasped, sucked in air, and swallowed painfully. Then she said, 'Hitch?' like it was a question or something."

Dr. Proxmire corroborated Frederic's testimony and added that Officer Eugene Spaid hung around as long as he could, impressing upon the doctors the importance of taking note of anything the victim might say.

In Spaid's words, "I told them that we simply had no idea where to begin our investigation into this horrible crime, and that anything she said, no matter how fragmentary or nonsensical, could be extremely helpful to us."

From everything I've found and everyone I've talked to over the years, what went on back at the Village Hall after Miss Knaak's body had been discovered and transported can only be described as a three-ring circus. "Chief" Rosenhagen had, literally, been begged to take on the police chief role as a favor to the town fathers. It's also not incidental to the unfolding events of this first day at the crime scene that Rosenhagen, a German immigrant, had very limited English skills. But his paltry command of the English language was vastly superior to his knowledge of how to manage a crime scene in what was about to become a full-scale investigation.

Take the fact that the gardener, the terrified man who had discovered Miss Knaak's body, was, soon after, directed by the chief to clear out the ashes from the furnace, put fresh coal in it, fill the external coal bin, and get the furnace started as soon as possible. The chief would subsequently explain his actions by noting that "the building was freezing, and the village clerk upstairs was already complaining about the cold." To Rosenhagen's credit, Louis did testify that he was told to do all that "without touching or disturbing anything else down there."

A second, equally stunning example of Rosenhagen's incompetence can be discerned in the fact that he didn't bother placing a call to the Lake County Sheriff Lawrence Doolittle nor to State's Attorney A.V. Smith until almost 1:00 p.m. that afternoon; that's a full six hours after Miss Knaak was discovered at 7:01 a.m.

At 1:45 p.m., at almost the exact same moment, these two highly agitated officials pulled into the Lake Bluff Village Hall. State's Attorney Smith arrived in his typical, loose-fitting, gray pinstriped suit, unbuttoned in the front, and a matching fedora. Sheriff Doolittle was always and only seen in the khaki uniform of the department he headed, and this particular day was no different. He and Colonel Smith were more than familiar with each other, as their respective jurisdictions overlapped constantly.

Much to Chief Rosenhagen's chagrin and subsequent embarrassment, the first thing Sheriff Doolittle reported seeing as he approached the crime scene was the ashen bucket Chris Louis had used to thoroughly empty the furnace of ashes. Seeing the gardener nearby, the Sheriff testified that he asked him directly, "Son, what is this bucket doing here?"

"That's the bucket we use to empty the ashes from the furnace each morning, sir," Louis responded.

"You emptied the ashes this morning? You emptied the furnace ashes this morning, today?" This was probably the first of many moments that the calmer State's Attorney Smith had to remind Sheriff Doolittle that this was the tiny, sheltered town of Lake Bluff, not the "big city" of Waukegan, where crimes happened on a much more regular basis. Smith did tell a *Waukegan News Sun* reporter, "We got to the scene of the crime as soon as we could. But keep in mind that Barney waited almost six hours to call us in on the case."

A third blatant example of the Lake Bluff force being in way over their heads on the Knaak case is the fact that it was the outsiders—Smith and Doolittle—who first made the connection that this "Hitch" the victim kept mentioning might actually be Charles Hitchcock, Spaid and Rosenhagen's co-worker.

While Hitchcock's name was kept out of the earliest newspaper reports as a person of interest, by late Tuesday afternoon the actor was named as a possible suspect by Smith.

Both Smith and Doolittle later reported that Chief Rosenhagen gave them a thorough tour of the crime scene. Doolittle noted that while the chief answered all their questions, he was "visibly shaken and emotionally distraught" over what he had seen.

Coming to Rosenhagen's defense, Smith told the same *Waukegan News Sun* reporter that, "It's hard even to describe what a body looks like that has been burned over one third of its surface. It's a horror that few can look upon without collapsing."

Looking back on that first morning of the case, Smith would later write, "I'm still trying to figure out how you would get anywhere near a third of any adult body into that furnace opening, even one piece at a time. I would be hard pressed to get more than either of my arms into this opening, much less my entire head." He later admitted to being most baffled by the complete absence of any signs of struggle as the investigation got rolling.

In this first meeting between Rosenhagen, Doolittle, and Smith, the three men determined that Deputy Dispatch Hitchcock would be the first person questioned. That interview was scheduled for the very same afternoon.

CHARLES HITCHCOCK AT HIS HOME, TUESDAY OCTOBER 30TH, 1928
DN-0086790, Chicago Daily News negative collection, Chicago History Museum

Chapter 31 — The First Interrogation of Charles Hitchcock
Lake Bluff, IL — October 30, 1928

By 1:45 p.m. on Tuesday, October 30, the same day Elfrieda Knaak's burned body was found in the Village Hall furnace room, the entire village was in a state of panic. School, which had met as usual in the morning, was called off in the afternoon, once news of the burned body began to leak into the community.

I remember Miss Arbuckle and almost all the housemothers meeting us just outside the school that day and making us all walk home with them in single file lines, according to what dorm we were in. And orphans weren't the only ones who got escorted home on October 30; just about every kid in the school had parents waiting at the school's front door when the early dismissal bell rang.

As we got to the downtown area, I remember seeing shopkeepers pulling their shades down and locking their doors, as if it were the end of the day. Very quickly the streets got quiet, and by the time we got to the orphanage, all we were told was that there was some sort of problem with the water and sewer lines at the school. But there was no hiding the eerie tension all around LBO. The housemothers were huddling and whispering the rest of the day, scrambling to find ways to keep us occupied. Miss Arbuckle made an announcement about "a whole orphanage clean-up," followed by "games and puzzles if we made the place sparkle."

Even all these years later, I still remember how sick I felt that afternoon. More and more I kept picturing the horrible images of that woman's charred body. It was like a movie in my mind that just wouldn't shut off. I asked Miss Harvey if I could lie down in my bed for a while. She felt my head with the back of her hand and nodded, with concern creasing her forehead.

But being alone back in my bed made me feel even worse. I was restless and agitated and just couldn't get still. I was short of breath and felt like I was being choked.

Meanwhile, according to a police report I gained access to almost ten years later, at the very moment I was tossing and turning in my first floor bed at Wadsworth Hall, three officers of the law were making their way to the home of Charles Hitchcock. The Hitchcock residence was a mere two-and-a-half-blocks from the Village Hall on the very same street. The three-man police delegation consisted of Eugene Spaid, State's Attorney Smith, and Sheriff Doolittle. While the transcript didn't include it, I have to believe that it was Doolittle who took the lead once these three arrived at the Hitchcock home.

The threesome arrived just after 2:30 p.m. and were admitted into the home by Mrs. Estelle Hitchcock and shown to the room in which the deputy was convalescing. Because I had been in the Hitchcock home a dozen or so times that same year, I can still picture what those three would have seen on their short walk from the entry hall to the back bedroom.

The Hitchcock abode was not exactly the model of organization and neatness. Their entryway had newspapers and books aplenty that were in leaning piles on a bench beside the coat closet. The closet's door wouldn't even close due to all the stuff hanging out of it. Mrs. Hitchcock must have been embarrassed that day when three unexpected visitors showed up. The fact that they were officers of the law would have made things even worse.

The following conversation between the officers and their leading person of interest was preserved in the police records:

Doolittle: "I understand that you serve the village as the night dispatch deputy."

Hitchcock: "I most certainly do. Yes."

Doolittle: "And when did you last work?"

Hitchcock: "Well, ordinarily, I would have been there Saturday night, but my little accident occurred last Thursday, so I haven't worked since then."

Doolittle: "Mr. Hitchcock, do you happen to know a woman by the name of Elfrieda Knaak?"

Hitchcock: "Eugene, would you please shut the door behind you … all the way, please."

Doolittle: "Mr. Hitchcock…?"

Hitchcock: "I'm sorry. Yes, I do know Miss Knaak. Why? Is she in some sort of trouble?"

Doolittle: "In what capacity do you know this woman, Mr. Hitchcock?"

Hitchcock: "Miss Knaak is one of my students, just as you were, Mr. Smith, up in Waukegan. Fritzie…Miss Knaak has been an able, exemplary student."

Doolittle: "And does your relationship with this exemplary student extend beyond the classroom?"

Hitchcock: "I did tutor her from time to time, Sheriff."

Doolittle: "When you did this tutoring, was it just the two of you—you and Miss Knaak?"

Hitchcock: "Yes. Yes it was. All my tutoring is one-on-one. It's most effective that way, I find. Please, Sheriff Doolittle, I must know. Why all these questions about Miss Knaak?"

Doolittle: "I'm getting to that, Mr. Hitchcock. Can you tell me how often you and Miss Knaak would have these tutoring sessions, and when and where the most recent one would have been?"

Hitchcock: "Oh, my. I'd have to consult my appointment book for the specifics. It would have been late September, early October perhaps…Look, I don't mean to sound secretive about all this, but it's important for you to understand that my wife was never particularly comfortable with my tutoring students."

Doolittle: "And why was that, Mr. Hitchcock?"

Hitchcock: "Estelle knew…knows that we desperately need the money. But she would prefer that I make it some other way."

Smith: "You mean some other way that doesn't involve meeting privately with young, single women half your age?"

Hitchcock: "Yes. When you put it that way, I suppose that's exactly what Estelle would say."

Doolittle: "So these tutoring sessions with Miss Knaak, where would they take place?"

Hitchcock: "The Village Hall. At my…in the basement of the Village Hall. I know it probably was a poor choice for me, meeting Miss Knaak there when I was technically on duty…But as Officer Spaid knows, nine nights out of ten we receive no calls of any kind over there, save the occasional frazzled parent, whose teenager is out shooting at squirrels over in one of the ravines. Gentlemen, I do regret using the Village Hall as our meeting place, and I assure you that it happened, at most, a half-dozen times. But I'm sure you can see why meeting here would not have been an option."

Doolittle: "I believe I can see why you two would choose not to meet here. But, again, just to be completely clear, the last time you saw and were with Miss Knaak was when, exactly?"

Hitchcock: "I'm sure it would have been almost three weeks ago."

Doolittle: "Not last night then, Mr. Hitchcock?"

Hitchcock: "No, absolutely, not! I was here. Right here. In fact, my good friend Oscar Kloer stopped by for a drink. You can check with Oscar."

Doolittle: "Well, your student was found last night, badly injured. Burned, in fact...almost beyond recognition."

Hitchcock: "No! My God, no! Burned, you said? Oh, dear God, not burned! Please, not burned...Is she...all right? Is she alive?"

Smith: "Barely, Mr. Hitchcock. Just barely,"

Hitchcock: "Where is she? Where did this happen?"

Doolittle: "Alice Home Hospital down in Lake Forest. But she was found in the Village Hall...in your office, Deputy. So, Mr. Hitchcock, getting back to your question, we are here looking into an assault that may, in a very short time, become a murder."

Smith: "We're not jumping to any conclusions, Mr. Hitchcock. We're not sure what the hell happened. We've never seen anything like this, not in Lake Bluff, not even in Waukegan. Our best guess at this point is that some vagrant might've done this horrible thing to Miss Knaak somewhere near this village and then dragged her to the basement to die."

Doolittle: "Just so we can completely rule you out, Mr. Hitchcock, can you tell us where you were last night, between the hours of, say, six and midnight or so?"

Hitchcock: "Yes, certainly. I was right here, doing pretty much the same thing you see me doing now. And, as I mentioned before, my friend Oscar Kloer came over to see me for a while."

Doolittle: "So, you weren't anywhere near the Village Hall last night or before dawn this morning?"

Hitchcock: "No, no. I have really only gone between here, the bathroom across the hall, and the kitchen for the last four days."

Smith: "Can anyone verify your whereabouts last night and in the predawn hours of this morning?"

Hitchcock: "My wife, I suppose. And two of my girls as well, Charlene and Helen."

Doolittle: "You should know, Mr. Hitchcock, that the only reason we are here at all is because of something Miss Knaak said in the ambulance, when Officer Spaid was en route with her to the hospital. It was only one word...and it was your name."

Smith: "So I'm sure you can understand why we are starting with you. We're just hoping you can give us some sort of help here."

Hitchcock: "I'm afraid I...I just don't know. I am certainly in a state of shock over this, but nothing is coming to mind."

Smith: "Can you tell us, Mr. Hitchcock, did Miss Knaak ever speak of any male friends she might've known, or did she ever mention any unusual acquaintances in your time of knowing her?"

Hitchcock: "No. She spoke only of her brothers and sisters. She's from a very close and loving family."

Doolittle: "Mr. Smith, why don't you go have a word with the lady of the house, while Officer Spaid and I stay here with Deputy Hitchcock."

Smith: "Be happy to, Sheriff."

I'd managed to get on pretty good terms with Deputy Hitchcock's second oldest daughter Helen during my year in Lake Bluff. She was over at the Hitchcock house most days when I was working over there. Plus, I'd see her in school quite a bit. As I pieced together what must have been going on in the hours and days after the body was discovered, I couldn't help but wonder what it must have been like for her: police coming over to their house, pictures and reports in the newspaper, and constant allegations about her father's "inappropriate relationship" with Elfrieda Knaak.

I remember seeing her in school about a week after Miss Knaak's burned body had been discovered. I asked how she and her family were faring.

"My daddy's just not the same," she said. "He's constantly on edge, and at times, he becomes…well, almost crazy." And that was just the beginning of the trauma her father would put her and her family through.

"You may remember, Detective Hargrave, that you actually provided me with a summary of A.V. Smith's brief interchange with Mrs. Hitchcock when the State's Attorney left the Deputy's room to ask Estelle a few follow-up questions. Those notes verified that Mrs. Hitchcock was away at work, down in Highland Park, from about 8:00 in the evening until almost 12:30 on the night in question."

"That's right," Hargrave interjected. "And, as I tried and tried to get Smith and Doolittle to understand, that gave Hitchcock over four hours without his wife around. Crutches or no crutches, he could have left."

"Yes," I said, "but Mr. Hitchcock said his two older kids were in and out of his room checking on him until almost 10 p.m. So that really only leaves about a two to two-and-a-half hour window when he was alone."

"His wife was not at all keen on any of us talking to the children. I remember that," Hargrave said.

"So what became of all this, the inquiry over at the Hitchcock place?" I asked.

"Nothing much, I'm afraid," Detective Hargrave chuckled. "But Smith and Doolittle hightailed it over to Alice Home Hospital right afterwards, to see if they could talk their way into Miss Knaak's room."

George Hargrave paused, shook his head and said, "I gotta take a leak."

ALICE HOME HOSPITAL — LAKE FOREST, ILLINOIS
Photo courtesy of the Lake Forest-Lake Bluff Historical Society

Chapter 32 — A Hospital Visit
Lake Forest, IL — Alice Home Hospital — October 30, 1928

According to the police reports and testimony from several hospital employees, State's Attorney Smith and Sheriff Doolittle walked into the elaborate main entrance of the Alice Home Hospital in Lake Forest, Illinois, at approximately 3:30 in the afternoon on October 30. A receptionist greeted them and showed them up to Elfrieda Knaak's second floor room. The greeter noted that the men "announced that they were on an urgent investigative matter." She delivered them to the hallway just outside the room, where they then had words with Dr. Proxmire, the attending physician.

"I was reluctant to let them in the patient's room," Proxmire testified. He explained to the Sheriff and State's Attorney that the patient was "incoherent, in and out of consciousness, rarely responsive in any way." The doctor was concerned about Miss Knaak's excessive weakness and was reluctant to "risk anything that would agitate her or drain what little fighting energy was still within her."

Smith testified that he and Doolittle inquired after the patient's condition, and that Dr. Proxmire reported, in no uncertain terms, that it was tenuous at best. In Smith's words, "I think the doc's phrase was 'hanging by a thread, and not much of one at that.'"

Obviously, Doolittle and Smith's concern was getting as much information from Miss Knaak as possible before she expired. Dr. Proxmire had previously described her condition as "extremely dire," and had conjectured that "she may not make it through the night."

In Proxmire's words, "You have to understand, the human body is not designed for fire. It can absorb a lot of blows, breaks, and even gunshot wounds. But to have burns over this much of one's body makes the chance of survival negligible at best."

Doolittle apparently pressed Proxmire hard about getting into the patient's room in order to question her. As the Sheriff would later tell the *Waukegan News Sun*, "It was our belief that there was a crazy moron out there somewhere—somewhere in Lake Bluff or the surrounding area. This animal, whoever he was, had lighted Miss Knaak on fire and then watched her burn. We had every reason to believe that this maniac could strike again." Given that the attending physician had put the victim's chance of survival somewhere between slim and none, the two officers felt justified in pushing for the interrogation. "We had to balance our concern for the victim's condition with our responsibility for public safety," Sheriff Doolittle explained.

Dr. Proxmire later revealed that it was the presence of the victim's two brothers, Otto and Alvin, keeping vigil at her bedside, that ultimately led to his refusing to admit Smith and Doolittle to the patient's room. However, Smith and Doolittle's efforts that first afternoon were not completely in vain, for it was there that Dr. Proxmire handed the two men a list of every word Miss Knaak had uttered in the hours since being admitted to the Alice Home Hospital. The list read as follows:

> *Hitch*
> *I'm sorry*
> *Hitch, oh, Hitch*
> *I did this to myself*
> *Frank threw me down*
> *I didn't do it…They did it*
> *I'm sorry*

I wonder…I wonder…who did this to me
The pain…Oh, the pain

In looking back through my notes and this list of the victim's ramblings, I found some of the questions the State's Attorney had about Miss Knaak's words:

—The 'Hitch' references were one thing; we'd sorted them out before we ever got to the hospital. But Miss Knaak's apologies—what in the world would she be apologizing for?
—What about "I did this to myself?" Can't be talking about the burns, can she?
—"They did this to me?" Who is "they?"
—Who is Frank? Need to follow up on every Frank in Miss Knaak's life.

The only other thing the two officers were able to accomplish that first afternoon at the Alice Home Hospital was a brief conversation with Alvin Knaak, one of Elfrieda's older brothers.

"While Doctor Proxmire wouldn't let us into the hospital room, he did consent to call one of the two Knaak brothers out to answer a few questions for us, provided we promised to be respectful of the delicacy of this awful situation," Doolittle said. The sheriff is also on record at the Coroner's Jury inquest saying that, "We introduced ourselves to Alvin Knaak, apologized for what he and his family were going through, and asked him if he had any idea who could have done this to his sister." Doolittle continued, "He clearly didn't. He went on to describe his kid sister as 'the nicest, kindest, most giving person I know.'"

"Yes, that's right," Hargrave replied, standing up and walking over to the window. "That's how I remember it."

I pulled out another list from my file. "I've got this short list of additional facts Doolittle and Smith were able to take away from their brief interview with Alvin Knaak." I handed it to Hargrave and watched as he read.

—The victim works for her brother Theodore at their late father's pharmacy

—She lives with and takes care of her 75 year-old mother

—She teaches Sunday school at the family's church in Deerfield

—She keeps incredibly busy selling encyclopedias door-to-door, taking self improvement classes at the Waukegan YMCA, and working with a tutor on her sales and presentation skills

—She may have a music teacher named Frank

—She was last seen by a pharmacy employee at 10:30 a.m. on October 29

When I could tell he had finished, I continued. "Smith told the *Waukegan News Sun*, 'We came away from that conversation with Alvin Knaak convinced that we needed to be looking for a stranger, a vagrant, some crazed moron who did this horrible thing to Miss Knaak without knowing her at all.' It wasn't much to go on, but the two officers agreed to send a couple of men to start working the likely train and bus stations Miss Knaak might have used on Monday afternoon and evening. They would provide their men with a recent picture of Miss Knaak. The two also agreed to track down the music teacher with the first name of Frank."

Hargrave came back to his desk but didn't sit down. He put his large hands on the back of his chair and looked down at the floor.

"There's even a note from you here, Detective." I slid my notebook across his desk and he read it aloud.

"*Miss Knaak's words 'I did this to myself' have continued to eat at me, and I'm sure they're eating at Smith and Doolittle as well.*" Hargrave chuckled and added, "It was true then, and I dare say it's just as true today, Griff."

THE FURNACE — LAKE BLUFF VILLAGE HALL BASEMENT
Photo courtesy of the Lake Bluff History Museum

Chapter 33 — Another Conversation With Charles Hitchcock

Lake Bluff Village Hall — Chief Barney Rosenhagen's Office —
November 1, 1928

On Thursday, November 1, two days after Miss Knaak had been found, Smith and Doolittle brought Deputy Dispatch Hitchcock into the Village Hall for a second round of questioning. While Hitchcock was still on crutches, in a splint of some sort, and staying close to home, Rosenhagen had learned that his deputy had recovered enough mobility to get up and down steps and in and out of a car. So the State's Attorney sent Sheriff Doolittle over to the Hitchcock home to bring the actor to his place of employment, not to mention the scene of the crime.

Though I'd entertained irrational fantasies about sneaking out of school in order to hang around the Village Hall early that Thursday morning, playing hooky at the local police station didn't strike me as a solid plan. But I sure wanted to see Mr. Hitchcock on his crutches and maybe even hear what the Sheriff and State's Attorney were asking him.

Instead, I was stuck over at Lake Bluff Elementary School, where the kids, the teachers, and even the custodian blabbed non-stop about the mysterious case of the burned woman from Deerfield.

> ...*I heard the lady was burned so badly, they thought she was a negress!*
> ...*They said the gardener who found her had to use a hoe to scrape her off the furnace.*
> ...*And when the ambulance fellas came and started to pick her up, one of her arms just fell off, along with her ear!*

The teachers were a bit more discreet, for their interests seemed to lie with apprehending the perpetrator.

> ...*They haven't a clue who this crazy killer is, and he may be loose in this very town!*
> ...*I don't know why they don't search every house in the village to apprehend this assassin!*
> ...*The fact that we even have school seems irresponsible to me. Why, these children and all of us are at risk simply by being here!*

I remember Lake Bluff becoming a circus, ever since the chief and his gardener discovered Miss Knaak beside that furnace. Reporters from every Chicago and Illinois daily, along with radio reporters, were swarming around the village, asking questions to people on the streets, patrons in downtown shops, and even train commuters. There were cars and trucks parked in every available downtown spot, and some of the more aggressive reporters had even parked right on the Village Green.

From everything I've been able to read and get my hands on in the years since 1928, it seemed to me that the purpose of the second interview with Mr. Hitchcock—two days after the body had been discovered—was to find out what he knew or thought about the possibility that Miss Knaak might have done this to herself.

Hargrave interrupted me. "That's right. A major reason the Knaak family hired me in the first place was that they were so steamed up about the fact that, in addition to the predominant theory of a crazed moron on the loose, Doolittle and Smith just wouldn't let up on this angle of spiritual purification and suicide."

The official record of the second conversation between Deputy Hitchcock, the State's Attorney, and the Lake County Sheriff reads as follows:

Doolittle: "Well, let's get right to it, Deputy Hitchcock. We've learned a bit more about your friend and student, Miss Knaak."

Hitchcock: "Please, how is Miss Knaak? There have been conflicting reports in the papers. One says she's on death's doorstep, and the next claims that she's prattling on and on in incoherent gibberish."

Smith: "It's pretty grim, Mr. Hitchcock. The doctors have done everything they can think of. But it's not likely to be enough. Deputy, did Miss Knaak ever indicate to you that she was interested in any sort of purifying religious rituals? Did she ever talk about burning herself, for example?"

Hitchcock: "No, sir. I never heard about anything like that from her. Why do you ask?"

Doolittle: "In addition to your name, one of the other things she said a number of times, both on the way to the hospital and once admitted, was 'I did this to myself.'"

Hitchcock: "I have no idea about that. I can't see Elfrieda doing something like this to herself."

Smith: "If you never talked about such things with her, can you think of anyone who might have had such spiritual conversations with her?"

Hitchcock: "She did mention a woman to me a few times, a woman with an odd name. She may have been an author or writer...I think her name began with B or perhaps her name was B...Yes, B. Lock, I believe it was. I seem to remember Elfrieda mentioning some writings of this B. person that were of a spiritual nature."

Doolittle: "You seem to have known the victim pretty well. So you don't give any credence to the idea that she may have done this to herself?"

Hitchcock: "I...I...don't think so, no. She was very serious about her religious faith. It was extremely important to her—what she read, what she wrote, what she talked about. She was one of the most devoted people I've ever encountered. But killing herself, burning herself...I can't imagine it."

Smith: "Now, Mr. Hitchcock, we must ask you about the furnace. You've worked beside it. You've...instructed Miss Knaak beside it. She was well aware of its location by the night of October 29. Did she ever show a particular fascination with it or seem to be studying it, observing it carefully, or asking you how it worked?"

Hitchcock: "She warmed herself by it, as anyone would coming in out of the cold...But, no...I don't recall anything other than that."

Doolittle: "We appreciate you coming in, Deputy. We'll have Officer Spaid run you home."

Smith: "And if you think of anything, and I mean anything that might be helpful to us..."

Hitchcock: "I will let you know at once. But please, gentlemen, do keep me posted on Miss Knaak's condition."

"I remember one of our conversations—yours and mine, Detective—the one where we reviewed this particular testimony. I remember you emphasizing over and over that, even though Chief Rosenhagen wasn't in on that interview and was constantly pushed aside throughout the entire investigation, you believed that the chief still had significant influence on what Smith and Doolittle concluded where Charles Hitchcock was concerned."

"That's exactly right, Mr. Morgan. That half-wit Chief Rosenhagen kept insisting that his deputy was innocent, and that's what led the two investigators to dismiss Hitchcock as a suspect in the case," Hargrave said.

"But I'm finding that so hard to believe, Detective. I can't even imagine that either the County Sheriff or the State's Attorney would have given any sort of credence whatsoever to Chief Barney's views on anything. He was a sewer and water man, for Christ's sake! You said, yourself, that he was in way over his head; the chief knew it and both Smith and Doolittle knew it as well. Even during the entire time Rosenhagen was serving as Lake Bluff's Police Chief, ninety percent of the calls that came into his office still had to do with roads in need of repair and water leaks around the village," I said. "He was constantly pushed to the sidelines of the investigation. Why would they have listened to him about Hitchcock's innocence?"

Detective Hargrave shook his head and turned his palms upward. "You got a better explanation for why Hitchcock walked, Mr. Morgan?" He stood up and started pacing. "We're talking about a guy who was having an illicit and secretive relationship with the victim. This same man worked in and had keys to the very office where the crime occurred. You, yourself, can verify that Mr. Hitchcock was seen either in or going into that very office with the victim on more than a half-dozen occasions. Heck, the scoundrel admitted to it under oath! And despite Miss Knaak being found there—right there, in that very room where she had only ever been with Charles Hitchcock—and despite her being found there severely burned in a manner and to a degree that no human could ever have done to herself, neither State's Attorney Smith nor County Sheriff Doolittle ever went after Deputy Charles Hitchcock as a suspect in the death of Elfrieda Knaak. It's utterly unconscionable, Mr. Morgan...unconscionable. And yet, somehow it's the truth."

"You're probably right, Detective," I said, shaking my head right along with him.

It still sticks in my craw that no one in the law enforcement community paid enough attention to the essential facts about Charles Hitchcock. They may have noticed them, but no one pressed him on these matters, at least not hard enough. Even though he should have been considered the prime suspect, his connection to the town, to the Lake Bluff Police Department, and all his convenient alibis allowed him to skate through all the proceedings without ever having to reveal what he knew, what he saw, and what he did. Neither the State's Attorney nor the Lake County Sheriff recognized that, whether Charles Hitchcock perpetrated this horrific crime or not, he must have, at the very least, been a party to it taking place in his office

.

LAUNDRY BUILDING — LAKE BLUFF ORPHANAGE
Photo courtesy of the Lake Bluff History Museum

Chapter 34 — A Death in the Village
Lake Bluff Orphanage Laundry Room — November 2, 1928

On Friday, November 2, just after dinner, Johnny, Knox, Billy, and I were down in the laundry with Mr. Spader. We all liked to go down there to "help" him with the laundry, which really just meant we sat around in the various laundry carts and listened to his favorite radio programs with him. This particular Friday, a brand new kid named Phillip Rutherford was already down there when we arrived. Mr. Spader was in the only actual chair in the laundry, a big, stuffed, blue one with a high back and arms. He was smoking his pipe and staring off, as *Amos and Andy* came on the air. Mr. Spader's burning pipe had a hickory smell that I always liked. He often smoked it on our trips to Crab Tree Farm, and whether I was in the cab with him or back in the flatbed, I always enjoyed breathing it in.

We were all quietly gathered around the Federal Telephone and Telegraph A-10 Orthosonic radio. There were three or four other radios scattered throughout the orphanage, but all the others were tightly controlled, and we'd never get to listen to anything fun. Mr. Spader was different. He loved to laugh and to get us laughing too.

The programs he listened to were entertaining, while Miss Arbuckle listened to opera and Miss Harvey had a penchant for violin concertos.

Mr. Spader's favorite program by far was *The Amos and Andy Radio Hour*. It began with a fifteen-minute opening segment, followed by a minute or two of commercial messages from sponsors, and the occasional newsbreak about a half an hour into the program from the WMAQ newsroom, right down the road in Chicago. On this particular Friday evening, the news segment grabbed us more than the show itself.

> *Tonight's news begins in Lake Forest, Illinois. In the ongoing investigation of the burning of The Furnace Girl, 30-year-old Elfrieda Knaak from Deerfield, sources report that Lake Bluff's Deputy Dispatch and former star of the silver screen Charles Hitchcock was rushed to the victim's bedside at approximately 3:30 p.m. this afternoon. State's Attorney Colonel A.V. Smith told WMAQ that Mr. Hitchcock was both a friend and teacher of Miss Knaak, and that he had been brought to the Alice Home Hospital in the hope of getting some useful information from the victim before she expired.*
>
> *As we reported yesterday, WMAQ obtained a series of unusual remarks the victim had uttered in the last 48 hours, while in a state of disorientation and semi-consciousness. Lake County Sheriff Lawrence Doolittle told WMAQ that while police were following up on every possible lead, none of what Miss Knaak had said since being found in the Lake Bluff Village Hall basement on the morning of Tuesday, October 30, had resulted in pointing authorities toward a possible perpetrator.*
>
> *Bringing in Mr. Hitchcock was a risky proposition, one that the attending physician, Dr. T.S. Proxmire, only consented to reluctantly after consulting with the victim's family. A representative of the Knaak family noted that, "For the safety and peace of mind of the community, we certainly want to help the authorities track down this maniac. But at the same time, we don't want to worsen Elfrieda's fragile and tenuous condition."*
>
> *WMAQ sources reported that Mr. Hitchcock's visit with the critically injured victim lasted less than five minutes, and that while Miss Knaak appeared to recognize Mr. Hitchcock, she was unable to respond to any of his questions, questions that had been carefully scripted by the State's Attorney. Colonel Smith told WMAQ, "We*

wanted to learn anything we could about who might have done this to Miss Knaak and how that person or persons obtained access to the locked Village Hall that late on Monday evening." Sheriff Doolittle even removed his shoes and followed Deputy Hitchcock into the victim's room silently, in hopes of hearing something that might guide their search for the perpetrator.

WMAQ sources further reported that it was a phone call that came to Chief Barney Rosenhagen's office at 3:15 p.m., informing him that Miss Knaak was failing that led to this last ditch effort to elicit information from the victim. Apparently, the only other non-family visitor the victim's family had allowed in Miss Knaak's room was her closest friend, a Miss Marie Mueller of Waukegan, Illinois, who spent ten minutes at her friend's bedside earlier this afternoon.

Detective George Hargrave, a private detective who has been called in by the Lake County Sheriff to assist with this gruesome and mysterious case, told WMAQ that he was at the Alice Home Hospital this afternoon, speaking to one of the Knaak brothers, when the officers showed up on the second floor with Charles Hitchcock in tow. Hargrave noted that, "State's Attorney Smith was hoping that since Hitchcock knew her, he might unlock some of what was inside her, before it was too late."

We all looked at the radio, then at Mr. Spader, and finally at each other. No one spoke. *Amos and Andy* resumed with Kingfish at the mic, but none of us were listening.

Finally, Mr. Spader broke our silence. "I'm sure this is very hard and scary for you boys, particularly having met Miss Knaak here in the orphanage a time or two." Again, we said nothing. I looked down at the worn, gray carpet. "I know there is a lot of fear around town, as we wait for the police to catch up with this…this criminal," Mr. Spader continued.

My head started pounding and my forehead heated up. I didn't dare look up. I could only imagine what my face looked like, as the images of that night flashed through my head, one after another, like a nightmare.

The radio program was interrupted a second time.

We interrupt this program. This just in…We regret to inform our audience that at 5:53 p.m. this very evening, Elfrieda Knaak of Deerfield, Illinois, passed away in the Alice Home Hospital in Lake

*Forest. The cause of death seems to be complications from excessive burns. No further details are available at this time. We now return to our regularly scheduled program...*Amos and Andy, *already in progress...*

I rose as if in a dense fog. I heard voices around me—Kingfish's on the radio and the other fellas around me in the smoke-filled laundry room—but I wasn't making out any words. I stumbled toward the back door, bounded up the single stair, opened the heavy door, and ran out into the November night. I ran up Scranton into town. I ran past the Post Office, and cut north toward Crab Tree Farm. I ran right across Sheridan Road without stopping or even looking both ways. I had no jacket on. I just kept running.

I turned in the long, gravel drive of Crab Tree Farm and finally stopped, out of breath, between the main farmhouse and the Reddington's guesthouse. The lights were on, and I peeked in two different windows looking for Lily, but I didn't see anyone.

I ran on up the path into the orchard, up and over the crest of the hill, and all the way down to the water's edge. I stood in the very spot where the boat had unloaded those cases of bootlegged whiskey into the fake milk trucks. I grabbed stones and started chucking them as far out into the dark Lake Michigan water as I could. I couldn't see where they landed and didn't care. I just grabbed stone after stone and threw until my arm wouldn't move any more.

"Griff, is that you?" It was Redd's voice, fighting to be heard through the wind and rolling waves. I felt his hand upon my shoulder, as I bent over in exhaustion. "What's going on, buddy?"

I stood up and stared back out over the water, hearing the waves crashing in on the shore. I felt my shoulders start to jerk, and I bit down hard on my lower lip. But it was no use. Tears began to gush out of my eyes, and I couldn't even speak to answer his question. I cried longer and harder than I ever remember crying.

The next thing I knew, I was in the Reddingtons' house, on their living room couch. I had no idea how I even got there. Lily was next to me, and Redd was in the kitchen, getting us some iced tea.

"She's dead, Lily," I said. "She's dead! Miss Knaak...she's dead." I felt her lean into me, and she started to whisper something in my ear, something I couldn't make out, when her father returned with a tray of drinks.

"Let's calm down and enjoy these drinks, and then I'll run you back to LBO, Griff," Redd said.

Until he said it, I hadn't even realized that I had just run out of the orphanage. It was past curfew time, so Miss Harvey would be howling mad at me. But none of that mattered. All that mattered was that as of 5:53 p.m. this evening—November 2—whatever was going on in the Village Hall, that Lily and I had practically witnessed Monday night, October 29, had become a murder. We'd been right outside while an innocent woman was killed, and we had a pretty good idea who did it.

I looked over at Lily, who returned my gaze with an intense glare, shaking her head, ever so slightly, back and forth. I know, I thought. We can't tell anybody.

It was half past nine when Redd drove me back over to LBO. The front door was locked and he knocked persistently until Miss Harvey opened it. I looked down at the concrete stoop and waited as Redd stepped inside pulling Miss Harvey in with him. I made out only their whispers until my housemother said, "Let's get you inside and warmed up, Griffin. You must be freezing." Her only other words to me came ten minutes later, when she came in my partition and said, "This will all be behind us soon, Griffin. Now you just try and get some sleep."

I tossed and turned all night.

The Furnace Girl

DOWNTOWN LAKE BLUFF
Photo courtesy of the Lake Bluff History Museum

Chapter 35 — Rumors, Peppers, and Ghosts
Lake Bluff, IL — November 3, 1928

I guess it didn't really surprise me to find out that Lily hadn't been more than five feet from her own back porch since sneaking back up those steps the night we'd been outside the Village Hall. The terrifying images from that night must have been just as relentless in their attack on her mind as they'd been on mine. They played like a movie in our minds all through the day and then got even worse in the night.

She told me her father had asked her again and again, "What's the matter?" But Lily told me all she'd ever say in response was, "I'm not feeling well," or "Nothing, Daddy. I'll be all right." But anyone who had spent any time at Crab Tree Farm knew that when Lily Reddington wasn't outside in the orchard, around the milk house, or with the cows, something was wrong.

So on Saturday morning, the day after Miss Knaak's death was announced and I had cried like a baby over at their place, Redd had insisted that she go with him to the Lake Bluff Fruit Market. "If there's truly 'nothing wrong,' and you're 'going to be all right,' then help me take a load of apples and vegetables to the weekly market.

279

It's the last outdoor market Saturday of the year, Lily. We'll be home in no time." Her father had worn her down, she told me later, and she just didn't want to keep having to explain herself.

It must have been about 9:15 a.m. when she hopped in the green CTF truck to head into town with her father. I was already downtown myself, doing errands for Miss Harvey and Miss Arbuckle. They'd been pretty easy on me after Redd dropped me off so late on the previous night. I wasn't the only kid at the orphanage who was struggling with all this Elfrieda Knaak news. But I sure was the only orphan who'd seen much of what happened down in that basement furnace room.

I was in the crowd on the Village Green when I saw the dark green Crab Tree Farm truck pull up. Lily wore a floppy, blue cap that had been her mother's, one of a handful of items Redd simply couldn't part with. Being a bit too large for Lily, the hat sat low on her head, placing her eyes in the shadow of its broad bill.

As I looked around the circus that downtown Lake Bluff had become, I hoped that Mr. Reddington had thought to warn Lily of what she was in for. I remembered what Miss Arbuckle had told me before letting me out the front door. "All this news brings reporters, police, and maybe even some G-Men or officers of the Bureau of Investigation. Don't go sticking your nose anywhere it doesn't belong. Just get the items on my list and come right back. There'll be more chores awaiting you."

I slithered my way through the throng of people, making my way toward the Crab Tree Farm truck.

I saw Lily open the truck door and knew she must have been shocked by the chaos and noise. The only time I'd ever seen Lake Bluff this crazy was on the Fourth of July, just before the parade got started. From her spot next to the truck, I'm sure Lily could see the huddles of reporters flipping their notebook pages, policemen clearing the entryways to merchants' stores, and photographers snapping pictures of everything under the surprisingly bright November sun.

"Lily!" I heard her father call. He was now behind the truck, motioning to the flatbed, where the bushels of apples and peppers were stacked. She nodded and made her way to the back end of the truck. I kept catching snippets of the conversations that swirled around the Village Green.

...They're saying The Furnace Girl did it to herself...
...Would that have even been possible? In that furnace? How?
...Charles Hitchcock? It can't be...
...I know. Such a handsome man with a moving pictures career!
...In the Village Hall, of all places!
...Defiling our precious, all-American town!

"Lily, I need you, dear." I heard Redd's familiar voice calling out to her above the din. She hopped up and quickly handed down the first bushel. As Redd disappeared with it around the corner, she turned back toward the surrounding conversations.

...An encyclopedia salesman...
...Who could do that to themselves?
...No one from Lake Bluff would ever have done something like this.

When her father returned, I saw Lily hand him the next bushel. "You OK up there, hon?" he asked with a wink. Lily nodded. Out of the corner of her eye, she must have seen the crowd I was trapped in start moving. It was pushing me over toward the Village Hall.

"Chief Rosenhagen is about to make a statement!" someone behind me said, as the crowd neared the dark, majestic building. I moved with it.

"The chief is coming out? When?" another voice to my left said.

The reporters moved the fastest, with the photographers close behind. In a matter of seconds, Scranton had totally cleared out. I looked back at the CTF truck just as Redd had come back for another bushel. He must have wondered where everybody had gone.

I saw Lily point toward the Village Hall. Then she shrugged and handed down the next bushel. She slid the next one out to the back edge of the flatbed and must have decided to run that one in herself. As she did, I saw the familiar, long, black Packard coming around from Center onto Scranton. It slowed as it came by the double-parked CTF truck. The passenger side window cranked down slowly, and I knew the haunting face that it would soon reveal to Lily. I heard myself say, "No!" and I started pushing back through the crowd to try to get to her. It was a struggle to gain any ground. All I could do was watch, as Lily froze and then dropped an entire bushel of peppers all over the sidewalk. Her hands covered her face, as the long, black car slowly disappeared.

"Lily? What happened?" Her father asked. "Are you all right?" Lily was trembling uncontrollably and had crouched down over the now inverted bushel. "Lily, what is it?" her father asked with both his hands on her shoulders. I could see her shoulders beginning to jerk up and down and saw tears streaming down Lily's face. Redd bent down beside her, keeping one arm around her shoulder. With the other, he flipped the bushel back over and placed a few of the peppers that were within reach back into it.

"Don't you worry about these, honey," Redd said. "We brought more than they need, and the bruised ones will make great treats for Chance and Truth."

"I want to go home! Please, Daddy, can we just go home?" She pushed herself up from the concrete. "Now!" Lily walked determinedly to the passenger side of the truck, opened the heavy door, and climbed in, leaving the scattered peppers to her father.

Scranton began to fill back in, as the crowds from the Village Hall filtered back after Chief Rosenhagen's short and apparently unsatisfying statement. As Redd picked up the last of the peppers, he probably heard the same murmurs I was hearing from those who had heard the chief's update.

> ...*No suspects? How can they have no suspects?*
> ...*When did he say the Coroner's Jury would rule on The Furnace Girl's cause of death?*
> ...*How can they still not know what she was doing in our Village Hall?*
> ...*What about the blood on the back sidewalk?*
> ...*Have there really been phone calls threatening the life of Chief Rosenhagen?*
> ...*The deceased woman was from Deerfield, the pharmacy family.*

Redd climbed in beside his daughter, who had her head in her hands and her elbows on her knees. She looked out the window, and her eyes finally fell upon me. I was standing with my mouth open, trying to communicate something to her, but I didn't know what. I think we were both wondering if we'd ever be able to tell anyone what was eating us up from the inside out. I'd wondered that very thing about a thousand times in those first five days, and I haven't stopped wondering it in the twenty-nine years since.

ELSIE KNAAK, 75, MOTHER OF ELFRIEDA KNAAK, AT HER
DAUGHTER'S FUNERAL IN DEERFIELD, ILLINOIS
(HER SON THEODORE KNAAK IS HOLDING HER ARM)
Photo courtesy of The Chicago Tribune

Chapter 36 — The Funeral of Elfrieda Grace Knaak

Deerfield, IL — November 5, 1928

Just after 12:30, when I had finished my lunch at LBO and everybody else was hustling back to Lake Bluff Elementary, I waited patiently just inside the front door of Wadsworth Hall in my very best church clothes. Miss Arbuckle was by my side, as we watched for Mrs. D.'s yellow Ford to pull up to our front walkway. Mrs. D. was going to drive us down to Deerfield for the memorial service of Elfrieda Knaak.

I'm still not sure how it came to be that I was going to Miss Knaak's funeral. I think their decision must have had something to do with a sense that the orphanage needed to be represented at this memorial—and not just by an adult either, but by one of us kids. Because of the many things Miss Knaak had done for all of us at LBO, since that first day she showed up with the encyclopedias, I bet Mrs. D. had suggested that an orphan child needed to join the two of them. Given that I had become Mrs. D.'s favorite farmhand, I'm guessing she lobbied hard to have me join the two matrons at this incredibly sad event. In the days leading up to the funeral, the housemothers had made an enormous sympathy card and gotten every single kid from LBO to sign it. Miss Arbuckle proceeded to lug it outside once Mrs. D.'s car came sputtering up Scranton.

I can still remember what a chaotic scene it was once we got within a couple blocks of the Deerfield Presbyterian Church. Police officers were everywhere, directing traffic. There were even cars pulled off the road, trying to park in front of businesses and storefronts. Many of these cars had photographers leaning out their windows to take pictures. I remember Mrs. D. calling them "vultures."

It took us a full twenty minutes to walk just two blocks from where we'd parked, due to the thickness of the crowd, and I offered to carry the big card this time. As we neared the dark brick church building, I saw two large delivery vehicles parked next to a side door, and men were carting flowers inside by the boxful. With less than fifteen minutes to go before the service was to begin, the bouquets and arrangements just kept coming. I heard Mrs. D. say that every single business in downtown Deerfield had sent both flowers and a delegation to this service.

When we finally made our way inside the church, we were greeted by ushers wearing black suits with white flowers pinned to their breast pockets.

"I have to go to the bathroom. Can you please tell me where to go?" I blurted out to one of the men. He pointed to my left, and I turned to hand the gigantic card to Miss Arbuckle.

"We'll wait right here for you, Griffin," I heard her say. "Hurry along now." I nodded and then turned to weave through the crowd.

I passed offices, cloak rooms, and even a nursery. One dark wooden door said "Reverend. Mark J. Andrews, Pastor." It opened quickly, startling me, and two tall men in dark suits came out, as the robed reverend held the door for them.

"I can assure you," the reverend said, "that I understand your concern, and I have no intention of fanning the sensationalist flames this afternoon with any cause-of-death talk. I'll only communicate the comfort and assurance that the gospel provides at such a time as this." The two men nodded and the shorter one said, "Thank you, Reverend. Our mother has been through enough already, without having to wonder if her daughter's heavenly salvation is in question." I looked down and continued on toward the bathroom and slipped in quickly to relieve myself.

As I re-entered the hallway to head back to the main entrance, I heard sobbing and sniffling and turned to see a large, crowded sitting room. It was completely filled with a huddle of at least 25 or 30 people, all dressed in black. In the middle of it all was an old, hunched-over woman, holding a handkerchief to her nose. Her hands were gloved in white, and a black veil covered her face. The two dark-suited men I'd seen coming out of the pastor's office each had a hand on her shoulder. This had to be Miss Knaak's family.

Just then, the reverend brushed by me, heading toward the room where the family was waiting. He was carrying a Bible and a black folder. One of the ushers I'd seen at the front door caught Reverend Andrews just as he was crossing the threshold into the sitting room.

"Reverend, if I might," the pudgy usher began, gesturing toward the hallway with his chubby fingers. "The crowd is unusually large today, sir, and it seems that it may well take another five to ten minutes to get everyone in and seated."

Reverend Andrews withdrew a gold pocket watch and flipped it open. "It's 1:55 now. Why don't I take a little more time with the family, Stan, and then lead them in at about 2:05."

The usher nodded, half bowed, and backed away. I followed Stan, the usher, all the way back to where Miss Arbuckle stood impatiently.

"Are you ready, Griffin?" she whispered as she gestured toward the sanctuary. "Mrs. Durand has graciously saved us seats."

It was a large, echoey room with a cold, tile floor and incredibly high, arched ceilings. Behind the pulpit were ornate stained glass windows with life-size depictions of Jesus and the disciples. We made our way up the center aisle, but there were two side aisles as well on the other side of some massive cylindrical pillars that ascended all the way up to the ceiling. Black-suited ushers were shuttling chairs up those side aisles to make room for the overflowing crowd.

Mrs. Durand scooted over to make room for the two of us. I turned around in my seat to see the span of the room and to get a look at the crowd of mourners. Slowly, the two rear doors opened, and Reverend Andrews stood in front of the entire Knaak family, lined up, two-by-two, behind him.

The organist took their entrance as her cue and began playing the first notes of Chopin's Funeral March. The little, old woman I'd seen earlier in that family lounge clutched Reverend Andrews' right arm with both her trembling, gloved hands and leaned heavily on the reverend, all the way up the long, central aisle.

After seating Miss Knaak's mother, Reverend Andrews ascended the three stairs, angling toward the pulpit. He scanned the entire sanctuary, taking in the enormous crowd before beginning. "Dearly beloved, we are gathered here on this sad, November afternoon to remember and celebrate the life of Elfrieda Grace Knaak, to mourn her passing, and to give testimony to our belief in the resurrection." His opening words wafted through the pews, and the reverend appeared to make eye contact with each and every one of us in the packed room. But his gaze returned to and settled upon Elise Knaak, Elfrieda's mother.

"Let us pray," the reverend said. "Gracious and ever present God, your ways are not like our ways. Your plan is shrouded in mystery. Our limited, human brains cannot penetrate your providence. But by faith we gather here this day, struggling to believe in your promises, yearning to see some sign of hope…" I don't think I was the only one wishing he'd just get to the "Amen."

When he finally did, Reverend Andrews took his seat, and the church seemed as silent as the stones that formed its walls. Slowly, an older couple rose from their seats in the choir loft and sang, "Softly and Tenderly, Jesus is Calling." Though I didn't like the tune, I did recognize it from our forced weekly attendance at the Methodist Church in Lake Bluff.

The sobbing in the Knaak family pews became most audible during the reading of a strange poem that came next. It was from one of St. Paul's epistles and began with something about "speaking in tongues of men and angels" and then moved on to talk about what love is and isn't. But it was the poem's end that became Reverend Andrews' focus, and the pastor repeated it three times for emphasis: "For now we see in a glass darkly." He paused and repeated this line that would form both the title and the refrain of his message. "For now we see in a glass darkly." Reverend Andrews closed his black Bible, exhaled, sipped from a glass of cold water, and, once again, made eye contact with Elise Knaak before beginning his homily.

"Elfrieda Knaak was a gift to her family, to the town of Deerfield, to this church, and to the world. Look around this crowded sanctuary, and you'll get a sense of just how many lives were positively affected by this vivacious, generous, young woman. There are people here from her office at Compton Publishing. There are several pews filled with her fellow students from up at the Waukegan YMCA, where she took night classes to improve herself. Right up here, near the front, I can see almost three entire rows of her Sunday school students—and those are only her current pupils. I imagine there are some alumni of Miss Knaak's classes scattered about this room as well."

He shook his head compassionately and took another sip of water. Sweat droplets had formed on his brow, and I watched one particular droplet that hung there at the end of his nose, refusing to fall. Reverend Andrews made no attempt to wipe it away. "I cannot begin to explain why the life of this faithful servant came to such a tragic end," Reverend Andrews continued. "But I do know that we live in a world cloaked in mystery, a world where the forces of wickedness threaten to overtake us at every turn, unless we turn to God. There is mystery all about us. But it is our lot in life to see only through a glass darkly, through a foggy mirror. Seeing only a murky picture is a part of what it means to be human. We never get the full picture from earth's humble shores. But God's vision, God's view of things, is altogether different. Today we must remember that nothing is hidden nor kept from His sight. Nothing is beyond His understanding." Reverend Andrews paused and looked at the entire Knaak family. "We may see through a glass darkly…but God sees without limitation.

"Jesus said, 'Come unto me all who are weary and heavy laden, and I will give you rest.'" Andrews continued to look directly at the Knaak family pews. "This is our consolation...This is the balm, the salve God provides. It is not much, but, perhaps, it is enough."

Reverend Andrews descended the steps of the pulpit, gave a subtle nod to the organist, and sat down. A man whom the bulletin identified as "Mr. Alden Winter" rose, positioned his tall, slender frame to the right of the organist, and adjusted the height of a black music stand. He ran a hand through his reddish-gray beard and began to sing in a sweet, tenor voice. "I come to the garden alone, while the dew is still on the roses." As he sang, six identically dressed young men rose and made their way slowly forward toward the casket. They were listed in the program too, the "Pallbearers: Ralph Hornberger, William Krumback, Ralph Peterson, A.W. Meyer, Harry Muhlke, and C.E. Huhn."

As Mr. Winter sang the chorus one final time—"And he walks with me and he talks with me, and he tells me I am his own..."—the six men I'd later learn had been high school classmates and friends of Elfrieda Grace Knaak hoisted the maple-stained casket and began their slow march down the center aisle.

As the music ended and the casket had cleared the rear doors of the sanctuary, Reverend Andrews reminded the congregation of the details of both the forthcoming burial and the meal to follow. Having instructed the faithful to rise, he began the benediction.

"In one of his last moments with his disciples, our savior said, 'Let not your hearts be troubled. Neither let them be afraid. In my father's house are many mansions...'" When he finally finished, the reverend removed a single, long-stemmed rose from a vase on the communion table and took it directly to Elise Knaak. He offered her the rose, followed by his right arm, and led the grieving mother down the aisle. Her family followed behind, looking like exhausted zombies, the walking dead.

"I was there," Hargrave interrupted. "At the funeral, sitting in the balcony."

"I didn't know that," I said. "So I guess this isn't the first time we've been in the same room together." I tried picturing the sanctuary and the balcony of The First Presbyterian Church of

Deerfield on that November day, but I came up empty as far as finding Detective Hargrave in that crowd.

Anyway, as we rose to exit, I heard the cluster of night students from the Waukegan YMCA whispering after the family had passed them. They were mostly in their 20s and 30s, though one woman appeared closer to 50.

"Where is Mr. Hitch? I was sure he'd be here," said one of the young women.

"Me too!" said another. "He was always talking with Elfrieda after class in Elocution, and she told me he tutored her on the side as well."

One of the men in the group shook his head. "Now, girls, let's not make any assumptions about old Mr. Hitchcock." He wagged a finger at the one closest to him. "I have it on good authority that he had some sort of accident and is still home recovering."

That was no accident, I thought, remembering Walter's story. Those thugs beat up Mr. Hitchcock on purpose.

A striking young woman with a feathered blue hat made her way down the center aisle. She looked familiar somehow. She stopped, overhearing the same conversation of the students as I had. She made some sort of adjustment to her hat and then leaned toward the students without facing them.

"What sort of accident?" asked another of the adult students.

"Is he all right? Is he in the hospital?" begged another.

"Excuse me," the woman in the blue hat interrupted them. "Are you speaking of Charles Hitchcock? Has something happened to him?"

The tallest of the male students stepped toward her. "Have we met? I'm Nathan Reid."

"No, no, I'm sorry," she said, blushing a bit. "I didn't mean to barge in. I'm Marie Mueller, a very close friend of Elfrieda's." She paused, adjusting her hat with her left hand. "I am also a friend of Charles's, uh, Mr. Hitchcock's rather." This Miss Mueller was beautiful, and I suddenly remembered her. She had been with Miss Knaak on that day we made those burning bush crafts in Hobbs Dining Hall. But I sure didn't remember her being quite so beautiful that early Saturday morning.

The group of students began to walk out, following the flow of mourners. Nathan Reid continued. "I believe Mr. Hitchcock has a broken leg or ankle or something. I'm sure he'll be fine, but we were all hoping to see him here."

"Yes...so was I," Miss Mueller said. A look of concern came over her heavily made-up face. "I'll have to send him a card."

I felt Miss Arbuckle's hand on my shoulder, nudging me forward as the line before us finally began to move again. We were nearing the double doors that separated the sanctuary from the narthex, and I could see outside through the heavy open doors of the main entrance. Reverend Andrews had positioned himself at the very back of the narthex and was shaking hands with each and every mourner that filed out of the Deerfield Presbyterian Church. As we neared him, I saw the reverend shaking hands with a short, stout woman in her fifties. She had an endearing smile, but her eyes and forehead were wrinkled with grief.

"It was a wonderful service, Reverend," she said. He nodded and smiled. "My name is Luella Roeh," the woman continued. "Elfrieda and I had a wonderful and spiritual friendship." She hesitated for a moment, clenching both her hands into fists. "I just can't accept that my friend is gone." She shook her head and looked down. "Anyway, I appreciate your words." The portly woman waddled past Reverend Andrews, and he watched her depart with a look of concern.

The reverend turned back to the long receiving line with us now at the front of it. He seemed stunned to see Grace Durand waiting to shake his hand. Mrs. D. was pretty well known. Even down in Deerfield, people had heard of this rebel farmer, who had held off the State's Agricultural Commission at gunpoint and was also the wife of famous Chicago financier Scott Durand. I knew—and I'm sure Reverend Andrews did too—that not only was Mrs. D. not a member of the Deerfield Presbyterian Church, she wasn't a member of any church at all.

"Mrs. Durand, so nice to see you. What is your connection to the Knaak family?" the reverend asked, probably noticing, as I had, that she was the only person in attendance not dressed in black. She wore a colorful, print dress with a bright red shawl.

"It's not much of a connection, I must admit," she replied, wincing a bit. "Everyone in our little town just knew her as 'the seller of encyclopedias.' Why, there wasn't a door in Lake Bluff Elfrieda didn't knock on trying to sell those darned books. She had been to a few meetings at the farm, but, sadly, we didn't really know each other particularly well." She shook her head. "I despise door-to-door sales people, almost as much as my husband does. But there was something about Elfrieda, something spiritual…something almost magical." The penetrating eyes of Grace Durand looked beyond Reverend Andrews, up into the graying November skies.

She squeezed the reverend's hand. "Reverend Andrews, let me introduce you to two of my friends from the orphanage. This is Miss Jessie Arbuckle, the chief administrator of LBO." She stepped aside so Miss Arbuckle could shake the pastor's hand.

"You did a fine job today under very difficult circumstances, Reverend," Miss Arbuckle said.

"It is a pleasure to meet you, Jessie. I've certainly heard a lot about your terrific work with the children," the reverend said.

"Jessie is a town treasure, indeed. And she has one of her prize residents with her," Mrs. D. said, pulling me forward. "This is Griffin Morgan, who, in addition to living at LBO, works for me at the farm." Miss Arbuckle nudged me even closer to the reverend, and I reached to shake his hand. "Griffin is one of my very best farmhands," Mrs. D. said.

"Well, Griffin, it is a pleasure to meet you, boy."

"Thank you, sir. We brought a card, a really big one. The whole orphanage signed it for Miss Knaak…or for her family, I mean," I said.

"How nice, Griffin. Thank you and all of your friends back at the orphanage," he said, smiling.

"Yes, Reverend, it was rather large," Miss Arbuckle explained, "so I gave it to one of your ushers with instructions to pass it along to the Knaaks."

"Well, we are holding up the line," Mrs. D. said, winking at the preacher, and urging us on our way.

"I'll see to it that the Knaaks get your card, Griffin. Many thanks!" Reverend Andrews said, as he reached for the next hand in line.

LAKE BLUFF VILLAGE HALL — POLICE & FIRE STATION
Photo courtesy of the Lake Bluff History Museum

Chapter 37 — Enemies Closing In
Lake Bluff Orphanage — November 7, 1928

The second time I actually spoke with Lily after our Village Hall nightmare, she was more hysterical than I had ever seen her. She had snuck all the way over to LBO late on a Wednesday afternoon, and instead of coming up to the front of our campus, where she surely would have been turned away and sent home, she went directly into the laundry area and found Mr. Spader. He was the one person at LBO who knew Lily, given all the time he spent taking us over to Crab Tree Farm. She also knew that Mr. Spader was somewhat indebted to her father and to the Durands. Her hope must have been that he would come find me and allow us to talk.

After settling her down a bit, Mr. Spader found me in the front yard, throwing pop flies to myself and catching them.

"Griffin, I need a little help in the laundry room," he said, and I followed him.

When we got to the laundry room door, he paused at the single step and said, "There's someone here to see you. I'll be right here." He looked back over his shoulder and around the yard before adding, "You two won't have much time." Mr. Spader nodded toward the door, put his hands in his pockets, and took several steps away from the door.

Lily was pacing at the far end of the laundry room. Her fiery hair was down, without pigtails for the first time since we'd met almost a year before. Her eyes were puffy and red. She rushed toward me with both hands covering her mouth.

"Griff! Griff! Oh God! Where have you been?" More than a week and a half had passed since the night of the crime and almost five days since I'd run over to Crab Tree, when we heard on the radio that Miss Knaak had died. I'd wanted to get over there more than ever in the past week, but with the exception of the funeral, going to and from school, and a couple of quick errands downtown, all of us were pretty much on lockdown at LBO. Miss Arbuckle and the orphanage board had held a special meeting and decided that until the perpetrator of Miss Knaak's murder was apprehended, they wanted all of us on the orphanage property at all non-school times. So this time Lily came to me.

"Oh, Griff, I can't...I can't believe it. It's terrible. I...I don't know what to do, Griff!"

"Calm down!" She was talking so fast and choking up so often, that it was hard to make out much of what she was saying. But as the story flooded out of her mouth, I came to understand that she had been sitting in the milk house, tending to Lucky, when she'd heard voices outside. She'd recognized two of the voices right off: one—her father's—and the other—Mr. D.'s. But as she'd worked her way to the doorway that looked out to the porch and the kitchen entrance to the main farm house, Lily heard a third voice—*the* voice. And it was that throaty, raspy, damaged voice that brought her running over to me.

"The creepy guy...the thin one with that awful skin and ... and ...the throaty, hollow voice." She took in air. "He was there, at the farm! At our farm! The three were talking, even laughing...like they were friends! My daddy and Mr. D. were talking to him. That creep had his arm around Mr. D., Griff!" She was gasping and clutching my wrist.

"OK! OK!" I said, thinking as fast as I could. "But what were they saying? Could you hear what they were talking about?" I pressed.

"The scary one…the man had a dark blue, pinstriped suit on. He was holding his hat in his left hand and was gesturing all around with it. He made Mr. D. and my daddy laugh. I heard them laughing a lot, Griff. A lot!" She wiped her nose with her coat sleeve and then started to cry again.

I gave her several seconds, hoping she'd compose herself. "But what did you hear? Can you tell what they were saying or laughing about?"

"The creepy one, said, 'I'm glad we have an understanding.' It was so horrible hearing that wrecked, hollowed-out voice again, Griff. I hate him! I hate that voice and his creepy skin! Then he said, 'If there is anything at all that my organization can do to help you in your many important endeavors, it would be our pleasure to return the favor.' What was he talking about, Griff? What organization? What favor?"

"What else?" I blurted. "Did you hear anything else?"

She was shaking her head, like she was trying to rid it of all the images that had taken over her mind in the last nine days. Finally, she settled a bit and said, "The creepy one pulled out two envelopes, one really fat one that he gave to Mr. D. and a medium fat one that he gave to my daddy. Mr D. said something…He said, 'I'm sure we will be in touch.' Then they all shook hands, and the creep got in the car with that big, huge guy, the one with the sausagey hands, and drove away. That's when I ran over here."

I put my head in my hands and closed my eyes, just trying to think.

"What are we gonna do, Griff? Huh? What can we do? I can't believe my daddy and Mr. D. are friends with this…this…criminal!" She reached up above her forehead and pulled her hair. "What if it was money, Griff? I think it was money that guy gave them!"

"I don't think they're friends," I said, though I wasn't sure of anything anymore. "I think they must be in some kind of business together or something. Maybe they were just meeting about the bootlegging? Maybe...maybe Mr. D. just lets them use that far corner of his property?" I added, thinking out loud.

"Yeah! And maybe that's the favor these guys want to return!" Lily said, almost yelling.

I nodded and looked behind me to make sure the wooden back door to the laundry was still closed and that we were still alone. "I don't think your father or Mr. Durand had anything to do with Miss Knaak's death, if that's what you're thinking."

"I sure hope not, Griff. My daddy is all I have left...I know he drinks too much and all, but...I don't want him going to jail." She grew quiet for almost a minute. Then she blurted out, "Maybe we should tell them—my daddy and Mr. D.—that they shouldn't be doing anything with these bad guys!"

"No!" I practically shouted. "We can't tell anyone! You heard what the voice said that night. We're the only ones who saw what we saw, who sort of know what happened—the only ones! That means if anyone else finds out, it'll be 'cause we told 'em."

She nodded, looking defeated. "It's OK," I said. "It's all going to be OK. We just have to think and talk only to each other." I turned and looked right at her until I knew she was looking right at me. "We talk only to each other about this, Lily, OK?"

Her eyes fogged up with tears. Then she gritted her teeth and nodded.

I gave her a hug and watched her cut back through the trees behind the laundry toward Sheridan Road.

It wasn't fair that Lily had to deal with all this. To have seen what she saw and hear what she heard around the Village Hall that night was bad enough. But to have her father in cahoots with bootleggers and the likes of this onion-skinned ghoul was way more than any young girl could bear.

Anyway, after she left, I stood up and turned to go back outside. Mr. Spader was puffing on his pipe just a few feet from the door.

"Is everything all right, Griffin?" he said.

"Yes, sir. Thank you so much for coming to get me and for allowing us to talk." I looked down at the grass and stuck my hands in the pockets of my pants. "I guess it's been a really hard day over at the farm," I said and headed back across the lawn to Wads.

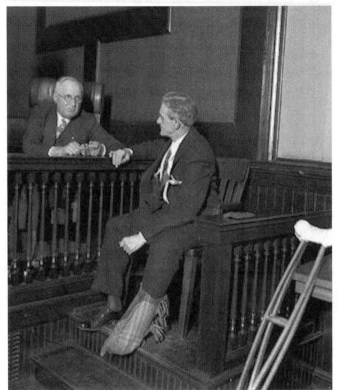

CHARLES HITCHCOCK TESTIFIES AT THE INQUEST
INTO THE DEATH OF ELFRIEDA KNAAK
Photo courtesy of The Chicago Tribune

Chapter 38 — The Coroner's Jury Inquest
Waukegan, IL — The Lake County Courthouse — November 10, 1928

I exhaled a deep breath and prepared for the next part of my story, the part that held the most frustration and mystery for me. "Almost immediately after Miss Knaak passed away, I remember that all the talk in town, in the newspapers, and on the radio turned to the inquest of the Coroner's Jury that was to take place just over a week after her passing.

"Of course, back then I had no idea what a Coroner's Jury even was, so I turned to our encyclopedias, which is where I found that this kind of a jury would tell us the manner or cause of Miss Knaak's death. The man to lead this jury was Manfred Trayner, whom I'd first seen at the Magical Palace Fundraiser at the Cooks' house that summer. When Miss Knaak was pronounced dead at The Alice Home Hospital on Friday, November 2, Dr. Traynor was called and asked to certify her death. Then, later, he would have to investigate the death in order to issue a ruling as to what caused it."

"Yes," Hargrave interrupted, "I knew Manny well. No one envied him and what he was asked to do in ruling on this bizarre death." I'd never heard anyone except the judge refer to Coroner Traynor as "Manny." There was something informal and almost disrespectful to the way the detective referred to him.

I knew Detective Hargrave had been in the courtroom on Saturday, March 10, both as an observer and a testifying witness. I didn't know how well he knew Manfred Traynor. I was anxious to see if my notes from that day were accurate. "Do you mind, Detective, if I run through my notes from the Coroner's Jury? You were there, and I wasn't. I'd appreciate you setting me straight in the event that you remember things differently."

Hargrave ran his hand through his hair and shook his head. "It was one of the craziest, most chaotic courtroom scenes I've ever witnessed, Griff. Reporters and photographers moving this way and that, taking pictures from every conceivable angle. It was hard simply to hear what was being said at the witness stand at times, with all the noise." The detective pinched the corners of his mouth between his thumb and forefinger, and then squinted, as if he were trying to see the courtroom through the haze of years that had passed. "I remember it all though, that's for sure." He closed his eyes and shook his head another time. "Go ahead, shoot," he said.

I shuffled my papers, and reflected on those confusing, frustrating days. "It's astonishing how much I still remember about the days leading up to the coroner's inquest and how vividly I remember it. On the way to school the Friday before the inquest, Bobby and Billy O'Neil were arguing about the investigation. Bobby didn't understand what a Coroner's Jury did, and thought it was a big waste of time, considering we all knew she'd 'burned to a crisp,' as he so bluntly put it. But Billy set him straight, and told him that the jury would decide if it was a murder, an accident, or a suicide. I'll never forget good old Knox speaking up: 'There's no chance Miss Knaak burned herself, especially not in that furnace! No human could even stand to touch the outside of that furnace! How in the heck could she stick herself inside it?'"

Hargrave rolled his eyes. "That's the question we all were asking ourselves back then and the question I'd still like to ask that jury today."

"I know," I responded forcefully. "My buddies from LBO may have been only 12 or 13 at the time, but in that brief conversation on the way to school, they actually hit on what would become the essential facts of the case. In fact, as I would learn years later through a ton of research, theirs was the very same argument that was playing out in all the newspaper and radio reports from November 3 right up to November 10, the day Dr. Traynor's jury had its inquest. At the end of it, that misguided, six-person jury had to listen to the evidence presented and determine if Elfrieda Knaak's death had been self-inflicted or foul play"

"Yes," Hargrave said, "your young friends were right. That was the essential argument that the whole thing boiled down to. And I've never been able to get my head around the fact that six intelligent men could consider that Elfrieda Knaak actually may have done this to herself." He stood and began to walk around his desk. "Continue."

"By all accounts—and, yes, I have read them all," I told him, "on Saturday, November 10 at 9:00 a.m., the Lake County Courthouse was jam-packed. According to every reliable newspaper I've managed to find, a minimum of 200 people had squeezed into that small, Waukegan courtroom, simply to listen to the testimony of over 33 witnesses and, at the end of the day, to Dr. Traynor's ruling on the final cause of Elfrieda Grace Knaak's death."

"As I said before," Hargrave interjected, "it was a total circus in there. Cameras flashing, reporters checking with each other in attempt to get their quotes right. I would have cleared that courtroom of all but the witnesses if I were Manny."

I continued, "I had no idea back then that coroners' inquests were actually open to the public; anyone could attend." I pulled out my papers and handed them to Hargrave. "Here is the official list I kept of who was in the courtroom that day, the 33 witnesses summoned to testify." Hargrave skimmed over the paper:

- *Charles Hitchcock, Deputy Dispatch and tutor of the victim*
- *Estelle Hitchcock and her daughters, Charlene and Helen*
- *Oscar J. Kloer, Charles Hitchcock's good friend, who claimed to be with the deputy on the night of Oct. 29 in Hitchcock's home*

- *Sheriff Lawrence Doolittle*
- *George Hargrave of the Edward Hargrave detective agency of Chicago*
- *Mrs. Maud Hartman, Maynard Schram, Mrs. M. Conder*
- *Mrs. Kromer*
- *Mrs. Wagner, Highland Park*
- *Mrs. Pottinger, Franklin Nursery in Deerfield*
- *Chris Louis, the Lake Bluff gardener, who found Miss Knaak by the furnace*
- *Police Chief Barney Rosenhagen*
- *Patrolman Eugene Spaid*
- *Members of the Knaak family, including Theodore, Alvin, Otto, Edward, Rudolph, Emily, and Ida*
- *Miss Marie Mueller, Miss Knaak's closest friend*
- *Frank T. Mandy, Miss Knaak's violin instructor*
- *Dr. C.A. Barnes, who helped perform the autopsy*
- *Dr. A.J. Rissinger, who was the first to attend to Miss Knaak at Alice Home*
- *Dr. T.S. Proxmire, who also attended to Miss Knaak at the Alice Home Hospital and attended to Hitchcock for his fractured ankle*
- *Sylvia Carlson, owner of the Highland Park Bookstore where Mrs. Hitchcock is employed, and who took Mrs. Hitchcock home the night Miss Knaak was found*
- *Mr. James Carter of the Compton Publishing Co. in Chicago, where Miss Knaak was employed*
- *Mr. Jack Johnson, a Deerfield taxi driver*
- *Mr. L.F. Wenban, a Lake Forest undertaker*
- *Mr. Ray Spaid, brother of Patrolman Spaid, who was around the police station the day Miss Knaak was found*

After he looked at it, I pushed on. "Now, it's always seemed a little curious to me that all of these witnesses had already been questioned—in some cases several times—by law enforcement officials in the investigation involving Miss Knaak. But I guess that's just how these coroners' inquests worked back then. Each of the important witnesses who had been questioned during the initial investigation would then have to give their testimony in public, answering direct questions from the two representatives of the Coroner's Jury."

Hargrave nodded. "You'd be surprised how often a witness's story will change, even in a matter of a week or two, Griff," he said. He came back around the desk and sat, this time putting his long legs up on his desk. "I'd questioned many of these people myself since getting involved with the case, and on the stand that day I heard things that had not come up in my interviews." The detective ran his tongue along his lower lip and then continued. "It's not that people are lying or consciously changing their story; it's that each time they are asked, different details emerge." Hargrave took in a deep breath and tilted his head back. "That's why we question witnesses over and over, often asking the same questions."

"That makes sense," I reflected, and returned to my story. "Having gone back over this enormous volume of articles, police reports, and interviews countless times, what is still so hard to fathom even today is that only 12 days before this inquest, no one outside of Deerfield, Illinois, had ever even heard of Elfrieda Knaak. But after the storm of publicity generated by this ghoulish case, everyone in the entire Chicago area—and even beyond the Chicago area—had become familiar with 'The Furnace Girl,' who was found burned and barely alive in the Lake Bluff Village Hall."

"It's not a kind of fame anyone would ever want to have," Hargrave responded with a grimace.

"I know this case pretty well, Detective, but I still don't know what it was actually like to have been in that crowded courtroom. You were there. You were able to hear the tone of the questions they asked Hitchcock and to see the expressions on his face when he answered. I keep trying to picture what it must have been like for him, having his own wife and daughters in that courtroom, listening as his 'relationship' with the 30-year-old Miss Knaak was dissected. I want to hear Chief Rosenhagen's German accent and see Chris Louis's face, as the two of them described finding Miss Knaak that morning. I want to hear with my own ears which clues they noticed first in that furnace room and which ones they might have missed. But the best I've ever been able to do is to read and reread the newspaper reports, review the radio transcripts, and, eventually, interview as many people as I could who were either in or at least closer to that courtroom on November 10, 1928, than I was able to be."

"Well, I was there, as you've mentioned, but I can't provide details on much of what you seem to want, and that's because my eyes were on Hitchcock ninety percent of the time. I was completely convinced that he had done it, Griff, and I wanted to see him squirm." He shook his head in resignation. "But I'll save you the suspense, Mr. Morgan. Hitchcock never cracked. He just sat there like the trained actor he was, doting on his wife, putting an arm around his daughters." Hargrave wiped his nose with the back of his hand and then motioned for me to continue.

I obliged. "All anyone would need to confirm the abundance of reporters on hand that Saturday morning is the file I have on this case. It wasn't just the Chicago reporters either. Writers from various reporting agencies were there too, sending their impressions across the wire to New York, Boston, Cleveland, Detroit, and even Los Angeles. The transcripts from the WMAQ radio reports the morning of November 10th described the press corps as 'strung throughout the back and side aisles of the overflowing courtroom.' The same report said that the noise produced by all the cameras and flashbulbs going off 'interfered with the jury's ability to hear the testimony of several witnesses.' *The Chicago Gazette* reported that 'the photographers practically tripped over each other in an attempt to get close-ups of the Knaak family members as they filed in.'"

"That's exactly right, Griff," Hargrave said with a look of disgust. "I saw that very thing happening, and it appalled me." He clenched his fists. "Can you imagine what all this was like for the Knaak family who had already endured Elfrieda's funeral? I wished then—and I still wish now—that they all could have been spared the additional pain from this hearing, not to mention its ultimate ruling," Hargrave said.

I understood his concern for the family. I'd read all about the mayhem in that room. "Articles from the day of the coroner's inquest said that the in-court reporters were equally desperate for any photos they could click of 'former star of the silver screen' Charles Hitchcock. When I think back to what all of the guys at Wads and I thought of him when we first saw him up at the Waukegan YMCA, I guess we were pretty star-struck. But so much has happened since then, Detective, that I don't need to tell you that I'm a long way from enamoured with Charles Hitchcock. Even so, I've always believed that, for many in that courtroom, there must still have been enough in Hitchcock's face in 1928 to kindle memories of his glorious Essanay Films' days."

"It just about drove me nuts, I tell you," Hargrave interrupted. "This no count weasel was still some sort of media darling, all because of his movie career. Seeing reporters fawning over him and watching him mug for every photographer in the room, disgusting is what it was." The detective pounded the table and fumbled for the last cigarette in his pack.

"Every time I pore back over the details of the testimony from Hitchcock, I think about his daughters Charlene and Helen," I said. "I'd gotten to know them over at the Hitchcock home when I was working there. How confused they must have been by their father's unseemly connection to Miss Knaak. I can only imagine what Estelle Hitchcock thought of the proceedings."

Hargrave nodded sadly. "All the years I've spent as a detective have taught me how to read faces. Estelle Hitchcock was not buying her husband's act. Not one bit, I tell you," Hargrave said. "And those girls, his daughters...they were just young kids. What the State's Attorney was thinking when he subpoenaed them that day is beyond me." Hargrave banged his hand on his desk and rose. "Yeah, the girls substantiated their father was home that night, at least as far as they were aware. But that had already been established in the discovery phase. Kids that young have no business being subjected to the kind of content that was covered that day." He came within a foot of me and pointed his long finger right at my face. "I'll give you ten-to-one odds Hitchcock didn't object to their presence, because they made him look like an upstanding family man." He shook his head and lighted another cigarette.

"I got my first look at some of these news reports all the way back in 1928, though I clearly wasn't supposed to," I said. "Many of the articles in my Elfrieda Knaak file came from the papers I got from my classmate Ricky McSwain, the newsy. Now, of course, they are yellowed, crinkled, and still carry a hint of that musty smell I associate with LBO." I pulled one out of my file.

"I have one of those articles here," I informed Hargrave. "This one came from the Sunday edition of *The Chicago Daily Star* on November 11. It's chock-full of information about the inquest." I handed it to him for review. He leaned back in his chair and looked it over. Staff writer Lloyd Dunniston described the beginning of the proceedings as follows:

> *A door opened to the left of the judge's bench, and a hush descended on the courtroom. Six men walked into the chambers looking somber. They wore dark suits and carried notebooks and folders. The witnesses and spectators quickly took their seats. A seventh man came in through that same door, about a dozen paces behind the others. He pulled the door shut behind*

him, and walked to the center of the courtroom, cleared his throat, and offered a forced smile to the gathered crowd.

He introduced himself as "State's Attorney A.V. Smith." Gesturing to his left where a tall, slender, bald man stood and nodded, Colonel Smith continued, "This here is the County Coroner, Dr. Manfred Traynor." Smith went on, "The purpose of today's proceedings is to hear information concerning the death of Miss Elfrieda Knaak." Mr. Smith then walked over to the coroner and leaned down to ask him something.

The State's Attorney resumed his opening remarks. "Coroner Traynor's jury will listen to all of the testimony brought before them today. Once all the evidence has been heard, the jury will deliberate, and we'll take a recess as they do. When the Coroner's Jury returns, they will make a formal and official ruling on the cause of death, the options being suicide, homicide, accidental death, natural causes, or undetermined causes. The coroner has asked me to remind all of you that the ruling rendered here today carries no civil or criminal significance. This is an inquest, not a trial, in other words."

Those last two sentences had caught my eye and confirmed what I'd originally found out in Compton's Pictured Encyclopedia. A Coroner's Jury is not like a regular courtroom jury; the coroner's team doesn't decide a criminal's guilt or innocence, and what it decides doesn't carry any legal weight. The six men just had to decide what caused Miss Knaak's death. But I'm still not sure how many people who walked into that courtroom on that Saturday morning in 1928 fully grasped the implications of what the effect would be if that jury were to rule that Miss Knaak died by accident or by suicide. If the cause of death ruling was either of these options, it would result in the stoppage of all further official investigation into Miss Knaak's death. And, perhaps most importantly, if Dr. Traynor's jury were to rule in favor of accidental death or self-inflicted causes, then all those involved in the crime, along with Deputy Hitchcock, would never be held accountable for the death of Elfrieda Knaak.

Hargrave finished the article and handed it back to me with uncharacteristic silence. He took a breath and huffed it out. "November 10th was a long day in that Waukegan courtroom. Questioning the witnesses lasted over six hours. The state's attorney and the coroner alternated in questioning the 33 witnesses, to try to be as brief and efficient as possible. Most of the them answered one to three questions."

I nodded encouragement, and handed him my next article. "Some fairly extensive summary from the day's testimony was included in the *Waukegan Daily Sun* the following day." Hargrave looked it over

Lake Bluff Police Chief Barney Rosenhagen testified that on the night before Miss Knaak was discovered, with Deputy Hitchcock on short-term injury leave, the chief himself handled the building security circuit, making sure that the Village Hall, the Post Office, and other municipal buildings were all locked up. "It was probably between 11:15 and 11:30 that night that I checked the main doors of the Village Hall. They were locked."

The questions then turned to the discovery of the body the next morning. Rosenhagen reported that there was no evidence of a struggle or any sort of violence in the furnace room office, where the body was discovered. Only later, once they got the hallway lights working, did he and Officer Spaid notice the bloody footprints heading up and down the stairs leading to the furnace room. "Our best guess from examining them is that the victim was alive after her encounter with the furnace and tried to get out of the building. But finding the door locked, she apparently went back down to the furnace room."

When asked why the ashes from the furnace were emptied that morning when they could have contained valuable evidence, an embarrassed Rosenhagen acknowledged, "That probably shouldn't have happened, but we're not used to this kind of thing in Lake Bluff." The State's Attorney also pressed the chief about Miss Knaak's heavy, blue coat and hat that she was wearing when she left home the morning of October 29, but the chief confirmed that no such articles were found at the scene.

Rosenhagen's assistant, Officer Eugene Spaid, was only asked whether any evidence at the scene led him to believe that Miss Knaak's death came as a result of violence. Officer Spaid answered in the negative but noted, "We did find a small trail of blood on the back sidewalk, but we have no way of determining whether that blood is Miss Knaak's or not. What I can't quite understand," Officer Spaid continued, "is why there was no smell in the building the morning we found Miss Knaak. I keep wondering if she could have been burned somewhere else and then brought to the Village Hall."

"You know," I considered, as I saw Hargrave finish reading, "I had never thought about the smell in the building that next morning. I've never smelled a human body burning, but I'm sure it leaves quite a stench. I ended up deciding that lack of odor could probably be explained by the fact that Miss Knaak was burned in the furnace boiler that supplied hot water to the building and not the furnace that heated the building. Had she been burned in the furnace that supplied heat to the building, any smell from within would've traveled throughout the air ducts, and the odor of burning flesh would have traveled through the entire building."

Hargrave nodded in agreement. "That makes sense to me, too."

"And another key detail in all this," I went on, "which I happen to know know for a fact, is that the coal chute was left open that night, and if those back cellar doors were also propped open, as some reports indicate they were, that would have provided plenty of airflow, as windy as that night had been, to minimize any lingering odor. The record of the testimony that day has both Rosenhagen and Louis testifying that when they first opened the Village Hall doors the morning Miss Knaak was found, a blast of cold air greeted them."

Hargrave returned the article, and I handed him the next piece from my collection. The Star's coverage included other witnesses' testimony as well. He glanced over it:

> State's Attorney Smith even questioned Miss Knaak's violin instructor, a Mr. Frank R. Mandy. Mandy was only brought into the proceedings because of his first name. One of Miss Knaak's repeated ravings after she was found was "Frank threw me down!" Mr. Mandy, a slender, soft-spoken, bespectacled musician, hardly looked the part of a cold-hearted killer. Wearing both a bow tie and a trace of a smirk, Mandy said, "Elfrieda was one of my students—period. We had no dealings of any kind outside of our lessons."

"I still remember the next witness," Hargrave said, rubbing his face with his hand, "because he was one of the last people to see Miss Knaak alive: Mr. James Carter of the Compton Publishing Company."

"That's right," I jumped in. "According to the police timeline, Elfrieda left the Compton offices at approximately 6:00 p.m. on Monday, October 29. Mr. Carter confirmed seeing her at approximately 4:30 p.m. on the day in question and remembered nothing unusual about the woman he considered one of his 'very best employees.' Carter also established that Miss Knaak had given a 'first rate sales presentation at a workshop for the entire Compton Publishing sales force' just before Carter left on the day in question, indicating that Miss Knaak had every reason to have left work in a very positive mood. Mr. Carter also confirmed that there were no 'Franks' employed at Compton Publishing, other than the company's owner, a Mr. Frank T. Compton. To me, the most important aspect of Carter's testimony involved that same blue coat Chief Rosenhagen had been asked about. Carter said that as he was preparing to leave on that Monday, he saw 'Miss Knaak's long, blue coat had been left in the presentation room, so I took it over to her desk and handed it to her before I left.'"

"Ah, yes," Hargrave reflected. "The vanishing blue coat. But then we got to hear what was, without question, the most important medical testimony of the day from Coroner Traynor's assistant, a Mr. C.A. Barnes. He and Coroner Traynor had performed the autopsy together, exactly one week before the inquest, with the assistance of Dr. A.J. Risinger. While the entire jury viewed the body after the autopsy, the details of Miss Knaak's death, however, had not been made public. It was C.A. Barnes's job to explain those gory details in layman's terms."

I interjected to display an entire column from the Star, which was dedicated to his testimony:

> When asked to summarize his findings, Barnes began with the unequivocal statement that "Miss Knaak had clearly not been attacked nor beaten. Our thorough post-mortem examination revealed nothing that would either contradict or support her story of self-burning." The Assistant Coroner went on to explain that the victim's brain had been sent to Victor Memorial Hospital, where a team of doctors led by Dr. James Whitney Hall, a University of Chicago neurologist, found "no evidence of any violence, nor any indications of any mental disease." Barnes reported that while there may have been some "blunt trauma, the skull itself had not been cracked."

When asked about Miss Knaak's fractured right arm and what could have caused it, Barnes surmised that it may have been the result of her falling, "perhaps while trying to walk on extremely charred feet."

State's Attorney Smith proceeded with a question about a wound the autopsy revealed on the back of the victim's neck. Barnes described it as "a half-inch wide and extending from the middle of the back of her neck to the right." He called the indentation "the possible result of a blow from a blunt object or a compression."

But State's Attorney Smith interrupted Mr. Barnes, saying, "Didn't you just say that she hadn't been attacked or beaten?"

Barnes readily admitted that the entire Coroner's Jury had debated this very point during the autopsy review. "Some of us saw it as externally inflicted, perhaps a poke or blow with a blunt object. But I'm inclined to believe it was more likely the result of Miss Knaak being awkwardly positioned for a sustained period of time, perhaps leaning her head back against the opening of the furnace grate." Here Barnes' testimony got increasingly technical, as he elaborated on the particular shape and kind of burns on the victim's head. "It is my judgment that that she did not ever place her head directly on the coals. We noted that while the burns on her head were severe, much of her hair was not even singed. The same was true of her eyebrows," Barnes continued. "Though they were in close proximity to very badly burned areas of her head, again, the eyebrows themselves were not even singed. Similarly, her eyelashes were also inexplicably not burned at all. Our best conclusion about this would be that the burns on her head were likely the result of reflected heat rather than direct contact with fire or coals. This kind of reflective burning could have resulted from her placing her head too close to the fire while she was burning other parts of her body, such as her hands, for instance."

The State's Attorney asked, "Are you suggesting, Mr. Assistant Coroner, that all the wounds noted in the autopsy were self-inflicted?" The entire gallery leaned toward the witness in anticipation of his reply. The Assistant Coroner hesitated only for a moment before saying, "Well, nothing we found suggested violence or even a struggle. And many of the curious details and anomalies between the victim's burned and unburned areas are more consistent with their being self-inflicted."

While I didn't come close to grasping the details Mr. Barnes referred to in his testimony back in 1928, I would certainly come to understand in later years that his professional opinion very well may have turned the tide of the entire case.

"I believe you followed Mr. Barnes, right, Detective?" I asked.

"That's correct," Hargrave replied. "But my testimony didn't seem to matter much at this point."

"How do you mean?" I asked.

"The Coroner didn't ask me much," the detective said, shrugging. "All they were really after was my take on whether there was any evidence of a struggle or the presence of another party in the furnace room that night."

"And what did you say?" I asked.

He took a deep drag on his cigarette and shook his head. "I said, 'you mean any evidence in addition to the fact that no human being could ever put one limb at a time into a fiery furnace until most of her body is burned?'" Hargrave flicked the lengthening ash from his cigarette. I shook my head in utter amazement at this one fundamental fact, a fact that no one on that jury must have been willing to consider.

"Old Manny was none too happy with my tone or my innuendo," Hargrave said, smirking. "All he said after that was 'You may step down, Detective,' and that was that." Hargrave exhaled an exasperated breath.

"I'm sure your testimony, though it may not have swayed Dr. Traynor's jury, certainly led the Knaak family to hire you for further investigation," I said.

The detective stood up again, snuffing out his cigarette in what was now a full ashtray. He motioned for me to continue and walked over to the window behind me.

"The next witness was Marie Mueller, and she was introduced as 'Elfrieda Knaak's closest friend,'" I said. She was that same attractive woman with the blue hat, whom I had both seen and heard at the tail end of Miss Knaak's funeral. "You remember her testimony was short and played no role in the jury's decision. But, I would, in later years, consider the lack of attention to Miss Mueller one of the great bungles by those who handled the case."

I stood up from my chair to pace the back of the office and went on. "I still maintain that the phone call from Miss Knaak to Miss Mueller late Monday afternoon changed everything, for it motivated Elfrieda to board that train in Highland Park that was bound for Lake Bluff. Something Miss Mueller said must have influenced Miss

Knaak to pay a visit to see Charles Hitchcock rather than keeping to her previously scheduled appointment in Deerfield to sing with her sister Ida."

"It's a fair observation, Griff," Hargrave interrupted, "But when Coroner Traynor questioned Miss Mueller, he covered very little ground." I handed him the next excerpt from my collection--a very short one--and explained, "Only *The Lake County Journal* saw fit to include an account of this exchange, and you can see that there isn't much there."

> *Miss Mueller testified that she and the victim were best friends and "had been for years. We even took classes together here in Waukegan at the YMCA." Coroner Traynor proceeded to ask the witness if she had been worried about her friend, her state of mind, or her general contentment. Miss Mueller said, definitively, that Miss Knaak was "very happy and enthusiastic about her life." Mueller was dismissive of the suggestion that Miss Knaak might have done this to herself for spiritual reasons. "She never mentioned anything of the sort to me."*
>
> *Coroner Traynor then proceeded to ask Miss Mueller about her visit to the Alice Home Hospital on the morning of November 2. "Did Miss Knaak say anything to you?" Miss Mueller winced, fought back tears, and replied, "No. She was...too far gone."*
>
> *Miss Mueller did confirm her friend's tutorial relationship with Mr. Charles Hitchcock, saying, "Elfrieda was very excited to have the opportunity to do additional work with such a great and gifted instructor, as am I, for he tutors me too. Both Elfrieda and I have Mr. Hitchcock to thank for our improvement in sales."*

"I only have a few more articles, Detective," I shared, and I filed the paper. "You must remember we are reaching the end of the witness list, and it was the two final witnesses of the day who provided the most emotion. The first, of course, was Mr. Charles Hitchcock, and here is the article that covers it. *The Waukegan Sentinel* was none too kind to Lake Bluff's favorite son." I handed it to him and he leaned back in his chair:

> *A.V. Smith began his interrogation of the aged, former actor-turned-deputy by asking him to confirm that the deputy had met with*

Miss Knaak "several times" at the Village Hall for tutoring purposes. Smith then sought to determine if the two had planned to meet at the Village Hall on the night of October 29. Deputy Hitchcock replied, "No. It wouldn't have been possible with my leg."

"And how exactly did you injure your leg, Deputy Hitchcock?" the State's Attorney asked.

"I was on a ladder in my home, and I slipped off it." Hitchcock went on to claim that he had had to cancel all of his appointments and obligations for several days due to the severity of his injury. Additionally, Hitchcock had "no idea what Miss Knaak could have been doing at the Village Hall" on the night in question.

The Deputy was then asked if he could explain how the victim might have gained access to that furnace room, which the State's Attorney called, "your office." At this point, Mr. Hitchcock swallowed hard but, again, claimed to have "no idea."

"Is there anybody you can think of, Mr. Hitchcock, who a) could have wanted to hurt Miss Knaak, and b) might have had access to that room?" Mr. Smith asked.

Deputy Hitchcock replied that "Miss Knaak was an angel of a woman, a Christian of impeccable character." Hitchcock then added, "I'm simply at a loss for how this could have happened, and I can't imagine anyone doing such a thing to any other human being, least of all to Miss Knaak."

A.V. Smith then opened up a file and withdrew a piece of lined paper, identifying it as having come from one of Miss Knaak's nurses. He explained that the list contained some utterances of Miss Knaak just a day before her death. The State's Attorney then read one of the entries in which Miss Knaak said, "I'm sorry, I did this to myself." Colonel Smith asked Deputy Hitchcock if he could "shed any light on this."

The former silent movie star took in a deep breath and exhaled before replying. "No sir. I'm afraid I can't. Miss Knaak was a devoted Christian woman. I simply cannot imagine her ever wanting to inflict harm upon herself."

At this point, the State's Attorney took up a more mystical line of questioning. "Deputy Hitchcock, do you have the training or capability to put another person under a trance or hypnotic spell?" The spectators gasped, and Mr. Hitchcock appeared to be shocked. "No, I most certainly do not," the actor proclaimed.

Colonel Smith continued undeterred. "It has been suggested, Deputy, that in order for someone to inflict severe bodily harm on him or herself—such as putting one's own body into a fire—that person would have to be put in an hypnotic state. So I need you to be clear as to your familiarity with such matters."

"I have only come across one person in my entire life with such an ability, and that was the great Harry Houdini. While I did know and have an association with Mr. Houdini, I never ascertained how he was able to put so many people under his hypnotic spells. And, as far as I know, no one saw Mr. Harry Houdini in or around the Village Hall on the night in question." There was a snicker throughout the courtroom, and Mr. Hitchcock seemed to smile for a moment.

The State's Attorney then walked slowly over to the bench, where the beleaguered witness sat. Colonel Smith apologized for the difficulty and intensity of the questioning, but asked the former actor one final question. "Can you confirm one final time for us that on the night of Monday, October 29, you were not in the Lake Bluff Village Hall, and that you neither saw nor had any contact with Elfrieda Knaak?"

Deputy Hitchcock responded without hesitation, "Yes, sir, I can. I was not in the Village Hall at all that night, nor did I have any contact with Miss Knaak." And with that, Charles Hitchcock was excused from the witness bench and returned to the third row on the right in the gallery, where he sat alongside his wife and two daughters. The daughters and spouse had already been questioned earlier in the day, verifying that Mr. Hitchcock had, indeed, been both home and immobile on the night in question, still recovering from a very recently broken knee and ankle. Mr. Hitchcock's friend, Mr. Oscar Kloer, had also confirmed, earlier in the day, this same fact in his brief testimony.

When I saw Hargrave look up, I went on. "Even though I knew, all the way back in 1928, that Mr. Hitchcock was lying, I wasn't initially mad at him for doing so. He hadn't killed Miss Knaak, any more than Lily or I had. He was just there, and he'd seen it. He'd been beaten up by these thugs, and that must have scared him pretty good. But over the course of the next twenty years, I got plenty angry at him, especially when I would learn that Hitchcock was arrested less than a year after the Knaak case for robbing houses in Lake Bluff. Several newspaper articles confirmed this, along with the fact that Estelle Hitchcock, his wife of twenty-some years, divorced him in 1933, and, after that, Hitchcock wound up marrying Marie Mueller-that very same former student of his, and not to mention, the very best friend of Miss Elfrieda Knaak!"

Hargrave's revulsion couldn't be contained. "Even if he didn't do it, he's guilty of plenty. I didn't like him from the first time I laid eyes on him."

"Here we have our final witness, Detective: Elfrieda Knaak's older brother Theodore, the one who ran the family pharmacy after his father died. The November 11th *Chicago Daily Star* reported this final testimony." I slid the article across the desk:

The Coroner, himself, Dr. Manfred Traynor, called the day's final witness, Mr. Theodore Knaak, Jr. The tall, angular brother of the deceased walked slowly and deliberately to the witness bench. The coroner began by offering his heartfelt condolences to Mr. Knaak and his entire family for their "unthinkable loss." Theodore Knaak only nodded somberly. He craned his neck to check on his sisters Ida and Emily, both of whom had sobbed uncontrollably throughout the day and had even left the courtroom on several occasions. They were, however, both in attendance for their brother's testimony, albeit in a noticeably shaken and grief-stricken state.

Dr. Traynor began by asking Mr. Knaak to identify any enemies his younger sister may have had. The question struck the victim's brother as preposterous, and he told the Coroner so. "My sister was a gentle, caring, Christian woman. Her entire life was dedicated to serving others and making the people around her more comfortable."

The coroner nodded vigorously and then altered his line of questioning. "We've heard that time and time again today, and I, for one, have no doubt that Elfrieda was an exemplary citizen in every way." Traynor paused. "But given the absence of any known enemies, how do you feel about the possibility that your sister may have...may have done this to herself? For example, did you see any signs of her unhappiness, or might she have been struggling with deep, psychological pain perhaps?"

The eldest Knaak brother reddened and his jaw clenched, as if he were going to erupt at Dr. Traynor's question. He said, "My entire family and I resent the implication that Elfrieda may have done this to herself. Our Fritzie was filled with a zest for living from the time she was a tiny girl, and that love for life never waned." He puffed his cheeks, and his teeth clenched for a moment before he continued. "The only thing more outrageous than the idea that our sister had enemies who would do such a…such a horrible thing to her is this ridiculous speculation that she would have or could have done this to herself." Mr. Knaak crossed his arms defiantly and shook his head in disgust.

Coroner Traynor seemed to recognize that he was on treacherous ground with this witness. He gathered himself and asked the next question as gingerly as he could. "I understand, sir. But, if I may, if having any enemies who could have done this is not an option, and if doing this to herself is equally untenable, where, exactly, does that leave us? What other options are there in terms of a possible cause of death?"

Theodore Knaak Jr. rolled his eyes and shook his head. "There are all kinds of crazy morons out there. One of them happened upon our sister." For a moment, it looked like Knaak was rising up out of the witness bench. But he stiffened and halted, becoming still in the seat. "Don't waste any more time on this ridiculous theory of suicide! Get out there and find my sister's killer!" he demanded.

At this, the State's Attorney rose and took control of the proceedings. "Thank you, Mr. Knaak. That will be all," Colonel Smith said preemptively. He patted the coroner on his shoulder and then steered him back toward the judge's chambers. The State's Attorney then informed the entire courtroom that there would be a recess of undetermined length, after which the Coroner's Jury would return and render its decision.

"I remember sneaking into the laundry room to listen to the verdict on the radio. WMAQ reported that it was just after 3:00 p.m. when the recess for deliberation began. And by 3:40 p.m., the 200 spectators and witnesses jostled their way back to their seats. The radio reporter noted that the Waukegan courtroom 'was just as packed at 3:40 p.m. as it had been at 9:00 a.m., with four notable exceptions: the entire Hitchcock family did not return to hear the verdict.'"

"Yeah, that was no surprise," the detective interrupted. "I saw that no count, good-for-nothing slink out of the courtroom at the recess and knew he wouldn't be back."

My final clipping represented the most dramatic report of what transpired after the recess. It was in the November 11th Sunday *Chicago Post*. I handed it to Hargrave.

A gradual hush descended on the courtroom, as Coroner Traynor stood beside the judge's bench. After calling the room to order, he nodded decisively to his chief juror. Thomas Eastwood, a tall, slender man with sandy hair, rose soberly and cleared his throat. He looked down nervously, as he unfolded his sheet of prepared remarks.

"We, the jurors, sworn to inquire into the death of Elfrieda Knaak, on oath do find that she came to her own death by burns, which appear, from all the evidence presented, to have been self-inflicted."

There was an eruption of sound: cries of disbelief, expressions of shock, and even a few screams of "No!"

Coroner Traynor quickly ushered his jury out of the courtroom through the door to the judge's chambers.

The Knaak family huddled together. Only Otto looked over his shoulder at the chaos around his family and shook his head in obvious disgust. Theodore helped his sisters up from the bench and led them quickly down the packed center aisle, using his long arms to part the bustling throng of observers. Tears were evident on both Ida's and Emily's faces.

Rudolph, the youngest Knaak brother, yelled, "What a load of horse manure! How could they think Elfrieda or anyone could do such a thing to herself?" His deep voice carried above the din, as his rant continued. "I'd like to see one member of that jury hold his hand on a hot stove for five seconds, for Christ's sake!"

Several minutes later, after the chaotic courtroom had cleared, dozens of reporters crowded around the steps of the Lake County Courthouse, hoping to get a statement from the exiting spectators and witnesses. As the Knaak family emerged, flashbulbs popped, and questions flew at them from all sides. Theodore Knaak lifted his long, left arm to quiet them.

"Please!" he screamed. "We have nothing to say at this point, except that we find the jury's conclusion preposterous and unacceptable. We have already hired Detective George Hargrave and plan to garner all the resources of the Hargrave Secret Service Agency in order to find the madman who murdered our sister. Now, if you'd all please excuse us and make way, it's been a long and exhausting day." And with that, Theodore, Alvin, Rudolph and Otto Knaak each put an arm around their sisters and descended the seven steps of the courthouse.

Hargrave slammed the article on his desk, crushed out his cigarette, and said, "I need to get some air." He stormed out of his office without closing the door.

THE LAKE BLUFF FAMILY

THESE are typical of our Lake Bluff family, — regular boys, genuine girls, wholesome, bright, ambitious, growing, normal in every way.

But unhappy fortune deprives them of home, of love or care. Some are from families good like yours; and ambition and brains like yours; with life to justify.

Lake Bluff Orphanage hopes that their rugged childhood will wind its way into your heart.

LBO POSTCARD
Courtesy of the Lake Bluff History Museum

Chapter 39 — Unexpected News
Lake Bluff Orphanage — November 12, 1928

It was just a couple days after the Coroner's Jury fiasco that I trudged up the steps of the Mackey Memorial Building, with no clue of what I was in for. On my way to breakfast, Miss Harvey had stopped me.

"Griff," she'd said, "after breakfast Miss Arbuckle would like to see you over in her office, before you go to school." There was no discernible tone or emotion in the way she delivered the message, but I couldn't help but worry.

"Any idea what she wants to see me about?" I asked. I'd been extremely anxious and out of sorts since the horrible event of fourteen days ago. All the stuff on the radio, in the newspapers, and in the gossip around town had made everything for Lily and me that much worse. Once Dr. Traynor's jury added their unfathomable decision to the already boiling pot, I couldn't even eat or sleep.

It didn't help that I'd only seen Lily twice since that dreadful night, and on both occasions, we couldn't talk much about what we'd seen. My mind raced as I approached Miss Arbuckle's office. What if this meeting had something to do with that night? I was pretty sure no one had seen or heard me come back in, and I knew I'd been able to keep Ernie from ever delivering the note to Betty and Ceilia. Assuming he hadn't blabbed to anyone about my runaway plan, I'd thought I was in the clear.

But when the solid oak door to Miss Arbuckle's office opened, and she motioned for me to come in, I felt like I was going to be sick. She was dressed in a gray skirt that came down just below her knees. She had those blue knee socks on that she always wore and a navy blue, high-necked sweater.

"Please sit down, Griffin." She went around to the other side of her desk and sat in her high-backed chair. Picking up her glasses from the desk, she put them on her long nose. She had a single, brown file on her desk, and she opened it, removing several documents.

"It seems, Griffin, that I have some...good news. You have acquired a rather wealthy patron," she said, without looking up from the papers.

"I'm sorry, ma'am?" I said. "I...I don't understand."

"Well..." she took a breath, "someone has taken a very special interest in your and Betty's case." She set the document back on top of the file, smiled, removed her glasses, and looked straight at me. "What this all is," she said, gesturing at the contents of the file before her, "is an expedited petition to have both you and Betty placed together with a nice family in Oak Park, Illinois." She scratched her hair with her left hand, just behind her ear. "You and Betty have been adopted, Griffin. Isn't that great?" I couldn't tell if she was happy or confused.

"What? What family?" I asked, trying to make some sense of this.

"It is the Tosto family." She put her glasses back on to read the names. "Mario and Francesca Tosto. They have wanted children for quite some time but have been unable to produce them."

"How did they find out about Betty and me?"

"That is a very good question, one I'm afraid I can't answer. But isn't it great! You and Betty will be together." Miss Arbuckle thumbed through the papers briefly and then stacked them neatly, putting them back in the brown file folder.

"Have you met them, Miss Arbuckle?" I asked, biting my lip. I felt my forehead heat up and wrinkle with worry. I clasped my hands tightly between my legs under the table. "They haven't even met Betty and me. How can they know they want to adopt us?"

She cocked her head to one side and smiled reassuringly. "I haven't met the Tostos personally, but I know how this process works and how incredibly careful the State of Illinois is when monitoring potential adopting families. I am sure this will be a terrific home for you and Betty." She exhaled and added, "I think we have every reason to be optimistic about this."

I looked down, and, for the first time in a long time, thought of my mother. "My mother...Does she know about this?" I didn't look up for the answer.

I could feel Miss Arbuckle considering her words carefully. "Yes, she does, Griffin. And this is what makes the speed of this particular adoption a bit curious." She rose from her chair and turned to look out the window behind her desk. "I asked your mother, when she was last here back in August, to sign some papers authorizing us to find a suitable home for your sister and you." Turning back to face me, she continued, "But she refused. Yet, here, in this petition, I see the signed authorization, bearing your mother's name. And your mother's signature is, indeed, necessary to make this placement to the Tostos in Oak Park possible." Miss Arbuckle removed her glasses again and shook her head. "So, it seems that somehow...the proper authorities obtained your mother's permission."

"What are we going to do, Miss Arbuckle?" I asked, standing up to pace in the tight area between my chair and the door that led back out to the entry hall.

"Why, Griffin, this is a wonderful opportunity," she said. "It is very rare, indeed, for a brother and sister to get to live together when they leave LBO." She turned back to the window and looked back out at the gray, November day. "I should also tell you, Griffin, that this expedited petition for adoption is not for a typical foster type situation." She paused and turned to face me again. "Usually, children who leave here do so on a somewhat temporary or trial basis. That's what foster families do." She picked up the folder again and waved it in my direction. "The Tostos have petitioned the court to adopt you and Betty permanently: no trial period, no provision for returning you to us in the event of things not...well, not working out."

I stopped my pacing and looked down at the floor. I could feel my head shaking back and forth, and I bit down so hard on my lip that it drew blood. By the time I looked up at Miss Arbuckle, tears had completely filled my eyes. I could feel my lips trying to form words, but all that came out were sharp bursts of air.

"I know this is a lot for you to think about, Griffin," Miss Arbuckle said, "but this is very good, very good indeed!" Coming around her desk and placing her long hand on my shoulder, she continued. "I'd like to be able to tell you to take some time to think about this. But the Tostos—and whoever else is…involved in this— seem to be in a bit of a hurry to make this all official. And, of course, we'll have to tell Betty." She hesitated. "I thought it best to have this talk with you first."

At the mention of Betty's name, I straightened myself, nodded, and took in a couple of deep breaths. I said, "How soon…? I mean, when would we leave?"

Miss Arbuckle removed her hand from my shoulder and clasped her hands as she stood facing me. She took a deep, slow breath. "Tomorrow, I'm afraid. Tuesday, November 13. I also want to let you know, Griffin, that I did contact your Aunt Rose, who has been extremely supportive of you and Betty, even from a distance."

I thanked her and told her I needed some air. She dismissed me with a hug, the warmest and longest one she'd ever given me, and it felt good. I opened her heavy office door myself, stepped across its threshold, and walked that long, echoey hallway to the front door and out into the November wind.

That night at dinner, Miss Arbuckle called Betty and me forward to the the head table when everyone was still standing to say grace. Just over a year ago, the entire orphanage sang us "We Welcome You." But tonight they had a different song to sing us. It was to the tune of the old hymn, "Blest Be the Tie that Binds."

We're sorry you're going away
We wish that you could stay

We surely will miss you
We know God will bless you
We're sorry you're going away

Finally, on that one night—our last night in LBO—Betty and I got to eat together at Miss Arbuckle's table.

By the time I returned to my room that night, a small, brown, leather suitcase sat on my bed, packed and closed. I had no idea where the fancy piece of luggage had come from, but I know it was filled with all my stuff, everything I had in the world. The only thing that hadn't fit in it was the baseball glove that the Freidles had given me the previous Christmas. It, along with the baseball inside its webbing, was resting on top of the suitcase.

The Wads boys received the news of my departure with a mix of shock and happiness. Everyone knew how Betty and I had been dumped at the orphanage and what a loon our mother was. As Dennis had reminded me, I'd talked non-stop about wanting to get out of here, especially now that Danny, Dick, and Artie were all gone.

For the next few minutes, all I could think about was the farm—Lily, Mrs. D., and even Redd. Who would tell them? How could I thank them? What would Lily do? I ran to the next cubicle and got some writing paper and an envelope from Knox. I had a pencil tucked under my pillow, so I grabbed it and starting writing. I signed it then sealed it with blood from my finger.

Dear Lily –

By the time you receive this letter, Betty and I will be gone. All I know is we got adopted by a family in Oak Park named the Tostos. Miss Arbuckle just told me today, and we're getting picked up tomorrow. I'm going to ask Mr. Spader to make sure you get this, but you probably won't get it for a day or two. I don't know their address, but PROMISE ME you'll find a way to get this back to me !

I probably won't see you again. So in case that's true, I want us to make a pact. I want us to both swear with our blood to keep what we saw that night a secret... We know what could happen if we don't. So here is the pact:

On this day, November 12, 1928, we hereby swear with both of our blood to keep our secret a secret forever and ever. No matter what happens or who asks us, we will never tell.

Griff Morgan   Lily Reddington

A pact like this has to be sealed with both our blood. Prick your finger with a needle and press it on the paper above your name like I did and send it back to me.

Goodbye, Lily.
Signed, Your Friend, Griff

I tucked it in the envelope and then licked it really good. I wrote "Lily Reddington" on the front in big letters and then wrote "Private" on the back. I ran down the stairs two at a time and went out and over to the laundry. I smelled Mr. Spader's pipe tobacco and let myself in.

"Well, Griffin. We sure are sorry to be losing you, but it seems good fortune has smiled upon you."

"Mr. Spader, I'm not going to be able to get over to the farm before I leave."

"And how can I help then?" He smiled, just like he always did, tamped down his tobacco and relit the bowl.

"I just wanted to see," I said, "if you'd deliver this to Lily for me. It's real important and…well…private." I extended my letter across the clothes hamper to him.

"Well, I certainly understand." He tucked it in the breast pocket of his work shirt and then patted it, so I could see where he'd put it. "You can count on me to carry out this vital errand."

"Thanks, Mr. Spader. Thanks a lot." I turned to leave.

"Best of luck to you and your little sister, Griffin. You will be missed."

"Thank you, sir," I said, turning back for a moment. He patted the letter in his pocket once again and nodded before returning to his laundry folding. His dark pipe was pinched between his teeth at the left corner of his mouth. It was one of the only moments in my entire year at LBO that I wish I had a picture of. Mr. Spader was a good man, and I knew I'd miss him.

LAKE BLUFF ORPHANAGE DINING HALL
Photo courtesy of the Lake Bluff History Museum

Chapter 40 — Moving Day
Lake Bluff Orphanage — November 13, 1928

I stood, frozen, next to the bedside table, staring out the window of Wadsworth Hall. I was waiting for the car that would take my sister Betty and me to the home of Mario and Francesca Tosto in Oak Park, Illinois.

I remember being more than a little shocked that Miss Harvey had helped me strip my bed, and she'd even brought me the broom, dustpan, and cleaning supplies I needed to scrub the floor. It was definitely the nicest Miss Harvey had ever been to me, and I was grateful for it.

At about 9:15 a.m., my eyes were drawn to a slow movement coming from the west. It was a long, sleek, green car, moving very slowly down Scranton. It turned around and pulled up close to the curb between Wadsworth and Judson Halls. The driver, dressed in a dark, pinstriped suit, got out and walked up the walkway toward Judson Hall. This was it. I grabbed my bag and walked nervously out of my cubicle and down the main Wads' stairway one last time. The hall was completely empty, for it was a school day, and all the kids had left for school just over an hour ago. There were only two goodbyes left to say.

At the bottom of the stairs stood Jessie Arbuckle. She smiled at me. "Well, this is a big day for you and Betty, Griffin." I forced a smile and nodded. "I've asked Miss Jaeger to bring Betty down and to meet us at the car." I nodded a second time.

I hadn't anticipated this moment. But I stopped and set my suitcase down at the landing. "Miss Arbuckle...I really want to thank you for all you've done for my sister and me." I looked down, hoping desperately that I wouldn't crack.

"Why, you know that it has been my pleasure, Griffin. All of us at LBO have enjoyed having you and Betty as a part of our family." She brushed some lint off of the shoulder of my coat. "I know this is a big step for you and your sister, but if there is one thing I've learned about you, Griffin Morgan, it is that you are a resilient and adaptable young man." She reached into her coat pocket and pulled out a small piece of paper. "This is from your Aunt Rose. She wanted you and Betty to have her new address and phone number in Chicago if you should ever need anything at all." I tucked it into the pocket of my trousers.

The front door of Wadsworth Hall opened, and the man I'd seen getting out of the car looked in and nodded at Miss Arbuckle, who nodded back at him. He picked up my suitcase and led us out the door to the awaiting car. I held my ball glove under my right arm with the baseball tucked tightly inside the webbing. Betty was already next to the impressive green car, holding her housemother's hand and pointing at the shiny green vehicle. She soon heard our three sets of footsteps and turned to see me, her one and only brother.

"Griffy! Look at the car!"

I put my arm around her. "Isn't it beautiful, pumpkin?" The driver put the two small suitcases into the external luggage compartment on the back of the 1928 Rolls Royce. Miss Arbuckle hugged Betty and gave me one last squeeze on the shoulder. She and Miss Jaeger stepped back, as the driver opened the rear passenger door to help Betty and me in. I shook Miss Jaeger's hand, thanked her for caring so well for Betty, and said my last goodbye.

It was only then, when we were in the car with the door closed and moving slowly, that I noticed the skinny, silent man, sitting in the front passenger seat. He sat perfectly still, looking straight ahead. He wore a dark suit and an even darker hat. I couldn't see his face, even when I scooted as far across the rear bench seat as I could.

Both Betty and I looked out and waved to Miss Arbuckle and Miss Jaeger, who were waving feverishly. I turned to look ahead, up Scranton to where the train station lay immediately before us, and our car turned left onto Sheridan Road to head south. Not until we passed the sign welcoming us to Lake Forest did the silent man in the front seat turn slowly toward us and begin to speak in his unmistakable, throaty, raspy, and damaged voice.

"You must be Betty," he said looking at my little sister. "I bet you're excited to meet your new family and see your new home." Betty giggled and nodded at the raspy-voiced man. I put my left arm around Betty and pulled her as close to me as I could. I was trembling and unable to breathe. I couldn't believe I was looking at the very same face that had stopped Lily and me dead in our tracks the night of the Village Hall nightmare.

The man with the pale, oniony skin and wrecked, raspy voice reached his left arm around and placed his bony, yellowing hand behind the driver's head. I did everything humanly possible to avoid making eye contact with this ghoul with the paper-thin skin. I could feel his hollow, throaty voice pursuing me. There was nowhere to hide from it. I was in a moving vehicle with my little sister; the orphanage was long gone, and the man in the front seat had been a part of stuffing a live woman—a woman I knew—into a furnace less than two weeks ago.

"Where are we going?" I demanded.

The man turned even farther around to look squarely at me. He gave me a toothy and ominous grin, revealing his yellowed, jagged teeth, lined up like crooked tombstones. "To your new home," he snickered. "Your new family."

"Who are they? How do they even know about us?" I pressed.

"Griffy! Griffy! Look at the pretty houses!" Betty blurted, oblivious to the man in the front seat and the effect he was having on me.

"Yes, Betty, lots of pretty houses," said the raspy-voiced man. "Just wait till you and your brother see the house you'll be living in! Talk about pretty!"

I was sweating profusely. I tried to lower the window just to get some air.

"You see, Griff, we took care of finding a terrific family for you and Betty." The man had turned back around to face the front. His voice had a way of seeping through the car like a poisonous fog. "We know how hard it's been for you living at the orphanage, not having your own rooms and in separate buildings." He turned his ghastly face back toward us and continued. "We wanted to do something for you, to solidify our little agreement from the night we met…over at the Village Hall. You remember that night, don't you, Griff?" he said with a sick smile. He cleared his throat, but that had no effect on the haunting sound of the voice.

"Think of it this way, Griff." He reached his slithering hand around the seat again, placing it behind the driver's head. "You like being with your sister, right? You wouldn't want to have be separated from her, would you, Griff? Wouldn't it be a shame if little Betty, here, went to one family and you went to another? Or worse yet, if something were to happen to little Betty…" He let his haunting words hang until he was sure I'd grasped the full force of their threat.

"So for now, you and your sister get a nice place to live together, with a real family. And all you have to do is keep that little secret you and your friend Lily have…a secret. But if not…if you start talking, then I'm quite sure you'll soon discover that the Tostos have inexplicably lost interest in one of their two adopted children…the boy will have to go," the ghoul explained.

"What about Lily?" I asked.

The bony man turned all the way around and looked at me. "Believe me, your friend Lily and her father will be well taken care of for a long, long time. Mr. Reddington has been and continues to be instrumental to the success of our transportation business. In fact, if that weren't the case, I don't think you or your little girlfriend would still be…well, would still be." He winked at me and smiled.

My mind raced. I couldn't get enough air. We traveled in silence for the next sixty minutes or so. Betty held my hand and settled into the quiet.

Shortly after I'd seen the sign for Oak Park, a new voice chimed in. "Boss, we're here." The driver pointed to the house at the corner of Superior and Cuyler.

"Is this our new house?" Betty asked excitedly.

"This is it, Betty. What do you think?" The raspy voice asked.

"It is beautiful!" she said in amazement, as the driver turned off the car and jumped out of the seat onto the driveway of the Tosto property. The monster in the front passenger seat got out and opened my door for me, but as I got out, he blocked my path. I looked up at the same sick face. One last time, the voice spoke.

"Do we understand the rules here, Mr. Morgan?"

I took in a deep breath, steeled myself, and looked up at the man blocking my path. I gave him the toughest stare I could muster. I stared right into his little eyes and tombstone teeth and nodded. Then I walked around him to meet my new family.

I only looked back over my shoulder once, as the dark green Rolls Royce pulled away.

DETECTIVE GEORGE HARGRAVE —
THE HARGRAVE SECRET SERVICE AGENCY
Photo courtesy of The Chicago Tribune

Chapter 41 — Tying Up Loose Ends With Detective Hargrave

Chicago, IL — The Hargrave Secret Service Agency — October 19, 1948

We returned to Detective George Hargrave's office after lunch.

"Are we nearing the end of this tale, Mr. Morgan?" the detective asked.

"We're in the home stretch," I said. "You've been incredibly patient."

He rubbed his hands together. "Well, at least I understand now why you've been so invested in this unsolved case over the years." He scratched the back of his head, adding, "I knew it was more than just some 20th Anniversary article."

"Yeah," I nodded. "And I wanted you to understand why I've kept quiet about my connection to the case for so long, twenty years to be exact."

Detective Hargrave stood, picked up his fresh cup of coffee and strolled around to my side of the desk. "Here's how I see it. You're writing this piece on the anniversary of this crime for your little paper in St. Paul. But what you're really after is trying to honor a good woman—a woman you knew personally—by finally getting to the bottom of her wrongful death, her murder."

"That's pretty much it, Detective. Like I said before, this case made me want to be a detective. But I'm still just a reporter," I said. "And now you know that I've been working with a little more at my disposal than just instinct and hunches." I said.

Detective Hargrave came back around his desk and sat in his chair, as he reached for a handful of 8x10 photographs. His brow furrowed, and he took in a long, deep breath.

"What is it, Detective?" I asked. He exhaled audibly and glanced down at a few of the photos in his hand.

"I'm not sure you're going to want to see these, Mr. Morgan, especially so soon after eating." He bit his bottom lip as he looked down at the top photo. "I bet I've seen these things over a hundred times, and they still sicken me."

"What are they?" I asked.

"The autopsy," Hargrave said, "Miss Knaak's body. They'll give you a look at Miss Knaak you won't ever be able to forget."

"May I?" I asked, reaching my hand across his desk cautiously.

"It's your lunch," he replied, sliding his desk trash can over to my side of the desk with one hand, while he slid the photos toward me with the other.

I couldn't believe what I was holding. As much as I'd always wanted to see this kind of evidence, I was hesitant to actually look at them. I was also completely baffled as to why these original photos were in a private detective's office, rather than in the county courthouse or the coroner's office. Hargrave read my mind.

"They were never admitted into evidence, out of respect for the Knaak family," Hargrave said. "I made an agreement with Coroner Traynor." He rubbed his eyes, shook his head, and filled his cheeks with air. As he expelled it in frustration, he continued. "I didn't see the point of the Knaaks having to see these, and they would have, if they'd become a part of the official evidence of the case. Once the State's Attorney and the Lake County Sheriff had seen them, we all thought it best to let the testimony of the medical experts and those who had performed the autopsy 'speak for itself,' as Sheriff Doolittle had put it. And Dr. Traynor's jury had all seen Miss Knaak's body first-hand in the autopsy anyway, so there was no benefit to their seeing the photos either," Hargrave concluded.

The first photo was of Miss Knaak's hands and forearms. Bone was visible through the darkened char. There were stumps for fingers, each missing the final portion from the last knuckle up. The hands looked more like rounded claws or even a deer's cloven hooves.

The next photo showed a similar angle, but of her two feet, and they were in a similar state. Several toes were partially burned off as well. Several of the bones in her feet were completely visible and intact, like a Halloween skeleton, but with random patches of charred or even missing skin.

Hargrave awoke me from my horror. "You OK, Mr. Morgan?"

I nodded, trying to convince myself as much as him that I was all right.

"Can you imagine someone doing that kind of burn damage to herself?" he asked. "Holding her own arms in a raging, hot fire long enough to do that?"

"And then pulling each of those appendages back out," I added, shuddering at the thought.

"How could she have burned one foot, then stood on that burned foot while she burned the other one?" Hargrave asked. "If you ask me, this whole 'Furnace Girl' thing was a real stretch."

The next photo was of Miss Knaak's head, a front view. At first, it looked almost normal—the closed eyes, eyebrows, eyelashes all normal and untouched. But then I saw that she only had hair on one side of her head. The other side was completely burned off. I set that particular shot on the table and, as anticipated, came to another headshot, but this time from behind. There was a clear and fairly straight line that ran across the bottom of her neck that looked both burned and bruised.

"What did you and the coroner make of this?" I showed him the rear head shot.

"Well, at first, some of the jurymen thought it was a blow of some kind, maybe a blunt instrument. But since the front of her face had so little burn damage, Coroner Traynor speculated that if she were crouched with her back to the furnace and attempted to put her head in by leaning back into the opening, that line could be from the weight of her head pressing her neck down against the lower edge of that hot furnace opening."

I tried to picture that furnace that I'd been in front of so many times back in '27 and '28. I remembered from my research that that feeder door was twelve and three-quarters inches by nine and three-quarters inches. "Could a human head have fit through that opening?" I asked.

"Just barely," the detective nodded. "Not a lot of room to spare though."

I stood up and pushed my chair back awkwardly. "So you're telling me that the entire coroner's jury saw these pictures, along with the autopsy itself, and still managed to rule that these were self-inflicted burn wounds?" I realized that I was practically yelling. Detective Hargrave looked alarmed, but I continued. "The State's Attorney and the Sheriff saw them too, and nobody put up a fight about the decision?" I turned away from Hargrave and looked out his office window.

"That's what I'm telling you, Griff." He got up and came around to my side of the desk and began to gather up the photos. "It's the darnedest thing," he muttered. I turned to face him, and he looked away for a moment, as if considering whether to continue. "But the tests they did on the brain…" He paused.

"I didn't know they'd done tests on her brain until I got a hold of the transcripts from the Coroner's Jury," I interrupted.

"Yeah, Coroner Traynor removed the brain and sent it away to be tested at some neurological hospital." Hargrave put the photos back in his file and walked back over to his file cabinet. "All the tests they did for trauma came back negative, even that crease on the back of her neck. There were no fractures or cracks in her skull, but there were some signs that her head may have sustained some minor, blunted blows."

I turned away again, this time remembering what I'd seen that night—October 29, 1928—through that window with Lily.

"Griff, you sure you want to go any further on this?" the detective asked.

"I'm fine, Detective—really," I replied.

Detective Hargrave leaned back in his chair and folded his large hands behind his head. He tilted his head to the right, took in and then expelled a big breath, and said, "You've got me thinking, Griff. You've really got me thinking." Suddenly, Hargrave leaned forward in his chair, put both hands flat in front of him on his desk, and stared straight at me. "I've heard your story, Mr. Morgan, most of it anyway, about your year in Lake Bluff." He paused. "But now it's time I heard your theory. What do you think happened that night?"

I hesitated, took in a deep breath of my own, and decided to let it rip. "Here's what I think, Detective. I think that Hitchcock was definitely involved, but I don't like him as the killer. He's an actor, a dishonest one at that, but he's no killer. I know he and Miss Knaak were in the Village Hall that night and something went wrong, horribly wrong. I also know there were others down there with them, maybe not at first, but eventually." I turned away from the detective, bit down on my lower lip, and looked outside before continuing.

"What if…what if Hitchcock was involved with some criminal types, some bootleggers or something?"

Hargrave rubbed his chin."You think he was?"

"Well, everybody knows the mob was running booze through most of the small towns along the lakeshore in '27 and '28, right? Hitchcock was the night watchman, the perfect contact for some thugs to lean on. Am I right?"

Hargrave was nodding. "Go on."

"Remember those two guys you mentioned that people had been seeing around town late at night in the weeks and months leading up to Miss Knaak's death? I think you said their names were Pirelli and Donato?" I turned back toward Hargrave. "What if Hitchcock was on their payroll, and his job was to smooth things out for them as they came in and out of Lake Bluff? And then suppose they came upon their guy in his office one night…and found him with a woman. And what if that woman was in the process of purifying herself by means of the fire in that furnace boiler? The way I see it, Detective, Miss Knaak had a couple reasons to subject herself to the refining powers of fire that night. The first was all that spiritual stuff she had corresponded with B. Lock about. The second was that she felt she was losing Hitchcock's affection to her friend Miss Mueller, and Miss Knaak was desperate to prove the superior quality and depth of her love to Deputy Hitchcock.

"So these smugglers arrive, already a bit twitchy, because the Chicago P.D. was turning up the heat all over the area, and the city and suburbs were now crawling with G-men. Pirelli and Donato weren't about to take any chances with somebody like Charles Hitchcock's lady friend getting wise to their operation in Lake Bluff."

"So you think it was Pirelli and Donato who burned Miss Knaak that night?" Hargrave asked, his eyes narrowing.

"They certainly didn't show up that night intending to burn anybody, Detective. Their purpose was to pay a visit to Hitchcock and make sure that he received the message their beating from a couple nights before was meant to deliver."

"But what they found in the Village Hall basement that night was not what they expected," Hargrave said, thinking out loud.

"That's correct," I replied. "Seeing Hitchcock's lady friend down there with him would have immediately signaled to the mobsters that the deputy had not received the gist of their message, not at all. And the fact that Miss Knaak was naked and already flirting with the fire gave them the perfect means to try a second time to get Hitchcock to keep his mouth shut about their operation."

Hargrave leaned back, folded his hands at his chest, and stared at the ceiling thoughtfully. "In one sense, all they did was help her do what she was already in process of doing...the Refiner's Fire." The detective's words trailed off, and we were silent for a long time.

"But why does Hitchcock lie on the stand? Why doesn't he finger anybody else? Why doesn't he squeal?" the detective asked.

"Because he saw what they did to Miss Knaak! What those thugs did to 'The Furnace Girl' was as much a message to Charles Hitchcock as it was for her. After witnessing what those animals did to Elfrieda Knaak, there was no way the deputy was ever going to open his mouth about what happened down in that furnace room."

Detective Hargrave rose from his chair, put his hands in his trouser pockets, and walked toward the window. "What about the Coroner's Jury though?" he asked.

"What about them?" I said.

"If the victim was forced into that furnace by a couple of mobsters, you don't think they would have seen signs of that in her remains?" he asked.

"You just showed me the autopsy photos. We both agreed there was no way Miss Knaak or anybody else could have done that to herself. Neither of us could even conceive of how or why that jury came to the conclusion they did." I paused again and leaned on the detective's desk. "What if their verdict was predetermined?" My question hung in the air for several seconds.

"You're saying the mob bought off Traynor's jury?" Hargrave asked.

"I'm saying that's the only explanation that makes any sense to me after all these years. I thought then—and I still think now—that there's only one way that particular verdict and conclusion could have been reached, and that's if there was an interested party out there with the juice to exert his influence on the Coroner's Jury. Could Dr. Manfred Traynor and his six-person team have been persuaded or leaned on to render a verdict that would cease all further police inquiry into the case? For if they could, then whoever actually committed the crime would never have to worry about being caught. And as you and I both know, Detective, nobody ever has been arrested or charged in the death of Elfrieda Knaak."

He gestured with his free hand for me to continue.

"Doesn't it seem odd to you, Detective, that even without the letters you showed me earlier and without any knowledge of the victim's important, spiritual relationship with this B. Lock, Dr. Traynor's jury still ruled that the victim did this to herself, without a shred of evidence to suggest it? To me, that smells like corruption, like a predisposition to arrive at the ridiculous verdict, with absolutely no evidence to lead them to it."

"But who would have the juice, the means to influence a jury like the one in 1928?"

I drew in a deep, long breath, let it out slowly, and said, "Not Charles Hitchcock." I let those three words drift slowly through the smoke. Hargrave stared out the window at the gray, October skies. His right hand tapped rhythmically against the window frame, while his left held the stub of his cigarette between his first two fingers.

"That is why I can't see Hitchcock as the perpetrator," I continued. "I mean, I understand your reasons for liking Hitchcock for the murder back then. I really do. But the ruling that came down is so outrageous, given the facts, that I am much more inclined to think that whoever did this must have had the wherewithal to get to this jury and to influence them to render the one verdict that would essentially shut down further investigation into this obvious crime."

He paused, and I felt his stare burrowing into me. "You just might be onto something, Mr. Morgan, something that could actually get this case reopened." I gasped and leapt to my feet before realizing I had done so. These were the words I'd dreamed of hearing ever since the Coroner's Jury rendered their ridiculous verdict more than two decades ago. The faint prospect that this freezingly cold case might someday be reopened had fueled virtually everything I'd done in the last twenty years. And now the man who was best suited to petition the court for a complete review of the Elfrieda Knaak case had uttered the magic words.

Hargrave's voice shook me out of my reverie. "But nobody in their right mind would lead that charge," he said.

I felt my shoulders slump and all the air seep out of my lungs. "What? What do you mean, Detective?" I gestured to his enormous file and to the autopsy photos. "You'd be the perfect man to head up a renewed investigation."

Hargrave shook his head, scratched the back of his neck, and then pointed right at me. "You said it yourself, Mr. Morgan, not two minutes ago." He paused searching for my words. "Hitchcock didn't squeal because 'he saw what those thugs did to Miss Knaak?' That there was 'no way the deputy was ever going to open his mouth about what happened down in that furnace room.'"

He reached for his cigarettes and tapped another one out of the pack. "You think I'm going to risk my own neck? I might have ten or fifteen years ago, when I was on my own, but not now." He paused and rubbed the bridge of his nose with his thumb and index finger. "Would you, Mr. Morgan?" He lit up and inhaled, as he walked back toward the window.

I had sat back down into the chair and dropped my head into my hands, certain that my head was about to explode. I wanted to yell at Hargrave, maybe even throttle him for his cowardice…and I probably would have had he not said those four final words: "Would you, Mr. Morgan?" He and I both knew that the last twenty years of my life had already answered that question. Heck, the story I'd just taken an entire day to tell him was nothing if not a resounding answer to that question. I expelled the most frustrated breath of my life and finally looked up at the detective.

"I hate these thugs every bit as much as you do, Griffin," the detective continued. "But there's no statute of limitations on when the mob can take revenge. Guys like Pirelli and Donato don't limit their revenge to the person who crossed them; they go after the family too. I've got a wife and kids, just like you do." He took a long, slow drag on his cigarette. "These are the type of guys who can show up on your doorstep with a Tommy Gun at any moment."

The detective ran a tired hand through his hair and came back around his desk to sit down. He more collapsed than sat in it. "But between you and me, Griff, nothing would make me happier in retirement than to pick up my evening paper someday and see the headline, '1928 Knaak Mystery Finally Solved! Murder Not Suicide!'"

1953 SWIFT HEALTHCARE CENTER NURSING STAFF WITH LBO KIDS
Photo courtesy of the Lake Bluff History Museum

Chapter 42 — Back Home to the Orphanage
Lake Bluff, Illinois — October 19, 1953

Lily and I had a hard time staying in touch over the years, once I moved away from Lake Bluff. I wrote her a few letters the first couple of years after I left, but I wasn't sure she was even getting them. They all went unanswered. Given how Redd was in cahoots with the bootleggers, I wondered if he'd been instructed to intercept them. There was one letter I got from her. In it she'd somehow managed to enclose the signed pact, sealed with a spot of her blood right beneath her signature.

Miss Arbuckle made a point of checking in with the Tostos a time or two the first few months we were in Oak Park, just to make sure Betty and I were doing well. And we were. The Tostos were a great family. I still call them "Mother" and "Father," and they're my Artie's grandparents too, plain and simple. Mario Tosto turned out to be one of the only men in my life I could trust. From my father to Charles Hitchcock, and from Mr. Pirelli to Mr. Donato, there weren't a lot of men in my life that I could look up to. But I've got to hand it to Mario Tosto. He was kind-hearted, hard-working, and a man of his word. He, along with Mr. Spader, redeemed the word "man" for me, and I'm forever indebted to them for doing so.

As for my birth parents, my mother was pretty much dead to me from the moment she walked out of Mackey Memorial the second time and moved down to Nashville with her "new family." Father wound up dying the year before my Artie was born. Aunt Rose called to tell me that he'd been found dead in a flophouse on the southside of Chicago. She didn't want to give me a lot of details, but we both knew that whatever end my father had come to, there was no way it had been pretty.

Mario and Francesca Tosto were terrific parents for my sister Betty. She lived in their dark brick home all the way through college. When she was accepted at DePaul, she chose to commute rather than reside in the dorms, largely because she didn't want to move away from our folks. Betty lived in the Tosto home, right up until the day she died—March 11, 1947—at the horribly young age of 23. Contracting pneumonia in mid February, Betty died three weeks later. Aunt Rose came to Betty's funeral and got to hold my Artie, who was only a baby at the time. God Bless Aunt Rose. She's been an angel behind the scenes through all of my life, working for my benefit for a long, long time.

The Tostos were shattered by Betty's death, every bit as much as I was. Having no real parents for as long as Betty and I did brought us much closer to each other than the average brother and sister. Betty is buried in a beautiful plot over in The Woodlawn Cemetery, just outside Oak Park in River Forest. I visit her grave several times a year.

In the summer of 1949, just a year after my final conversation with Detective Hargrave, I was at my newspaper office in Stillwater, Minnesota, reading through the morning news on the A.P. wire, when I came across the report of Grace Durand's passing. Mrs. D. had tracked me down barely a year before this, thanks to the article

I'd written on the 20th anniversary of the Elfrieda Knaak case. The Chicago papers had picked up my piece off the wire and republished it with my byline. That was the same conversation in which I told Mrs. D. about Betty's death. We eventually got around to talking about Lily, and she told me Lily had married and was living down near Peoria, a town called Morton.

Mrs. D. had earned her reputation as a hard-nosed, straight-shooting, no-nonsense woman. Her work with the WCTU and her dabbling in matters of the spirit only added to the intrigue surrounding her. But to me and a lot of other orphans, she was a good, kind woman, generous and fair. I was saddened by her passing.

The only time I went back to Crab Tree Farm and to the orphanage was in August of 1953, when my son Artie was seven. I wanted to show him where I'd grown up, so I took him to Oak Park first, both to the Tosto place and over to Betty's grave. He'd been to his grandparents' place a number of times, but he'd often heard about my time at the orphanage and wanted to see that place for himself.

Pulling into Lake Bluff was almost surreal for me. The town looked pretty much exactly like I remembered it—the train station, the downtown shops. I even drove by the Village Hall in spite of myself. Despite the horror I had witnessed there, I couldn't help but notice its stunning and majestic beauty. Pulling up to the front of Mackey Memorial was more emotional than I'd anticipated. Having Artie in the back seat kept me from giving in to the moment.

The orphanage campus looked different, quite a bit bigger. There was a new building right across from Wads that had been built for preschoolers. The sign said "Ann M. Swift Hall." Then, over where the old dining hall once stood, was a brand new baseball field. Plus the playground area had been expanded and updated. Artie headed straight for the swings and some sort of merry-go-round. After giving him a few minutes to burn off some energy, we went into Wadsworth. I half expected Miss Harvey to come down the stairs, but it was actually a Mr. Donaldson who asked us if he could be of service.

I learned from him that there were no longer housemothers at LBO but "house parents." It was part of a larger effort to "create a home and family-like environment for the kids," with both a mother and a father figure in each dorm. Mr. Donaldson hardly looked to be of parenting age. I judged him to be in his early twenties at most. He was working on a seminary degree down in Chicago and used the school days, when the orphanage was empty, to tend to his studies.

"When did you live here, Mr. Morgan?" the Wadsworth housefather asked.

"Just one year—1927 to '28. Is Miss Arbuckle still around?"

"No. I'm afraid not. She retired in '47 and then died shortly after that in 1948," Mr. Donaldson replied. "But hers is a name that is often heard in these halls. Jessie is a legend, indeed."

"I'm beginning to wonder if anyone from my year is still around," I said, putting my arm around Artie."

Almost as if on cue, a tall slender man came down the stairs with a pipe in his mouth, wearing a tool belt and carrying a bucket. I knew immediately who it was.

"Mr. Spader?" I said, moving toward him.

He coughed for probably twenty seconds before he could answer. "Yes, sir?" he replied, clearly not remembering me.

"Jim," Mr. Donaldson said, "this is one of our former residents, Mr. Griff Morgan, and his son Artie." Mr. Spader still showed no signs of recognition.

"It was a long, long time ago, sir," I said. "1927 and 28 to be exact."

Mr. Spader smiled and shook his head, and then another coughing fit set in. "I'd say darn near two-thousand boys have been through here since then. So you'll have to forgive me for not remembering." He cocked his head for a moment, as he plucked out a pouch of pipe tobacco from his breast pocket and began to dip the head of his pipe into it. "1928…wasn't that the year we lost a boy down at the lake?"

I pulled Artie closer to me and nodded somberly. Hoping to change the subject before any names were mentioned, I interjected, "Do you still take boys over to Crab Tree Farm to work, Mr. Spader?"

"As a matter of fact, I do. 'Course, the dairy operation over there is kaput, now that the Durands are gone." He lighted and puffed life into his pipe. "But there are still some meaningful chores for us to do over there a couple days a week." He puffed hard on his pipe, and the hickory smell of his tobacco transported me back through the years. Mr. Spader noticed Artie peering into his tool bucket and handed Artie a cloth measuring tape to play with.

"I'd sure like to take my son over to Crab Tree Farm, if you think that would be all right," I said.

Mr. Spader nodded. "I'll take you over there myself in a few minutes, if you'd like."

I responded. "Do you still have the old brown truck that leans way over to one side?"

"Hah! I'm afraid not," he chuckled and then coughed. "She was a beauty though, wasn't she?" He bent down to help Artie finish up his measurement of the coffee table. "You must have worked for Redd back at the farm in '27 then, huh?" he asked.

"Yes, sir," I said, looking down, remembering his passing.

Mr. Spader took another slow pull on his pipe, winced a bit, and shook his head, looking down at Artie. "Yeah, old Redd passed on quite a while ago, back in '32, I believe. They found him on the farm property, way down by where the orchard meets the lake." Mr. Spader exhaled an exhausted, sentimental breath and shook his head. "The cause of death was never determined. Redd was always healthy as a horse as far as I could tell."

I remembered the spot, right where Lily and I had watched those smugglers unloading cases off the boat, and where they'd leave a single crate after each delivery for Redd.

"Redd was always good to me," I said. "Lily and me...we were...we were good friends." It always bothered me that no matter what words I used to explain my connection to Lily Reddington, they just never seemed to come out right.

Mr. Donaldson had walked out of the room briefly but returned with a small, brown, leather notebook. "Mr. Morgan, if I could get you to record your name, address, and telephone number in our LBO alumni register, I'll make sure it makes it over to Mackey Memorial, and we'd be able to contact you with any information about people from the year you were here and send you news updates and the like."

"Sure," I replied. "That would be just fine." I knelt down to Artie's recently measured coffee table and filled in the register for the Wadsworth house parent. He glanced at his watch and began to rush.

"Oh my," Mr. Donaldson said in a bit of a panic. "The kids will be home for lunch any moment. I'm afraid I have to scoot over to Wesley Hall, our new dining facility."

"Yes, I noticed that building. Awfully impressive. May I assume the food has improved significantly since the old Hobbs Hall days?" I said, winking at him.

He smiled, shook my hand, and patted Artie on the shoulder as he excused himself. I thanked Mr. Spader for his time and passed on his offer of a ride to the farm.

I wanted Artie to get a look at the kids as they poured in from the Lake Bluff Elementary School, so we went outside and headed back to the playground Artie had been on when we first arrived. From there we'd have a good view of the children's return. No sooner had he scaled the jungle gym that we heard the crescendo of voices and the pounding of shoes on the pavement. I watched Artie from my perch on the bench and saw his jaw drop at the throng of children coming "home" for lunch.

"All these kids live here, Dad?" he asked.

"That's right, buddy, just like your Aunt Betty and I lived here when I was twelve and she was four."

"But how can that many kids not have parents?" he asked, attempting the math in his head. I couldn't come up with a good, seven-year-old response to that question. Artie was posing more and more unanswerable questions since turning seven back in July.

I watched as he slowly came off the playground apparatus and moved slowly toward Wesley Hall, where the last of the students were disappearing inside the new dining hall.

"How can Mr. Donaldson and Mr. Spader take care of all these kids?"

"Well, they have some help, Art. There's Mrs. Donaldson and a House Mother and Father for every building, maybe even every floor."

"Oh. That's good." He came over and grabbed my arm. "You and Mom are lucky you only have to take care of me."

"Your mom and I are so lucky, Artie Morgan! We're the luckiest parents in the world!" I tousled his hair, and we headed out to the car. I drove all the way down to the lake on Scranton and then came back into town on Center. I slowed way down as we passed the Village Hall, wondering where Charles Hitchcock was, and if he were still up to no good with men in dark suits, dark hats, and dark cars—men I would forever associate with the night.

We headed up Sheridan Road and drove part way in the Crab Tree Farm driveway. The farmhouse was on the left, and I inched in just far enough to see the guest house on the right, tucked back behind the milk house. "When I worked here, Art, I was eleven or twelve years old," I said, without turning back toward Artie. "Mr. and Mrs. Durand lived in that big white house there, and my friend Lily lived with her father in that little house there, on the other side of the driveway." I pointed to the right. "We picked apples, milked cows, and did all sorts of chores."

"And then went home to the orphanage?" he asked.

Hearing the words "orphanage" and "home" so close together struck me as odd somehow. But all I said was, "That's right, buddy. Home to the orphanage."

After we left the grounds of Crab Tree Farm, I turned south on Sheridan Road and headed into Lake Forest. I drove into the gated entrance of the Lake Forest Cemetery.

"Dad, are we going to see Aunt Betty's grave?"

"No, son. Aunt Betty is buried down in Oak Park. This is Lake Forest."

"Well who's buried here that we know?" he asked.

I took a deep breath and swallowed hard. "One of my very best friends, Art." I pulled all the way back to a remote section of the cemetery, where the single graves were and parked the car.

I pointed to our left and said, "You see all those headstones, like Aunt Betty has? Those are the graves of people with families and with some money too." Then I pointed to the right. "Over here are lots and lots of people who died who didn't have any family."

"Or no money too, right?" Artie said.

"That's right. No family and no money." I reached for his hand, more for my benefit than his. My voice and chest were trembling. "Most of these people buried in this part are children."

"Orphans like you and Betty were?"

"Well, some of them, yes. But there are also a lot of kids buried here who died from a deadly disease all the way back in 1918."

"Did your friend die in that big disease?" Artie asked, looking down at the tiny, nondescript gravestones.

I thought back to that hot, August Saturday on the Lake Bluff beach, to Roderick and Olive Stavenhagen, to that scrappy, little dog

Bandit, and to the 23 of us kids, who walked down the well-worn path to the beach…and the 22 of us who made it back. I could still see that lifeguard pushing hard on Artie's chest, trying to breathe life back into him, and poor Johnny Dee looking down at the sand when Olive Stavenhagen asked, "Who was Artie's buddy?"

I let go of Artie's hand and put my arm around his small, narrow shoulders. "No, buddy. Artie…my friend didn't die in the pandemic. My friend from the orphanage drowned." I choked on the final word, and Artie felt it. Tears ran down my cheeks, and I removed my glasses and wiped hard and fast with my sleeve.

"Sorry, Dad." My son turned to hug me, his head just below my waist.

"Me too, son…Me too."

LUDWIG MORTUARY — MORTON, ILLINOIS
Photo courtesy of the Ludwig Mortuary

Chapter 43 — Things Left Unsaid
Morton, IL — August 12, 1954

It was about ten months after our trip to Lake Bluff, when I'd signed my name to the LBO alumni register, that the call came. My phone in Stillwater, Minnesota, rang at almost 10:30 at night.

"Griff?" the voice said on the other end of the line between coughs.

"Yes, this is Griff. Who is this?"

"It's Jim Spader from LBO," he said before a 30-second coughing fit set in.

"Mr. Spader," I said, "is everything all right?"

"No, Griffin. No it isn't." The line got quiet for several seconds.

"There's no good way to tell you this, Griffin, but your friend Lily Reddington passed away two days ago." His voice was tight. I thought I could make out a few sniffles at the other end.

"Aw, no...not Lily. What happened?" I felt my throat constrict, and tears coated my eyes in an instant.

"Cancer...It just plain ate her right up," the orphanage handy man said.

"Is she still down in Morton? Last I heard, that's where she was."

"Yes, Morton...Morton, Illinois," Mr. Spader coughed out. "The wake is on Thursday, Griff. I remember you saying that you two were friends, when you and your son came through last year. Anyhow, I thought you'd want to know." He paused again before sputtering on. "Truth is, now that Redd is gone and Mrs. Durand is gone, I've been wondering if anybody from this chapter of her life will be there to pay her respect. That's when I thought of you."

"That's very thoughtful of you, Mr. Spader." My cheeks were already slick with tears, and I needed to get off the phone. "I'd best be going now. It's late here. Thanks again, Mr. Spader, for taking the time to let me know about this...and for being so good to me...and to all of us who have came through the orphanage." I was crying hard and couldn't hold back.

"I was good friends with Lily's father, as you know, Griff, and worked closely with the Durands for over thirty years," Mr. Spader said. "But I can't make it to the wake on account of my emphysema." I thought of all those pipes filled with of tobacco that Mr. Spader had smoked, day and night, in and around the orphanage. The line went quiet again.

"Do you know the whereabouts of Lily's wake?" I asked, not knowing what else to say.

He took a while to respond. "It's at the only funeral home in Morton, Ludwig's I think it's called. This Thursday at noon. If you're able to go, Griff, please pay your respects for...for all of us, won't you? Her married name is Young, Lily Young"

"Thanks, I'll do what I can, Mr. Spader. I'll do what I can."

Three days later, after my stop to visit Betty's grave at the Woodlawn Cemetery in River Forest and my folks in Oak Park, I drove down Illinois Highway 55 to Illinois 74 and over to Morton. I'd forgotten how beautiful Illinois' wide-open farmland was, and down this far south, everything was so lush, rich, and green.

It was just before eleven in the morning when I saw the sign welcoming me to Morton, Illinois. Morton was the only town for miles, and I would have found the Ludwig Mortuary even if I weren't looking for it. It was oddly shaped, a one-story building with red brick on one half and stark, white wood siding on the other. The single word "Ludwig" was stuck on the white-sided portion in long, slanted silver letters.

I parked up the street from the funeral parlor and wandered the downtown area in search of hot coffee. I found Houter's, a classic downtown diner, narrow side to side but as long as forever. The counter was filled with men, mostly in overalls, retired farmer types, I suppose. They were shelling and munching on peanuts.

A saggy-eyed woman with bleached blond hair and bright red lipstick nodded at me and smiled from behind the counter. She took a quick glance down the long surface, cluttered with coffee cups and peanut shells, and motioned me toward a single remaining stool I hadn't seen at first.

I made my way over, accepted her offer of a cup of coffee, and asked her if she could point me in the direction of the Young place. Her apron said "Rita" in bright, red script.

"Less than a half-mile out'er town, 'atta way," the man just to my left said.

The similarly clad man next to him reached across behind me, pointing south. "Just go to Conibear's Drugstore and go left," he added. "You'll see a nice white farmhouse with yellow trim and a freshly painted barn behind it."

"Thank you," I nodded to both men.

A third man, clear at the far end of the counter, chuckled and chimed in. "You'll know it's the Young place 'cause it don't look like anybody's ever used the barn for nothin' but decoration." There was some muffled laughter up and down the counter.

Rita chided them. "Now, now. Let's have some respect, gentlemen, on account of the occasion, on account of the occasion." She looked at me and shook her head. "Don't pay no mind to these old coots, sir. You must be a friend of the family's then?"

I nodded as I sipped the hot, stale coffee. "Yes, ma'am. I worked with Lily Reddington when we…I mean Mrs. Young, when we were just kids."

"Nice lady, she was," another of the farmers said. "Always kind and put on no airs, that one." There were nods up and down the counter.

"If you see David," Rita interjected, "do pass on my condolences. He graduated from Morton High with my son just this May. Sweet boy." She pulled out her lipstick and added, "I so wanted to attend the wake myself, but, as you can see, I have to work."

"I'm sure he'll understand. I'll be sure to pass your condolences along, ma'am. Thank you," I said. Turning to the rest of the counter crowd, I added, "Thank you kindly, gentlemen."

I had a half hour at least before I'd need to be back at the funeral home, and I wondered if I'd see any of the men at the counter at the wake. I hoped I hadn't overdressed.

It was sunny and hot, and following the farmers' directions, in less than eight minutes, I had reached the long entrance to the Young place. The bright, yellow mailbox bore their name, and a gorgeous, plump robin sat on top of it in the sun. The whole property had a finely manicured look about it. A young man hurried out from the right side of the farmhouse in a dark suit, carrying a folder in one hand and some freshly cut yellow flowers in the other. He saw me before I could move, and I froze. I looked up and down the street, and he called to me.

"Can I help you with something, sir?" He had red hair and freckles, the spitting image of his mother, as I remembered her.

I shook my head and mustered an awkward smile. "Oh, no. I'm just admiring your property."

He came upon me quickly, nodded, and turned toward town. "Are you David Young, by any chance?" I asked. He stopped and looked at me, trying to place me.

"Yes, that's right. Who are you, sir?" he asked politely, though I could see he was in a hurry.

"I'll walk with you, if it's all right. I'm Griff Morgan, and I'm here to pay my respects at your mom's wake."

"Sure, walk with me, Mr. Morgan. I definitely remember my mom talking about you. I'm sorry I'm in such a hurry. I'd forgotten these." He held up the flowers. "How did you know my mother?" he asked.

I smiled and nodded, but looked down as I did. "We...we were...we worked at a farm together when we were young kids."

"Crab Tree Farm? The Durand place, you mean?" he asked.

"Yes, that's the one. You know it then?" I asked, as we quickened our pace.

"My mother loved that place. Talked about it all the time," he said, smiling nostalgically. "I think it got on my dad's nerves sometimes. He felt that we could never get our place to measure up to Mom's recollections of Crab Tree Farm."

"It was a special place, for sure. But you've got a great plot here too." I added, "I'm truly sorry for your loss."

He tucked the flowers under his left arm and extended his right hand to me, all without slowing his pace. "My mom showed me a picture of you, over at the farm, I think."

"Your mother…your mother was a good friend, probably the first good friend I ever had."

"How long did you live in Lake Bluff, Mr. Morgan?" he asked.

"Please, call me Griff," I said. "Just a year, actually."

"So did your parents move a lot or something?" he asked.

I hesitated, and I think David sensed the tension. "Actually, I was at the orphanage there, until my little sister and I got adopted."

"Ah, the orphanage. Mom always used to threaten to take me to the Lake Bluff Orphanage if I got out of line." He paused. "But you seem to have come out all right."

"She ever take you up to Lake Bluff?" I asked.

"Naw, but Lake Bluff seemed to come to her, at least once a year, anyway." His countenance changed, and he paused for a moment. "I'll never forget the first time." He pointed off to our right to a dirt lot behind the Pick-n-Pay Grocery. "My buddies and I were building a jump for our bikes with palettes and two-by-fours, jumping pumpkins end to end. I was on my bike, right about there." He pointed to a spot on the dirt lot, right beside the end of the paved parking area. "Around that corner," David turned and pointed to the corner by Conibear's Rexall, the very corner we were approaching, "I looked up to see the most amazing car I'd ever seen: a long, sleek Rolls Royce, deep green. I pedaled after it for all I was worth to get a better look. Where was it going? My house! Our farm! Pulls right in the drive. I duck behind a tree off to the left, ditch my bike, and sneak up as close to it as I can. Out comes my mom, motioning for my pop not to come with her, and she doesn't see me. She walks out with her arms like this, crossed real tight against her chest, and this expression on her face like she's seeing a ghost."

David and I turned right onto Main Street and could see the townsfolk pouring into the mortuary just ahead. My head was spinning with the possibilities of what he was about to tell me.

"Here we are," David said, as we reached the sidewalk in front of the mortuary. "Maybe we can talk more later."

"Oh…but…Why, yes, yes, of course. Please, don't let me keep you." I said, angling my head toward Ludwig's. "You were awfully kind to let me walk with you, David."

"Not at all. It's good to meet someone who knew my mom back then, when she was a little farm girl." David looked down at the concrete, and I saw grief color his face. "It's really good of you to come all this way, Mr. Morgan."

"You go, David. I'll leave you to it."

He nodded, took a deep breath, and leaned toward the front steps. I watched him slowly disappear behind the big front door of Ludwig's Funeral Home. I glanced up the street toward Houter's Diner and then tilted my head back to squint at the August sun. An older couple came up from the curb. I made way for them and followed them up to the entrance.

The minister from the Morton Methodist Church was there to greet people. I shook his hand and nodded awkwardly. There were only a few seats left, and I took one near the back. It was only a couple of minutes before David rose and said a few welcoming words to the capacity crowd. He included several brief, personal stories to honor his deceased mother. The picture he painted of Lily Reddington Young was quite a bit different from the little farm girl I had known all those years ago. But there's bound to be a difference between a 12-year-old girl and 39-year-old mother. I felt sad not to have known the woman he spoke of—caring, resourceful, generous, community-minded, but always serving behind the scenes—never in the spotlight. David spoke of his mother's willingness to do "whatever was necessary for those she loved." I could tell she'd been a great mother.

But I could also detect a strange tension under the surface of these proceedings, something not quite right in her husband's demeanor, something I couldn't quite put my finger on, and it made me wonder how close their marriage had been. William Young seemed to be floating above the family and friends who had gathered somehow, like he was not quite there, not really engaging with those who had come to pay their respects. I'm not sure what it was that was on his face and in his voice, but it sure didn't seem like the sadness of grief. In my brief exchange with him, there was nothing of the warmth and recognition his son had given me. Lily's husband seemed utterly disinterested in Crab Tree Farm or in the particulars of my connection to his deceased bride.

Most of the town had turned out. I recognized two of the men from Houter's Diner, both still in their overalls. They shared stories, ate heartily, and all wondered who in the heck this stranger was from Stillwater, Minnesota. I'm not sure if I was the only out-of-towner in the bunch, but I sure felt like I was.

The trouble with wakes is that there's almost always an open casket. And where there's an open casket, there's the accompanying expectation that every mourner is going to go over to it and say his final goodbyes to the deceased. I hadn't seen a lot of dead people in my life, but I'd seen enough to know I didn't want to see Lily laid out like that. I definitely didn't want to stand in line waiting my turn, as everybody talked about how "good" she looked. Dead is dead, and no matter how well the embalmer does, he can't change that. But, there was something I had come to do, just the same. And I could only do it if Lily's casket was open. So I took my place at the very back of the line, because in spite of everything, I still wanted to say goodbye to Lily Reddington Young.

There's a tradition in some religions and cultures where friends and loved ones can drop a small token or special item in the casket before it's closed. I've seen everything from small flowers to pictures placed gently alongside the deceased. I watched the folks in the line ahead of me, in hopes that I'd see at least one or two of them indulge in that practice, for I, too, had brought something I wanted Lily to take with her.

I fingered the worn, crinkled piece of paper in my right pants pocket, going over its 26-year-old words in my head, seeing in my mind's eye the dried, brownish blood at the bottom of the page, where Lily and I had pressed our fingers after signing it back in 1928.

When I'd finally reached the front of the mourners' line, I turned to confirm that nobody was behind me. I cupped the pact in my right hand, still in my pocket, and leaned toward Lily's head. Her red hair was beginning to gray, and most of the freckles I remembered were gone. There was a trace of a smile that Mr. Ludwig had managed to fashion on her otherwise frozen face. I looked at it one last time, searching for a trace of the 12-year-old I'd met beneath the farmhouse window, raking leaves that first December day.

"Hey! I'm Lily Reddington. Who are you?"

"I'm Griff…from the orphanage."

"I know you're from the orphanage. Every boy who works here is from the orphanage. Tell me something I don't already know!"

My eyes began to well up, and I closed them against the tears. Leaning down toward her face, I whispered, "I miss you, Lily. I've always missed you. And I'm sorry...I'm so very sorry that...that because of my hair-brained notion to run away that night, you had to see what happened to Miss Knaak at the Village Hall." I paused to wipe my eyes and draw another breath. "I kept our pact...well, mostly...and I know you did too...and...and I want you to take it with you." I drew my cupped hand up out of my pocket slowly and rested it on the inside edge of the casket. I pressed the folded paper against the padded wall, released it, and said, "Goodbye, Lily."

When most of the mourners had finally departed, David Young approached me by the punch bowl. There was a familiarity and kindness in his manner that was astonishing for a seventeen-year-old at his own mother's wake.

"I'm walking back to the farm now. Would you like to walk with me, Mr. Morgan?" he offered.

"Sure, but don't you and your father have some commitments?" I said, looking around the funeral parlor for his father.

"Dad has to run Aunt Sally to the bus station and check on things over at the restaurant, where we're having a little family meal. I'm on my own for about an hour," he said. He took a final glance back at his mother's casket, now closed. "You came farther than anyone to get here, Mr. Morgan, and there are a couple things of Mom's I think you might like to see."

David held up one finger at me, while he dashed over to thank Mr. Ludwig, the gray-faced funeral director, before catching up with me at the front door. We walked most of the way to the Young farmhouse in silence, enjoying the hot sun and August breeze.

He finally spoke as we rounded the corner at the drugstore.

"So I was telling you about the first visit of this guy in the Rolls. He pulls up into our driveway and doesn't even get out of his car. His voice was so throaty and hoarse, I couldn't make out much of anything he said from behind my tree. But I could see his pasty arm and his long, skinny fingers reaching into his coat pocket and pulling out a fat manila envelope. He hands it to my mother, nods to her, and slowly drives away." I shoved my hands in my pockets to hide from David how badly they were shaking.

"That man came back in his green Rolls every August, every single year with another envelope. No matter how old I got, Mr. Morgan, my mother never let me near him or his car. She'd send me up the stairs to my room, where I couldn't hear a thing, except the sick sounds of his wrecked voice. Then after he drove away, I'd watch her slip into a sadness that neither my dad nor I could ever seem to pull her out of." David scratched the back of his neck and finally loosened the striped tie he'd had on all day.

I didn't know what to say, so I just stood there silently. I don't know how much time passed, when David tapped me on the shoulder and said, "Let me show you something, Mr. Morgan," and led me to the stairway. I followed him up the narrow staircase and over to a short doorway. It opened into a sort of attic crawl space that was stuffed with boxes. David pulled out the first three boxes and stacked them in the hallway. Then he pointed to an unusual box draped in a plaid wool blanket. He pointed to it, shaking his head.

"You see that box? It's been right here a long, long time, but, to my mother's credit, neither my father nor I had ever even noticed it." I cocked my head and held my hands out with my palms turned up.

David continued. "Two days ago, my dad and I met with the estate's attorney downtown. My mother had left him specific instructions to have her last will and testament read to both Dad and me together. After going through all of the usual preliminaries, he reads us the last section, which basically says that there's a box in the attic crawlspace covered with a plaid blanket." David gestured to the box he'd uncovered but left in place. "My mom specified that the contents of the box are to go to me, to help cover my four years of college and a down payment on my first home." Again David gestured toward the box, this time adding, "Go ahead, Mr. Morgan...pull it out and open it up."

I looked at him curiously and then leaned in the four-foot doorway and slid the box toward us. Pushing the blanket off its top, I opened the flaps of the box and saw that it was jam packed with manila envelopes. I picked up the one on top and opened its unsealed flap. In it were twenty $100-dollar bills.

"Two-thousand dollars?" I asked.

"That's right, Mr. Morgan, two-thousand dollars...in each and every one of those manila envelopes. I'll save you the counting; there are 22 of them."

"One per year since 1932, the year your grandpa Redd died," I said to myself but not silently. I couldn't figure why this boy, Lily's son, who had only met me a couple hours before, was trusting me with all this sacred and secret family stuff.

"Each one personally delivered by the creepy-looking man in the green Rolls Royce." David added, shaking his head.

"Did the lawyer say anything about where the money came from?" I asked. "Did he know about the deliveries?"

"No. He just said that it was from an 'unusual insurance policy' going back to mom's father, Alex 'Redd' Reddington." David scratched the back of his neck and blew out a long, audible breath. "Unusual is putting it mildly."

"Life can get complicated sometimes, David." I said, desperately wanting to offer some sort of plausible explanation. "You know the Durands were very generous people," I said. "They loved your grandfather very, very much and may have loved your mother even more. They counted both of them a part of their family." I paused, trying to gauge David's reaction. "Isn't it possible that they just wanted to help your mother or continue their support of her, especially once your Grandpa Redd died?"

"Yeah, I've thought about that. But the problem with that theory is what would this creepy delivery guy be doing working for a nice family like the Durands? And have you ever heard of any legitimate insurance company delivering a payout this way, in unmarked manila envelopes?" This time he paused to gauge my reaction. I just held my two hands up and shook my head. David resumed. "And why would that kind of generosity and help from old friends make my mom so sad?" I had nothing to say. I just shook my head slowly and stared at my feet.

"I hope you can forgive my dad for being less than cordial at the funeral home today. As you can imagine, this unexpected revelation of $44,000 in his attic, which his wife never even told him about, has him rather upset." David stooped in front of me and began to replace the box, re-covering it carefully with the blanket, and then with the two other boxes. He closed the little crawl space door and gestured for me to lead us back down the stairs.

As we entered the kitchen, David said, "I've only got one more thing to show you. Have a seat here." He pulled out one of the chairs at the kitchen table. Just beyond the table, sitting on top of a small oak bureau, was a photo album with a lacy front cover. David picked it up, brought it over, and opened it for me. The first few pages were all pictures from Lily's days at Crab Tree Farm. I saw Mrs. Durand with her arm around Lily. There was one of Lily blowing out birthday candles on a large cake. There were pictures of Redd and

Mr. Durand. The next page had Lily on a milking stool with a flabby udder in her tiny hands. But then David pointed to a picture on the top of the next page. It was of Lily with her red pigtails and freckles, squinting in the sun, standing with her arm around a scared, awkward looking, twelve-year-old boy.

"Well, I'll be," I said, trying to remember when the picture of us had been taken.

"Would you like to have it, Mr. Morgan?" David was reaching to peel it out of its page. "I'm sure my mom would be happy for you to take it. I remember when she showed it to me. She said your name, and I could tell she had a real fondness for you."

"Well, I…" It was in my hand before I could answer. "Thank you, David. Thank you." I took another look at the two, innocent 12-year-olds. Who were we back then? What did we know about anything? What business did we have spying on smugglers or witnessing a murder? And how…how different our lives might have been if we hadn't…if I hadn't tried foolishly to run down to Wilmette that night, that horrible, dark, life-changing night?

I slid the photo carefully into my breast pocket. "I should probably be heading back," I said. "I have a long drive ahead of me, and you've got all kinds of people to greet." My voice was cracking like an adolescent's.

"You're welcome to stay and join us for dinner, if you'd like," he offered warmly.

"Oh, no. I'm afraid I need to be on my way." We rose from the kitchen table together, and I closed the scrapbook gently. We turned back toward the door out to the driveway, and he opened it for me. Outside, I looked west over the pumpkin fields, over to where the neighbor's cornfield rose. The sun was starting its westward slide, throwing yellow-gold light on everything we could see.

"Your mother was a very good woman, David. I know you know that," I offered, sounding a little more patronizing than I intended.

I swallowed hard and looked down at the driveway. With the August heat and humidity, the air seemed just as stale and thick outside as it had in the house. I thought of that pact I'd just tucked in Lily's casket, the pact I'd finally violated in '48 with my conversation with Detective Hargrave. I hated to think of all the possible explanations David had come up with over the years to explain those annual cash deliveries and the sadness they brought out in his mother. And it pained me to know that all of David's scenarios were probably way worse than what his mother had actually done. For Lily Reddington hadn't done anything; it's what she didn't do that some might judge. She witnessed something she never should have had to see—especially as a twelve-year-old—and then didn't tell anyone what she'd seen. And she'd only seen it because of me.

"Mr. Morgan..." David said, staring at me. "Are you all right?"

"David, I didn't know your mother very long, and, of course, it was a long, long time ago when I did know her. But I feel very strongly that she didn't do anything wrong or untoward for that money." I paused and exhaled without meeting his gaze, wondering if I were telling the truth or lying. "That sadness you saw every time this man came around...it could have been about any number of things. I'm guessing that it might have had more to do with what it all reminded your mother of." I looked at Lily's son, trying desperately to see if what I'd said had satisfied him in any way. "But I have to believe your mother would be very happy knowing that you now have everything you need to make a fine start in life."

In the silence that followed, I remembered the promise I'd made to Mr. Spader. "Oh, Mr. Spader asked me to be sure and pay you and your father the respects of everyone from Crab Tree Farm and the orphanage. He worked with your mother for many years at the farm and knew your grandfather too."

"Thanks," David said.

"Thank you, David," I replied. "You've been very generous with your time today." I searched for the right words and stumbled on. "I came here to say goodbye to a really special, childhood friend. And somehow the sadness of doing that has been...well, a little lessened because of you." The August heat made me sweaty and lightheaded. As I looked at David Young's face, seeing his mother more clearly than I had in years, I added, "She's alive in you, David. I see that now, and...and it helps."

He took in a long, slow breath, and turned away, staring out over the pumpkin fields. He wiped a tear from his eye.

"Well, I'll be going now, David. Please give my regards to your father again."

Lily's son turned back to me and smiled. He extended his right hand for me to shake, and I took it in both of my hands.

"It was awfully nice meeting you, Mr. Morgan." I nodded in agreement. "Oh, and one more thing..."

I stopped and turned back. "What's that?" I asked.

"His name was Frank," David said.

"What? What do you mean? Who?" I asked.

"The guy with the green Rolls, the one with all the envelopes. I remember now. At least once, I remember hearing my mother call him Frank."

I nodded once and turned away, not wanting David to see whatever look it was that was taking over my face.

I walked out the long driveway of the Young Farm property and took a right, back toward town. I walked past Connibear's Drugstore, past Ludwig's Mortuary, past the Cliftwood Restaurant and Houter's Diner. By the time I reached my car, I felt like I'd been holding my breath ever since I heard the name...Frank.

My hand was shaking so badly, it took me more than a minute to get the key into the slot to unlock my car. It was like an oven inside with that damned black upholstery. I rolled down the windows on both sides and started the car. I got out of that town as fast as I could, heading back up toward 55.

I tried everything I could think of to get his haunting face out of my head, but that oniony skin, those tombstone teeth, and that damned voice were just as clear the afternoon of Lily's funeral as they were that night at the Village Hall, when Lily and I first met Frank Donato.

I thought of Lily again and hoped she'd approved of the conversation I'd had with her son, of what I'd said and what I'd left unsaid. And I hoped that, in the end, in that final reckoning that Lily had already faced and that still awaited me, I hoped that we wouldn't be judged for the things we'd left unsaid.

Afterword

Before we share the rest of the story with you—where all our real life characters ended up after the events of 1928—there's a story I mentioned in the foreword that requires further elucidation. In 2011, as I finalized the research for my documentary on the history of the Lake Bluff Orphanage, I interviewed a gentleman whose mother had grown up on the Crab Tree Farm property. The man, whom we called "David" in the book, shared an unusual and compelling story with me, a story that provided the final puzzle piece in a theory I'd been developing for years, a theory about what really happened to Elfrieda Knaak on October 29, 1928.

David said, "You know, Kraig, I haven't told a lot of people about this, but when I was growing up in a small farming town near Peoria, there was a strange man who came into town each and every August from Chicago. He rolled into town in a deep green Rolls Royce. Now, you've got to understand, Kraig, down where I grew up, about the only thing we ever saw coming down our streets were John Deere tractors and beat up Ford pick-ups. So this Rolls Royce was something we all took notice of. Nobody knew who the man in it was, but we all sure looked forward to seeing his fancy car every year. And we weren't the only ones who did. Each August, as it slowly made its way down Main Street, just about every shopkeeper in town stopped what he or she was doing and stared in amazement at this mysterious and beautiful car, wondering who the driver could be. But I knew more about that guy in the Rolls than anybody else in town, and that's because the place he was going each and every August was our farm. He was on his way to see my mother."

David would go on to recount for me the details of this annual visit, details David's own mother refrained from sharing with him for a great many years. These details included an annual cash payout that dated back to some sort of business relationship between Al Capone's bootlegging operation and his mother. David suggested that Capone's gang was actually running booze through the Crab Tree Farm property from the late 1920s into the early 1930s.

It was after my conversation with David that I knew this was a story that needed to be told. I owe a big thank you to Toby for doing such an incredible job writing it and bringing it to life.

– Kraig W. Moreland

What became of the real life people and places in this story?

Charles Hitchcock
Photos courtesy of the Lake Bluff History Museum

Deputy Charles Hitchcock's position as Night Dispatch officer had been seriously compromised by his court-confirmed relationship with Elfrieda Knaak. The impropriety of "tutoring" his young student, while supposedly on duty as the village's night watchman, proved to be Hitchcock's undoing, as far as the Village of Lake Bluff was concerned. After the Coroner's Jury ruling, he was asked for his letter of resignation, and on November 30th, 1928, the village board accepted it.

Though Charles Hitchcock was never charged with any wrongdoing in Elfrieda Knaak's death, he and his son Raymond were later charged for other, unrelated robberies less than a year later. Yet, inexplicably, Charles Hitchcock's robbery charges were dropped by State's Attorney A.V. Smith.

In the five years following the Knaak case, Mr. Hitchcock's marriage to his wife Estelle completely fell apart. Estelle divorced him in 1933. While she continued to live in Lake Bluff at the family home on Center Ave. until her death, her estranged husband moved to Highland Park.

Marie (Mueller) Hitchcock
Photos courtesy of the Lake Bluff History Museum

Miss Marie Mueller, the same Marie Mueller who was Elfrieda Knaak's best friend, married Charles Hitchcock in 1943. Years after the case, Marie Mueller's niece wrote to the Lake Bluff History Museum, stating in no uncertain terms that her aunt Marie and Elfrieda Knaak were simultaneously involved in a love triangle with Charles Hitchcock. The two women vied for his attention and affection. This complex tryst was taking place at the very time of Elfrieda's death. Marie told her niece definitively that she knew Charles and Elfrieda had been romantically involved at the time of Miss Knaak's death, and, more importantly, that Marie knew who killed Elfrieda but would never talk about it. Charles Hitchcock, to whom Marie referred to as "my dearly beloved god," remained married to Marie Mueller until his death in June of 1960. Marie passed away in 1994.

Miss Jessie Arbuckle *(left)*
Photos courtesy of the Lake Bluff History Museum

Jessie Arbuckle faithfully served the Lake Bluff Orphanage from 1924 until her death in 1948. It's estimated that nearly 3,000 children were under her care during her tenure as the orphanage's second superintendent. In 1949, the chapel on the second level of the Mackey Memorial building was dedicated in her honor, in recognition of her 24 years of selfless service.

George E. Hargrave *(middle)*
Photo courtesy of the Chicago Tribune

In 1932, George E Hargrave took over the detective agency his father Edward had founded in 1888. Hargrave Secret Service Agency would later change its name and franchise several branches across the United States and overseas under the name Hargrave Secret Service and became "Chicago's Leading Detective Agency." In 1979 George Hargrave passed away at the age of 82 in Pinellas, Florida.

Luella Roeh - a.k.a. "B. Lock" *(right)*
Photo courtesy of the Lake Bluff History Museum

Luella Roeh, the woman whose letters to Elfrieda were discovered by Miss Knaak's brother's in the bedroom of her family home, faded into obscurity. After she was brought into A.V. Smith's office and questioned as to the spiritual relationship she and Miss Knaak shared, Ms. Roeh was released due to insufficient evidence to connect her to the crime. The bungalow where she lived when Elfrieda came calling with her box of encyclopedias—412 Park Lane (now Rockland Road or Route 176) in Libertyville—has long since been razed and replaced with a car wash.

Scott & Grace Durand

Photo - Chicago History Museum - ICHi-065046, Mr. and Mrs. Scott Durand walk along sidewalk in coats followed by their servant, Helen Duncan

Scott Durand, Chicago sugar magnate and proprietor of Crab Tree Farm, was indicted in February of 1933 with 75 other persons. The charge was conspiracy in attempt to violate the laws of prohibition. The 42 counts in these indictments linked 75 people, including Durand, with the Capone liquor syndicate. Allegedly, between 1929 and 1932, thirty-million-pounds of sugar were provided by Durand's company for the express purpose of producing illegal alcohol. Durand would eventually be acquitted of all charges. Grace Durand passed away in 1948, and Scott died one year later in 1949. The two are buried, side by side, in the Lake Forest Cemetery.

Officer Eugene Spaid *(left)*
Photo courtesy of the Lake Bluff History Museum

On November 30, 1928, only a month after the Elfrieda Knaak incident, the Lake Bluff Village Board voted to promote Officer Eugene Spaid to the post of Lake Bluff Chief of Police. Spaid would continue serving the village in this capacity for the next eighteen years, until his retirement in 1946. Spaid took all of the files related to the case with him upon retirement, which was a common practice for police chiefs at that time. Eugene Spaid passed away in 1982. After Spaid's death, his son was contacted by a Lake Bluff Police sergeant, Mr. Murray Michelsen, who was passionately involved in trying to solve the Knaak case. Spaid's son said his dad never stopped searching for a key to unlock the Knaak case throughout his tenure as Lake Bluff Chief. But He went to his grave believing Knaak had been the victim of foul play. The only known case files were believed to have been stored in an old trunk at Chief Spaid's home. His son, however, was never able to locate them.

Chief Barney Rosenhagen *(right)*
Photo courtesy of the Lake Bluff History Museum

Barney Rosenhagen began to experience severe heart problems shortly after the Knaak investigation. The Lake Bluff Village Board voted to relieve him of all duties as police chief at the same meeting they promoted Spaid. While the purported reason for this demotion was the chief's emerging heart illness, there was also wide speculation that his mishandling of the crime scene and the subsequent investigation had become an embarrassment to the village. Rosenhagen died on December 20, 1928, less than two months after discovering Elfrieda Knaak next to the furnace. He was 62.

Col. Ashbel V. Smith *(left)*
Photo courtesy of the Lake Bluff History Museum

Colonel A.V Smith served as State's Attorney until 1933, three successive terms. Smith was highly regarded for the work he did for Lake County during the prohibition years. While Smith was finishing his third term as State's Attorney, he became a Republican candidate for congress but was defeated. He was defeated in his bid for a fourth term as State's Attorney in 1933 and returned to private practice. Colonel Smith died of a sudden heart attack in 1936.

Sheriff Lawrence A. Doolittle *(middle)*
Photo courtesy of Chicago Tribune

Sheriff Lawrence Doolittle was elected and served two terms as Sheriff of Lake County, Illinois, one from 1926-1930 and his second from 1934-1938. Sheriff Doolittle gained national attention by successfully leading an army of law enforcement deputies into battle against a group of armed strikers. He retired to Wisconsin, where he became a farmer and developed a special breed of chicken— "Doolittle White Plymouth Rocks." He passed away in September of 1955.

Christ (Chris) Louis *(right)*
Photo courtesy of the Lake Bluff History Museum

Christ Louis, the village gardener and public workman, who was the first to discover Miss Knaak in the Village Hall on the morning of October 30th,1928, continued to work for the village as a public works employee. He, like Chief Rosenhagen, passed away barely a year after the death of Elfrieda Knaak in 1929.

Marion Claire Weber *(left)*
Photo - Chicago History Museum - ICHi-065046

Horace and Grace Cook's only child was a daughter, Marion Cook, who was an internationally known opera singer in the late 1920s and early 1930s. She performed under the stage name Marion Claire. From 1926 to 1929, Claire performed in Italy, France, and Germany. Ms. Claire did, in fact, perform at her own home for the benefit of local causes.

Doctor TS Proxmire *(right)*
Photo courtesy of Lake Forest – Lake Bluff Historical Society

The attending physicians to Elfrieda Knaak at the Alice Home Hospital, Theodore Samuel Proxmire and Arthur J. Rissinger served as the town physicians in both Lake Forest and Lake Bluff from the 1920's through the 1940's.

The Lake Bluff Village Hall
Photo by Kraig W. Moreland

The majestic and historic building, once used as the headquarters of Lake Bluff's Police & Fire Departments along with the village clerk's office, still stands today as the centerpiece of the village. While the front of the building looks exactly as it did in 1928, the back of the building has been modified significantly. The window that once looked into the basement is gone, as are the cellar doors that Elfrieda Knaak may have used to gain entry to the building on October 29, 1928. When the Village Hall was renovated in 1997, the chandeliers that once hung in the Lake Bluff Orphanage's dining hall were reclaimed and moved to the Village Hall board room. On Halloween from 1989 until 2012, the Lake Bluff History Museum used the Village Hall for its famous "Ghost Walk." During this village-wide, spooky celebration, the mysterious and chilling tale of Elfrieda Knaak's death was recounted and often considered the highlight of the event.

The Lake Bluff Orphanage
Photo courtesy of Lake Bluff History Museum

The Lake Bluff Orphanage changed its name to the Lake Bluff Children's Home in the late 1950s. As care for parentless children in the 1960s America shifted away from orphanages and toward foster homes, the Lake Bluff Children's Home closed its doors and moved its administrative offices to Chicago, where most of the families it served lived. The Village of Lake Bluff trustees were then left with the task of dealing with these large, abandoned buildings. The entire block was sold to a developer, and the buildings were razed in 1979.

In today's Lake Bluff, a 16-home housing development encompasses the block where The Lake Bluff Orphanage/Children's Home once was. In November of 2010, a Lake Bluff Children's Home plaque was dedicated on the corner of Evanston & Scranton Avenues, the very corner where the orphanage's first wood-framed building was erected in 1894. The plaque is intended to honor the children and staff who once lived and served there.

Copies of Kraig Moreland's documentary, *A Childhood Lost & Found—A Journey Back to the Lake Bluff Children's Home* are available at the Lake Bluff History Museum.

Crab Tree Farm

Photo courtesy of Crab Tree Farm Foundation

In 1926, William McCormick Blair and his wife Helen Bowen Blair purchased an eleven-acre portion of the farm from the Durands. The parcel overlooked Lake Michigan, and the Blairs eventually commissioned architect David Adler to design a summer home for them there. Over the course of the next decade, the Blairs purchased the rest of the farm from the Durands but allowed Grace to run the Crab Tree dairy operations until her passing in 1948. There have never been dairy operations at the farm since.

In 1985, the Blair estate sold the farm buildings and most of the farmland to the current owners John H. and Neville Bryan. The Bryans have endeavored to restore all of the buildings on the property to their original state. Many of the old dairy buildings have been repurposed as workshops that support the art of antique woodworking and handcrafted furniture for various woodworking artists.

The Lake Forest Alice Home Hospital *(left)*
Photo courtesy of Lake Forest-Lake Bluff Historical Society

The Lake Forest Alice Home Hospital, was, in fact, where Elfrieda Knaak was cared for before her unfortunate passing. The hospital, formerly a private residence, was a gift of the Henry C. Durand family in 1899, who were relatives of Scott & Grace Durand. It stood on the grounds of what is now the Lake Forest College campus. In 1942, a new Lake Forest Hospital was built approximately 3 miles away on 25 acres west of Route 41 and north of Deerpath Road on land donated by the A.B. Dick family. The Alice Home Hospital was then turned into a woman's dormitory at Lake Forest College until 1965, when it was razed. The foundation of the Alice Home Hospital can still be seen on the east side of campus, near the edge of the ravine.

Knaak Pharmacy - Deerfield, Illinois *(right)*
Photo courtesy of Deerfield Historical Society

Following their sister's death, the Knaak family continued to run the family pharmacy, located on the SE corner of Waukegan Road and Deerfield Road in Deerfield, Illinois. Theodore Knaak, the eldest of the Knaak brothers, took charge of his late father's business. Another of Elfrieda's brothers and a sister also helped Theodore at the drug store. The Knaak pharmacy continued to operate until the 1940s, when it became the Ford Pharmacy. As of 2017, the plot on which the pharmacies once stood has become a major retail development space.

The Cook / Marion Claire Weber estate
Photo courtesy of the Lake Bluff History Museum

The Marion Claire home still stands at 700 Center Ave., almost exactly as it looked after Marion and her husband took ownership of the family home in 1936 and remodeled it. To this day it is still known to many Lake Bluff residents as "the castle house."

Knaak Investigation & Autopsy Files
Photo courtesy of Lake Forest-Lake Bluff Historical Society

Despite the Elfrieda Knaak case being a national media sensation and, to this day, one of the top ten unsolved mysteries of the early 1900s, virtually no official records of the case can be found. During the writing of this book, the Lake County State's Attorney's office was unable to locate or produce any records pertaining to the case, despite records of other cases from this time period being readily available. All records involving the official investigation, from the coroner's inquest testimony to the autopsy report and death certificate, have completely vanished. The autopsy report photos have also inexplicably disappeared from the Lake County Coroner's office in Waukegan. They have not been found in Springfield, Illinois, either, even though all autopsy reports from anywhere in the state are to be scanned and stored in Springfield as a part of the official State of Illinois records.

The Furnace
Photo Chicago Tribune

Pictured above, a reporter from the *Daily Independent* Alma Sioux Scarberry demonstrates how difficult it would have been for Elfrieda Knaak to burn herself in the Lake Bluff Village Hall on Oct. 30, 1928. The *Chicago Tribune* reported on Nov. 1, 1928, "To believe her story you would first have to believe these facts," Dr. A. J. Rissinger told Detective Hargrave: "That she had placed her right foot in the furnace and kept it there for several minutes. Then that she stood on the burned foot and put the other one in the fire, after which, standing on the two injured feet, she thrust head and arms into the fire. The pain would have been excruciating, and she would probably have fainted after the first feeling of the flames." Records obtained by the Lake Bluff Village Engineer George Russell indicate that the famous boiler furnace that Miss Knaak was burned in was removed and replaced in 1952.

Acknowledgments

As I traveled the country meeting with former residents of the Lake Bluff Orphanage, I was struck by how willing people were to help with this project. I am particularly grateful to all who invited me into their homes and lives, sharing what they knew about the case and offering details and theories. To my friends at the Lake Bluff History Museum – you never tired of my requests for more photos, more articles, and more artifacts that could shed light on the case. Your dedication to local history is the reason we could bring this story to life. Finally, to all the people who took an interest in helping us tell this story, thank you for your feedback and enthusiasm.

I am especially grateful to all the real LBO alums who shared stories and granted us permission to use their real names as characters in this story. The characters' backgrounds and life events were combined or switched to protect their privacy. Below is a list of their names and the years they resided at the LBO:

Griff Morgan: 1939-1942
Richard "Dick" Moley: 1938-1944
Ernie Van Es: 1947-1954
Dennis Bradley: 1948-1956

Dan Thompson: 1958-1969
Walter "Steve" Spitzer: 1957-1962
Heather Madsen: 1961-1964

Griff Morgan | Richard "Dick" Moley | Ernie Van Es | Dennis Bradley

Dan Thompson | Walter "Steve" Spitzer | Heather Madsen

Photos courtesy of the Lake Bluff History Museum

Leslie Basedow, Michael Bright, and Margaret Kelley—for editing this book

John Borta—for technical assistance with the interior design

Tom Dickelman—for offering assistance and support throughout the entire project

Lindy Jensen— for her assistance with the photos from the Lake Bluff History Museum

Marianne Mather (*Chicago Tribune* Photo Archivist)—for identifying and making available key photos from the Tribune's collection

Cathy McKechney —(Lake Bluff History Museum President) for her years of leadership in the Lake Bluff community and for inspiring me to tackle the orphanage documentary that subsequently led to this book

Murray D. Michelsen (Lake Bluff Police Dept Sergeant from 1971–1999)—for spending so much of his career as a Lake Bluff policeman searching for clues to solve the Knaak case (Sergeant Michelsen passed away in 2014)

Janet Nelson—for finding and making available so many of the artifacts from the Lake Bluff History Museum

Judy Nickels—for her voluminous and wide-ranging historical research

Kathy O'Hara—for sharing the incredible collection of photos and articles from the Lake Bluff History Museum

Phillip Ross—for the cover art and photo editing, and restoration

George Russell (Lake Bluff Village Engineer)—for providing copies of the original blueprints of the Village Hall and uncovering the serial and model numbers from the 1928 furnace and boiler.

Helen Sedwick (Business Attorney, author of *Self-Publisher's Legal Handbook*)—for legal consultation

Peter Sims—for serving as our opera consultant

Wally "Steve" Spitzer—for his assistance with the photos in the book

Kay Wolff—for creating the line-drawn maps, illustrations, and charts

Our army of readers—for spending hours, days, and weeks of their valuable time going over countless drafts. Their input was instrumental in bringing this story to its current state:

Louisa Baddeley	Craig Jones
Leslie Basedow	Steve Jones
Cristin Berns	Margaret Kelley
Laura Boshart	Angie Larned
Michael Bright	Melissa Ludwa
Steven Cohen	Judy Nickels
Russell Dann	Kathy O'Hara
Jean Dickelman	Mary Tompson
Graham Greer	Bob Whelan
Zachary Hancock	Brennan Young
Nanette Jenkins	Brian Zeeman
Darci Johnson	David Zimmer
Beth Jones	

David D. Belmonte (current Lake Bluff Police Department Chief of Police) and the Lake Bluff Police Staff — for having an exceptional team of law enforcement professionals protecting the community of Lake Bluff every day.

Photo Acknowledgements

Lake Bluff History Museum
Lake Forest-Lake Bluff Historical Society
Chicago History Museum
Chicago Tribune
Chicago Daily News
Waukegan History Museum
Deerfield Historical Society
Ludwig Mortuary, Morton, Illinois
Winters Publishing Company
Aeroplane View of Lake Bluff, drawn by H.S. Whyttle 1913

Sources

Newspapers
"33 Witnesses Called In Death Inquiry - Torture To Be Probed; Call Many, Authorities, Relatives And Lake Bluff Residents To Testify Here Saturday In Knaak Death Quiz," *Waukegan Daily News*, November 8, 1928

"Autopsy May Aid Fire Death Quiz." *Waukegan Daily News*, November 3rd, 1928

"Burned Girl Succumbs At Lake Forest," *Waukegan Daily News*, November 2, 1928

"Burned; See Mystery! Found Nude in Station of Village," *Waukegan Daily News* October 30, 1928

"Charlie Hitchcock Gave Delightful Entertainment at Winona Last Night," *The Warsaw Union* July 15, 1922

"Conflict in Torture," *Waukegan Daily News*, October 31, 1928

"Death Seals Girl's Lips," *Waukegan Daily News* November 2, 1928

"Elfrieda Knaak Burned Herself - This Is The Verdict Of Coroner's Jury, State Continues Investigation," *Waukegan Daily News*, November 12th, 1928

"Father, Son Out On Bond, C.W. Hitchcock And Raymond Released Through Efforts Of Friends," *Waukegan Daily News* August 15, 1929

"Find Mystery Clue - Book May Explain Why Girl Burned Self," *Pittsburgh Post Gazette* November 13, 1928

"Frank Threw Me Down - Teacher Says - Give Suicide As Motive In Furnace Case," *The Sheboygan Press* November 1, 1928

"Funeral Services Set for This Afternoon at Girl's Church in Village of Deerfield," *The Lake Forester* November 5, 1928

"Girl Burned Self, Belief - Doctor Has Opinion Of Knaak Death, Dr. Arthur Rissinger Said Possibility Miss Knaak Inflicted Burns; Repeats Story Told By Girl," *Waukegan Daily News* November 10, 1928

"Girl Sticks to Spiritual Tale - Young Book Agent Near Death Tells Fantastic Story of Attempt to Burn Self," *The Cornell Daily Sun* November 1, 1928

"Girl Tells Doctor She Burned Self, Officials However Work On Theory, She Was Forced In Furnace; 3 Sought; Death Is Near," *Waukegan Daily News* October 31, 1928

"Girl Tortures Self in Furnace as Love Test," *Luddington Daily News* November 2, 1928

Grossman, Ron, "Unsolved: Did Elfrieda Knaak fatally burn herself in a furnace in 1928?" *Chicago Tribune* November 27, 2016

"Hitchcock Query Not Answered, Miss Elfrieda Knaak Fails To Enlighten Former Teacher In Touching Scene Just Before Her Death," *Waukegan Daily News* November 2, 1928

Hiertz, Jack F., "Believe Miss Knaak Struck With Hot Bar Authorities at Lake Bluff Say Depression on Neck of Furnace Victim Gives Clue - Suicide Theory Entirely Dropped," *Pittsburgh, Post Gazette* November 3, 1928

Hiertz, Jack F., "Mystery Not Decreased In Furnace Case, Girl's Conflicting Statements Throw No Light On Her Burning," *Pittsburgh Post Gazette*, November 4, 1928

"Hold Knaak Inquest Waukegan, Saturday Nothing New Found," *The Lake Forester* Nov 9, 1928

"Indict Chicago Sugar Broker, Durand Named By Government As Leaders in Alcohol Conspiracy, Yielding $2,000,000 Profit Per Year," *Wisconsin Rapids Daily Tribune* February 17, 1933

"Knaak Case Probe Being Continued - Inquest Verdict Given - Jury Finds Burns Self-Inflicted as Far as Testimony Shows; New Developments are Reported," *The Lake Forester* November 16, 1928

"Knaak Case Revived By New Arrest - Raymond. Son of Charles Hitchcock Confesses To Robbing Several Homes In Lake Bluff In Past Months," *Waukegan Daily News* August 14, 1929

"Man Unable To Tell Of Miss Knaak, Oscar Kloer, Visitor At Hitchcock's Night Of Tragedy Collapses, Did Not Know Girl," *Waukegan Daily News* November 5, 1928

"Mental Experts Discuss Miss Knaak Case," *Waukegan Daily News*, November 1, 1928

"Milk of Astral Kindness To Save Durand Calves, Woman Cattle Fancier Says Spirit of W.T. Stead Advises Her," *Chicago Daily Tribune* June 24, 1917

"Miss Knaak Near Death Late Today, Authorities Seek To Trace Movements Of Victim, Check Made Here By Detectives; Girl Holds To Story," *Waukegan Daily News* November 1, 1928

"Murder Theory In Knaak Case Grows Stronger - Elfrieda Knaak Carries Secret of Torture Chamber to the Grave," *The Waukegan Daily* November 2, 1928

"Probe New Clue in Knaak Case at Lake Bluff - Report That Oscar Kloer, Friend of Hitchcock Is Being Questioned - Authorities In Denial," *The Lake Forester* November 6, 1928

"Rapid Growth of Lake Bluff Seen," *The Lake Forester* February 22, 1924

"Scott Durand Named in Rum Ring Indictment," *Chicago Daily Tribune*, February 17, 1933

"Scott Durand's Jail Foster Son As Liquor Thief," *Chicago Daily Tribune* September 11, 1921

"Suicide Plan Is Discounted, Friends Of Deerfield Girl Victim Of Torture, Believe Another Responsible," *Waukegan Daily News,* November 2, 1928

"The Weird Case of Elfrieda Knaak." *Chicago Daily News* November 25, 1944

"Tip" Offered In Knaak Case - Amateur Clairvoyant Tells Col. Smith Her Vision After Furnace Torture," *Waukegan Daily News* Thursday, November 8, 1928

"To Bury Miss Knaak Monday, Services To Be Held At Home And Church In Deerfield; Mother Stunned," *Waukegan Daily News* Friday, November 2, 1928

"W.C.T.U Leader Approves Home Used Brew, Light Wines All Right Roo, Says Mrs. Durand," *Chicago Daily Tribune* September 7, 1930

"Young Hitchcock Placed On Trial In Lake Bluff Theft Case Today," *Waukegan Daily News* October 29, 1929

Magazines
Heller, Rosalie, "Mrs. Durand's Modern Dairy," *The Field Illustrated,* February, 1926

Lane, Clem, "Did This Woman Burn Herself Alive? The Strange Truth About Elfrieda Knaak and the Furnace," *Chicago Daily News True Detective Mysteries Magazine,* June, 1931

Books
Chicago Central Business and Office Building Directory. Chicago: The Winters Publishing Company, 1928

Christ In You. London: J.W. Watkins, 1918

Coventry, Kim. *The History of Crab Tree Farm.* Chicago: The Coventry Group, LLC, 2012

Durand, Grace G. *Sir Oliver Lodge IS Right, Spirit Communication a Fact.* Lake Forest: 1917

Holohan, Dan. *The Lost Art of Steam Heating.* Bethpage, NY: Holohan Associates, Inc., 1991

Lake Bluff Illinois - A Pictorial History - The Village of Lake Bluff. Lake Bluff: The Village of Lake Bluff Centennial Committee, 1995

Reichelt, Marie Ward. *History of Deerfield Illinois.* Glenview, IL: Glenview Press, 1928.

Vliet, Elmer B. *Lake Bluff The First 100 Years.* Chicago: R.R. Donnelley & Sons & Co., 1985

Reading Group Discussion Questions

1.   As you began your journey through *The Furnace Girl*, which suspect or suspects did you think perpetrated this heinous crime and why? Did your hunch change as you read on, or was it confirmed?

2.   Much of the novel takes place in the Lake Bluff Orphanage. What scenes and moments from the orphanage stood out to you and why? Were there moments of tenderness and grace at LBO?

3.   What did you think of the narrator Griff Morgan? What drew you to him? His web of relationships in the novel is wide-ranging. Which of his relationships were most interesting to you and why?

4.   Griff's relationship with Betty is central in this novel. How does this relationship direct and compel the narrative?

5.   The vast majority of *The Furnace Girl* is a story Griff is narrating to Detective George Hargrave. Did that impact how you experienced Griff's story?

6.   What were your early impressions of Charles Hitchcock? How did those impressions evolve over the course of the novel? At any point in the story did you feel sympathy for Hitchcock? Why or why not? How did the information in the Afterword affect your view of him?

7.   In Chapter 14, "A Complex Character," we are introduced to Elfrieda Knaak. In what ways is she complex? What was most interesting to you about this young woman of the 1920s? What drew Elfrieda into mystic spirituality and

communication with the dead? Is the notion of the Refiner's Fire a plausible theory for her death?

8.   There were many significant female characters in this novel. How were the various women portrayed? How did they compare to women in other novels set in the 1920s? (*The Great Gatsby, The Age of Innocence, This Side of Paradise, The Sun Also Rises, Mrs. Dalloway*)

9.   Griff likes to sneak out by himself at night, where he imagines family life in various Lake Bluff homes. What effect did these flights of imagination have on him?

10. The character of Helen Morgan only appears in chapters 2 and 23, and yet, somehow, she still seems to be a major character in this novel. What role does she play in the story, even in the chapters in which she doesn't appear? What were your feelings toward her? Did they change at all?

11. At the end of Chapter 23, on the heels of his mother's visit, the older Griff, reflecting back, writes:

I suppose, though, that the passage of time, becoming a father, and doing the kind of reporting I've done over the years has softened my heart a bit where Helen Morgan is concerned. My mother, like many single mothers, was faced with some horrible choices in this life, and I'd like to think that she did the best she could. I want to believe that, anyway. But my mother's choices and actions have always haunted me more for Betty's sake than for my own. None of what our mother did to us ever made a lick of sense to Betty, and unlike me, Betty wouldn't live long enough for her heart to soften toward our mother.

How did you react to this passage and why?

12. The theme of forgiveness is central in the novel, particularly for Griff. Who are the characters Griff forgives over the course of the narrative? Are there people he struggles to or even fails to forgive? Do you think Griff ever forgives himself?

13. The illegal trafficking of alcohol was a significant part of America's prohibition years. Towns like Lake Bluff had WCTU chapters coexisting with smugglers. A great many people got sucked into the vortex of the illegal activity. Redd Reddington is one such character. What were your impressions of and feelings toward him?

14. Grace Durand was a fascinating person. If you were to have coffee with Mrs. D., what would you most want to ask her? Why?

15. As a grown man, Griff becomes a father. Were you surprised that he named his son after Artie? Why or why not?

16. Lake Bluff, Illinois is the town that lived through this entire story. What kind of an impact would a gruesome event like this have had on such a town? Are there any modern day parallels?

17. In the final chapter, while talking to David Young and referring to the payouts Lily received, Griff tells David that he's sure Lily didn't do anything wrong in exchange for the money. Immediately after, though, Griff tells the reader that he couldn't decide if he was telling the truth or lying. In what ways might Griff's statement to David be a lie? In what sense is it the truth?

18. The novel ends as follows:

I thought of Lily again and hoped she'd approved of the conversation I'd had with her son, of what I'd said and what I'd left unsaid. And I hoped that, in the end, in that final reckoning that Lily had already faced and that still awaited me, I hoped that we wouldn't be judged for the things we'd left unsaid.

Why do you think the author chose to end the story this way? In what sense is *The Furnace Girl* a novel about things left unsaid?

19. This entire novel is Kraig Moreland's theory of what really happened to Elfrieda Knaak. Do you find his theory compelling? Why or why not?